# THE SEA WRAITHS

## AND OTHER TALES

# SEAN ELLIS

ADRENALINE PRESS

The Sea Wraiths and Other Tales

Cover art by J Kent Holloway

ISBN-13: 978-1-940095-55-4

Published byAdrenaline Press
www.adrenaline.press

Adrenaline is an imprint of Gryphonwood Press
www.gryphonwoodpress.com

Printed in the United States of America

# OTHER THRILLERS BY SEAN ELLIS

## Mira Raiden Adventures
Ascendant
Descendant

## The Nick Kismet Thrillers
The Shroud of Heaven
Into the Black
Fortune Favors
The Devil You Know (novella)

## The Adventures of Dodge Dalton
In the Shadow of Falcon's Wings
At the Outpost of Fate
On the High Road to Oblivion
Against the Fall of Eternal Night

## The John Thomas Rourke Survival Academy
Camp Zero

## Chess Team/Jack Sigler Thrillers
(with Jeremy Robinson)
Callsign: King
Underworld
Blackout
Prime
Savage
Herculean

**The Jade Ihara Adventures**
(with David Wood)
Oracle
Changeling

**Other Works**
Magic Mirror
WarGod (with Steven Savile)
Hell Ship (with David Wood)
Destiny (with David Wood)
Flood Rising (with Jeremy Robinson)

# CONTENTS

**In 2006, I** was in a strange place both literally—I was in Afghanistan on a military deployment, and figuratively—in the unexplored country of trying to decide if I had any kind of future as a writer of adventure fiction.

I had written five—count 'em, FIVE—novels, and only one of them was in print, and only because I took a chance with a rather shady print-on-demand service—I think it sold maybe a dozen copies. I wasn't going to give up writing, but I also knew that what I was doing wasn't working. But I really didn't know what else I could do/.

An answer came when a friend of mine told me about a small pulp reprint press that was going to be doing a series of anthologies centered on less-well known classic pulp characters who were in the public domain.

A few words of explanation about pulp heroes and public domain. Back in the 1930's, when people wanted some light escapist entertainment, they turned to the pulp magazines. Some featured one-off stories of sci-fi, romance, mystery, and others had recurring serial characters—The Shadow and "Doc" Savage probably the most noteworthy. A lot of really famous (and a few infamous) authors got their start writing for pulp magazines—Louis L'Amour, Robert Heinlein, Isaac Asimov, and perhaps the most prolific of all, L. Ron Hubbard, to name just a few.

Most of the pulp magazines ended before the onset of World War II, and those few that survived have since dwindled, but you still hear about them every now and then, particularly when Hollywood needs a "new" blockbuster. The rights to the most noteworthy characters were retained by savvy publishers who recognized that they still had some potential, but for every headlining pulp hero, there were a dozen or so who didn't make the same impression on our collective consciousness. The rights to those characters passed into the public domain, meaning that any author who wants to write a story featuring one of those characters can freely do so.

As an example of how this works, Sherlock Holmes is in the public domain (though there is some debate about this) so anyone can write and publish a Sherlock Holmes story without having to pay licensing fees to the owner of the rights to the character, and without any creative limitations. James Bond on the other hand, is not in the public domain—at least not in the United States at the time of this writing—so anyone wanting to write a James Bond story must have the explicit permission of the rights holder if they want to publish and sell it. Alternately, an author can release the story for free as "fan fiction" or create a pastiche character. (I did something along the lines of the latter with the creation of the Dodge Dalton character, which was intended as an homage to Doc Savage).

The prospect of working with some classic pulp characters was instantly appealing to me. I had already staked a claim in pulp country with the (at the time unpublished) first Dodge Dalton novel and saw this as a chance to raise my profile in the burgeoning pulp community, and maybe even find a publisher and some readers for Dodge Dalton. But when I saw the list of available characters, I balked. None of them were anything like what I wanted to write.

Most were costumed vigilantes like Green Ghost, Black Bat and Moon Man— all of whom doubtless inspired some of the comic book superheroes that are still with us today. There was Doctor Satan, an occult uber-villain (a la Rohmer's Fu Manchu) with a silly devil costume, and Ki-Gor the Jungle Lord, presumably a Tarzan knock-off. The only one that seemed even remotely interesting was Secret Agent X, and only because of the words "secret agent"; I was hopeful that I could spin a Bond-style yarn in the pulp-era. As I soon learned, Secret Agent X was also more superhero crime fighter than action hero superspy. Still, if I wanted to make my mark with the pulp crowd, I needed to do something, so I committed to writing a 15,000-word novella about a character I knew almost nothing about.

Actually, I knew even less than nothing because in my preliminary research, I confused Secret Agent X with a newspaper comic strip hero named Secret Agent X-9, created by Dashiell Hammett and drawn by Alex Raymond. They were most definitely not the same character.

Although popular in its time, the Secret Agent X magazine never achieved the same level of success as some of the more well-known hero pulps, but collectors and aficionados kept the Agent's memory alive, and eventually I was able to find some of the original adventures which gave me a better idea of what I had gotten myself into.

### Who is Secret Agent X?

**Created by author** Paul Chadwick in 1934, and written by several different authors under the pseudonym Brant House, Secret Agent X appeared in 41 adventures over the course of his five year run.

He was a dedicated crime fighter with extraordinary abilities, almost unlimited resources, and a cadre of loyal assistants, but one thing set Secret Agent X apart from the rest. Like many masked vigilante crime fighters that graced the pages of both pulp magazines and comic books of the day, Secret Agent X kept his true identity a closely guarded secret. But unlike the rest, that secret was kept from readers as well. That's right, we still don't really know who he really was.

Nevertheless, over the course of his adventures, many details about Secret Agent X's past, as well as his many unique abilities, were revealed. Readers learned that he had fought in the First World War where he evidently was both a flying ace, and later a courier who undertook numerous dangerous missions. During one, he suffered a nearly fatal chest wound, which left an X-shaped scar over his heart. That wound would prove to be something of an Achilles's Heel for the Agent, leaving him vulnerable to episodes of debilitating pain. Upon returning from combat, this unnamed hero began working with a secret government agency to battle fantastic villains threatening the safety of his city. In some stories, he received his marching orders from a controller named K-9, but more often than not, it was understood that Secret Agent X was beholden to no one.

X's signature ability was his mastery of disguises; his tag-line, "the man of a thousand faces" was no exaggeration. Using theatrical makeup, he could, with almost preternatural skill and speed, assume any identity. He was also skilled in hand-to-hand combat, and possessed the unique ability to hypnotically control—or at least subdue—wild animals. X did not use lethal weapons, but instead employed a "gas gun," which was described as looking like an ordinary semi-automatic pistol, but fired a jet of anaesthetizing gas. He also wore a virtually impervious chest plate which both shielded him from bullets and protected his vulnerable heart.

But the most effective weapons in the Agent's arsenal were his friends and associates. Foremost among these was Betty Dale, intrepid reporter for The Herald and X's star-crossed romantic interest. Private investigator James Hobart was another resource that X cultivated utilizing one of his regular aliases. More impressive however was the vast network of operatives, controlled by a man named Harvey Bates, who remained ever at the Agent's beck and call.

## Taking on Secret Agent X

**Though it took** me awhile to fully embrace the idea of writing what was basically a comic-book superhero story, I soon began to see a lot of potential in writing about a character who could be anyone except himself. Once the creative juices started flowing, I came up with the outline for Masterpiece of Vengeance, a crime caper inspired in part by the infamous theft of Edvard Munch's painting, The Scream, from a museum in Oslo, Norway.

Even before I finished Masterpiece, I had the idea for another Secret Agent X story—The Scar—which takes the matter of Secret Agent X's unknown identity to a whole new level. I also had the first glimmers of an outline for a novel. The original magazine series ended before the start of World War II, which to me raised the hypothetical question: What would Secret Agent X have done during the war years? Of course, those adventures are probably still classified, but I am pleased to include The Sea Wraiths, a short Secret Agent X novel in its entirety in this collection.

I pitched these ideas to the editor of the anthology, and was somewhat dismayed to learn that all the slots in the first volume had already been filled. Masterpiece would be in the second volume, which wouldn't be in print for several months, and a third volume was too far off to even be on the horizon and there was no guarantee that The Scar would be included. He then suggested that what he really needed was a story about a team of WW I flying aces known as The Three Mosquitoes.

## Flying Aces

**There is something** about the early days of aerial combat that evokes an almost mythical nostalgia. The fighter aces of World War I were like knights of old, charging into battle, their planes painted in sometimes outlandish schemes like the heraldic livery of medieval warrior lords. My earliest memory of encountering these legendary figures comes from the Peanuts comics, where Snoopy, decked out in scarf and an old-fashioned leather aviator's helmet, endlessly flew his doghouse into battle with his arch-nemesis, the Red Baron. I seem to recall owning a model of Von Richtofen's distinctive Fokker triplane—a cartoonish version produced under the Peanuts license. I wonder whatever happened to it? Like many other fancies of childhood, my interest in the fighter aces waned and slipped into the dusty corners of the memory attic.

I was up for the challenge of writing a story of aerial combat in a slightly different era and dove in headfirst, but there was even less information about the Three Mosquitoes than there had been about Secret Agent X. Just a few paragraphs in an online pulp encyclopedia, which offered little more than their names—not even their full names. At the time, I figured this would work to my advantage; if nobody else remembered The Three Mosquitoes, then who would question my interpretation.

Unfortunately…no, scratch that…fortunately, the flying aces anthology that would have featured my Three Mosquitoes story never materialized. I say "fortunately" because in the years that followed, the original Three Mosquitoes stories by Ralph Oppenheim finally emerged, and I quickly realized that, while I had written what I believed to be a cracking good adventure story, it wasn't a Three Mosquitoes story.

There was a simple fix of course. I changed the names and a few other details—the Three Mosquitoes became the Wolfpack—but much of the momentum had been lost, and for a while, The Sorcerer's Ghost was relegated the memory attic along with my model of Snoopy's Red Baron.

### Doctor Satan

**"Doctor Satan…where** have I heard that name before?"

Well, if you're a horror film fan, you probably recognize it as the name of a serial killer mentioned in Rob Zombie's "House of 1000 Corpses." Much less likely, you recognize the character who appears in The Prisoner.

After finishing up the flying aces story, I went back to the anthology editor and asked if there were any other upcoming books that needed more stories. By this point, I was more than ready to tackle some of the characters I had earlier dismissed. He told me what he really needed was a story with Doctor Satan.

Doctor Satan was a pulp villain created by Paul Ernst in the 1935 for Weird Tales magazine. Although human, Doctor Satan was a master of both science and black magic, and used these diabolical abilities for crime. Opposing him was the equally talented criminologist Ascott Keane—a sort of occult Sherlock Holmes.

Imagine if A. Conan Doyle had chosen to write "Moriarty" stories, in which the villain took center stage, used magic and wore a silly red costume; that's pretty much Doctor Satan in a nutshell. There's a reason he was billed as "The World's Weirdest Villain."

As with the others, there was very little information to be found on this character. I couldn't even get my hands on one of the original stories, and much of what I did turn up was confusing and contradictory. My perception of the character however nicely dovetailed with an idea I had been kicking around for a long time, namely how would our criminal justice system deal with a murder who used supernatural abilities that most people don't even believe in? Thus was The Prisoner conceived.

If it sounds like I've disparaged the source material a bit...well, you're probably right, but I love this story, and I'm proud to include it here. Suspend disbelief...think Holmes and Moriarty if it helps, and enjoy a little slice of pulp horror!

### DOA and a New Lease on Life

**In publishing, as** in everything else, things happen that are beyond our control. The pulp anthology series stalled. The volume featuring Masterpiece of Vengeance was eventually released, but the other titles never saw the light of day. It would have seemed like a writing year wasted if not for the fact that, in December of 2006, I signed a contract to publish The Shroud of Heaven, the first Nick Kismet adventure, and that got me back on track writing-wise.

My interest in the pulp era—what I call "the Golden Age of Adventure"—endures, but I've mainly focused on my original character, Dodge Dalton. Readers of the latter series will note some crossover appearances. The Fraternis Maltae—the brotherhood of assassins in Masterpiece of Vengeance, show up again in The Adventures of Dodge Dalton at the Outpost of Fate. Tyr Sorensen, the villain from The Sorcerer's Ghost comes back from the dead in The Adventures of Dodge Dalton on the High Road to Oblivion. And something tells me we haven't seen the last of the diabolical Wu Sun.

Still, I loved writing those pulp stories. Looking over them now, I'm frankly amazed that I came up with these ideas. My greatest regret is that only a handful of people ever got to read them. To remedy that, here at last, collected in once volume, are the fruits of that very strange writing year. I hope you enjoy reading them as much as I enjoyed writing them.

Sean Ellis, October 2016

*Classic pulp crime fighter Secret Agent X, the man of a thousand faces, encounters a villain from his past and a deadly brotherhood of assassins who will stop at nothing to destroy him...*

# SECRET AGENT X: MASTERPIECE OF VENGEANCE

# *PROLOGUE*

**No one saw** the figure in black lingering in the North Gallery, despite the fact that he made no special attempt to conceal his presence. He had situated himself in a corner of the great hall, out of the way to be sure, but in plain view of anyone who might have happened to glance his direction. Of course, no one did; people came to the Metropolitan Museum of Art to look at renowned works of paint and sculpture, not to peer into musty vacant corners. Even fewer eyes strayed to the corners where the wall met the ceiling, some sixteen feet overhead, which was in fact where the dark-clad man waited, secured by a rig of ropes and hooks screwed into the plaster, biding his time until the museum closed for the night.

The North Gallery was busy that day, as it had been for the past two weeks, owing primarily to the exhibition of Rembrandt originals on loan from the Rijksmuseum in Amsterdam, but the crowds thinned out with the onset of afternoon and before the last rays of the summer sun dimmed into twilight, the Museum was all but deserted. The man in black however, did not stir. Only when the lights were turned down and the watchman had completed his first sentry round did the man in black leave the roost he had occupied since the early dawn hours before the first visitors began touring the museum.

He moved with an economy of motion, dropping spider-like from his fixed line, and crept stealthily toward the one painting he had been watching throughout the day: The Night Watch. He did not pause to admire or appraise the arrangement of oil on canvas; it was merely an object he wished to possess. He was far more interested in what lay behind the image.

The display frame, he knew from careful planning and hard bought intelligence, was part of the museum's protective system. It was no mere construct of wood, but rather was connected to an elaborate network of electronic detection measures. Any attempt to lift the frame from its mount would immediately sound an alarm. Likewise, if a burglar were to try breaking the frame apart in order to remove the canvas itself, the result would be an immediate clamor. Even the swiftest thief could not hope to gain the exit with his prize before the uniformed security guards swept in like a flash flood. Success in this venture hinged upon defeating the alarm system, which was why the thief had spared no expense in learning the intricacies of the device. And because forewarned is forearmed, he had brought exactly the right tools to complement the knowledge he had acquired.

With deft precision, he exposed the electrical filaments imbedded in the segments of the frame, splicing in extra lengths of wire to bridge the connection and maintain the circuit. Only when he was satisfied with his handiwork did he began separating the ornately carved pieces of the frame.

The last bit required extreme care. A pressure sensitive switch behind the painting itself was keyed to sound the claxons if the canvas was lifted away, but the burglar knew exactly how to fool the system. He took a long strip of metal, thinner than the blade of a surgeon's scalpel, from his tool satchel and insinuated it into the imperceptible gap between the canvas and the wall. His sensitive fingers felt the slightest resistance as the shim slid across the pressure switch and a faint smile crossed his lips.

Success!

Still cautious, he lifted the bottom of the painting, sliding his fingers along the metal strip to maintain the illusion of normalcy for the sensors beneath, until the wall was completely exposed. Laying the portrait aside, he crossed the shim with a thick piece of adhesive tape to secure it in place, and with that final touch, was done. The painting was as good as his.

No one saw the black clad man lingering in the corner of the North Gallery, and no one saw him leave. The theft was not discovered until more than hour after he crept through the 53rd street exit with his prize wrapped in a piece of dark velvet, and despite the best efforts of museum staff to hide the deed, news of the daring escapade made the front page of the late edition of The Herald. The scandal was the talk of the town for more than forty-eight hours as frustrated policemen and insurance investigators chased endless leads to fruitless conclusions. It seemed destined to become a crime for the ages.

Then the unimaginable happened. Following up on a vague telephone call from an anonymous tipster, a beat cop discovered the canvas, still wrapped in a swatch of black fabric, in a public restroom in Central Park, less than ten blocks from the museum's main entrance.

"The rascal was feeling the heat," Police Commissioner Foster explained to reporters. "The moment he tried to fence the goods, we would have had him, and he knew it. Giving the painting back was the only thing he could do."

The affair of the stolen masterpiece quickly slipped from headline to footnote, and although the thief was never apprehended, interest in bringing him to heel soon waned in the face of more immediate crimes and misdemeanors. As far as everyone was concerned, the story was over.

Of course, the real story had only just begun.

## CHAPTER 1-THE ART EXPERT

**Betty Dale sat** primly in the hard wooden chair, her petite form seemingly immune to its intentionally uncomfortable planes and angles, and regarded the man across the desktop with a curious expression. Without breaking eye contact, she slid a hand into the deep recesses of her purse and, by touch alone, found a pack of Beeman's gum. Her nimble fingers unwrapped the foil and with a minimum of effort, brought forth the slim white stick of candy. Her ruby lips parted in a wry smile as she popped the gum in her mouth and began chewing.

The man on the opposite side of the desk, the one man for whom the museum theft was not old news—Detective Malvern—watched the performance as if hypnotized, and for a moment completely forgot what it was that the slim blonde reporter had just asked him.

"Ah, no," he finally managed, shaking his head in an effort to bring himself back to reality "Nothing new on the case, but I'll be dam…er, pardon my language, Miss Dale…but I'll be danged if I give up on this one. That scoundrel made a mockery of the museum's security. He might not have gotten away with it this time, but there's nothing to stop him from doing the same thing to a bank vault or a jewelry collection. I'll warrant he'd have a much easier go of fencing the Hope diamond than he would have that painting."

"If he was such a smart fellow, why didn't he realize that from the start? There's something fishy about the whole thing, Jim."

"You're telling me, Betts."

Betty popped her gum thoughtfully. She was no stranger to the crime beat, and the time she had spent following and chronicling the exploits of some of the city's most diabolical villains had given her unique insights into the criminal mind. Out of the corner of her eye, she glimpsed a well-dressed man entering the precinct station house. The newcomer, almost youthful with a shock of tousled blond hair and a pair of wire rimmed glasses looked out of place in the dreary environs of the police station. Betty watched him gaze around the open area until their eyes met, then snapped her attention back to the detective. "How do we know he didn't swap it for a fake?"

Malvern smiled confidently. "Give us a little credit. That was the first thing we thought of. The museum is putting together a panel of art experts to go over that canvas inch by inch."

"Ah, excuse me…"

Malvern looked up to the source of the soft interruption; the sandy-haired newcomer now stood a few steps to Betty's left. "Be with you in a moment, pal."

"Yes, quite." The man's tone was affable, but he did not retreat. "I do have an appointment, detective."

Although he had spoken only a few words, Betty did not fail to peg his British accent, and was immediately intrigued. Her keen instincts told her that this fellow was not here to report a petty crime.

Malvern's eyebrows came together in a crease. "Oh, you must be the fellow from Lloyds."

"Indeed. Well met, sir." A pleasant grin cracked the blond man's countenance as he proffered a business card. "Jonathan Rhys-Reynolds at your service."

Malvern stood, took the card and politely extended a hand, which Rhys-Reynolds grasped and shook in a quick business-like manner.

"Hiya!" Betty chirped, interposing herself between the men. She scrutinized his face, memorizing every detail right down to the mole below his left eye, and seized his hand as soon as Matheson let go. "Betty Dale from The Herald."

Rhys-Reynold's smile did not falter. "Charmed," he answered, inclining his head. "The Herald, you say? Then you are a journalist?"

"Betty covers the city crime beat," Malvern intoned, and then enunciating clearly so that there would be no mistaking his meaning, added: "She was just leaving."

"Not on my account, I hope." The Englishman gave a light chuckle. "There's no reason to conduct this business under a veil of secrecy, detective. Miss Dale's readers might find the business of art appraisal less than sensational, but I see no reason to keep her in the dark."

"Great! It's settled then." Betty threw a triumphant glance at Malvern then looked back to the newcomer. "So, you're the guy who's going to authenticate the painting?"

"Oh, good heavens no. I wouldn't know a real Rembrandt from a cigar box lid. No, I am simply a representative from the insurance company, here to observe the panel of experts."

"One of our early theories," explained detective, "was that the thief might have been in cahoots with one of these experts. Switch the original with a fake, and then have an expert authenticate the phony. Mr. Reynolds is here to make sure that no shenanigans of that sort are in the works."

Betty raised an eyebrow. "Do you really think that's possible? An art expert turning into an art thief?"

Rhys-Reynolds waved airily. "Oh, probably not. Doesn't hurt to check though."

Malvern shuffled some papers on his desk and then passed over a small bundle held together with a paper clip. "Here's the list. Everyone seems to be above suspicion; all native citizens in good standing… except for the last one, Professor Richard. He's actually a Belgian immigrant. Still, nothing out of the ordinary there."

The Englishman flipped through the papers quickly—too quickly for more than a cursory examination. "Jolly good, detective. You seem to have everything well in hand."

"So you're not going to check up on these guys?" Betty challenged, chewing her gum with an unconscious intensity.

"Oh, I'll probably do a little investigating on my own, especially this Richards fellow, but I see no reason to interfere with the appraisal." Rhys-Reynolds tucked the sheaf of paper into a small leather portfolio, then again extended his hand to Malvern. "Thank you for your cooperation, detective."

"No problem."

Betty's instincts were buzzing. "Mind if I tag along?"

The Englishman's mouth parted in an expression that lay somewhere in the middle ground between amusement and dismay. "I'm not certain that it would be proper…"

"Ah, come on pal. This is America and I'm a big girl. Why don't you buy me a cup of coffee, and we'll call it a date?"

Rhys-Reynolds seemed about to choke and Betty expected his cheeks to flush with embarrassment, but strangely his pale complexion remained unchanged. He shook his head in apparent consternation, and then offered his arm to her.

As Detective Malvern watched them leave a low whistle escaped his lips. "That Betty Dale is a spitfire," he said to no one in particular. "No doubt about it."

**Ever the perfect** gentleman, Rhys-Reynolds opened the passenger door of the sedan and offered a helping hand as Betty slid into the seat. The pretty journalist was a bit surprised to find that the visitor from across the Atlantic had his own automobile, even one as bland as the brown 1935 Ford Tourer, and said as much once he was seated behind the wheel.

"A hired car," he explained. "And please, if this is to be a date, then I must insist you call me Jonathan."

Betty laughed. "Don't get the wrong idea, chum… Jonathan. You're sweet and all, but I'm here for the story."

Rhys-Reynolds started the engine and decisively pulled out into traffic. "I wouldn't have it any other way."

Although she made small talk during the drive, Betty observed that her foreign companion navigated the city streets with the surety of an inveterate taxicab driver. He never once consulted a map or appeared to scrutinize street signs as he traveled main thoroughfares and side alleys, some familiar and others totally alien to the city girl beside him. She filed the inconsistency away for future consideration and silently congratulated herself for having made this play; there was a lot more to Jonathan Rhys-Reynolds than met the eye.

In short order, they found their way to Fifth Avenue, and it wasn't long before the grand Beaux-arts façade of the Metropolitan Museum of Art hove into view. Betty had spent more than a few afternoons admiring the exhaustive collection of artwork on display, but since the theft, she had spent an inordinate amount of time in the vaulted halls of the Met. Nevertheless, she had a feeling that the man driving the sedan knew far more about the inner workings of the fifty-odd-year old institution than she did.

"The Rembrandt is under constant guard in a private viewing room," he explained as they left the car, and made the short hike down the sidewalk and up the chiseled marble steps to the entrance. "The appraisal will be closely supervised and each one of the judges will be permitted only fifteen minutes with the painting. The museum director personally chose this panel of experts, so I don't anticipate any problems."

"What happens if they discover it's a forgery?"

"Oh, I think that quite unlikely. You see, this is a mere formality. The director has already conducted a cursory examination of the painting and declared it authentic."

"Uh, huh. Okay, so what happens if they discover it's a forgery?"

Rhys-Reynolds chuckled. "Why then, Miss Dale, you'll have a front page exclusive."

**There was little** time to admire the architecture of the vast museum complex, much less its priceless collection of art both contemporary and antique. The Englishman briskly led Betty past the grand galleries to a section of the Met she had never before seen. The corridors they traveled were less elegant than the public area, but retained a bit of its old world charm and featured assorted pieces of art and ancient relics, though there was a sense that these works were of inferior value and purely decorative. At one point, she chanced to catch a glimpse of the interior of one adjoining room and saw what appeared to be a small classroom, but Rhys-Reynolds whisked her along before she could get a better look.

"It's right up here," he explained, directing her attention to another non-descript doorway. The only difference this time was that two uniformed guards, with large holstered pistols on their hips, stood to either side of the portal. The guards admitted them, a terse nod the only form of communication that was exchanged. The insurance representative escorted her into a chamber that was nothing like the modest classroom she had spied moments before.

The anteroom had been richly appointed with velvet wall treatments, extravagant cherry-wood tables and several divans upholstered in dark leather. Betty felt her heels catching in the nap of the rug and looked down to find the elaborate designs of an honest-to-goodness Persian carpet. Yet, despite the trappings, she detected a hastiness about the décor; it was as if this room had been slapped together on the spur of the moment. Betty made a mental note of this bit of theatre, adding it to her already deep suspicion that something was fishy about the whole affair.

There was a second door leading out of the sitting room, and two more guards posted there, but aside from that pair and Betty and her guide, the room was empty. The Englishman gestured to one of the sofas positioned at the back of the room, facing a large courtyard window, and took a seat beside her. Not long thereafter, the first door opened and an older man with the demeanor of a college professor entered the room. Rhys-Reynolds stood and greeted the fellow as if they were old friends, then introduced him to Betty as the museum director.

The older man sat with them, and over the course of the next few minutes, several more people entered the room. Each time, the director supplied a name, which prompted the Englishman to consult the documents in his portfolio. One by one, the art experts arrived and took their turn in the second guarded room. Without exception, each man emerged from the viewing chamber with a confident smile and a nod to the director.

"Well that's that," the older man said. "Not that I had any doubts."

Rhys-Reynolds smiled, then as an afterthought, consulted his papers. "Wasn't there supposed to be one more...? Ah, yes. Professor Richards?"

A nerve in the director's cheek twitched. "Professor Auguste Richard," he said with a sigh, correcting the Englishman and pronouncing it Ree-shard, "is a very private man; a bit of a recluse. I didn't have much hope that he'd actually put in an appearance, but he's the absolute authority on the Dutch masters so I had to extend the invitation."

Rhys-Reynolds shrugged. "No matter. We have five perfectly qualified experts who all say yea; I think the case has been made adequately." He got to his feet and offered Betty a hand up. "It seems all of this was much ado about nothing."

The director grimaced. "If nothing else, we were found wanting in our security precautions. The police are still at a loss for how this devil got in and out without attracting notice…"

The older man's voice trailed off as the guards opened the door admitting two more people. Betty's gaze snapped to the second of the pair, a young woman dressed to the nines. A spark of innate jealousy caused the reporter's shoulders to tense up as she watched the other woman stride confidently into the anteroom; this lady was a Grade A knockout. Not a strand of her stylishly cut auburn hair was out of place beneath the spiffy green trilby, which perfectly matched the lady's handbag and shoes and nicely accented her dark red suit. She tore her gaze from the woman and glanced at the Englishman, expecting him to be likewise entranced, but to her surprise, Rhys-Reynolds was staring transfixed at the other newcomer. The intensity of his scrutiny prompted her to then give the lady's companion a closer look and as she did, she heard the director's muted exclamation:

"My goodness, it's him!"

Like the young woman beside him, the man was immaculately dressed, though his perfectly tailored charcoal gray suit was a good deal more subdued than hers, appropriately enough since he was old enough to be her father.

"Professor Richard, I presume?" the Englishman asked, quietly.

The director nodded, still breathless in amazement. "I didn't dare to hope… The young lady must be his daughter Amelia. I've not seen her since she was a child."

Professor Richard inclined his head toward the director, giving Betty her first real look at the elusive art expert. His erect posture, along with a mane of silver hair and a slightly darker Van Dyck beard lent an air of regal majesty to his countenance.

Betty cleared her throat impulsively. "I thought this guy was a hermit."

Richard did not loiter, but moved immediately toward the viewing room doors, while his daughter took a station near the window, casually assuming a pose to rival a department store mannequin.

The director shook his head. "Perhaps I misled you. Professor Richard stays out of the public eye, but he is a man of means to be sure. He has donated several of the pieces that are now in our permanent collection, but those are a drop in the bucket compared to the private collection he keeps at his estate in the Hamptons."

Betty glanced at the Englishman again. "A wealthy reclusive art collector and he's keen on Rembrandts? Sounds like the sort of guy who might want The Night Watch for himself."

Rhys-Reynolds continued to watch the door of the viewing room, oblivious to her comment, but the director came quickly to Richard's defense. "Miss Dale, I'd think twice if I were you, before making such a libelous accusation in your newspaper. Professor Richard is a man of the highest character."

The Englishman nodded absently but said nothing, and an uncomfortable silence ensued, until after what seemed an eternity, the viewing room door opened and Richard emerged, his magisterial face now wearing a mask of reverential awe. He caught the director's eye and nodded.

"There you go," exclaimed the museum official. "Six of six."

Abruptly, Rhys-Reynolds took a step forward. "I say, Professor, might I have a word in private?"

Betty gasped at the sudden turn of events, and was almost speechless when the Englishman turned to her apologetically. "Forgive me, Miss Dale, this won't take a moment."

Betty's eyes flashed from the now confused countenance of the art expert back to her own companion. "No trouble at all," she said, with a wan smile. "In fact, I should probably be running along anyway. Gotta scoop The Clarion with the big news that the painting ain't a fake... not that it's really news." She was rambling and she knew it.

"But I promised you a cup of coffee..."

Betty grinned. "Rain check. Gotta make the evening edition."

She hastened from the room, stealing a look over her shoulder as the sandy-haired Englishman and museum director moved off to stand next to Richard. The latter's daughter remained where she was and with placid indifference, took a cigarette from a silver case, lit it, and pressed it to her painted lips. But as Betty opened the exit door, she paused and affected a dizzy expression. "Whoops! Forgot my pocketbook."

She turned back inside, but now her strides were as stealthy as a stalking panther. No one in the anteroom paid her heed or even seemed to notice as she returned to the divan and knelt as if to search for something lost. She lingered there a moment, out of direct view of the others, then crept forward until she could hear their voices.

The director was making introductions. "Professor, this is Mr. Jonathan Rhys-Reynolds of Lloyds—"

"Your faithful servant," the Englishman exclaimed quickly. "Forgive me, but what I have to say is for Professor Richard's ears only."

"Ah, I see." The director was clearly disappointed at the dismissal, but regained his composure. "Professor, it was good to see you again. We must arrange for a future rendezvous."

"It would be my pleasure," answered a third voice, a rich baritone, faintly accented, that could only belong to Richard.

Betty crawled closer, straining to hear the voices that now dropped to barely a whisper, and what she heard made her fingertips tingle in anticipation. She hastily fetched her notepad and pen and began scribbling furiously.

"Professor Richard," began the Englishman. "I apologize for deceiving both your honored self and the director, but I am not from Lloyds of London, and my name is not Jonathan Rhys-Reynolds ..."

**Andre LeMartre stood** in the grand central lobby of the museum, nervously fingering what looked to all appearances like a large crucifix depending from a silver chain around his neck. Aside from the religious icon, his attire was plain; he seemed no different that the hundreds of other tourists wandering the vast repository of aesthetic treasure. But LeMartre's dark eyes did not seek out works of art on display; his gaze was fixed on another man, similarly dressed to blend in, and somewhat less conspicuously, also wearing a large silver crucifix. Though nearly a hundred yards separated them, the two men were deep in conversation.

"This is the man we seek," the second man observed, confirming their suspicions.

LeMartre nodded, then replied: "Do nothing. I will attend to this."

The other man's face was a mask of concern. "This place is too public..."

LeMartre looked away, effectively silencing the protest. Had anyone in the museum cared to observe the men, they would have noticed no strange behavior, and certainly nothing they would have understood as communication. The entire exchange of had occurred without the use of spoken words—their common tongue was a language of signs and gestures, which to the untrained eye seemed like little more than the tics of a nervous man fidgeting anxiously. It was just one of the skills that made LeMartre and his comrades into one of the most effective infiltration and espionage forces on the planet.

There was no need for the young man to explain himself; though he was only a second tier apprentice, he was still senior to the other operatives spread throughout the museum, and more importantly, he had been given complete oversight of the mission. His success would guarantee his ascension to the first tier—perhaps even a leap forward to knighthood; he wasn't about to let anything prevent or delay the accomplishment of his sworn task. And there were other reasons why he longed to see this mission finished as quickly as possible.

Gripping the upright length of the crucifix in his left hand, he strode from the lobby and hastened through the maze of exhibits and dioramas to the section reserved for offices and classrooms.

The guards spied him from a long ways off, but failed to see the obvious warning signs in his determined stride and the intensity of his gaze. It was only when it became plainly obvious that he was heading for the very door they protected that one of them stepped forward to block him. It was an error in judgment he would never get the opportunity to repeat.

LeMartre closed with the guard and tugged at his crucifix with his right hand. The seemingly solid piece of silver came apart—the long vertical shaft of the cross still depended from a chain about his neck, but the cross piece and upright came away in his hand, along with a deadly revelation. He swiped the metal across the guard's throat, and then pirouetted on his left foot like a ballet dancer, spinning completely around and slashing the second watchman before the first one even realized he was dead. A sharp tang of iron filled the air as the stricken men sank to their knees, struggling in vain to stanch the pulsing flow of crimson. LeMartre lingered long enough only to unlimber a holstered revolver from one of the slain men, and then burst through the door.

He surveyed the sitting room in an instant, his eyes alighting on the target of his quest, but not remaining fixed there; there would be time enough to savor that blow. He dismissed the young woman near the window and the young blond-haired man as posing little threat, but a second pair of guards demanded his full attention. Like their ill-fated counterparts in the corridor, the two men were slow to recognize the danger they were in, but one of them spied the revolver in LeMartre's hand and instinctively reached for his own sidearm. The killer however, had the element of surprise on his side and used it decisively,

The stout little police model revolver thundered twice in the confines of the anteroom, and two well-placed rounds punched the watchmen back against the wall. The young woman at the window let out a shriek of alarm, but the sound was lost in the ringing echo and miasma of cordite.

A triumphant grin broke across LeMarte's face as he strode boldly forward to confront to silver-haired man. He exchanged the gun in his right hand for the bloodstained cruciform object in his left and looked the man squarely in the eye. "For Mont Sacre!" he cried, and then struck with all his might.

## CHAPTER 2-THE LONG RUN

**My name is** Alec Devine, and I'm an agent of Interpol—the International Police agency."

Professor Richard's eyes narrowed defensively at this strange admission. "Interpol? Am I some sort of trouble?"

"You may well be, sir. Have you ever heard of an organization called The Fraternis Maltae—"

That was all the sandy-haired Englishman got out before the door burst open and hell exploded into the room. Richard stood still as a statue, seemingly paralyzed with fear as the dark-eyed killer dispatched the two guards then hastened toward him. In a moment frozen in time, he saw rays of sunlight streaming through the window—where his daughter stood likewise transfixed in terror—and glinting on the red-tinged metal blade in the assassin's right hand. He barely heard the man's exclamation as the dancing reflection began to move. But the blade never reached his throat.

Faster than lightning, the man who had identified himself as both Alec Devine and Jonathan Rhys-Reynolds—and yet was neither—thrust his hand out to arrest the deadly arc. An iron grip stopped LeMartre's slash mere inches from its intended victim, and before the killer's dark eyes could confront the source of the interference, an open-handed blow struck him in the sternum. The assassin staggered backward, falling over the back of a couch and momentarily disappeared from view.

"Come with me if you want to live."

Richard stared dumbfounded at the man. At first blush he had taken the Englishman to be merely some kind of functionary, but the cold steel of his gaze and the quick efficiency with which he had thwarted the surprise attack told a much different tale.

"Amelia!"

Devine gestured furiously for the red-haired girl to join them and as she crossed the room, he stooped to retrieve a cross-shaped object from the rug. When father and daughter were reunited, the trio raced toward to exit door, still ajar from the killer's dramatic entrance. The girl gasped in horror as her eyes alit upon the spreading pools of scarlet, in which lay the lifeless forms of the first pair of guards. Devine's eyes however were scanning the far end of the hall; he didn't like what he saw.

Three more men were racing down the length of the corridor, silver crucifixes depending from their necks. The Englishman regarded the object in his hand; an ornate knife fashioned to resemble Christ on the cross. It seemed too beautiful to be anything but ceremonial, yet the dark stain on its scalpel-sharp edge indicated a more utilitarian purpose, and something told him the fellows racing their way shared that purpose. He extended an arm to block the path of his new companions.

"Back inside!" When they failed to immediately comply, he gave them a firm shove, thrusting them past the scene of carnage and once more into the anteroom. As he pushed in behind them, he removed a handful of what appeared to be tiny glass marbles from his pocket and scattered them in the path of the attackers, before pushing the door firmly shut.

None of the three apprentices in LeMartre's murderous organization comprehended their blond foe's final action, but the foremost of them got a quick explanation when his foot chanced to crush one of the glass spheres. Even as his shoe ground the fragile glass into sand, a cloud of white vapor swirled up in the hallway, rendering the trio unconscious almost instantaneously.

The gas, a potent anesthetic in aerosol form, was the signature tool of a man known only by the sobriquet: "Secret Agent X." That he was in fact a "secret agent" was not something that could be proven; no one knew his true identity, nor were his allegiances understood. According to the police, he was a master criminal, but many a criminal genius had been brought to heel by his surreptitious investigations, and not a few members of the press—Betty Dale foremost—publicly championed his cause. Yet no one knew if he was an American, working on his own behalf or on behalf of some government agency like the Secret Service, or if perhaps he was a foreign agent provocateur. The only thing that was known to be factual about "X" was that he was a master of disguise; he could literally be anybody. At this moment, X's true face was concealed beneath a thin layer of liquid plastic make-up, a blond wig and pair of wire spectacles.

Richard halted abruptly inside the room and whirled on his savior. "We cannot get out. There is no exit from here."

"There's a window," X answered, his voice and accent perceptibly different.

Still crouched behind a sofa, Betty Dale held her breath in anxious anticipation. Shooting, murder and mayhem… she was smack dab in the middle of the biggest story of the week, if she could survive long enough to post it. As the fugitive trio approached the window, she sidled around the opposite end of the couch to stay out of their view.

"We're on the second floor," moaned Richard. "I can't make that jump."

X frowned, then cast his eyes around the room, looking for a better answer, but there was only the long divan. "That's it!"

Richard and Amelia retreated from him as they might a lunatic on the sidewalk, but there was a method to X's madness as he grasped one end of the couch and hauled it toward the window. Betty choked back a squeal and scrambled behind a second piece of furniture, but her presence continued undetected. For his part, X scooted the heavy sofa toward the window, and with a mighty heave, pitched one end through the pane.

Amelia shuddered at the high-pitched crack of shattering glass, but X wasn't finished. He hastened back to the opposite end of the couch and lowered his shoulder to it like a football linebacker ready to meet the opposing team's charge. With a torturous sound of fabric ripping and wood splintering, the large piece of furniture began to slide across the windowsill and out into the air above the courtyard.

At just that moment, the door to the sitting room burst open again and two more men—ordinary looking fellows except for the unique accoutrement they shared with the stunned killer laying a few feet away—rushed in brandishing their knives. Their eyes roved the room, quickly alighting upon Richard.

X gave the sofa a tremendous shove and it scraped to the tipping point, where it slid of its own accord out into the courtyard. All the Secret Agent could do at that point was guide its descent in order to keep it positioned against the exterior wall. Once it was beyond his reach, beyond his control, he whirled to face the two killers and met them with his gun in hand.

The men were almost upon the defenseless Richard, brandishing their blades with murderous glee in their eyes. There was no time to warn them off; X aimed his pistol and fired. One of the assassins glimpsed the gun in X's hand, but before he could make a single move in his own defense, the weapon discharged.

There was no explosive report however; no eruption of flame and lead from the barrel of the gun. Instead, there was only a jet of pressurized anesthetic gas, which formed a narrow cone of white mist across the intervening space and swelled about the heads of the two would-be murderers. At the edge of the gas cloud, Amelia gasped and slumped to the ground, joining the senseless pair that had received the full dose.

X muttered a rare oath, then sucked in a deep breath and waded into the lingering haze of fumes in order to retrieve the girl. The gas was a substance of his own design—a vapor similar to nitrous oxides but which acted much more rapidly—and the gun an alternative to the lethal methods he had once employed in defense of freedom. The gas was now his preferred weapon of choice, and not merely because its employ spared him from the ghosts of those slain by his own hand. It was after all, much easier to gain essential information from someone who was merely rendered temporarily unconscious than from the dead. He had no doubt that Amelia Richard would be alert and on her feet again in a few minutes, but what had to happen in that period was what concerned him most.

"Out the window," he growled to Richard, hefting the girl's limp form onto one shoulder. The stately patron of the arts seemed rooted in place and it took a gentle shove from X to get him moving.

The silver haired professor swung one leg onto the windowsill, and then extended his head out into the courtyard. The couch remained tilted up against the wall, affording a flat surface upon which to stand, but the distance between the couch and the window was greater than Richard's full height.

"Go!" X urged. "There are bound to be more of them and they won't stop until you're dead."

"Who?" pleaded the older man. "Who wants me dead? And why"

"You mean you don't know?" X stared back, fixing the man with his unflinching iron eyes.

A strange look passed over Richard's face—it was neither terror nor confusion—and then he shook his head negatively.

X grimaced. "We'll sort that out once we're safe. Right now, we need to get out of here. Go!"

The command brooked no refusal and Richard surrendered himself to gravity. Once in motion, he seemed far more agile than his years, dropping onto the couch and then sliding down to the lawn of the courtyard. X cautiously hefted his burden through the window, and threw a final glance back into the chaos of the sitting room. The two assassins lay unmoving near one wall, while the first of their number writhed in agony near the center of the room, struggling to get his wind back.

Then X spied another form that he had missed in the confusion, huddling behind a divan. Though she did not recognize him, her face was well known to the Secret Agent; there was an unfathomable bond between X and Betty Dale. He met her gaze and with one forefinger, traces two intersecting lines in the air to form an "X." Then he was gone.

**The tumult in** the viewing room had not gone unnoticed by museum visitors idling in the courtyard. A small knot of them, mostly the clientele of the open air coffee shop situated against an adjacent wall, stared in mute disbelief as the fugitives made their escape, but none dared interfere. X steered Richard toward the crowd; there wasn't much chance of simply melting into the throng, not with the dazed Amelia slung over one shoulder, but perhaps it would be enough to hide them from the strange group of assassins.

The Agent felt the burden he carried shift abruptly and called Richard to a halt, just inside the cafe. Amelia had awakened with a start and her first impulse had been to struggle against an imagined captor. X eased her to the ground, allowing her father to soothe her rattled nerves. The anesthetizing gas was a powerful defensive weapon, but the Agent knew from experience that its effects could be short lived, especially when the initial dose was very small. The girl had breathed only a few wisps of the vapor, so her rapid return to consciousness was not surprising. X knew that the assassins were likely stirring as well.

"We have to keep moving."

Richard held his daughter's hand a moment longer then faced their savior. "I have a car in the staff parking lot."

X nodded and gestured to the open archway that led into the museum proper. "Let's go."

A short walk led them back to the main lobby where they were no longer subject to the stares of amazed tourists. They moved briskly back through the maze of exhibits to a service corridor, and from there to the staff parking lot. X had maintained a constant vigil as they moved, but saw no more silver crucifixes, nor any indication that the group of assassins was monitoring their escape. As soon as they left the building complex however, his wariness increased.

"Where's Ashby?" Amelia asked.

"Who?"

"Our driver," Richard explained, slightly out of breath from the hasty egress. He pointed to a black Towne Car about fifty yards from where they stood. "He usually waits outside the—"

The Agent cut him off. "This is a trap. Quickly, to the street."

"A trap?" Amelia asked, but instead of explaining X simply grabbed her arm and directed her away from the parked vehicle. Immediately as he did, three menacing figures emerged from behind it and took up the pursuit.

X brandished his gas gun at the men. He had little thought of actually using it; in the open air, the concentration of gas would probably dissipate too quickly to be effective. Nevertheless, the mere sight of the weapon, which looked like an ordinary automatic pistol, was enough to send the assassins diving for cover. The Agent kept it trained in their general direction as he has trotted along behind Richard, easily keeping pace with the winded older man as they skirted the edge of the massive gothic structure and rounded onto the sidewalk opposite Central Park. There was no sign of the trio from the parking lot, but as they moved in front of the museum, a different group of men, led by the killer that had dispatched the guards, emerged at a near run, scanning the street for the fugitives. It didn't take long for them to spot their quarry.

"Head for the brown Tourer," instructed the Agent. "It's mine. We can make our getaway in it."

It was Amelia who seemed to respond first, grasping the old man's hand and tugging him along at a pace that was, for Richard at least, almost a dead run. It wasn't nearly fast enough.

"Keep going," X shouted, and then abruptly sprinted ahead of them, crossing the busy avenue and stopping onrushing traffic with a raised palm. He reached his parked car in a matter of seconds and slipped behind the steering wheel, but saw to his chagrin that Richard and his daughter were stranded on the sidewalk in front of the museum, unable to find a break in the flow of cars, and seemingly unaware of the malcontents closing on their position.

With a loud blast of the Ford's horn, X whipped out into the stream, triggering a sympathetic cacophony of screeching tires and horn blasts. The brown sedan carved a direct line across the macadam, still blaring its trumpet alarm, and bounced up onto the sidewalk, scattering tourists and assassins alike. He drew to a stop beside Richard and threw the door open.

"Hurry!"

The father and daughter pair barely made it inside ahead of their pursuers. The killer—LeMartre—caught the door before Amelia could pull it shut and attempted to wriggle his way inside. He would have succeeded too, but for the quick thinking of the man behind the wheel. X opened the throttle wide and the Tourer shot off the sidewalk like a rocket, yanking the assassin violently forward and spilling him into the street. The brown automobile fishtailed across the pavement for a moment, then straightened and charged forward.

Their elation at the narrow escape was short lived. A glance in the side mirror revealed a familiar looking automobile—Richard's Towne Car—bursting onto the main thoroughfare. X didn't need X-ray vision to know that it was being driven by one of the assassins, but when the elegant vehicle pulled up short to admit the leader of the group, his suspicions were confirmed.

"Hang on," he shouted and whipped the Tourer into a sharp right turn. The big brown sedan left smoking trails of rubber as it skidded around the corner. There was a loud crashing sound as the front end blasted through a short wooden barricade, and then the car was abruptly swallowed by the greenery of Central Park.

Under the strong guiding hand of Mayor LaGuardia, Central Park had been reborn, restored from a shabby wasteland into an emerald jewel on the crown of the city's collective pride, where children and adults alike played and relaxed in an island of tranquility. That tranquility was now about to be completely shattered.

X trumpeted the horn again, warning park goers of the relentless machine of destruction that was now charging down the service access road. About five seconds later, the bigger Towne Car crashed through the entrance as well, and its driver was far less concerned about running down innocents. That complete lack of regard for human life translated into an advantage of speed for the gang of killers; they were closing fast.

The mayhem continued unchecked. X kept one eye on the side mirror, watching anxiously as the Towne Car moved inexorably closer. He wasn't surprised at all to see a figure lean out from the passenger side and point a small dark object at the fleeing Tourer.

"Get down!"

Almost simultaneous with his warning, a tiny spurt of flame signaled the escalation from chase to running gun battle, followed immediately by a loud thump as something struck the rear of the Ford. The Agent wasn't overly concerned for his own safety or that of his passengers; the Ford was one of his specially modified vehicles—modified with, among other things, heavy manganese-steel armor plating and extra-thick window glass treated with a special chemical to make it bullet resistant. But every bullet that ricocheted from the impervious exterior of the car might very well strike an innocent hundreds of feet away. It was time to end the pursuit once and for all.

The spires of Belvedere Castle loomed ahead over the treetops, and X steered toward that landmark, a plan taking shape in his mind. The road they currently traveled would bring them abreast of the castle in a matter of seconds, and that seemed as good a place as any to make a stand against the assassins.

The Agent brought the car around a corner, momentarily removing himself from his foes' line of sight, and tapped the brakes. As the Tourer slowed, he flipped a switch under the steering column, releasing a smoke grenade from a compartment hidden behind the rear bumper. A cloud of white smoke began to billow in their wake, completely obscuring the roadway.

The smoke was just that—a chemical substance that burned rapidly to produce a screen to mask their escape. Yet the Agent continued braking and the brown car came to a complete halt about twenty yards from the roiling mist.

"What are you doing?" Amelia shrieked, still hidden in the well behind the driver's seat.

The Agent did not answer, but continued to watch the mirror, one foot resting on the accelerator poised for action. He was taking an awful risk, but if the gamble paid off....

A moment later, the front end of the Towne Car emerged from the smoke. In his eagerness, the driver had not eased off one bit. Now, as the sight of the motionless Ford filled his view, he reacted instinctively to avoid a collision, stabbing the brakes and twisting the steering wheel to the left. His panicked maneuver wasn't enough to prevent a crash, but as the rear end of the Towne Car sloughed around, certain to strike the Tourer, X stomped the gas pedal and the brown car shot forward out of the path of danger.

The Towne Car went into an unrecoverable spin, leaving the paved surface to crash through the low stone wall that guarded an embankment. As it scraped over the rubble in a shower of sparks, the remains of the bulwark tore out the underbelly of the elegant vehicle, and in a nightmarish instant the spilled fuel ignited in a tremendous explosion of flames. The rolling pyre continued its doomed course, crashing down the steep rocky face into the reservoir below the castle.

The Agent saw very little of this as he sped away, but the roar of the explosion and the column of black smoke in the mirror adequately told the tale. He drove more cautiously now, searching his memory for the quickest route out of the park, where they would be able to blend in with the flow of traffic.

"It's over. You can come up now."

Both of his passengers complied cautiously, peering through the windows as if unwilling to trust their savior's declaration. After a few moments, Richard broke the silence. "Mister...ah, Devine did you say?...I am certainly grateful for you actions on our behalf, but I should like that explanation now. Just what the devil is going on? Who were those men?"

The Agent fixed him with a steely glare. "Those men are part of an organization called the Fraternis Maltae—the Brotherhood of Malta. Does that ring a bell?"

Richard shook his head, a little too quickly, the Agent thought. "The Brotherhood of Malta is an old organization—they've been around for centuries—loosely tied to a monastic order based in France. They are mercenaries—spies and assassins for hire—but until now, they've stayed on the other side of the pond. Two weeks ago, Interpol received a tip that the Brotherhood was after someone they identified only as 'the Art Expert;' a man evidently living in the United States."

"And you think I am this expert?"

"Are you?" Receiving no answer, X turned his attention back to the drive, but continued speaking. "It is quite possible that the Brotherhood is unsure of the identity of their target. The museum theft might well have been designed to draw their quarry into the open. It seems plainly obvious that they believe you are their man, Professor, so I need you to be completely honest with me. Can you think of any reason why these men might want you dead?"

"This is outrageous," Amelia intoned from the back seat. "My father is a model of virtue; a man of the highest moral character."

"Good men are not exempt from the schemes of the wicked. Like it or not, the Brotherhood has fixed their sights on you. Until we can bring them to heel, you are going to have to trust me to protect you." X steered the car through an opening in the perimeter and waited for a break in traffic. "Uh, oh. Looks like we're not done running."

Honking the horn once more, he accelerated into the flow, cutting off a taxi that immediately swerved into a neighboring lane, sideswiping a second car. The accident caused a snarl behind them that allowed the Ford to quickly pick up speed, but it offered them only a momentary reprieve. The flashing of emergence lights and the blare of sirens quickly parted the way through the stalled vehicles, and black and white cruisers shot out in pursuit of the Tourer.

They may have escaped the assassins of the Fraternis Maltae, but now the Agent and his passengers were being hunted by the equally relentless men of the New York Police Department.

# CHAPTER 3—INVESTIGATIONS OF A MURDER

**Inspector John Burks** had never visited the museum until the brouhaha with the stolen Rembrandt erupted, and now only a few days later, he was looking forward to a time when he would never ever have to set foot in it again. It was a dimly lit torch of hope; a stolen masterpiece was bad enough, but now the esteemed repository of art had become a slaughterhouse. Two shapes, indistinct beneath the heavy tarpaulins that had been spread over them, lay to either side of the door he now approached, and he had been warned that two more lay just inside. Yet, the first thing he saw in the sitting room was not the corpses of slain security guards, but the familiar face of Betty Dale speaking with Detective Malvern. Burks moved over to greet the journalist.

"How'd you get here so fast, Miss Dale?"

"I was right in the thick of it, Inspector."

"Betty saw everything," Malvern supplied. "A gang of thugs was after one of the art experts. Evidently the man from Lloyds was actually an Interpol agent. He whisked the art expert and his daughter out the window and to safety."

Burks looked at his detective as though the man were raving. "Lloyds? Interpol? What the devil are you blithering about?"

Despite the horror she had witnessed, Betty managed a rueful smile. "Better let me explain, detective." She quickly outlined everything that had happened from the time she and the ersatz insurance appraiser left the precinct house. She did her best to reproduce the strange oath the killer had uttered, and did not speculate concerning what it might mean. The only piece of information she withheld was the revelation made by the man she identified only as "Alec Devine of Interpol" just before he slipped out the window. Her discretion however was rendered futile as one of Burks's uniformed officers burst into the room, just as she was wrapping up.

"Inspector! Detective Keegan just fainted in the hall!"

A frown crossed the senior policeman's weathered visage, but before he could move out to investigate, a second constable shouted an update. "He's okay! It looks like he stepped on a glass capsule filled with knockout gas."

Betty's heart sank as Burks correctly deduced the significance of this discovery. "Knockout gas? I might have known he would be in the middle of this."

"The Interpol fellow used knockout gas on the killers," Betty quickly supplied. "Gee, do you think he might have been Agent X?"

"Impersonating an officer of the law is something he excels at," Burks snarled, recalling an occasion when X had actually impersonated the inspector himself. "By God, we'll get him this time, and he'll answer for his crimes."

Betty bit her tongue and let the ace detective rant. It was no use defending the Agent to the police; despite the many criminal schemes that Secret Agent X had thwarted, Burks was determined to prove that the man of a thousand faces was a villain of the highest order. Yet, the inspector's prejudices were of only secondary concern to the reporter. She was in a unique position to set the story straight in her newspaper, exonerating X in the court of public opinion, if nowhere else, but was that what her old friend would want her to do? Might she inadvertently spoil his clever schemes by stripping away his false identity?

When Burks paused to catch his breath, Betty jumped in. "Need anything more from me, Inspector? If not, I'd like to get back to The Herald. There just might be time to make the late edition."

The policeman frowned but then dismissed her with a brusque wave and Betty hurried off, her mind turning like a machine, to find just the right words to tell the city the real story.

**Although their methods** were not as Draconian as those employed by the Brotherhood, the NYPD had a greater arsenal of resources at their disposal. The two police cars that dogged the Agent's sedan were in constant radio contact with a dispatcher who in turn maneuvered other patrol cars from all over the city to intercept the vehicle that had been spotted fleeing the scene of the museum murders. Secret Agent X had only one advantage over them: he knew where he was going.

Immediately as he had left the park road, he commenced navigating the urban maze to a secret location uptown. Getting there was going to be tricky—he knew the police were even now setting up road blocks in his path—but he still had a few cards up his sleeve.

They had only gone about twenty blocks when the first roadblock came into view, about 100 yards ahead. X scanned the street quickly looking for a means of escape but the police had chosen this location well. There were no alleys or cross streets the entire length of the block. By sealing the far end of the street, they had created a dead end from which it would be almost impossible for their prey to escape. But the Agent's steel-colored eyes saw something else that was almost as good.

"When I give the word," he said, never taking his eyes off the road. "I want you both to duck down."

Taking their silence as acceptance, the Agent immediately set his plan in motion. He thumbed the switch to release one of the smoke grenades, and as the white smoke billowed to fill the street with a cloud of impenetrable fumes, he pulled the handbrake and twisted the steering wheel sharply to the left.

Obscured by smoke, no one saw the brown Ford spin around 180 degrees, nor did anyone outside see the strange flash of light that burst from the vehicle. The Agent steered into the curb, slotting the car into an open parking space and hastily killed the engine.

"Now!" he shouted, heeding his own advice by lying flat across the seat. "Get down and stay that way."

It only took a minute or so for the smoke to clear. During that time, the passengers of the Ford sat motionless, hardly daring to breath, as the audible cry of nearby police sirens continued to assail their ears. Yet, the din of the claxons did not change during all that time; the patrol cars were wisely staying out of the blinding miasma.

"I don't understand," Amelia said, breaking the unbearable silence. "Why are we hiding from the police? We didn't do anything wrong."

The Agent had been wondering when one of his charges would pose that question; he wasn't surprised at all that it had been the daughter, rather than the father. Before he could answer, Richard jumped in. "It's better not to involve the local authorities in this matter, my dear. However sir, I fail to see how just sitting here will help our cause. The police are sure to recognize—"

"Just stay down," X reiterated in a tone that brooked no argument. The smoke had cleared now and the siren wails grew closer as the patrol cars slowly rolled up on them and then, inexplicably, went right past. The clamor of sirens was abruptly cut off and the trio in the Ford could hear shouts of consternation from beyond their hiding place. After what seemed an eternity, there was a roar of engines and the din outside ceased altogether. The Agent cautiously raised his head, and then sat fully upright and switched on the engine.

"All clear. You can get up now."

To the amazement of his passengers, the street was now open in both directions; there was no sign of police presence. X pulled out from his parking spot and drove at a considerably more restrained pace through the urban jungle. Less than five minutes after escaping the roadblock, he pulled the car into a large brick building decorated with a sign that read: "Murphy Bros. Auto Repair." As he eased into the garage, a fellow in greasy overalls, chewing on the stub of a cigar, moved over to greet them.

"Howya doin', pal?"

"Never better," X said, smiling as he got out. He opened the door for his passengers as the mechanic walked slowly around the vehicle.

"What can I do ya fer?"

"I'd like to get it painted. Something bright." He turned to the girl. "What do you think, maybe a nice fire engine red?"

Amelia didn't answer. She was staring dumbfounded at the car—at the charcoal gray Ford—which had brought her to this place. "Wasn't it…?"

The Agent grinned. The special "flash paint" has worked perfectly. The brown paint that had covered the Ford had been impregnated with a special chemical, not unlike the flash powder used by stage magicians, and with the application of a small electrical charge, had vaporized completely, exposing the dark gray underneath. "Red, it is my friend. Is there someplace we can relax while we wait?"

The grease monkey rolled the cigar to one side of him mouth and jabbed a thumb over one shoulder. "There's a little apartment upstairs. Make yourselves at home."

X steered Richard and his daughter toward the open staircase, then turned back to the mechanic and addressed him in a low voice. "Thanks a million, Murphy."

The other fellow just winked, and then drew a little "X" in the air with his finger.

**Typing like a** woman possessed, Betty Dale handed her story to the copy editor a mere fifteen minutes after returning to the Herald Building, but she could not escape the feeling that the hasty recap of the events she had witnessed was merely a prelude to something greater. Her notebook lay open on the desktop, a page filled with scribbled shorthand notes recorded both on the scene and during the taxicab ride back to the newspaper office. Two items had been circled and despite her best efforts at deductive reasoning, remained completely foreign to her; in fact, she was almost certain that they were words from another language:

"FRATERNIS MALTAY"<br>"FORMONT SOCK"

Realizing that the answer to the riddle wasn't about to appear magically on the page, she snatched up the notebook and headed down to The Herald's morgue— the musty cellar where every single issue of The Herald, all the way back to its inaugural edition, which announced the surrender of Confederate forces at Appomattox Courthouse, were filed, catalogued and cross referenced.

The archivist, Billy Hayes, remembered that first issue—a mere boy at the time, he had stood on street corners hawking the Herald to passersby. Though he had never received a formal education, he was one of the most knowledgeable people Betty knew; he not only read every column inch of The Herald, but also had dutifully cross referenced each article and filed them away for future reference. A kindly old fellow who always wore a red cable knit sweater, even on the hottest day of summer, and sipped continually from a chipped coffee mug—rumor had it that there was more than coffee in that cup—Hayes was Betty's best chance at unraveling the mystery.

"Heya, Billy."

"Ah, Miss Dale." Hayes was stooped over a large table where several issues of the newspaper lay spread out for his perusal. He took a swig of coffee then straightened to greet her. "Always a pleasure. What can I look up for you today?"

Betty flashed him a winning smile then showed him the notebook. The older man straightened his glasses, and then peered at the scribble intently. "Well, 'Fraternis' sounds kind of like 'fraternity.'"

"I thought the same. Some kind of secret society?"

"Hmm. 'Maltay.' That rings a bell." He scratched his stubbly chin thoughtfully, and then snapped his fingers in revelation. "Ever heard of the Maltese Cross?"

"I've heard of the Maltese Falcon."

Hayes winked at her knowingly. "In both cases, the word 'Maltese' comes from the island of Malta, and I wouldn't be at all surprised if your fraternity is somehow connected as well. Let's start there."

The old fellow shuffled down a row of card files to the beginning of the section marked "Ma." He flipped through it until he found a section of several cards all somehow pertaining to Malta. "Aha, this just might be the thing. There are several articles about the Knights of Saint John, also sometimes called the Knights of Malta."

He wrote the date of the most relevant articles on a piece of scratch paper then went off to pull those issues from the vault. In a matter of minutes, Betty was reading various news items pertaining to the Knights of Malta.

"Listen to this: 'The Knights of the Order of St. John of Jerusalem were at one time known as the Knights Hospitaller, owing to their practice of establishing hostels throughout the Holy Lands during the years of the Crusades. They amassed enormous wealth during this period. When the Knights of the Temple of Solomon were crushed by papal decree, much of their land holdings and vast riches fell into the hands of the Knights Hospitaller, who ultimately separated into several groups, including the Knights of Malta...et cetera... and the Fraternis Maltae.' That's it!"

"Is there anything about 'Montsock'?"

Betty scanned down the article. "Here it is. I just spelled it wrong. I think it's a French word. 'Most of the splinter organizations remain to this day, but some have fallen into ignominy, such as the Fraternis Maltae which was all but destroyed in the Tragedy of Mont Sacre in 1918.' Billy, we've got to look up Mont Sacre. That's the key to everything."

The archivist was already moving off to his card files and a few minutes later Betty was immersed in the tale of the siege and ultimate destruction of the French village of Mont Sacre. At first, she read aloud a few sentences that seemed important to their search, but after a minute, she fell silent and her eyes grew wide. When she finished, her initial elation had been completely sublimated. Now there was only a sort of horrified awe. She pushed the paper back to the archivist. "Billy, I need everything you can find about a man named Auguste Richard."

## CHAPTER 4-INTO THE SPIDER'S WEB

**Murphy Bros. Auto** Repair was just one of several legitimate businesses that served double-duty as part of Secret Agent X's vast underground organization. While they earned their daily bread providing necessary services for the residents of their respective neighborhoods, they also contributed to the war on crime and evil by using their skills to improve the Agent's arsenal of weapons and equipment, or to provide safe haven when the need arose. The Murphy brothers, for example, had worked to outfit several of the Agent's automobiles with flash-paint, smoke grenade launchers and several other useful accouterments. Like most of the men and women working on behalf of the Agent, they had little inkling of the scope of the organization; most of their contact came through a man named Harvey Bates, who was in fact, the director of the effort and answered only to Secret Agent X himself.

While Sam Murphy worked to refit the Tourer, Agent X was helping his charges get settled in. Richard had been strangely silent and Amelia had followed his lead, despite the curiosity burning in her eyes.

X however had little time to play the dutiful host. The Brotherhood's attack at the museum had been a big surprise; he had not expected something quite so audacious or foolhardy from an organization that had perfected the art of espionage centuries before. There had to be a compelling reason for their daring gambit and he needed to find out what it was. After encouraging Richard and his daughter to make full use of the amenities in the little flat, he excused himself and retreated to the tiny office in the downstairs garage. There, concealed behind a heavy bookshelf that appeared to be bolted to the wall, was the entrance to a small room, which contained only a special radio transmitter. The Agent seated himself before the radio and began tapping out a coded message summoning Harvey Bates. The reply came almost immediately.

"Chief, are you all right? The museum incident is already hitting the papers and they know you were involved."

Both men were as conversant in telegraphy as they were in spoken language and X responded without having to consult a Morse code chart. "Couldn't be helped Harvey. They struck without warning and it was all I could do to get Richard to safety."

"Then he is the 'art expert'?"

The Agent hesitated before replying, but not because of any uncertainty. "He's the one; no doubt about it."

"What do you need?"

"The location of the Brotherhood's headquarters in the city. They can't have pulled this together without some local help."

"Already got that for you. They're working out of the hall of the local chapter of the Knights of Malta. Here's the address."

X scribbled the street and number on a scratch pad. "Do the police know about them yet?"

"No," Bates replied. "They think this was all something you concocted to steal the painting."

"Good. That should keep them out of my way." X took out the cruciform dagger and studied it thoughtfully. "I need you to pull together everything we know about the Brotherhood and send it to drop point Violet."

"I'll have a runner deliver it within the hour. Anything else?"

Before X could reply, a chime sounded. It was a warning bell connected to the upstairs door; one of his guests was wandering. "That should do it. I'll be in touch."

He hastily signed off and crept back into the office just in time to see Amelia descending the stairs. He calmly exited the office and went to meet her. "Is something wrong?"

The girl averted her eyes guiltily. "No. My father… He's too old for this sort of excitement. He's resting. I wanted to… Well, thank you for everything."

"It's quite all right, Miss." He gestured to the stairs. "I think it might be well for you to rest, too."

"Are we still in danger?"

Something about her tone caught the Agent's attention. "Miss Richard, do you know something about all this?"

"Why on earth would I know anything?" she answered, but her reply came too quickly and she looked away again as she spoke.

"Amelia, I can't help you or your father if you're not honest with me." He placed a firm hand on her shoulder, compelling her to face him. "I think you want to tell me."

The pretty redhead sighed nervously and then fished a cigarette from her bag.

"You shouldn't smoke in here." He motioned to the stairs again. "Let's go up to the roof where we can speak privately."

A look of gratitude dawned on her face and for the first time, the Agent saw her, not as an empty-headed dilettante, but as a frightened and naïve child. Without another word, he guided her up the stairs, bypassing the apartment, and brought her to another set of steps leading to the open roof of the garage. The noise of the city was strangely soothing as they settled against the parapet, and Amelia waited only long enough to take a long drag from her cigarette before bursting into tears.

"When I was very young, he used to warn me that bad men might come someday… that we might have to leave everything behind. I thought he was just telling me stories to frighten me. We've always been so safe at the house."

X took her hand, soothing. "Start at the beginning. You weren't born in America, were you?"

"No. I was very young when we came here. I don't remember anything from before. Father told me that we had to leave because of the war. Everything was ruined there; America was the land of opportunity. After mother died, there was no reason to stay."

The Agent nodded and despite the urgency of his inquiry, kept his voice calm. "What about the 'bad men'? Did he ever tell you who they were, or why they might come after him?"

"I thought it might have something to do with his art collection. I may be young, but it wasn't too hard to figure out that he didn't come by everything honestly. But he's a good man; he's always used our wealth to help others. Anything he might have done in the past… well, he's not that person anymore."

The Agent maintained his compassionate expression. "Don't worry, Amelia. I'm not going to let these scoundrels hurt you or your father. I'm going to go out and see what I can learn about them. I need the two of you to stay here where it's safe. Promise me that you will."

She nodded, stubbing out her cigarette.

"Good. Now go back and get some rest yourself."

He escorted her back to the apartment and as soon as she was stationed within, hastened down to the garage where Murphy had a second car ready, this one a 1929 DeSoto that looked ready for the junk heap. X slid behind the steering wheel with a wry smile. It might not have all the bells and whistles of his modified automobiles, but the old DeSoto had its own kind of natural camouflage.

He did not drive immediately to the address Bates had supplied. Instead, he traveled across town to his own residence, a brownstone dwelling on the west side. Taking care that no one observe his entrance, he went in and stationed himself before a large three-way vanity mirror.

He chuckled to himself as the unfamiliar face of Rhys-Reynolds/Devine stared back from the glass. He wore so many faces that sometimes he forgot which one was his own. But in the unending battle against evil, his ability to disguise himself was his greatest weapon; his true face, his true identity, meant nothing in that struggle.

Well, he thought, almost nothing.

He closed his eyes, searching his memory for every detail of the face he now chose to don: that of the young assassin. There was a black wig in his kit that would require only a few snips with barber's scissors to be perfect. The rest he accomplished with a variety of prosthetic pads and a special cosmetic putty that he dyed with pigments to mimic the olive complexion of the young killer. The finishing touch was a costume from his extensive wardrobe that approximated the garb the fellow had worn. The final result would stand up to all but the closest scrutiny.

Leaving as discreetly as he had arrived, the Agent next drove to the place where he had directed Harvey Bates to leave the information about the Fraternis Maltae. Drop point Violet was just one of many such clandestine locations throughout the city where documents and equipment could be covertly picked up. In this case, it was a simple newspaper kiosk and the file had been secreted within the pages of the late edition of The Herald. X did not pause to read the front-page story about the murders at the museum, but returned to the relative privacy of the DeSoto in order to skim the more important papers hidden within.

Much of the information was already known to him; the history of the Brotherhood—a long and violent tale of espionage and assassination for hire. Despite their origins as a monastic brotherhood of the Church, the men who had taken vows to be part of the Fraternis Maltae seemed much more devoted to secular interests. For centuries, they had used their skills to alter the face of Europe, often betraying former patrons in favor of new and more powerful allies. They had even aligned themselves with Napoleon, in opposition to the interests of their parent order, and in so doing helped the Corsican become, if ever so briefly, the most powerful man alive. He read also of their apparent demise at the hands of a brutal

Prussian noble during the Great War, and how the man had learned of their secret treasure storehouse and savagely slaughtered every member... or so it was believed. The Agent skipped over most of this; his interest was in the more recent events.

The Brotherhood had not perished as believed, but stripped of their wealth, they had retreated into the woodwork to nurse their wounds. It had taken more than a decade to rebuild, and even now, they were a shadow of their former strength. Yet, what they lacked in resources, they had more than made up for in ambition. Through the tireless efforts of their Grandmaster, Yves Ste. Jean d'Arc, and the Chevalier Premiere or First Knight, Armande LeMartre, the Fraternis Maltae was once more becoming a force to be reckoned with.

The last page in the document was a detail of the most recent information about the First Knight's mission to assassinate 'the art expert.' LeMartre was leading the effort personally, along with more than a score of apprentices—men who, despite their lack of seniority in the organization, were nonetheless hardened killers. The Agent's own experiences verified this last assessment; the Brotherhood had shown no hesitation in killing innocents who stood in their way.

X drove to within a block of the Brotherhood's headquarters and finished the journey into the lion's den on foot. Despite his outward calm, a tremor of adrenaline pulsed in his veins; he had often walked in the lairs of criminal masterminds, imitating their minions so perfectly that no one was the wiser, but this time it was different. He knew nothing about the young man whose face he now wore. But for the brief utterance in the instant before the attack on Richard, he had never heard the assassin's voice, nor did he know any of the man's mannerisms. He would not even be able to answer to the man's name, if called, and there was a better than even chance that he might come face to face with the young man himself. His only hope at success was to get in quickly and quietly, and leave just the same way.

His first test came at the massive wooden door to the old chapel hall. A monk, replete with tonsure and the chasuble of a Benedictine acolyte, stood guard there, but gestured for him to enter when X held up the dagger—the mark of an apprentice in the Fraternis Maltae. The hall beyond seemed deserted; he could only hope that the itinerate residents were out combing the city for their prey.

He bypassed an ornate, centrally located door—no doubt some kind of office— choosing instead a simpler, unmarked portal further along, which opened to reveal an empty guest room. The Agent closed and locked the door behind him, then moved to a window that overlooked an inner courtyard, which like the hall, was devoid of human presence. He popped the window open, then climbed out and ducked behind a row of arborvitaes that skirted the perimeter of the building. The window to the office was slightly ajar, and in a matter of seconds, he hoisted himself inside.

His initial assumption about the room proved correct. Not only was it an office, it was the temporary headquarters of the Fraternis Maltae. A large oak desk stood directly in front of the window, and on its surface, along with a scattering of newspaper clipping, an overflowing ashtray and a pack of Gauloises cigarettes, was an elaborate sheathed sword, with a hilt fashioned in the form of a crucifix. The Agent gently moved the scabbard to one side in order to get a better look at the papers beneath.

The articles trimmed from The Herald and other daily tabloids were a brief history of the theft of the Rembrandt, beginning with the obnoxious front-page headlines and finishing with a few brief columns concerning the decision to bring in a panel of experts to verify the painting's authenticity. The information seemed sparse—too little by far to prompt the Brotherhood to launch such an open attack on Richard. In fact, nowhere was Richard even mentioned.

"What am I missing?" he murmured, glancing over the desktop once more. Then his eyes settled, not on the documents, but on the sheathed blade weapon. But for its length, it was identical to the dagger… The Agent took out the smaller blade—the badge of the apprentice knight. The sword was reserved for those who had earned higher rank in the organization.

The attack at the museum was led by an apprentice, he realized. There was no grand strategy behind it. I've badly overestimated them.

He turned toward the window, eager to be away from the lair of his enemies, but it was already too late. The click of the door latch froze him in his tracks and he barely had time to compose himself in front of the open window before the creak of the hinges signaled that he was no longer alone. He turned, affecting a casual demeanor, to greet the newcomer.

There was no mistaking the identity of the man that now regarded him from across the room; it was Armande LeMarte, the First Knight himself. His dark complexion looked haggard, as if burdened with great anxiety or grief, but when his eyes alit upon the disguised countenance of Agent X, a strange sort of recognition flashed in his eyes.

"Andre? But you are…" His expression seemed to roil like a mirage, before finally hardening into an emotionless mask. "What are you doing in here?"

X sucked in a breath. This was the moment he had dreaded. He opened his mouth as if to answer, but then launched into a coughing fit. It was stalling tactic, nothing more, yet it might just be enough to explain away the difference in his voice when he at last answered. As the ersatz paroxysm continued, he spied the cigarettes on the desk and in a flash of inspiration, seized one and lit up.

LeMartre's face flickered with something that was not quite bemusement. "When did you start smoking cigarettes, little brother?"

The question had been posed in French, a language the Agent had no trouble comprehending, but the last phrase felt like blow to the gut. The identity he had assumed in order to gain entrance to the headquarters of the Fraternis Maltae was none other than the First Knight's own brother. Now that the revelation was in the open, he cursed himself for not having seen the familial resemblance between the young assassin at the museum and the chief enforcer of the Brotherhood. He pretended to take a deep drag of harsh tobacco smoke, and then started coughing

SEAN ELLIS | 42

again.

"Today seemed like a good day to start," he answered in French, his voice gravelly between coughing spasms.

LeMarte nodded slowly, then started brushing at threads or lint on his shirt front... except that wasn't quite what he was doing. His eyes never left the Agent's face. "Indeed. It did not go well today."

"I believe I may know where the art expert is going next," X answered, taking a step toward the door. "I will make things right, First Knight."

The Chevalier Premiere did not move to impede him, but as he passed, LeMarte spoke. "A moment, Andre. Please, sit down."

X puffed on the cigarette again. "Yes, my brother?"

LeMarte did not meet his gaze this time, but moved toward the front of the desk, letting his hand rest on the scabbard of the sword. "Have you seen the late edition of the newspaper, my brother? A reporter has been kind enough to give us the name of the man we seek. Does that surprise you?"

It was a trap and the Agent knew it. "I have not had time to read the news."

"Oh, you should. There is a great deal of information about today's... debacle." LeMarte moved away from the desk and the Agent was relieved to see that the sword remained where it was. The First Knight continued moving about the room as he spoke. "Not just what happened at the museum. Oh, no. There is also news of men in cars racing through a city park. One of those cars crashed and burst into flames. All of the men inside were killed.

"You were killed, Andre."

The Agent started for the door, but something heavy crashed into the back of his head and night fell in the middle of the afternoon.

## CHAPTER 5-THE TRAGEDY OF MONT SACRE

**It was, he** thought, like the surface of another planet.

Everything was alien. A strange pall hung over the world; not quite mist, not quite smoke, but a stench of burning and decay. The ground was ragged with craters and hastily dug trenches. There were no trees anymore; they had all been hewn down for firewood and makeshift buttresses. What few structures that remained standing were on the verge of collapse, shot full of holes or alternately reinforced with sandbags so that they no longer resembled the work of carpenters. And everywhere the eye looked, there was wire—a twisting sculpture of barbed wire that surrounded the entire village—denying entrance, or more accurately, preventing escape.

He turned away from the strange tableau to regard the young prisoner, suspended between two of his soldiers. Like the village, the man was also wrapped in a sheath of wire. The metal strands surrounded his torso and extremities and blood flowed from dozens of minor wounds where the sharp steel thorns had torn his flesh.

"We caught him on the outer perimeter," one of the soldiers was saying. "The dogs drove him to the wire and he got tangled up trying to flee."

A wry smile crossed the jailer's face—the grin of a sadist. "There is no escape, my young friend. I would have thought that you would have realized this by now." He turned to the soldiers. "Bring him before the other prisoners. It seems I have been remiss in explaining the futility of escape to those in our care."

Though his expression remained defiant, the young man—an enemy courier wounded in an ambush and brought to the Mont Sacre prison camp a week previously—was on the verge of collapse. The soldiers dragged him through the labyrinth of wire and dropped him in a heap just inside the large holding area. The rest of the prisoners, an even mix of enemy captives and local citizens numbering about a hundred, had been marshaled in the yard and now stood under the ominous shadow of guard towers outfitted with Maschinengewehr 08 machine guns.

"Tie him to the gates."

The two soldiers hoisted the prisoner, still wrapped in his spider-web cocoon, onto the large swinging barrier spreading his arms wide like a crucifixion while the jailer gazed at the emaciated throng, allowing their collective dread to reach a fever pitch.

"Your attention, please. One of your number was captured this morning while trying to escape. Evidently, he did not understand the consequences of such an action. For this, I can blame only myself. Perhaps I did not make it clear to him, or to all of you, that such behavior cannot be tolerated."

He strode forward into their midst, barely able to contain his amusement as they shrank away before his deadly gaze. He made a circuit of the crowd, like a general inspecting the troops, then returned to stand before the captive hanging from the gate. Blood now oozed from the wire that dug into his wrists, but through the pain, the young man's eyes were clear and full of hate. The jailer's smile was as severe as the blade of a guillotine and although he spoke to the assembly, he held the prisoner's gaze with his own stare.

"It is fortunate for all of you that he did not succeed. You all know my standing order that, for every man that escapes, twenty of his co-conspirators must be executed. However, since he did not escape, it will only be necessary to punish ten."

The young man sucked in an agonized breath. "No! You can't…"

"Which ten shall it be?"

Despite his agony, the young man struggled against his bonds. "You can't do this. I'm the one who tried to escape. Kill me!"

The jailer affected a sad mien. "But how would that help you learn the folly of your ways? But I am merciful. You must help me decide which ten to choose. Shall I select ten of your brave comrades in arms? Or shall we take ten from among the villagers? Decide now, or I will rescind my generous offer and take ten of each."

The rage that suffused the face of the young captive was exquisite. At a gesture from the jailer, twenty souls were dragged from the crowd—ten wearing the torn and threadbare uniforms of three different enemy armed forces, and ten wearing the ragged remains of civilian clothes. The latter group included men and women, young and old alike.

"Which will it be, brave young soldier? I give you to the count of ten." He immediately began counting, his words metered to the tick of an invisible clock, each one falling like a scythe on the hopes of the prisoners.

The young man's hopeless anger quickly dissolved into helpless panic. "Please don't do this…"

"Six… Seven…"

"Choose us lad," one of the British officers called. "We all knew this war might be the death of us. Spare the women and children."

"Nine… Ten."

"Yes," cried the youth. "The soldiers. If you have no mercy in your heart, take the soldiers."

The jailer smiled his sad, mocking smile. "I'm sorry, but it's too late. I gave you ample time to decide." He turned to his own soldiers. "Shoot them all in the back of the head, then hang them up on the wall to keep him company."

The cries of protest chased after the jailer as he walked away, leaving his men to carry out the grim task. After the fourth or fifth gunshot however, the wailing faded away to nothing. For his own part, the jailer had already dismissed the incident from memory; he had other matters to consider. The search….

"Mein herr!"

The shout reached him through the door of the office he had appropriated from the town mayor. It belonged to his chief lieutenant. "Come in."

The man burst into the room, his face covered in sweat and grime. "Mein herr, we found it! We found the treasure."

The jailer was on his feet. "Show me."

The pair raced through the deserted streets of the village, their steps haunted by occasional echoes of gunfire from the nearby prison compound. As they entered a small chapel across the town square from the mayor's residence, the twentieth and final shot reverberated like thunder across the hills.

The lieutenant directed him to the altar at the front of the nave. The mensa had been pushed aside to reveal a dark hole leading directly down into the dais. "The entrance was here all along, but cleverly concealed. We found it by undermining the foundation, but once we broke through, it was a simple matter to open the secret passage."

The jailer did not hesitate to lower himself into the exposed passageway, where his feet quickly found the rungs of a ladder. He descended into the utter night, more than three fathoms down, until his boots at last came to rest on the hard surface of a sub-cellar. The flame of his cigarette lighter cast a dim glow into the chamber that was immediately returned by dozens of glittering golden surfaces.

The lieutenant joined him a moment later. "Is it not magnificent?"

"It is everything I dreamed it would be," the jailer answered reverently. "Who else knows of this?"

"Only the laborers. I have already seen to them."

There was no ambiguity about the euphemism. Both men had always known that the treasure, if it really existed, would be for them alone. None of the soldiers in the camp knew of their tireless search. And of course, the jailer's plans did not allow for an equal division of the loot with his subordinates, but there would be time enough to deal with that when it had been safely transferred away from this hellish place.

"Excellent," he breathed. "Then we are finished here."

"What about the camp? The prisoners? There must be some among the villagers who know of this."

"We are finished with them as well. Give them all an extra ration of food tonight, along with a generous helping of rat poison. If any remain alive in the morning, we will shoot them. After that, burn everything."

"Mein herr, some of the men... They have doubts about the way we have treated the prisoners. If we command them to do this..."

"We cannot allow anyone to bring the tale of what has happened here to the outside world."

The dull firelight made the lieutenant's horrified expression seem all the more hellish. "You mean to kill our own soldiers as well?"

The jailer took one last look at the treasure piled up in the chamber. "The price of glory is often paid in blood. Kill them; kill everyone."

**Richard awoke in** a cold sweat, gripping the cushions of the sofa as if they were the gunwales of a life raft, and he adrift in a raging sea. "Amelia?"

"I am here father."

He sat up and searched the room to find his lovely red-haired daughter. "Where are we, Amelia? What is this place?"

"Mr. Devine brought us here, father, after those men at the museum tried to kill you."

Richard rose unsteadily to his feet. "Yes. I remember. I must have dozed off. Where is Mr. Devine?"

"He went out to investigate the attack. He made me promise to stay here."

The old man shook his silver head. "No, Amelia. It is too late for that. We must get to the house, quickly, before they do. Where's Ashby?"

A strange sad look crossed the girl's face. "Father, Ashby isn't here. I think those men might have killed him."

"We shall have to call a taxicab then. Quickly, girl; there is no time to lose."

For just a moment, Amelia looked as if she might defy her father and keep her promise to their mysterious savior. But she had known the man calling himself 'Alec Devine' for only an afternoon; her father had protected her for all of her years. "The man working downstairs may try to stop us. We should go to the roof and leave by the fire escape. That way no one will know we have gone."

"Very good," Richard replied, a gleam of admiration in his eye. "We will return to the house just long enough to gather a few essential things, and then you and I will leave."

"Leave? Where will we go?"

"Somewhere safe, Amelia. Somewhere where you will be safe."

**A slap brought** the Agent back to consciousness, but also had the effect of exacerbating the throb of pain in the back of his skull. When he opened his eyes, he saw two of everything and despite his best efforts, the world refused to come into focus. Even through the blur however, he had no difficulty recognizing Armande LeMartre.

"Who are you?" the First Knight hissed. "Why do you look like my brother, who even now lies dead—burnt almost beyond recognition—on a coroner's slab?"

The Agent fought through the pain, rejecting the answers that came almost unbidden to his lips. A twitch of his cheeks confirmed that the mask was still in place; his captor had either chosen not to expose his true face or had failed to realize that the visage of his slain sibling was a construct of prosthetics and putty.

"Brother," he managed to say, slurring his speech to sound groggier than he actually felt. "What are you saying? It is I, Andre."

"Is that so?"

LeMarte's hands again moved, as if to pick at lint on his shirtfront, and it was only now that the Agent realized what the man was doing. The strange gestures were some form of sign language—a non-verbal method of communicating developed and used exclusively by the Knights of the Fraternis Maltae. His heart sank. "Brother, my eyes are not working. I cannot see what it is that you are saying."

"Your eyes were working fine before I hit you, pretender, but still you did not comprehend. Now I will ask you again; who are you?"

X blinked several times, willing the pain down to the level of a dull roar in his ears. His vision was clearing and he could now see that LeMartre had been joined by two other men, posted on either side of the bound Secret Agent. He further realized that he was now seated in a straight-backed wooden chair, with his arms bent around the upright backrest and his wrists bound together with what felt like packing twine. He also saw that his captor now possessed his gas gun, though it was unlikely that the man believed it to be anything but a common automatic pistol.

He evinced defeat with a heavy sigh, trying to distract his guards from what he was doing with his nimble fingers. "I am a policeman, LeMartre. We've been investigating the Brotherhood for some time now. We know all about what you've been up to. I was picked because of my resemblance to Andre, but we never meant for him or anyone to be killed. It's time to end this without any more bloodshed. If you kill me, you're bound for Old Sparky up at Sing Sing."

A corner of the First Knight's mouth twitched. "'Old Sparky?' I don't think so, detective… if you indeed you are a detective, which I very much doubt. We have allies in the police department, even in your government."

"No, I think rather that you are the man the newspapers call 'Secret Agent X.'" He held up a copy of The Herald. "It's all here. 'Secret Agent X Foils Murder Attempt at the Met.' You are the one who killed Andre, and now you are going to die."

As LeMartre had been speaking, X's fingers were working his watch crystal loose. The crystal was not a solid piece of glass, but rather a hollow capsule filled with the same anesthetizing gas as his gun. Yet it was not the vapor inside the crystal that he needed now, but rather the glass itself. Carefully transferring the disk to his thumb and forefinger, he went to work, sawing at his bonds, but he needed more time if he was going to get free.

"Tell me something," he said, seemingly oblivious to LeMartre's threat or to the gun barrel now pointing toward his face. "Tell me why?"

"Why?"

"Why are you after Richard?"

The hand holding the pistol wavered then moved away. "Richard? Yes, that is what he calls himself now. Back then, he had a different name."

One strand of the twine separated with a faint pop. The Agent shrugged his shoulders to hide the subtle release of tension. "You mean back at Mont Sacre?"

"Ah, you know about Mont Sacre? Then why do you need to ask? Von Reichardt razed our home to the ground, killed women and children, left us all for dead. We are mercenaries, true, but this is a matter of honor."

"Honor? Hah. Why don't you admit the truth, if only to yourself? You're after the treasure." Another strand parted… just one more.

LeMartre's eyes grew cold.

"Oh, yes," X continued. "I know all about the treasure. You're not after Richard or Von Reichardt…or whatever he's calling himself this week… for revenge. You just want the treasure so you can rebuild your criminal empire."

"The treasure is ours. It is our birthright. We will have it." LeMartre's righteous indignation simmered down to something more like grim determination. "The world is changing, Secret Agent X. New kings and powers are rising. The wise will seek the favor of the Fraternis Maltae, and in turn we will ensure that their dominion extends to every corner of the Earth."

The pistol came up again, mere inches from X's forehead. "Regrettably for you, it will not happen in your lifetime."

LeMartre pulled the trigger.

# CHAPTER 6-FINAL FLIGHT

**Instead of the** recoil of a gunpowder explosion, there was only a hiss like that of air escaping from a tire valve, and a blast of knockout gas splashed across the Agent's forehead. Although the gas was most effective when inhaled, at close range it could permeate the skin and cause localized paralysis. But the Agent had a layer of protective armor that prevented this from happening; the thin mask of cosmetic putty formed an impermeable seal across his face that kept nearly all of the gas from touching his skin.

In the same instant that LeMartre fired the gas gun, the final strand of twine parted under the relentless sawing of the watch crystal and the Agent's hands came free. He bolted from the chair, thrusting LeMartre aside even as the First Knight and his men unwittingly inhaled a dose of the gas, and launched himself through the open window.

As he crashed into the hedgerow outside, the pain at the back of his head returned with a vengeance. To make matters worse, the area around his eyes—the only part of his face not covered by the make-up—was growing cold and his vision was starting to blur. The dose of anesthetizing gas he had received might not suffice to render him unconscious, but his vision was going fast and if he did not make his escape quickly, he would wander blind through the midst of his enemies.

Eschewing the indirect route he had used to gain access to the office, he charged instead toward the wrought iron fence that separated the courtyard from the street. Despite that fact that it was only late afternoon and the sun still hung low in the sky, darkness was closing in at the edges of his eyesight. He careened blindly into tree trunks that were directly in his path and tripped over flower boxes and benches that lined a path he could no longer clearly distinguish.

He thought he heard the sounds of pursuit from the Hall behind him, but it was difficult to tell through the roaring in his ears. He caromed from yet another tree, and then abruptly fell onto the spiky tips of the metal fence. The decorative spear points were not sharp, but they were enough so to tear clothes and skin alike as he tumbled over the barrier and spilled onto the concrete sidewalk.

The street might have been deserted or he might have been the subject of a dozen amazed stares; he simply could not tell. With one hand resting lightly on the wrought iron fence to feel his way along, he set off at a near run in the direction of the waiting DeSoto. In his mind's eye, he saw the street as before. It was his only means of navigating, for now he was almost completely blind; all he could distinguish was a bright ball of light, hovering just above the dark silhouette of the skyline.

When he reached the place he believed the DeSoto to be, he veered cautiously to the curb and extended a hand until he found the familiar outline of the car's fender... at least he hoped it was his car. He continued probing until he found the door handle and climbed inside. He had no thought of driving, not until the temporary blindness subsided, but to sit idle in the car was to invite discovery. He had to find a way to conceal himself.

Acting on a flash of inspiration, he tore the dark wig away to reveal his own wavy brown hair and similarly rubbed off the mask and prosthetics that formed the likeness of Andre LeMartre. Although his true face was now exposed to the world, he would at least look nothing like the man that the Brotherhood now chased after. Feeling some relief at the small act of camouflage, he felt in his pockets for the small first aid kit he always carried and shook out several aspirin tablets to combat the swelling of pain at the back of his head. The bitter pills grated in his throat, but the simple act of taking them seemed to help.

With a window open to allow some fresh air into the vehicle, the Secret Agent rested his hands on the steering wheel, and then after a few moments, leaned his forehead against the rigid circle and waited for his eyesight to return. It was not long before the darkness in his vision spread like a waiting blanket to completely engulf him.

**How long he** floated in the embrace of sleep, he could not measure. When he stirred, his world was still in darkness, but now he could distinguish points of light scattered across his vision. His head still throbbed from the blow LeMartre had administered, but the pain was tolerable now. Nevertheless, it took him several minutes to realize that his vision was completely normal again. The darkness was natural; it was now nighttime.

He came fully awake in a state of near panic. Although he had escaped the clutches of the Fraternis Maltae, he had unwittingly given them a head start on securing their ultimate goal: the treasure of Mont Sacre. And now that LeMartre knew Richard's name, it wouldn't take long for the Brotherhood to reach the art expert's estate in the Hamptons and pillage his wealth. The Agent had a lot of catching up to do.

Through a supreme effort, he kept the DeSoto's speed at the legal limit as he raced back to his residence. He could not afford the delay of a police traffic stop nor did he wish to attract any attention to himself, unmasked as he was. He considered using the reserve of cosmetic putty in the heel of his shoe to don a new face, but rejected the idea; there simply wasn't time.

Upon reaching his brownstone, he moved immediately to his closet and removed a clear wave transmitter, identical to the one he had used at the garage, and called for Harvey Bates. The frantic pace of the other man's response immediately set off alarm bells in his head.

"Chief! Where have you been?"

"What's wrong Harvey?"

"Murphy contacted me on the emergency channel. That pair of birds has flown the coop."

The news would have struck him like a physical blow, were he not already so close to collapse from his earlier trials. "When?"

"Hard to say. He went up to check on them a couple of hours ago, and they were gone."

"I know where they'll go." Although he had taken a personal vow to defend the defenseless, the Secret Agent felt only ambivalence when he considered what would happen when the Brotherhood caught the man who now called himself Auguste Richard. But Amelia was another matter; the daughter had no share in the crimes of her father, and did not deserve the fate that LeMartre would unhesitatingly deliver. He had to get to Richard's house on Long Island ahead of the assassins, and there was only one way to do that.

"I'm going to need a few things, Harvey."

**Despite his advanced** years, Billy Hayes drove like a demon.

At a mere hint of a suggestion from Betty, he had bundled her into his old Model A Roadster and rocketed through the city as if the hounds of Hell were nipping at his heels. Once across the Brooklyn Bridge, he had somehow found a way to further increase the revolutions of the Straight-4 under the hood, until it sounded like it would break free of its mounts and shoot off into the twilit sky.

Under any other circumstances, the fearless blonde reporter might have found herself not quite so intrepid being whisked through the countryside by the elderly, somewhat near-sighted, and almost certainly inebriated archivist, but the information she had uncovered burned so brightly in her mind as to eclipse all her senses.

Her friend, Secret Agent X, was risking his life to defend one of the most horrible men that had ever lived.

It had not taken long for her to confirm her suspicion that Auguste Richard had sprung fully formed into existence at almost the same moment that Count Augustus Von Reichardt had vanished off the face of the earth. Von Reichardt, a Prussian warmonger directly descended from the Austrian Habsburg's, had served with distinction at the head of an Austrian regiment during the Great War, but shortly before the signing of the Armistice, for reasons no one could comprehend, he had transferred himself to the command of a makeshift prison camp in eastern France—a small village named Mont Sacre, the Holy Mountain, which no longer appeared on any map. Von Reichardt was the reason Mont Sacre had been erased from both the atlas and from existence period.

In the aftermath of the war and the defeat of Austro-Hungarian forces, the Count could not shield himself from the accusing finger of those who knew of his atrocities, both against innocent civilians and prisoners of war, so he had instead vanished into the night. A few months later, a wealthy Flemish art collector named Auguste Richard had purchased an estate on a remote corner of Long Island, and wrapped himself in secrecy and security.

It was fairly astonishing to Betty that no one had made previously made the connection; doubtless, Richard's wealth had served well to deflect the sort of inquiries that might have exposed him. Yet, while he had changed his name and nationality, the one constant in his life remained a love of European Renaissance art. In 1919, when the police had raided the Von Reichardt palace outside Vienna, they found that the entire collection of paintings—many of which were uncatalogued, and almost certainly priceless, early works from the Dutch Masters—was gone.

Betty felt a chill run down her spine when she thought about the silver-haired man she had briefly glimpsed in the museum. It was hard to believe that the reclusive art expert had at one time ordered the wholesale slaughter of an entire village, and she wondered what could have driven such a man—a nobleman and a lover of art—to such evil. Now, with the power of the printed word, she would bring Count Von Reichardt's crimes once more to the attention of the world, and more importantly to her friend, Secret Agent X.

Night closed in around them as they made the long drive to Southampton in Suffolk County. Despite Richard's penchant for privacy, he could do little to hide the fact of his ownership of a historic manor house where several of New York's earliest men of influence had at one time resided, and a quick search of the archives had turned up a lifestyle feature on famous houses of New York, complete with driving directions.

The estate was a few miles from the hamlet, situated on a bluff overlooking the Long Island Sound. Behind a forbidding wall of native stone, the property was dense with elm trees, creating an effective curtain to hide the residence from the eyes of curious passersby, but strangely on this night, the large iron gate stood wide open. Hayes pulled the Model A to a halt at the invisible line where the barrier would have crossed the drive.

"What now, Miss Betty?"

The blonde reporter shrugged. "An open gate seems like an invitation to me. Let's go in."

**In the cloak** of night, the city hid its rough edges well. The squalid slums were swallowed up by inky darkness and only the glittering jewels of neon light remained, presided over by the towering spires of the Chrysler and Empire State Buildings in midtown, and to the south, amid the shimmering water of the East River, the majestic Statue of Liberty.

The effect was especially profound from two thousand feet above.

Secret Agent X lingered at the window of the Lockheed 10-A Electra until the city lights were swallowed up in the distance. With a pair of 450 horsepower Pratt & Whitney engines pulling the airplane through the sky, that didn't take long.

The plane was one of a small fleet of aircraft used by the Agent's organization, under the direction of Harvey Bates, primarily to provide aerial surveillance and reconnaissance for his clandestine activities. Their use had proved invaluable on countless occasions, but now he was using one of the camera planes for an entirely different purpose.

"Flight time is about forty-five minutes," the pilot had announced shortly after take-off. "Make yourself comfortable. Might be the last chance you get."

With the city now well behind them and the journey half-complete, X began making his final preparations. Using his portable make-up kit, he went to work, layering metal plates and plastic compounds to both conceal his true identity and present a face that would be familiar to Richard and his daughter. When he was finished, he once more wore the sandy-blond hair and countenance of Interpol agent Alec Devine. But the disguise was the easy part.

"We'll be at the coordinates in five minutes chief," the pilot called back.

The Agent acknowledged the timeline with a shout of his own, then went to work pulling on the rest of his costume—in this case a pair of heavy coveralls, a bulky backpack, and a flight helmet which he carefully pulled over his blonde wig. He was fitting a pair of goggles over his eyes when the plane began descending, prompting him to move forward to the cockpit. "How is it down there?"

"No wind, not even a whisper of a breeze. It's a perfect night to... well." The pilot chuckled. "Chief, you ever done this before?"

"Once or twice."

The pilot shook his head. "If the bird was on fire and both wings gone, I'd still try to set her down rather than strap one of those things to my back and jump."

The Agent clapped a hand on the fellow's shoulder. "Try it, my friend. It's an experience like no other."

"Thirty seconds until we're there." He pointed through the windscreen at the barely visible place where the waves of the Sound crashed against the bluffs of the island. "That's where you need to go."

X thanked the pilot and headed to the rear exit, quietly counting down the seconds. A rush of air filled the fuselage as he opened the door, and the wind of the aircraft's passage through the sky chilled him, even through the heavy garments. When he reached zero, he did not hesitate to step out into the night.

## *CHAPTER 7—THE SWORD OF VENGEANCE*

**Armande LeMartre had** not forgotten Mont Sacre; not one moment of the horror had slipped from his memory. No matter what the rogue Secret Agent might say, the desire for revenge against the destroyer of his village was an all-consuming fire.

He had been a young man and only an apprentice in the order when the war came to Mont Sacre. There had been opportunities to escape, but to flee would have meant abandoning both his kinsmen and the sacred treasure to the enemy, so he and his young brother had remained prisoners of the siege. And then Von Reichardt had arrived.

The Prussian knew of the treasure—how, LeMartre could not imagine—and was bent upon discovering its whereabouts by any means necessary. Senior members of the order were identified and culled from the larger group, never to be seen again. That they did not break faith was evident only by the fact that the horror endured. When all of the Knights had been taken, the scope of the torture shifted to other senior men from the town; by some miracle, the apprentices to the Brotherhood were overlooked. Ultimately, the young LeMartre brothers knew that they had not escaped their fate, but only postponed it. Yet strangely, the depths of despair had been their finest hour. They had kept hope alive for their fellow villagers, comforted old women and frightened children and often shared their meager rations with the weak.

The end came without warning. The soldiers guarding the prison had been generous that night, slopping an extra portion of gruel into their bowls, which the brothers, according to their custom, had surreptitiously divided among the young-est children. Only when Andre had roused him in the deep hours of the night, frantically reporting that the children were gravely ill, did LeMartre understand how Von Reichardt had turned his noble act of charity into the vilest kind of murder.

The next morning, the streets of Mont Sacre ran red with the blood of those who had not died in the night—villagers, Allied prisoners of war, and then in a cruel betrayal, even the young soldiers who had guarded the camp. The brothers had feigned death by poisoning and in the confusion of the mass executions, had found a place of concealment to weather the final storm, and so survived not because of hope, but because of a burning desire for vengeance.

And now, Andre was dead, another victim of Von Reichardt's machinations.

LeMartre's apprentices swept through the estate like wraiths, slaughtering the guards and domestic servants with the same indifference the torturer of Mont Sacre had shown nearly two decades before. They formed a noose, slowly tighten-ing around the main residence, strangling every avenue of escape, but they did not enter the house. It was understood that the First Knight alone would administer the coup de grace.

LeMarte strode through the night and kicked in the heavy front door without even bothering to see if it was unlocked. The oak panels crashed inward and the assassin entered the abode of his enemy. A long foyer permitted access to several different parts of the house, but all of the rooms were dark save one. LeMartre moved toward that singular source of light; a great room on the opposite side of the mansion, which looked out over the Sound through an enormous picture window. There, as if poised for a final confrontation, the villain of Mont Sacre was waiting.

He was older now. Years of soft living had erased the lupine hunger that had once driven Von Reichardt to the lowest depths of evil. The contemptuous sneer that twisted his patrician face now seemed merely laughable, but the revolver in his right hand could not be regarded with such indifference. "I always knew you would come. Did you imagine that I would not be ready?"

LeMartre hefted the sword in his right hand. "Even now, you are without honor. So be it. You will die as you have lived."

"Stop it, both of you!"

The outcry caught both men by surprise. But whereas LeMartre's gaze merely flickered in the direction of the voice, Von Reichardt appeared genuinely stunned. The pistol lowered as he turned to face the red haired girl that now stood at the far end of the room. "Amelia! You should have stayed in the—"

The old man's protest turned into a gurgle of pain as the First Knight sprang forward, stabbing the tip of his sword through Von Reichardt's right shoulder. The force of the thrust drove the old man backward, into the wall where the point of the blade pierced deep into the plaster, pinning him there like an insect in a child's collection. The gun fell from his nerveless fingers and clattered on the floor.

Amelia shrieked upon witnessing the sudden act of violence, and heedless of any peril, rushed to her stricken father's side. "Don't touch him! Murderer!"

LeMartre's hand was still wrapped around the hilt of his sword and he looked as though he might, at any moment, wrestle it free and drive it through the old man's heart. "Murderer, you say?"

"Let her go," Von Reichardt croaked. "Spare my daughter. She knows nothing…"

"Just as you spared the children of Mont Sacre? I think not. Your cursed bloodline shall be forever erased, butcher." The First Knight drew a deep calming breath to bring his passions under control. "You remain alive this moment for one reason only. I will not subject you to the torments of the damned, as you did to the noble Knights of the Brotherhood all those years ago; no, I will simply offer you this one chance at expiation. Tell me where the treasure is, and I will allow you to go to your final judgment with a prayer upon your lips."

"Amelia… Let her go. I beg you."

That LeMartre did not immediately refuse the wounded man's plea might have indicated that a shred of mercy yet remained in his tortured heart. But whether it was his intent to spare an innocent or not would never be known, for at just that moment, Amelia laid hands upon the gun that had fallen from her father's grip, and without hesitation raised the revolver and fired point blank at the assassin.

The bullet creased LeMartre's ribs, leaving a bloody but superficial wound; the First Knight had endured much worse. Though the impact had driven the wind from his sails, he struggled to his feet, closing on the girl with his hands curled into bestial claws. Amelia however was not intimidated. With more care than before, she aimed the pistol at the center of his forehead and thumbed back the hammer.

"Amelia, no!"

The introduction of a fourth voice onto the stage stopped everyone in their tracks. LeMartre froze in place, poised to strike if the red haired girl's eyes left him for even a moment, but Amelia's sights did not waver.

"Who the devil are you?" she hissed, glimpsing a blond head from the corner of one eye.

The newcomer moved cautiously forward. "My name is Betty Dale. I'm a reporter with The Herald. I saw you at the museum this morning."

A chuckle forced its way through LeMartre's grimace of pain. "Ah, Miss Dale.

I very much enjoyed reading your account of what happened at the museum. I am grateful to you also for giving us the name of the esteemed art expert."

Betty ignored the killer's barbs and focused her attention instead on the one person in the room who she reckoned might be worth saving. "Amelia, don't do this. We can call the police—"

"No police," croaked the old man. "Shoot him, Amelia. He'll never stop hunting us."

"Don't listen to him," Betty pleaded. "He may be your father, but you don't know the horrible things he's done."

"It is true," LeMartre intoned, straightening from his aggressive stance and raising his hands as if in surrender. "The blood of an entire village is on his hands."

"It was a war." Amelia replied, but her tone lacked conviction. "Terrible things happen in war."

"It was no battle, cheri. Women and children, poisoned. The survivors slaughtered and left for the carrion birds. And for what? To steal our gold. Your beloved father is worse than a killer; he is a thief."

"It was a terrible thing to do," Betty interjected. "But more killing won't change what's already done. The victims of Mont Sacre want justice, not revenge."

"What do you know of justice?" the killer spat. "Have you spent a night with the dead, daring not even to breathe, as the butchers spill the blood of children and old women before your very eyes. More than a hundred souls… poisoned… shot… slaughtered like cattle."

"Quiet! Enough of your lies!"

Amelia's gaze never left LeMartre but tears were welling in her eyes and her grip on the revolver no longer seemed quite so resolute. The First Knight pressed his advantage.

"Did he never tell you? A bedtime story perhaps? On the last day, before he found what he was looking for, he executed twenty prisoners because one young soldier tried to escape."

"Stop it!"

"He hung them up on the wall to rot. The birds ate their eyes—"

"Stop it! Stop it!"

LeMartre struck like a viper, springing across the room to hammer the girl with his fists. Amelia never got a shot off. The assassin scooped up the revolver and turned it on Betty.

"Thank you for the timely interruption," he said, panting. He aimed the weapon at her heart. "I wish that I had a better way to repay you, but alas, it is not our custom to leave witnesses."

But before he could pull the trigger, another player stepped onto the stage; a blond-haired man that LeMartre did not recognize entered the room as calmly as if he was merely a curious tourist taking a stroll. His confident voice however was very familiar. "So the noble Knights of the Fraternis Maltae make war on innocent women. You must be proud of yourselves."

"Excellent. All of my enemies gathered in one place." LeMartre smiled, turning the gun on the newcomer. "Welcome to the execution, Secret Agent X."

## CHAPTER 8-THE DUEL

**It had not** escaped LeMartre's notice that both Betty Dale and X had somehow slipped through the noose of apprentices surrounding the house. In fact, 'slipped through' did not begin to tell the tale.

The Agent's parachute had deployed almost directly above Richard's residence. As he drifted down, he could not fail to notice the wave of assassins moving stealthily throughout the darkened estate. He was still more than two hundred feet from the ground when they dispersed in a ring about the main dwelling, and although they were unaware of his presence, he had little doubt that they would overwhelm him the moment he crashed down in their midst.

The capacious silk canopy had only one function: to slow his rate of fall to a survivable level. It was not designed for maneuverability, and while he anticipated a degree of drift, the windless night had kept him right on target. Now, he desperately needed to adjust to a different drop zone.

Twisting in the full-body harness, he gripped one of the heavy-duty nylon straps that secured his body to the web of cords blossoming upward to the parachute, and began to haul it in like a hawser. As that side of the chute was pulled down, the rush of escaping air cause him to lose lift and he began to plummet at an angle, away from the house and toward the dark woods. He held the line as long as he dared; knowing that to land at such speeds almost guaranteed serious injury. With the treetops seemingly brushing his feet, he released his grip and the enveloped snapped taut once more. An instant later, he crashed into the trees.

The elm branches were springy, bending rather than breaking, and while they formed a softer landing surface than the ground, the difference was negligible. The Agent was struck dozens of times, his legs slapped with repeated blows that felt like the swings of a baseball bat. Then, with a violent jerk that snapped him in his harness like the end of a bullwhip, his fall stopped. The parachute had become tangled in the treetops, leaving him suspended two stories above the ground.

There was no time to nurse his wounds. He cut free of the lines and made the bone-jarring drop to the forest floor. His eyes were well enough adjusted to the darkness now that he had no trouble navigating to the edge of the woods, and his dark overalls helped him go unnoticed by the apprentices of the Brotherhood who had now formed a defensive perimeter around the house.

He skirted the tree line until he reached the cliff overlooking the water. There were only three of the assassins there, loosely spaced to guard what was probably considered the least likely avenue of escape for anyone inside the house. It took the agent only a few minutes to creep from man to man and subdue each one with a dose of his anesthetizing gas. He continued moving stealthily around the house, overpowering the apprentices and binding each one with wire restraints. He was in the process of taking down the last of the group when a shift in the shadows alerted him to the approach of a vehicle on the main drive. To his utter dismay, Betty Dale had emerged from the car, and before he could warn her off, entered the house unchallenged.

Moving swiftly but with caution to avoid detection by Betty's waiting driver, he gained the front entrance just as a gunshot broke the silence. He rushed forward in a panic, just in time to witness Betty's arrival on the scene. He held back as long as he dared, believing that Betty's appeal to common sense and decency might actually win the day, but when LeMartre turned the tables on Amelia and regained the advantage, there was no choice but intrude.

The First Knight brandished the revolver at the Agent. "You must be very brave. I almost admire your nerve. But you are a fool to come here."

"Nothing particularly brave or foolish about it," replied X, calmly. "The police will be here in a matter of minutes."

"You will not live that long." LeMarte's eyes narrowed. "In any case, I believe that you are bluffing. Secret Agent X is not a friend to the police. They would rather arrest you than me."

"Perhaps. But they won't simply turn a blind eye to the fact that you murdered four unarmed people, and before you tell me how swiftly you'll vanish into the night, let me just add that it will take you considerably longer to free your apprentices than you might believe." He moved across the room to stand beside Betty. "Your only chance is to surrender now. Betty's right; revenge isn't the answer. It is time for Von Reichardt to face justice. Let the world know the truth of his crimes; let him stand trial in a court of law."

Even as he spoke, the Agent knew that his appeal had fallen on deaf ears. LeMartre had lived too long with the fire of vengeance burning in his breast, and as a member of the Fraternis Maltae, was a true believer in the ideology of violence as a means to an end.

"There will be no court, no trial. It ends tonight."

"I can't let you do that."

LeMartre stabbed the pistol toward him. "And how will you stop me?"

X nodded at the firearm. "Not a very honorable weapon for a knight."

"So it is a duel of honor you want?" For the first time since confronting Von Reichardt, a smile cracked the assassin's hard visage. He abruptly stuffed the gun into a pocket, and then took hold of the cruciform hilt of his sword, which still pinned the Prussian pretender to the wall. He wrenched it free, eliciting a moan of agony from the old man, who slumped to the ground. "Excellent. You are correct, of course. A gun is far too crude a tool. This blade begs for your blood."

"If it's to be a duel, then you'll allow me to choose a weapon—"

The Agent's statement was cut off as LeMartre sprang forward, slashing with the long blade in a strike that would have taken off his head if he had remained where he was. The First Knight's concession to the so-called "duel of honor" did not evidently extend to the notion of a level playing field. He sprang forward again, this time with feint followed by another hacking blow.

Although unarmed, X was by no means defenseless. Even if the killer had elected to shoot him, the Agent's manganese-steel bulletproof vest would likely have stopped the round, allowing him a decisive moment in which to overpower his foe. Likewise, he was not completely vulnerable to an attack from LeMartre's blade. As expert in the unarmed form of combat known as jiu-jitsu, Agent X was more than a match for any thug with a knife.

Except LeMarte wasn't merely a thug. He had not achieved the rank of Chevalier Premiere by default. On the day of the tragedy of Mont Sacre, he had been simply an apprentice in the Fraternis Maltae, but from that day forward, he had dedicated himself to the way of the sword and had studied under the tutelage of the finest saber masters in Europe. Against his blade, even a mastery of Oriental martial arts seemed insufficient.

Nor was the Secret Agent in top fighting form. He was still smarting from his earlier encounter with LeMartre, and added to those wounds were the numerous bruises and abrasions he had suffered during the parachute drop. Every time he dodged a thrust of the assassin's sword tip, he winced in pain. Fatigue was building in his muscles and he could feel his reactions growing slower with each attack.

But on the other side of the coin, LeMartre had failed to score a single hit against his unarmed foe, and the repeated stabbing and slashing was taking its toll on him as well. The wound to his ribs continued to weep blood and flashed with pain every time he extended his sword arm forward. He needed to end this fight quickly, before his own fatigue somehow gave the Agent the upper hand. It was time to change his tactics.

He launched a series of halting feints, designed to maneuver his foe's back to the wall—or in this case, the large picture window—and yet at the same time, lure the Agent into attempting a counterattack. When he had the man where he wanted him, LeMartre stabbed out in what appeared to be a foolish overextension, leaving his wounded rib cage exposed to his enemy. The Agent took the bait and when he launched himself at the assassin's unprotected flank, the First Knight drove his elbow down into the back of his foe's skull.

However, LeMartre had underestimated the canniness of his opponent. X was not fooled for a second by the swordsman's seemingly foolish attacks. When the other man gave him the opening, he took it, but not in the frantic desperate way that LeMartre expected. Instead of striking at the wound, the Agent instead wrapped his arms around the assassin, planted his feet firmly on the floor, and twisted the other man off his feet. Entwined together, both men crashed into the plate-glass and in an explosion of razor sharp splinters, tumbled out into the night.

The fall to the ground outside the house was no great distance—only about six feet—but it was enough to leave both combatants momentarily stunned. The Agent recovered quickly, perhaps because he had anticipated such a result from his attack, but LeMartre's hand closed on the hilt of his sword even as the former struggled to his feet amid a deadly garden of glass shards. In a matter of seconds, both men were up, and once more circling each other warily.

Removed from the confines of the house, the battlefield favored the Agent; he needed only to avoid the reach of LeMartre's blade and there was nothing but maneuvering room on the expanse of lawn between the whitewashed walls of the mansion and the edge of the bluff some fifty yards away. Inexplicably however, X stayed close, barely out of the deadly circle described by his foe's increasingly desperate attacks, retreating toward the precipice.

The First Knight now fought two enemies—the Secret Agent, and his own fatigue. Yet through it all, he did not forget his hard won skills. Every inch that X ceded to him was a small victory; he was the one shaping this battlefield, not his unarmed nemesis. Step by step, like a Queen chasing the King around the chess-board, he pushed the fight toward the edge of the cliff and toward the inevitable checkmate.

A low wooden fence had been erected at the brink of the fall; a guard rail to keep anyone wandering close to the edge from falling over. The Agent knew it was there, but did not dare risk a backward glance to fix its presence. Nevertheless, the increasingly loud rush of breakers on the rocks below alerted him to the nearness of his approach. He was almost exactly where LeMartre wanted him, and when he felt the barrier against his legs, he froze in his tracks as if only now realizing his fatal error.

The First Knight did not hesitate. With a strike as fast as lightning, he stabbed the ornate weapon into Secret Agent X's heart.

## CHAPTER 9-THE SCORPION'S NATURE

**Helpless to do** anything to assist her friend, Betty Dale had watched in horror as the strange battle moved ever closer to the bluff. She had seen X fight countless villains with her own eyes, and while it was unthinkable that he would not also win this battle, those same eyes beheld a different outcome. Frantic, she began search-ing the ruins of the great room for some kind of weapon with which to aid the Secret Agent. Her hand settled on a piece of the window sash, jarred loose when the struggling pair had crashed through—it wasn't much, but it might just make the difference—and she hefted it in preparation to climb out the opening and rush into battle… and that was when she saw it.

Hanging on the wall, directly above the shattered window, was an ornate, jew-eled sword that looked as though it might once have belonged to a Bedouin prince. The fearless reporter wrestled the decorative weapon from its mount and pitched it out into the night, following close behind. The weapon was heavier than she expected and she struggled to run with it on the springy grass. For every step she took toward the embattled men, they retreated a step away, closer and closer to the precipice. And then, when there was nowhere for them to go, she saw a sight that would haunt her dreams. LeMartre drew back his sword and rammed it dead center into her old friend's chest.

What happened in the next instant defied explanation.

The sword did not penetrate the Agent's body as it had Von Reichardt's. Instead, only the merest fraction of the tip pierced the fabric of his overalls, and then, with all of LeMartre's weight behind it, the long steel shaft bowed and with a sound like a gunshot, snapped in two. The Secret Agent's vest of manganese-steel armor was, it seemed, proof against more than just bullets.

The blade fragment against X's chest flipped into the air like the knife of a carnival juggler. The other shard, still attached to the hilt, which was in turn still held in the assassin's grip, lurched forward, gouging a bloody furrow across the upper surface of the Agent's shoulder.

LeMartre found himself falling forward into his seemingly impervious foe, but X was already twisting away from the fence and the collision that seemed certain to send both of them plummeting over the cliff. The assassin's flailing left hand managed to snare the fabric of X's clothes in the same instant that he pitched headlong over the fence, and just as with the window, both men crashed through the flimsy wooden barricade.

All of this happened in a split second. Betty Dale was still paralyzed by the horror of seeing the Agent stabbed, and it took the splintering sound of the fence collapsing under their combined weight to snap her out of it. She realized in that moment that X was still alive, but also saw that he was scant inches from what would surely be a fatal plunge. Throwing caution aside, along with the now useless sword, she dived after the men, grabbing hold of the Agent's foot as the edge of the cliff crumbled under him.

In that single fateful moment, everything changed. LeMartre's skill with a sword no longer gave him the advantage. His fate, and the fate of his enemy, was now beyond his ability to control. He hung, suspended only his fierce grip on the Agent's overalls sleeve, a hundred feet above the craggy rocks of the shoreline. The shattered remains of his blade, the badge of his office as Chevalier Premiere, remained clutched in his free hand, a broken and impotent symbol of his failure. He stared up into the steely eyes of his enemy.

Although Betty's petite physique seemed as insignificant to the matter at hand as a feather on a rock pile, it was just enough to halt the Agent's slide and allow him to wrap one arm around a fence post. LeMartre clung to him with a death grip and the strain from the added weight was unimaginable. Every one of his myriad wounds now felt as though they had been ripped open with fiery daggers.

"It's over LeMarte," he shouted into the other man's face. "Surrender now and live. Let go of the sword and give me your hand."

Even as he made the offer, extending mercy to an enemy who would most certainly never have done the same, he knew that the First Knight would refuse. Like the scorpion in the parable, he could not help but plant his sting, even if doing so meant his own death.

With a fearsome cry, LeMartre brought the broken sword up and hammered it toward the Agent's exposed back. Anticipating the treachery, X did the only thing he could. As he felt the other man's weight shift in preparation for the killing strike, he twisted away, pulling the fabric from the assassin's fingers. There was a flash of sparks as the steel of the blade struck only rock, and then LeMartre was gone, tumbling down the nearly vertical surface. The sickening sound of his impact on the rocks below was almost muted by the roar of the sea...almost.

## CHAPTER 10—FINAL JUSTICE

**Amelia was huddled** at her father's side, ministering to his wounds and offering what comfort she could, when Betty and the Agent returned to the house. She gave a little gasp when she saw them.

"The other man?"

"Gone," answered the Agent. He knew what had to come next, and for the girl's sake, he felt a twinge of regret.

The man who had called himself Auguste Richard stirred. "I am sorry... for everything."

The Agent knelt beside him. "Your apologies won't bring back the dead. Or change what you did at Mont Sacre."

Von Reichardt's face twisted defensively. "You don't actually believe that killer's lies—"

"He wasn't lying," Betty intoned. "What you did at Mont Sacre was... beyond human."

The old man sagged, his dignity in tatters. "You're right. I can't change what happened. I wish now that I could. I have tried so hard to atone..."

"It's not up to you to set the price for the blood you spilled," X answered unequivocally. "Lady justice will settle that account."

Dread overshadowed Von Reichardt's countenance. He glanced at his daughter who now sat as motionless as a statue opposite the Agent. "Please, let us go. You can have the treasure, all of it. We'll go somewhere far away... I'm an old man; what difference does it make if die in prison, or an exile?"

The Secret Agent looked at him for a long time before answering. "It makes all the difference in the world." Then he reached up with both hands and carefully peeled away a layer of his disguise.

Von Reichardt eyes widened in an expression of absolute horror. "No! It can't be. You're..."

A shudder passed through his body, and then another. The spasms intensified in a matter of seconds, and the old man's face drew into a rictus of pain as he clutched helplessly at his chest. "So," he gasped, forcing the words through clenched teeth. "You have your revenge."

"Not revenge. Justice."

Von Reichardt jerked once then thrust a hand out as if clutching at the last sparks of his life force. "Amel…"

The plea took his last breath. He did not draw another.

The red haired girl remained where she was, shell-shocked by the violence that had left her life in ruins, and perhaps moreso by her father's awful legacy. The Agent wanted to comfort her somehow, but knew that such a gesture would be futile. Instead, he got to his feet and limped toward the door.

Betty hastened after him. "What happens now?"

"Now? That's for the police to decide." He kept walking.

"But Amelia? She has nothing now. She didn't deserve this."

"She has her life, which is more than Von Reichardt gave his victims. The innocent always pay the price for the deeds of evil men."

As he reached the front door, Betty placed a hand on his shoulder; a light touch, but enough. He stopped and turned to face her. "I don't think I've ever seen you so…hard. You were there, weren't you? At Mont Sacre?"

The Agent did not reply. His silence was answer enough.

"What do you want me to do? How should I tell the story?"

"Tell the truth," he said simply.

"There's just one more thing I want to know. You're the one who stole the painting from the museum, aren't you?"

A corner of his mouth twitched in what might have been an agonized grimace. "I knew that Von Reichardt might emerge from hiding for a chance to see The Night Watch like that. Art was always his passion. But I never anticipated that the Brotherhood would act so openly and a lot of innocent people paid the price for it."

"It's not your fault. You said it yourself, the innocent pay the price for the deeds of evil men. You aren't evil. Justice is never evil."

"Justice," he echoed.

She reached up a hand to caress his cheek. "This is just another mask, isn't it?"

"There's always a mask, Betty." A faint smile graced his lips. He leaned forward to kiss her gently on the forehead, then turned and strode out into the night.

*End*

*The Wolfpack, a legendary team of WW I fighter aces, know that the only way to survive combat in the skies is to stick together. But when a ghost from their past returns, the bonds of friendship will be tested. Will Captain Colby Wyatt stay loyal to his country and friends, or will he be seduced by the summons from the Sorcerer's ghost?*

## THE SORCERER'S GHOST

# CHAPTER 1 - A BAD DAY

**The Wolfpack was** having a bad day.

It had started off all right. They had left the airfield at Issoudon just as dawn's light was breaking in the East, and were eager to get back to their home base at Chaumont. The first part of the mission, providing escort for Brigadier General Sanders's DH.4 had been thankfully uneventful. The aces were always eager to prove their mettle in combat, but drawing fire for the more cumbersome de Havilland two-seater and risking their boss' hide in the process, was not their idea of a good time in the air. Today however, returning home without the General, they were fairly spoiling for a fight. Captain Colby Wyatt, the intrepid leader of the squadron, had suggested a route that took their gray SPAD XIII's close to where the action usually was, and neither the older and wiser Lieutenant Jimmy Styles, nor the pugnacious Robert "Bull" Caine had demurred. They felt ready to take on the world

Then everything had gone to Hell.

They had been lucky in that first engagement. Bull had spied the pair of Albatros D.III biplanes before the enemy saw them, and after a signal to Captain Wyatt, had drawn first blood. An expert marksman—possibly the best in the service—Bull had torn one of the Boche planes apart in mid-air with a single burst from his Vickers guns. Wyatt had taken the second plane, raking its tail with a relentless torrent of .303 rounds, but somehow the canny Kraut had peeled off, and then to everyone's surprise, turned into them. The three Spad pilots all whipped their heads around at almost exactly the same instant that the Albatros speared right through the center of their V-formation.

The move was gutsy to be sure, but they had the advantage of numbers and more importantly, had honed their team flying skills to the point where each man knew exactly what the others were going to do. As agile as the fierce hunters that were their namesake, the Wolfpack planes separated and independently carved tight turns that brought them back into formation in a matter of seconds.

The German pilot was also trying to come around, but Wyatt's opening salvo had damaged his rudder and the Albatros was responding sluggishly. Wyatt's fingers were ready on the triggers of his twin Vickers, but Styles had the best shot and immediately let lead fly. That was when things started to go wrong.

Unbeknownst to the Lieutenant, the cooling hose to his left gun had burst sometime after takeoff. As hundreds of tracer rounds scorched the sky, seeking out the enemy plane, the barrel of the weapon grew red hot and acrid metallic smoke began to issue from it. As soon as he became aware of the malfunction, Styles let go of his stick trigger, but the damage was done and the opportunity was lost. He dropped back to let his comrades take the kill, but the pilot of the Albatros, realizing that he was badly overmatched was already on the run. Wyatt once more took the lead, charging after the slower German plane, and unleashed another storm of bullets.

The Albatros rocked under the persistent hammering. Dark smoke began to pour from its engine cowling, and the pilot responded immediately by putting the biplane into a deep dive. Tracers from Wyatt's guns continued to chase after the doomed plane but he broke off the attack, satisfied that German was out of the fight, and regrouped with his comrades.

Although victorious, the battle had left the Wolfpack in rough shape. Without water to cool his machine guns, Styles would be limited to short bursts of fire. Wyatt had shot roughly half his load of ammunition. If they encountered another enemy patrol during the remainder of their flight, they would be hard pressed to emerge with a second victory. As luck would have it, that was exactly what happened.

They were still about fifty miles out from Chaumont when the Boche planes caught them—Fokkers painted with the outlandish colors of Germany's most feared Jagd-Staffel: the infamous Flying Circus. Battered though they were, the Wolfpack pilots would not have even considered turning tail and running, even from these terrible masters of the killing craft, but their will to fight mattered little, for the Germans were on them before they knew what was happening. Six fighters, with Spandau guns blazing, swooped down from out of the sun and tore into the Wolfpack.

Styles felt the distinctive whoosh of bullets zipping past and knew instantly that they had been ambushed. Even before his eyes registered the tracers flashing by, he threw his Spad into a dive, out of the line of fire. The desperate maneuver saved his life but even as he nosed down, something slammed into the side of his head and for a moment he saw nothing but stars.

Bull saw his friend's abrupt stall and instantly divined that there was trouble. It didn't take him more than a moment to spot the Dreideckers but by then, he too was taking fire. Thinking quickly, he pulled back on the stick and started climbing. The effect on the enemy was immediate; their formation split into three pairs, a lead and a wingman for each of the Wolfpack flyers

In the cockpit of his Spad, Styles used his scarf to mop away the sticky substance that obscured his goggles but the effort was for naught. Through the red smeared lenses, he saw two of everything, and despite his best attempt to fix his stare on one object, everything kept swimming in and out of focus.

Well, at least I'm still alive, he thought darkly. The pounding ache on the left side of his skull was proof enough of that. But if he wanted to stay that way, he was going to need a miracle, and with his friends likewise locked in combat, that miracle was going to be damned elusive. Framed between the wings of the biplane, he saw nothing but the green fields of France, and realized he was still in a dive. He fumbled for the stick and pulled back, bringing the nose up, but almost immediately found himself peppered with enemy gunfire and was forced to dive again.

For his part, Captain Wyatt was swift to take action. There was a simple unspoken rule among the three aces: watch your friend's back and he'll watch yours.

Disregarding the enemy planes that dogged his own tail, he immediately nosed down and went after the pair that was chasing Styles. He led with his guns, stuttering out a strange battle rhythm as he swooped down like a diving falcon on the larger, faster triplanes. A stream of tracers slashed across the tail of the lead plane and it began rocking under the assault. Wyatt straightened his line and fired again, and this time saw the enemy pilot pitch forward in the cockpit, after which the Fokker lazily rolled over and began spinning out of control. The American ace banked right and brought the second plane pursuing Styles into his sights and squeezed the stick trigger once more. Tracers described an arc through the air that terminated in the engine cowling of the Fokker, and abruptly, the remaining plane of the pair belched a cloud of black smoke and broke off its attack. While Wyatt had chased after the German planes, the pair on his own tail had withheld fire for fear of hitting their comrades; now there was nothing to hold them back. As the Captain fell in behind his wounded friend, two Spandau machine guns blazed through the propellers of the Fokkers and chewed up the sky.

The Fokkers were fast, much faster than the Spads, but what their tri-wing design gave them in speed, it took back in maneuverability. Even the Spad, with its stubby wings and fuselage—built more for speed than aerobatics—could fly circles around a Fokker, especially in a dive. But Wyatt held his position, just a few hundred yards behind Styles and endured the withering assault; leaving Styles to the mercy of the Boche flying machines just wasn't an option.

Bull Caine wasn't having it any easier. He climbed into the sky, trying to loop around and drop in behind the Fokkers on his tail, but the German pilots would have none of it. Steadfastly dogging his tail, they climbed through a slightly broader loop, and quickly picked him up again, lashing him with steady fire. Unable to shake the Hun planes, Bull threw his Spad into a dive and raced headlong toward the other fight. Suddenly, his fuselage exploded in a spray of splinters as a lucky burst from one of the enemy guns raked his plane. Bull felt something strike his left shoulder, followed by a hot throb of agony, and his nerveless hand slipped off the stick. Gritting his teeth through the pain, he kept on course, expertly steering the Spad with his one good hand.

With two of the enemy fighters removed from the aerial battlefield, the odds were improving for the Wolfpack, but the German aces still held the advantage. Styles continued flying straight in a shallow descent, but hardly maneuvered at all to avoid gunfire. His friends knew that he was wounded but there was little they could to help him now aside from keeping the enemy at bay.

Bull angled his dive to intercept the Germans on Wyatt's tail. With a little help from gravity, he pushed the plane well beyond its limits, shooting across the sly like a rocket, and then plowed through the empty space between his captain's Spad and the Fokkers. That pair of planes saw him coming too late to do anything but veer off, and they nearly collided with the pair that had come in on Bull's heels.

The momentary confusion was just what the pilots in the gray Spads needed. Wyatt immediately broke off and twisted around to engage the enemy, and for a few moments it looked like the tide of battle had shifted in favor of the Wolfpack. But then Wyatt's guns abruptly went silent; he was out of ammunition. Bull was still choosing his shots carefully, but the Germans seemed to sense that their foes' luck, along with their supply of bullets, was rapidly waning. Bull continued to harass the Fokkers, but with only one good hand to wrestle the stick, that was the limit of what he could do and it simply wasn't enough. Like hungry hyenas, the Boche pilots began to circle closer, tightening the noose around Wyatt and Styles.

Suddenly one of the bright red planes blew apart in mid-air. Wyatt craned his head around in time to see a black cloud of smoking debris begin a meteoric downward journey. The three remaining enemy pilots likewise snapped their heads around, looking for the source of the killing strike, but in that instant another of the triplanes seemed to dissolve in flight. A stream of lead—no tracers, just deadly slugs moving faster than the eye could follow—shredded the left wing assembly of the German fighter. The struts holding the triple-stack of airfoils collapsed and the multiple wing halves, tethered to the fuselage by guy-wires, fluttered in the breeze as the doomed aircraft plunged earthward.

The distraction was enough for Bull to seize the advantage, and in an abrupt change of fortune, it was the Fokkers that were fleeing, with a single Spad hurling tracers in their wake. Yet, before he could walk his fire into the enemy, a dark shape swooped out of the sun and pounced on one of the Germans, strafing it with deadly and accurate fire. As the fuselage disintegrated, the black plane dove across Bull's path, seemingly right through the debris cloud. Then the unknown pilot rolled to the right in a triple-corkscrew and came up with guns blazing at the lone remaining German. It was over in a heartbeat.

Bull's finger slipped off the trigger as he watched the black plane carve up the sky with aerobatics and bullets. The plane had no markings but looked an awful lot like a German Albatros. Yet that was not what had put the Wolfpack's dead-eye marksman into a state of stunned paralysis. Rather, it was that distinctive corkscrew to the right that the victorious pilot had executed immediately after dispatching the enemy planes. Bull had seen that move before.

With the last of the enemy planes scattered across the French countryside, the black Albatros immediately climbed back into the sun, vanishing from sight before any of the Wolfpack flyers could think to pursue. Bull left off pondering the mystery of their anonymous savior and turned his attention instead to the very immediate problem of survival. After rejoining the formation and flashing the captain a tentative thumbs-up, he unwrapped his silk scarf from around his neck and stuffed it into the ragged hole in the blood-soaked shoulder of his leather jacket. As the thrill of combat gradually receded into memory, pain was quick to rush in and fill the void.

Styles was holding his own, but his eyes still refused to agree on a point of focus. Only the fearless and headstrong Captain Wyatt had emerged from the battle completely unscathed. As they made their way back to Chaumont, he flew close to Styles's plane, his wheels never more than a few feet from the other's top wing, and shouted words of encouragement at the top of his lungs to keep the lieutenant from slipping into unconsciousness,

"I can't see too good, Cap!" Styles shouted. "Landin's gonna be a little dicey."

"You can do it," Wyatt replied. "We'll talk you in."

The captain did exactly that. He stayed alongside the other plane until the landing strip was directly beneath Styles's wheels. "Hold her steady and ease off the throttle to stall in ten seconds. You'll set down light as feather."

Styles followed the instructions to the letter despite the fact that the airfield appeared to be canted at a forty-five degree angle in his left eye. He kept that eye closed, and counted to ten. The wheels bounced hard before he was ready, but he kept his nerve and steered the plane true down the grassy strip.

The other two fighter planes were on the ground a few moments later, and both men leapt from their cockpits before the planes had fully stopped, hastening to the side of their wounded friend. Despite the fact that his left arm hung limp, Bull scrambled onto the fuselage of Styles's Spad and began administering to the lieutenant's injuries while Wyatt shouted for a litter bearer.

As the ambulance men carried the tall Texan away, the captain took out two cigarettes and passed one to Bull. "You should get over to the field hospital as well," he declared.

"Yeah," the other man answered, taking a deep drag to settle his rattled nerves.

Wyatt looked at him through the growing cloud of smoke. "You saw it didn't you?"

"I saw... something, Cap."

"It was him, Bull. You know it was. That triple-roll was his signature; an artist signing his masterpiece."

Bull shivered as if someone had just walked over his grave. "It can't be him. It just can't be. We both saw him die. Tyr Sorensen died six months ago."

## *CHAPTER 2 - THE SORCERER'S APPRENTICE*

**Young Lieutenant Wyatt** was eager to prove himself in combat. He had spent weeks flying his Curtiss JN-4 over the scrub prairies of Texas, engaging in mock battles with other cadets, but that was just practice. He was itching to do some real fighting.

His hopes of joining the famous fliers of the 94th Aero Pursuit squadron had not come to pass, but he had heard good things about the unit to which he had been assigned. Today, he would find out if the rumors were true.

It had been a long journey from Texas—from the Galveston docks, all the way across an ocean where U-boats prowled like killer sharks, to England and from there, across the channel to France and ultimately, Chaumont, home of the 44th Pursuit Squadron. Hefting his duffel onto his shoulder, he strode across the rutted airfield toward his new home.

He located a tent hung with the formal crest of the 44th. Beneath it, on what appeared to be a piece of an airplane wing, was the painted likeness of a skull with jagged lightning bolts shooting from its eyes and the legend "the Flying Sorcerers." Just as he was about to go in, a compact fellow with the physique of a bulldog and wearing the chevrons of a Sergeant First Class emerged and almost collided with him.

The sergeant was quick to snap up a salute. "Good afternoon, sir. You must be our new flier. I'm Sgt. Caine, but everyone here calls me 'Bull.' I expect you will too, sir, if…" Bull winced as if realizing he had said too much. "Anyway, welcome to the Flying Sorcerers."

Wyatt could not resist a grin. "Glad to be here, sergeant. Looking forward to taking the fight to the Hun."

"You'll get your chance, sir. The Cap likes to throw the new boys right into the thick of it. He calls it the 'baptism by fire.'"

Wyatt raised an eyebrow. He understood now what the little sergeant had meant by "if." "If" he survived his first day as a combat pilot.

The next morning, he underwent the ritual of rebirth.

He had not yet met Capt. Sorensen. The leader of the squadron, the man everyone called simply "The Sorcerer." Thus far, Wyatt was a little put off by the man and his idiosyncrasies; Sorenson had refused to meet with him and had not even appeared at the briefing before the mission. But he liked the diminutive, soft-spoken Bull Caine and the pair walked together across the camp to their planes.

"Don't worry about The Sorcerer," Bull told him. "You prove you got what it takes up there, and he'll let you in."

Wyatt just nodded. He had no doubts about his abilities in the air, but he wasn't so sure he wanted to be "in" with The Sorcerer.

The Spad XIII wasn't that much different from the "Jenny" he'd flown in Texas and by the time they were ready to start their run, strafing German trenches from the air, Wyatt felt comfortable on the stick. As Sorensen's wingman, he took his place in line, and swooped down on the enemy position with guns blazing. It was the most exhilarating experience of his life… and then the real enemy arrived.

Instantly, the air was transformed into a weird battlefield where planes darted to and fro like mosquitoes. Wyatt tried in vain to find a target, but there were so many planes in the sky, shooting at him or swooping in front of him, that it was impossible to pick one. Worse, his fellow Flying Sorcerers were constantly crossing his line of fire and he dared not loose a shot for fear of hitting one of them. For several long minutes, he flew in circles, unable to engage a single enemy plane.

Drawing a deep breath, he tried to remember his training. He knew he was letting the chaos paralyze him; with so much going on, it was difficult to stay focused, but that was exactly what he had to do. When an Albatros darted in front of him, he immediately took off after it, concentrating more on staying with the German plane than in shooting at it. His entire world shrank until nothing existed but the enemy biplane, framed by the struts of his own wings and floating magically in and out of his sights. He followed the German through every turn, he banked, rolled, pitched and dived with the Albatros until soon, he began to anticipate the other pilot's evasive tactics. And then, when the moment was right, he squeezed the trigger and felt an almost tangible release as his tracers speared directly into the Albatros.

Only then did he remember that he was not alone in the sky. While he had tunneled his vision exclusively on that lone Albatros, other enemy planes had fixed his location and were now throwing 7.92-millimeter rounds at his plane. His elation turned to near panic and he threw the aircraft into a series of frantic maneuvers to shake the relentless enemy, all to no avail. Machine gun fire from the Hun plane splintered his rudder, and then began to creep along the tail section toward the cockpit. Wyatt realized in horror that his first battle was going to be his last....

The incoming fire ceased abruptly. Wyatt craned his head around just in time to see the German biplane spinning out of control. One of the Spads rose into view from below, twisting through an elaborate series of rolls, and then settled in beside him. Wyatt looked over to see the grim face of The Sorcerer staring back at him, and beneath the protective mask of his silk scarf, his cheeks flushed red with embarrassment. His victory against the Albatros seemed empty now; his singular focus had nearly cost him his life, and to make matters worse, his commander had been the one to bail him out.

He was still burning with shame as the squadron returned victorious to Chaumont, and as the other pilots climbed out of their planes, whooping and congratulating each other, he remained in his cockpit, sullen and dejected.

"Get out of the plane, Lieutenant."

Wyatt snapped erect, and then upon recognizing that it was Captain Sorensen barking the order, hastened to comply. He dropped to the ground beside his plane and snapped to attention.

Sorensen was a striking man, saturnine with jet-black hair and a perfectly groomed mustache. He might have been handsome, but his black eyes confounded the effect; his gaze was unendurable, a dark void which sucked the will out of anyone unfortunate enough to be caught in his stare. The captain of the Sorcerers took a step forward, peering deep into Wyatt's soul, and then his dark countenance was split by a mischievous grin. "Good shooting today, Lieutenant. I think I'll keep you."

From that moment forward, there was nothing that Colby Wyatt wouldn't do for The Sorcerer.

## CHAPTER 3 - THE VISITATION

**Captain Wyatt walked** out into the cool night air and gazed up at the starry sky as if searching for an omen. He fired up a Lucky and watched streams of smoke drift like phantoms around his head.

It had been a long day, fraught with concern for Styles. Though the bullet had only creased his skull, the lieutenant had suffered a severe concussion and lost a lot of blood. The doctors were frankly amazed that he had remained alert enough to stay aloft and subsequently land his plane. Wyatt didn't share their wonderment, he knew what kind of stuff the tall Texan was made of. Nevertheless, the captain had donated two pints of his own blood for the surgery and he was still feeling a little woozy from the procedure. Styles had not yet awakened from the long but successful operation designed to relieve some of the pressure inside his head, nor was he expected to leave the sweet euphoria of morphine any time soon. That was fine with Wyatt; he just wanted his friend back in one piece.

Bull had fared somewhat better. His left arm was in a sling across his chest, but the wound was insignificant compared to some he'd taken in prior battles. The only reason he allowed himself to remain a guest of the field hospital was in order to keep tabs on the lieutenant.

Wyatt's only wound was to his pride; the battle might have turned out very differently for all of them, but for the intercession by the mysterious black plane.

"Good shooting today, Wyatt."

The voice was a ghost from the past, but Wyatt was not startled; in some strange way, he had been expecting this visitation. His reply, a single word, embodied a thousand burning questions. "How?"

The voice chuckled and then, like an apparition, a figure materialized from the smoke. "I've so much to tell you."

"I saw you die. Is this a dream?"

The Sorcerer smiled, but his dark eyes possessed no humor. "I didn't die, Wyatt. But it was better to let everyone think I was dead. Now, I'm part of something much more important. A secret flying force that can strike at the heart of the enemy."

"You've captured one of their planes, the Albatros."

"Oh, there is so much more to it. I have many planes, but what I need is the best pilots in the service. I need you, Wyatt."

Wyatt unconsciously took a deep drag on his Lucky. "Tell me more."

"I will tell you everything, but understand that there can be no going back." The Sorcerer moved closer, fixing his compelling gaze on the captain. "I will return tomorrow night for your answer. Tell no one."

"Wait…"

But the Sorcerer was already gone.

**The ghost of** Tyr Sorensen visited Wyatt a second time that night, not in the flesh but in a series of fractured dreams. The captain's sleep was restless and he awoke to the brayed notes of reveille feeling completely exhausted; it was as if he had endured the longest battle of his life. Nightmare images crowded together with true memories, leaving him uncertain about the very ground beneath his feet.

He joined Bull Caine for breakfast and saw that his friend seemed likewise fatigued. Had the Sorcerer's ghost approached him as well, the captain wondered. Remembering the apparition's final admonition, he didn't ask. "How's Styles doing?"

"He'll pull through," Bull answered with a grim smile. "Might be a few days before he's in full fighting trim, but he's a tough old bird."

"That's good." Wyatt sipped at his coffee. "That was a close one."

"Yep."

The silence between them was ominous, but both men seemed afraid to speak lest their comments be interpreted as madness. In the end, Wyatt excused himself, citing a need to check on the repairs to their planes. Bull simply nodded and continued toying with his uneaten breakfast.

Bull had not in fact met with Sorensen's specter, but he had nonetheless been haunted through the night by dreams of his former squadron leader's demise. Sorensen had to be dead; Bull had seen his plane crash to earth and explode. But that did not change the fact that the pilot of the mysterious plane, who had pulled their fat from the fire, had almost perfectly imitated the Sorcerer's style of flying. If it wasn't Sorensen, then who was it?

He continued grinding the grist of the mystery as he made his way back to the field hospital. Styles was awake and enjoying the company of a pretty nurse, and Bull was about to make a quiet exit when the Texan called him over.

"Heya, Bull. Where y'all runnin' off to?" Styles's drawl seemed even more pronounced, doubtless a side effect of the morphine.

Bull gave a wan smile and moved over to join him, even as the nurse excused herself and moved along to the next bed in the line. "How are you feeling?"

Styles touched the swath of bandages that encircled his head like a Dervish's turban. "Ah gotta headache that won't quit. Usually when ma head hurts this bad, it means Ah had good time the night before. But Ah can't remember much of anything about yesterday."

"Do you remember the six Fokkers?"

Styles raised an eyebrow under the bandages. "Six? How in Gawd's name did you and the Cap manage to get us through that?"

"We had a little help." He proceeded to tell the tall Texan of their mysterious savior.

Styles did not fail to notice the change in Bull's demeanor as he described the Sorcerer's signature move. "You know who it was, don'cha?"

The burly sergeant gazed at the floor. "I... I know who the Cap thinks it was: our former squadron commander, Captain Tyr Sorensen."

Styles nodded slowly. "The Sorcerer. Ah heard all about him. He was one of the best."

"He died just before you came to the 44th. Captain Wyatt got his second bar and took command of the squadron—changed our name too, 'cause there could never be another Sorcerer—and then you came along to take the lieutenant's slot."

"So which is it? Is the Sorcerer still alive, or ain't he?"

Bull sat down on the foot of the bed. "I don't see how he could be."

Styles leaned back on his pillow. "Tell me what happened that day; tell me everything."

## CHAPTER 4 - BULL'S TALE

**The Sorcerer was** a living legend, a god who walked among men. And like a god, his glory blinded those who worshipped and adored him—blinded them to his faults.

Bull had known Sorensen longer than any of them, and while he certainly admired the captain's ability behind the stick, he also saw the man's dark side, and had watched that darkness grow like the long shadows of Autumn as the war dragged on. Sorensen was a natural in the air—he flew as if he had been born with wings—but on the ground, it was a different story.

Like many hard men, Sorensen lived, loved and drank hard. His licentious behavior was excused for the simple reason that it did not interfere with his warfighting abilities. If anything, it was understood to be an outlet for the stress of near constant combat. But that was changing. The new brigadier general was demanding more discipline from his officers, and made no secret of the fact that Sorensen needed to run a tighter ship, both with respect to the squadron and his personal life. Rumors were already beginning to circulate among the enlisted men that Sorensen might be transferred out of the 44th or even relieved of command. Bull Caine however feared that the coming storm might prove far more disastrous; the Sorcerer didn't do anything quietly.

Yet the intrigues of command could not be allowed to interfere with day-to-day operations; there were missions to fly and battles to be fought. Bull and the rest of the Flying Sorcerers lined up at their planes, taking their lead from Lieutenant Wyatt—something they seemed to be doing more and more often—and waited for the captain to join them on the airfield. After half an hour of waiting, some of the pilots began to grumble anxiously. Lt. Wyatt quickly took control.

"Denis, go find the captain."

The young Frenchman, a mechanic from the nearby town who had ingratiated himself to the squadron in general, and to Sorensen in particular, hastened to the captain's barracks.

When some minutes had passed without either the Sorcerer or the runner returning, Wyatt reluctantly donned his helmet. "Start 'em up, boys. There's a war to fight."

"Let's go!" Bull shouted, trying to distract the nervous pilots from their worried musings. The war cry had the desired effect. The pilots leapt into their cockpits and one by one the ground crew spun their propellers and filled the peaceful morning with the throaty noise of nearly a dozen Hispano-Suiza 220 horsepower engines. Wyatt rolled his Spad past the lone silent plane, and throttled up in preparation for takeoff. That was the exact moment that the Sorcerer appeared on the field.

He was dressed for battle and walked with a determined unapologetic stride. He did not look at any of the men as he passed, but kept his expression hidden behind his goggles and the distinctive gold scarf he wore over his face. For some reason, Bull's heart fell as he saw the captain join them; he had actually been looking forward to flying under Lt. Wyatt. The young officer was an excellent fighter pilot but more importantly a charismatic leader of men, a critical skill that the Sorcerer had somehow allowed to go fallow. Nevertheless, Sorensen climbed spryly into his cockpit and waved one of the ground crew over to start his engine. Normally that would have been Denis's job, but evidently the young mechanic and the captain had passed each other by. With his own plane roaring in harmony with the others, Sorensen rolled around Wyatt and took his place at the head of the line.

Once in the air, the awkward moments caused by the captain's tardiness were quickly forgotten. The Sorcerer set a break-neck pace, rushing toward the lines like a berserker of legend, and quickly put them back on schedule. In no time at all, they reached their destination, a known enemy supply route, and commenced strafing the long convoy of wagons on the road.

It was only at that moment, that instant on the precipice when a combat pilot commits to action against the enemy, that Sorensen hesitated. It was nearly imperceptible—Bull would later discover that he alone noticed it—but for just that briefest of moments, it seemed like the Sorcerer had forgotten what to do next. But then he was gone, screaming down out of the sky with guns blazing, and the rest of the Flying Sorcerers followed. Bullets stitched the road, killing soldiers and horses, tearing apart wagons and setting fire to munitions stores. In a matter of seconds, the German convoy was thrown into chaos. They made two more runs, twisting the knife in the enemy's wound, before Bull's sharp eye spotted the distant specks of approaching enemy aircraft. Less than a minute later, the great knights of the sky were joined in combat.

The Sorcerer charged into the fray. Bull saw immediately that Wyatt—the captain's wingman—was having trouble keeping in position. It was as if Sorensen had forgotten how to fly a formation and was merely charging headlong at the enemy. Bull signaled to his own wingman his intention to help out, and together they raced after their fearless leader.

The fighting was fierce, like nothing any of the pilots had ever seen before. Tracers criss-crossed the sky like lightning bolts and bullets seemed to be coming from every direction. All around them, planes burst into flame or spiraled into oblivion with dead men at the stick. Bull glanced back at his own wingman, received a thumb's up signal, and the gasped in horror as the young man's plane disintegrated before his eyes. Through the black smoke of burning oil, an Albatros rose into view, its guns winking like deadly fireflies.

Bull swung his gaze around and focused on the part of the battle he could actually do something about. Up ahead, he saw Wyatt's plane and a little farther out, the Sorcerer, zigging and zagging in pursuit of a Boche raider. Sorensen was relentless, fixating on that single fighter as if it were the only plane in the sky, hurling lead at the enemy as if he would never run out.

Then Bull saw something he would never forget. His perception of that instant stretched like taffy, as if some part of his brain knew what was about to happen and slowed down to record every detail. He heard a dull roar over the noise of the Hispano—it was his own voice, shouting a denial—and then saw the tracers, moving sluggishly from somewhere above and slicing through the sky toward the Sorcerer's plane. There was a slow eruption of splinters behind Sorensen's head, then another a few inches closer, then....

Sorensen's head snapped back in a spray of crimson, then lolled to the side. The Spad hung there for an eternity—a moment forever frozen in Bull's memory—and then lazily heeled over and floated like a feather toward the ground, eventually shrinking to a nearly invisible speck against the landscape. He continued looking, peering down into the void between earth and sky, until a tiny explosion far, far below pulled him back into reality with a violent snap.

Bullets were cracking and zinging all around. He felt the Spad shake under the impact as the upper wing was hammered by enemy fire. What happened next was an indistinct blur—to the same extent that he had witnessed Sorensen's demise with astonishing clarity, he now saw everything in a rush. His next clear memory was of the surviving planes—five left out of twelve—every one battered and war weary, touching down at Chaumont, one after the next. He knew only two things with any degree of certainty: Tyr Sorensen was dead; and Colby Wyatt had brought them back alive.

**"And that was** that. Lieutenant Wyatt became Captain Wyatt. We retired the Sorcerer's crest and became the Wolfpack. You know the rest."

"Ain't no way Sorensen could'a' made a parachute jump?" Styles inquired.

"He was dead before the plane hit the ground. It had to be someone else up there yesterday. Not just anyone either; an ace, someone who actually knows how to fly and fight."

Styles stroked his chin thoughtfully. "That young mechanic must'a' been the last person to talk to Sorensen."

"Denis? Maybe. I can't see how that matters."

The lieutenant gave an enigmatic smile. "All the same, I wouldn't mind talking to the fella."

"He lives in town, but since that day... well, he really admired the Sorcerer. I think he took the news pretty hard."

"What are you sayin'? He hasn't been around since Sorensen died? Interesting."

Bull's face creased in a perplexed frown. "I don't get it."

"It may be nothing, but then again..." The Texan shook his head, then winced as a flash of pain spiked through his skull. He took a few deep breaths until the agony subsided, and spoke again. "The real question is: why does someone want y'all to think the Sorcerer is still alive?"

Bull stared back for a moment, pondering the question, and then looked abruptly to the exit, as if expecting someone to walk through. "The Cap?"

"Somethin's rotten here, mah friend. And I think whoever is behind this is tryin' to bamboozle our Cap'n."

## CHAPTER 5 - CHASING GHOSTS

**Wyatt eased the** motorcycle to a halt in front of the old tavern and killed the engine. The short ride from the air base was not quite as efficacious as a turn behind the stick, but it did help him clear his head and put his thoughts in order.

The old stone building had been a public house and hostelry for hundreds of years, and had entertained soldiers from countless armies. War was good for business. Wyatt himself had only been to the tavern a few times, but he knew it to be one of Sorensen's favorite haunts. He wasn't sure exactly what he was looking for, but it seemed like the right place to start asking questions.

The tavern seemed almost deserted; the regular clientele would not show up until after sundown, but there was a scattering of men in uniform. One of them recognized Wyatt as a fellow aviator and hailed him from across the room. "Wyatt, old chap!"

The captain peered through the darkened environs and saw the familiar face of Archie Manners, a lieutenant in the Royal Flying Corps. He meandered over and joined the British flier.

"I say, Wyatt, I don't think I've ever seen you without your chums."

The captain's smile slipped a notch, guiltily. "They were, ah, indisposed."

Manners leaned over the table, his typical joviality abruptly replaced by something more cryptic. "They haven't... well... gone off, have they?"

"Gone off?"

The RFC pilot glanced around the room nervously. "Last week two of our blokes deserted. Out of the blue, just like that." He snapped his fingers.

"Anyone I know?"

"Trent and Worthington."

Wyatt's eyes grew wide. He knew them by reputation alone, but their reputations were legendary. These were not the typical malingerers and malcontents, hanging about the fringes of the war and fleeing when the heat of battle became too intense; Allan Trent and Hugh Worthington were tops in the Corps. The words of Sorensen's ghost came back to him: A secret flying force...the best pilots in the service.

So it was true.

**Wyatt's departure from** the base did not go unnoticed. Bull felt guilty for shadowing his commander from a distance, but the longer he watched, the more he began to realize that Styles's concern was justified. When Wyatt went into the tavern, he skirted the outside of the building and crept into through the kitchen where he saw a familiar face.

"Marie," he stage whispered.

The pretty bar maid turned cautiously toward him, but when recognition dawned, her apprehension vanished. "Robert! Mon dieu!"

He touched a finger to his lips and she dropped her voice, but not her smile. "I saw your capitan and wondered if you weren't lurking about somewhere."

"I don't want him to know I'm here, but I need you to do something for me."

Her smile broadened. "You know I would do anything for you, Robert. But I am working now."

"Not that... well, not right now at least." He flashed a grin, but then quickly regained his composure. "I need to know what the Cap is doing in there."

"You want me to spy on your capitan? Tres bien, but..." She raised a conspiratorial eyebrow. "I think now you will owe me a favor."

**Though the doctor** threatened to put him in restraints, Styles had no intention of lingering in a hospital bed, not while there was even a hint of danger to the captain. When it became apparent that he was going to leave with or without permission, the nurses changed his bandages and helped him get dressed. He took along a walking stick in order to help keep his balance; his equilibrium had not completely returned and the simple act of standing made him feel as though he were on the deck of storm-tossed sailing vessel.

He caught a ride into town and in short order found himself in the town square, standing in front of the rectory of the parish church. He caught the eye of a priest strolling toward the chapel and hailed him. "Bon jour, Padre."

The priest smiled and launched into a rapid fire greeting in French. Styles caught about every other word. "Beg'n' your pardon, Padre, but I don't parlez too much Francais."

The priest blinked at him, then seemed to comprehend. He raised a finger and said something that Travis took to be: "Wait one moment" and then he hurried back inside the rectory. A few moments later, he came out with a young novice in tow. The girl kept her eyes downcast, as if afraid that merely gazing upon a dashing pilot might tempt her to break her vows. The Texan chuckled inwardly at the thought; he certainly didn't feel very dashing at the moment.

"Bon jour, sister. Parlez Anglais?"

"Oui, I mean, yes."

"Good. I'm looking for someone that lives here in town, and I figured, seein' as how he's the local vicar and all, that this would be a good place to start."

The novice looked up at him, her brow furrowed in consternation. She understood English, true, but Styles's idiom was a far cry from what her neighbors across the channel spoke. Nevertheless, she turned to the priest and made a halting translation, after which she interpreted the reply. "Yes, what is the name of the person?"

"A young fella named Denis Renault. He worked at the aerodrome for a stretch."

The priest didn't wait for the girl to translate. His head snapped up on hearing the name and he began speaking rapidly. "We know the man you look for, but he has not been seen in the town for some time. His parents are very concerned. He dreamed of becoming an aviator—like yourself—and they fear he may have run off to join the Aviation Militaire."

"He hasn't contacted them? Written a letter or anythin'?"

"No, monsieur. This is not so strange. Many young men leave to fight and enlist using false names so that their families cannot prevent them. Monsieur Renault fears that something may happen to Denis, and no one will know his true name."

Styles gave a heavy sigh. He had known, almost from the moment that Bull had told the tale of the Sorcerer's final fatal flight, what had really happened on that day, and now he was certain of it. He managed a grim smile and nodded to the priest. "Merci. Tell him I'll pray for Denis."

He didn't know how to begin to explain that Denis Renault had indeed gone off to fulfill his dream of becoming a fighter pilot, or that he now lay dead in another man's grave.

**Bull mulled over** the report Marie had given him as he joined Styles for dinner. Wyatt had returned to the base, but somewhere along the way, had unknowingly eluded his shadow. It was unlike their captain to miss dinner or for that matter to absent himself from the company of his friends, and Bull was now very concerned.

"What did you find out?" he asked the Texan.

Styles leaned close so that no one would overhear their conversation. "Tyr Sorensen is still alive. As near as I can figure, young Denis couldn't find him that day and decided to dress up in his uniform and play hero. Got himself killed for his trouble, but everyone thought it was Sorensen."

Bull shook his head in astonishment. "Now that I think about it, it makes a lot of sense. It just didn't seem like him flying."

"Maybe Sorensen was too embarrassed to admit that the boy had died in his place, or maybe he had some other reason for keeping hidden."

"Actually, I think Sorensen was already gone. When I followed the Cap today, he was talking to Arch Manners about desertions. It seems a lot of top aces have been disappearing just like the Sorcerer did. Denis might have discovered that he was gone and tried to conceal the fact by taking his place."

Styles's brow furrowed. "Pilots deserting? Why?"

"I don't have the foggiest notion, but I'm afraid the Cap might be next."

The Sorcerer returned at midnight, and Wyatt was waiting.

# CHAPTER 6 - THE GHOST SQUADRON

**They walked on** foot for a long time, Wyatt hefting a small duffel bag carefully onto his shoulder and Sorensen stealthily leading the way until they were well beyond the perimeter of the airfield. No words were exchanged; the Sorcerer had never been a loquacious man and Wyatt understood that now was not the time to discuss what was happening. At length they reached a waiting motorcar and Sorensen gestured for Wyatt to get in.

"I expected we'd be flying out," Wyatt commented, breaking the silence.

Sorensen glanced sidelong at him. "Every time we fly in or out of our secret base, we risk discovery. But after tomorrow, that won't matter anymore."

Wyatt desperately wanted to know more, but knew also that knowledge was one of the puppet strings his former captain now used to control him. Better, he reasoned, not to let the Sorcerer know just how hot his curiosity was burning.

The drive took nearly two hours, during which time Wyatt surreptitiously oriented himself on the North Star. They were traveling away from the front lines, west into the rugged hill country. Wyatt casually took note of landmarks and did his best to approximate their pace in order to create mental map. While they remained on the main track, he had a pretty good idea of where they were, but after an hour of driving, Sorensen turned off onto a wagon road that meandered through farmland and then into an unrecognizable dark forest. After another hour of slow but unpredictable travel through the rough, the road abruptly ended.

"We walk from here," the Sorcerer said. After Wyatt debarked, Sorensen took out a tarpaulin, painted with streaks of green and brown to blend in with the surroundings, and spread it over the vehicle. "A little vanishing trick," he explained.

Using only the beam of a handheld electric torch, Sorensen led the way down a narrow game trail. Wyatt counted his paces and estimated that they had traveled nearly two miles when the trail opened into a broad clearing. In the gleam of Sorensen's torch, Wyatt saw more than a dozen airplanes parked in two parallel rows under an awning of canvas. Spread out on the ground were dozens of tarpaulins painted in the same fashion as the camouflage cover the Sorcerer has used to conceal the motorcar.

"Welcome to the Ghost Squadron," Sorensen said enigmatically. "Try to get some sleep if you can. Tomorrow will be a very busy day."

Before Wyatt could say a single word, the torch went out, plunging the world into darkness.

**Despite the admonition** of his former captain, sleep eluded Wyatt. His heart continued to hammer with the enormity of the decision he had made, and excitement about the adventure ahead. He had not failed to notice in the brief moments before Sorensen turned out the light, that the planes were an equal division of SPAD XIIIs and Albatros D.IIIs, each of which bore the distinctive markings of their respective Air Corps. He had little doubt that the Sorcerer's intent for the Ghost Squadron was to use the enemy's own weapons against them; a dangerous deception that violated the Hague Conventions and guaranteed immediate execution if captured. It was a bold play for the Entente Powers and carried great risk beyond the mission at hand; if the enemy learned of it, then they too might feel compelled to engage in similar methods of chicanery, and no one would be safe. Wyatt was still wrestling with the dilemma when, in the purple of twilight, he saw other figures moving around the planes.

"Cheerio, Wyatt!" one of the men cried. It was Hugh Worthington of the RFC. "Glad you could make it."

As introductions were made, Wyatt realized that Ghost Squadron was not limited to Allied fliers. In addition to the two Brits and a Belgian, there were also three German aces. Wyatt now understood how the Sorcerer had been able to lay his hands on the enemy planes, but wondered what sort of incentive had been offered to get the German officers to defect.

Sorensen made his appearance in full battle kit just as the first rays of dawn were peeking over the horizon. "Gentleman, the time has come for the Ghost Squadron to strike its first blow."

As he outlined the audacious plan, Wyatt's heart was once more hammering with anticipation.

**Six planes—Albatros** D.IIIs with 170 horsepower Mercedes engines and twin Spandau machine guns synchronized to fire through the propeller for greater sight-to-target accuracy—winged their way high above the French countryside, but although the wings and fuselage were adorned with the distinctive Maltese Cross of the German Imperial Air Service, the men flying them no longer owed their allegiance to the Kaiser. Trailing nearly two miles behind them in a pair of Spad's were Wyatt and a Belgian flier named Hans Bierdon.

The route was circuitous, taking them well away from populated areas and more importantly away from the spotters and anti-aircraft batteries of the Allied forces on the ground below. Timing was critical; the target was mobile and already at the far limit of their range. The German officers had supplied Sorensen with exact times and locations for their objective, and from that list, this one moment was chosen as having the greatest chance of success.

Wyatt and Bierdon were chosen to pilot the trailing vehicles for the simple reason that they were unfamiliar with the Albatros. It was not a difficult plane to learn, Sorensen had explained, but there were only six of them and so the task of flying them of necessity fell to the senior members of the Ghost Squadron and to the German defectors who already knew the planes well. When they succeeded in taking the objective—"when, not if," Sorensen said—they would add more enemy planes to their fleet.

They made the long aerial journey without incident, stopping only once to refuel according to plan. They flew at the very limit of their airplane's ceiling, nearly three miles above the ground, virtually invisible to anyone below. As they drew closer to the Western Front, the Spads moved forward, sweeping the path for possible patrols of friendly aircraft, but then dropped back as the formation entered the sky above German territory. Sorensen led the way from that point onward, moving in northerly arc toward their objective.

At a signal from the Sorcerer, Wyatt and Bierdon dropped back even further, until the six planes of the Ghost Squadron were mere specks in the distance. From their position in the sky, the target was indistinguishable from the clouds, but then that was the genius of the zeppelin's defenses. If all went according to plan, they would have to wait only a few minutes to begin their own approach, and by then it would be plainly evident whether or not the Sorcerer's covert assault was a success. When the prescribed time elapsed, Wyatt waggled his wings as a signal to the Belgian, and then throttled ahead to the rendezvous.

Even from a thousand yards out, the airship looked like any other cloud. Gradually however, the distinctive sausage shape of the dirigible became visible through the mist. The great gray body of the airship emerged from the cloud and soon dominated his overhead view. Wyatt angled the Spad down, bringing it in line with the length of the zeppelin and continued forward without slowing. He immediately felt a headwind buffet the plane, but he did not break off; everything was moving exactly according to plan.

The zeppelin was also moving into the headwind, and though its speed was only about half that of the fighter plane, the relative difference was crucial. Wyatt's plane seemed to float forward rather than racing, allowing him ample time to make the delicate maneuvers necessary for close-quarters flying. The target of his approach lay directly ahead; suspended by mighty hawsers from the enormous gas-filled body of the airship, was a landing strip.

As the Spad drifted into the tight confines, Wyatt saw that the rest of the Ghost Squadron planes had been pushed to the side and secured to the deck alongside a dozen more just like them. He feathered the throttle, pushing the plane into the gap, and gently nosed down until the wheels were rolling along the runway. When he felt the bump of contact, he cut the engine and extended full flaps. Two of his fellow Ghosts rushed out to help steer the plane out of the way so that Bierdon could land. It was only as Wyatt climbed out of the cockpit to stand on the suspended landing deck, that he realized the sheer scope of what the enemy had built; the zeppelin was a massive mobile airbase in the sky.

**Bull's face was** ashen as he came into the barracks shared by the Wolfpack. In his hand, he clutched the letter, the contents of which he still could not believe. Styles looked up when he entered.

"He's gone," Bull said, waving the letter. "I can't believe it."

The lieutenant took the missive and read it:

*My dear friends,*

*Captain Sorensen is alive. He did not die in the crash as we believed, but allowed everyone to believe him dead in order to create a highly secret squadron for special missions. He has asked me to join him and I cannot refuse his request. He has also asked me to tell no one, but that is something I cannot do. You are my closest friends and you deserve to know the truth.*

*The service will believe me to be a deserter. This is a shame that I must endure in order to fully accomplish the mission I have now undertaken. Do not try to clear my name of this reproach. No one else can know of this.*

*Please do not try to find me. Carry on the tradition of heroism that has distinguished our squadron. Make me proud.*

*Your friend eternal, Colby Wyatt.*

Styles lowered the letter to his desktop, then after a moment's consideration, took out his cigarette lighter and struck a flame. He touched it to a corner of the letter and held it carefully until nothing remained but a charred curl of black ash.

"What do we do now?" Bull asked, barely able to contain his emotions.

The Texan's normally genial face was as hard as a diamond. "Simple. We find him."

## CHAPTER 7—THE STORM CLOUD

**"She's called the** Sturmwolke—Storm Cloud—because she looks like a cloud and can deliver a storm of destruction from out of a clear sky."

Sorensen had been especially dramatic in the briefing earlier that morning. "She's a prototype, larger than anything the Hun has ever put in the air, built in secret at Tondern, and this is her maiden voyage. She's been outfitted with special cloud-makers to disguise her appearance and allow her to get closer to the target. Then, when she's close enough, bam! Fighters launch right off the deck and are on the objective before anyone knows what's happening.

"We're going to take her boys, and put the Sturmwolke to work for us!"

While the zeppelin was still nothing more than a cloud in the distance for Wyatt, Tyr Sorensen was the first to land on the enormous suspended airstrip. Two crewmen in overalls waved him on and then guided his Albatros into a slip where they hastily tethered the aircraft to the deck. The Sorcerer climbed out as they finished their task and watched as they rushed back onto the runway to marshal the next plane in the formation. When the last Albatros was aboard and secure, Sorensen beckoned the two crewmen to join him. The young German sailors were taken completely by surprise; distracted by Sorensen, they never saw the knives in the hands of the other pilots.

Sorensen had intentionally excluded Wyatt from this part of the operation. His onetime apprentice was deadly behind the stick trigger of a Vickers gun in the air, but to kill a man up close and personal, with a knife in the back no less, wasn't his style. Wyatt would get his chance for glory though, if he chose to take it.

"Stow the bodies somewhere out of the way," he instructed the German pilots. "Then bring our friends in. The rest of you come with me. There's still some dirty work to be done."

**Wyatt retrieved his** luggage and ascended the long ladder to the enclosed flight deck where the Sorcerer was waiting along with most of the Ghost Squadron pilots and three other men he did not recognize—two wore the garb of German pilots and the third wore the uniform and rank of an Aerokapitan of the German Imperial Navy. These three, members of the airship's original company, had been secretly working with the leader of the Ghost Squadron all along, passing information along and ultimately helping the assault force take over the dirigible.

"Congratulations, gentlemen," Sorensen stated pontifically. "The Sturmwolke is ours. The first phase of our bold endeavor is complete. Kapitan Doerner will put us on our new heading and by the evening, we will transfer all of our planes. Tomorrow, we will embark on the great adventure."

There was a round of hearty cheering and then the gathering broke up into little knots of conversation while Sorensen and the naval captain moved up to the control station. Wyatt drifted through the throng and approached his former superior officer.

"The great adventure," he echoed, glancing at the map table, where a representation of Great Britain lay spread out for reference. The Wolfpack pilot immediately felt the hairs on the back of his neck stand up. Something was dreadfully wrong. "Care to fill me in?"

The Sorcerer fixed him with relentless eyes. "Soon," he promised. "The magician never reveals his secrets to anyone… except of course for his apprentice."

Wyatt did his best to match the other man's stare. "Is that what I am?"

At that, Sorensen cracked a smile. "Perhaps you are ready to be more than that? I wonder.

"Tell me, Wyatt. Why are you here? I don't mean here on the Sturmwolke. Why did you enlist and join the air service?"

Wyatt's sense of dread was burning like a warning beacon. "I love to fly and I love my country."

The Sorcerer barked a short humorless laugh. "And does your country love you? Look where you are; your country sent you to the other side of the world, and for what? To fight somebody else's war? To go up and risk your life every day, and if you get shot down? So sorry, you're boy was a hero."

The Wolfpack captain held his gaze steady, not challenging the Sorcerer. "We all knew the risks."

"Well I'm tired of taking risks for other people; risking my life for kings and presidents who will never raise a hand in defense of their nation, but who don't even think twice about sending millions—millions, Wyatt—to die in this hellhole." Sorensen took a deep breath and brought his passion under control. "The others feel the same way I do. I know this must be a bit much to swallow, but if you'll hear me out, I think you'll come around to our way of thinking. We are the new gods, Wyatt; winged lords of the air, and this is our time."

"And this 'great adventure' of yours?"

Sorensen touched a finger to the map of England. "Simple really. King George isn't fit to wear the crown. So we're going to take it."

**Wyatt waited until** dusk to make his move. He stole down to the open landing deck and moved to the very edge, as if trying to peer through the veil of clouds to see the ground below. After a moment, he turned away and moved toward one of the Spads. He froze stock still when he realized that the Sorcerer was right behind him, along with Trent and Worthington.

"What are you doing, Wyatt?" It was plain from the dark rage that suffused Sorensen's face that he already knew the answer.

Wyatt made no attempt to conceal his purpose with a lie. "I can't let you do this, Tyr."

The Sorcerer raised his fist, pointing the barrel of his pistol at the other man's chest, while the two British aces circled around to stand behind him. "I saved your life, Wyatt. I saved it the first day you flew for me and I saved it two days ago… and this is how you repay that debt?"

"Tyr… all of you, listen to me. You don't have to go through with this. Sail the Sturmwolke to an allied airfield and hand it over. You'll be heroes."

"A hero? And what will that get me in the end? Do you know what a hero is? It's someone who does all the work, and then lets someone else take all the reward." Sorensen sighed. "You are one of the best pilots I know Wyatt… maybe the very best. I had hoped that you would understand and follow me instead of clinging to some outmoded idea of honor or chivalry. But I also knew that it might come to this."

Something heavy slammed into the side of Wyatt's head and then he saw nothing but stars.

**Styles and Bull** had spent a long and ultimately fruitless day searching for their missing captain. The quest had begun in the map room, where they had plotted a large circular area—the estimated range of the black Albatros plane that had saved them from the Fokkers—and selected a number of locations within that circle where Sorensen might have been able to shelter and launch the planes of his secret squadron; it was a long list, but the two Wolfpack aces were undaunted. When they rolled their Spads, patched up and refitted, onto the field, both men acutely felt the absence of their leader and swore that nothing would keep them from finding him. But twelve hours and hundreds of miles of flying later, with the sky growing too dark to see anything on the ground, they had admit that they would not do so this day.

Wearily they returned to their barracks to review the map. "We gotta use our heads," Styles declared, running his finger over relief image. "Sorensen was flying a German plane. What does that tell us?"

Bull puffed on his cigarette and nodded. "His base might be somewhere across the line. Or…"

"Or the Sorcerer might be workin' for the other side."

"Cap would never be suckered into doing that," Bull said, unequivocally.

"Nah, he wouldn't." Styles scanned the part of the circle that lay on the other side of No Man's Land, and rubbed his weary eyes. "So many possibilities."

The door to their barracks abruptly burst open and a young soldier wearing a runner's armband burst in, panting heavily. In his hand, he held a small scroll of cigarette paper. "Sir, message for you."

Styles took the paper and felt his heart skip a beat, for drawn on the outside of the roll was the image of three tiny flying insects. "Where did you get this?"

"One of our birds just flew in with it. We didn't even realize she was gone…"

"Birds?" Bull asked, likewise excited. "You mean a homing pigeon?"

"Yes sir."

Styles eagerly broke the seal and read the short message inscribed thereupon. When he looked up, every trace of fatigue was gone from his eyes. "Assemble the squadron, Bull. The Cap needs us."

## CHAPTER 8–THE ATTACK

**Wyatt awoke to** a bustle of activity. The first thing he realized as the fog of sleep receded was that he was still on the launch deck of the Sturmwolke, and the second was that he was bound, hands behind his back, to one of the massive hawsers that held the landing platform to the zeppelin overhead. His skull was smarting from the blow that had put him out—probably delivered with the butt of Trent's pistol—but the physical pain didn't sting nearly as much as his own humiliation, both at having been foiled in his attempt to escape the airship and at having been so easily duped by his former superior.

He tried to test his bonds but his arms ached and his hands were numb from hours of constriction. Daylight illuminated the fog created by the Sturmwolke's cloud machines; he had been unconscious throughout the entire night, and the noise that awakened him was indication enough that they were nearing the objective of the Sorcerer's mad mission.

As if reading his thoughts, Sorensen materialized from behind one of the Spads—Wyatt now saw that there in addition to the many German planes, there were six SPAD XIIIs, all freshly painted with the distinctive bull's-eye insignia of the British Royal Flying Corps—and walked over to where he lay.

"Sleep well, Wyatt?"

"Better than I had any right to," the Wolfpack captain replied. "So you still mean to go through with this?"

"There was never any question." Sorensen kneeled beside him, fixing his dark compelling orbs on the captive. "Do you know why I didn't kill you?"

"You'd miss my charming company?"

The Sorcerer chuckled. "As a matter of fact, that's not far from the truth. I like you, Wyatt. It would have been so much better if you had embraced my vision willingly, but like it or not, you are one of us. When we have succeeded today, the world will know our names—all of us."

"Ah, so it's fame you're after."

"Fame, money—I'll take those over heroism any day."

Wyatt shook his head disparagingly. "A famous pirate and outlaw. You'll be remembered in the same breath as Blackbeard and Billy the Kid. Is that really what you want?"

"You will learn, my friend, that the world loves a pirate. For every blustering bureaucrat who damns us, there will be a hundred ordinary people who will secretly dream of joining us." Sorensen stood and put his hands on his hips, gazing down on his prisoner. "I think you'll come around in time, but alas, today you will have to settle for merely watching. Enjoy the show, Wyatt."

**Six Spads rolled** off the hanging runway and dropped into the sky above London. Sunlight glittered off the Thames, helping the pilots orient themselves. The city's distinctive landmarks—the Tower Bridge and most importantly, the cluster of medieval structures known collectively as the Tower of London—appeared differently from above, but they were nonetheless fixed reference points that enabled the squadron to navigate to their goal. In the lead plane, Sorensen gave each of his Ghost fliers a signal, dispersing them to the four winds.

The strange aerial display drew hushed murmurs from pedestrians who saw only tiny shapes like gnats flitting about in the clouds, but to the sharp-eyed soldiers manning the anti-aircraft batteries dispersed throughout the city, the dark specks were immediately regarded with suspicion. Gunners began adjusting the elevation and traverse of their guns while spotters pressed binoculars to their eyes and peered heavenward. However, one after another gun was lowered as the spotters reported that the planes were friendly, and the soldiers charged with defending the city from enemy air attacks relaxed their guard and sat back to watch acrobatics.

The planes drifted apart at high altitude, but as the distance between them increased, they each began descending, lower and lower, until it was possible even for those on the ground to see their markings. The men at the AA batteries got a particularly close look, for the fighter planes seemed to be coming directly toward them. Some of the gunnery officers might have grown nervous, but none fired a shot as the planes drew closer and closer. Then, as the planes simultaneously passed the dispersed gun locations, the pilots dropped something from their cockpits. The soldiers barely had time to dive for cover before the small grenades exploded on their targets.

In an instant, the orderliness of city life was turned to chaos. All around the Tower district, gun emplacements were destroyed and their crews scattered. The six planes looped around and strafed the nearby streets with machine gun fire. Soldiers ran or died before the onslaught, and civilians fled in a panic, choking the main avenues and trampling any who stumbled.

The attack continued for several minutes more. Although the anti-aircraft guns had been destroyed by the initial assault, sporadic rifle fire from the ground chased after the planes as they made repeated passes. The pilots in turn were quick to home in on the resistance and answer it with a withering volley of .303 rounds. All over the city, the word was spread; police constables and soldiers alike fought their way through the rush of crowds, trying to reach the focal points of the air-to-ground battle, little realizing that they were all being drawn away from the real goal of the daring air pirates.

No one even noticed the strange cloud that seemed to be descending over the Thames.

**Though his perch** on the zeppelin was still shrouded in mist, Wyatt saw the large ailerons on the dirigible tilt up and felt the craft descending. He shifted position, trying to get a better view of the obscured landscape below, but also to restore the circulation to his arms. He discovered after some experimentation, that by bracing his back against the hawser, he could push up with his legs and after a moment, managed to stand up. The change was just enough to work out the kinks and send blood rushing into his numb extremities.

He now saw that he was not alone on the landing deck; the two German pilots that had joined the group after the successful taking of the Sturmwolke were poised at machine gun emplacements on either side of the landing deck, likewise peering into the mist. Wyatt quickly lowered himself back to a seated position. He didn't want the Germans to see what he was about to do.

The rope that held the landing deck in suspension was as thick as a tree trunk and its surface felt as rough as bark. Wyatt leaned forward so that the twine, which bound his wrists, was pressed against the hawser. With a deliberate up and down motion, began to rub the coarse surfaces against each other. The friction immediately burned his skin, but he gritted his teeth through the pain and did not relent.

He was still sawing away at the bonds when he noticed that the shroud of fog concealing the zeppelin was beginning to dissipate. Kapitan Doerner had turned off the cloud generator in order to bring the airship directly to its target. As the last of tendrils of mist evaporated into nothingness, Wyatt saw that they had indeed reached their goal, for directly below the platform were the old stone battlements of the Tower of London.

# *CHAPTER 9 - ASSAULT ON WAKEFIELD TOWER*

**The Sorcerer looked** out from his cockpit at the pandemonium his Ghost Squadron had wrought upon the city and smiled. Everything was going perfectly according to plan. He banked the Spad toward the center of the ring of chaos, where the enormous silvery Sturmwolke appeared to be settling down atop the structure known as Wakefield Tower. The broad brackish expanse of the Thames flashed by beneath his wings, and then he was over the Tower compound itself, a mere hundred yards from the zeppelin.

A scattering of people in the courtyard below, oblivious to the mayhem going on several city blocks away, stared up in amazement at the airship. Sorensen scattered them with a burst from his Vickers, then banked around the Sturmwolke for another pass.

On the landing deck of the big dirigible, he could clearly see the figures of the German pilots along with Allan Trent, poised to make the short leap from the landing platform onto the roof of the tower. The Sorcerer lined up on the court-yard again, but this time the grassy area was clear, just as he anticipated it would be. He cut back on the throttle and gave the little fighter full flaps. The Spad appeared to plummet from the sky, but at the last possible moment, he throttled ahead just enough to pull out of the stall, and then touched down feather light onto the lawn. He killed the engine and allowed the plane to roll the length of the courtyard before coming to a stop, but by that time, the Sorcerer had already leapt clear. The Spad had served its purpose; he would be leaving by a different route.

He ran with pistol in hand back toward the curved edifice that was his destination: Wakefield Tower, which adjoined to the Bloody Tower. To the left of his goal was a postern which afforded access to a stairwell with slotted windows where archers had once been stationed to defend the entrance to theTower Green. That entrance, a large arched passage with an iron portcullis, separated the courtyard from Water Lane, the broad cobbled street that ran along the Thames. When it had been built centuries before, it had been called simply the Water Gate, but through the years, it had earned a different name.

The Traitor's Gate, Sorensen thought bemusedly. How appropriate.

The Tower Green was now abandoned thanks to the strafing run and no one impeded his progress as he entered the postern and began ascending the tower. As he reached the second floor, he heard the sound of gunfire from the chamber beyond. He peered around the doorjamb to see a group of Tower Guardsmen firing at his three confederates who were attempting to enter the vaulted octagonal room by the roof stairs. The Sorcerer steadied his pistol and drew a bead on the back of the nearest liveried guard.

As soon as the man went down, his fellows realized that they were trapped in a deadly crossfire, but no quarter was asked for, nor was any given. Sorensen killed one more of the guards as that man indecisively vacillated between firing at the foes to the front and the enemy at the rear; Trent and the Germans gunned the others down. The British ace flashed Sorensen a triumphant grin, and then both of them took a step back to behold the treasure that had lured them into desertion, treason, piracy and now cold-blooded murder.

In the center of the grandly decorated room, protected by a cage of polished steel, lay the greatest collection of precious metals and jewels in the entire world: The Royal Crown Jewels.

"Get it open," the Sorcerer ordered.

The still grinning Trent, evincing no reverence toward the treasure of his native land, held up a single stick of dynamite which he tied to the lock securing the cage with a piece of twine. "Better move back," he said, still laughing, then touched a lit match to the fuse.

The four men had no sooner retreated to the stairwell than an enormous whump reverberated through the stones. A cloud of dust and the smell of burn stone and cordite filled the stairwell, but the men nevertheless hastened back into the grand chamber. The door to the cage had buckled in the middle and its hinges were twisted, but the damage to the priceless bejeweled artifacts in the center was minimal. The blast had merely knocked a few pieces onto the floor and scorched the red velvet display.

"See anything you like?" chortled the Sorcerer. "Have at it, boys."

Trent and the two Germans produced large canvas sacks and filed gleefully into the cage. The sacks were opened and into them disappeared the treasures of the Empire: St. Edwards Crown; the Sovereign's Orb; the Sceptre with the Dove. The elaborate Sceptre with the Cross, which contained the Star of Africa—at 530 carats, the largest cut diamond in the world—vanished into the bag as unceremoniously as a grocer's produce. The swords, bracelets, rings and even the pearl-bedecked Anointing Spoon—the oldest piece in the collection and one of only two items to survive Oliver Cromwell's revolution and subsequent tyranny—every piece of any value whatsoever was snatched up. When the last bag was full, the three men hefted their burdens and filed out of the room, ascending to the roof of Wakefield Tower to make their escape.

At the top of the flight however, the greedy pirates came to an abrupt halt. Sorensen, bringing up the rear, muttered curses under his breath and pushed through, but then froze in horror as he saw what had caused his confederates to stop in their tracks.

The zeppelin was rising into the sky and moving away from the Tower. The *Sturmwolke* had left them behind.

Wyatt's wrists felt as though they were on fire; he could even smell something like smoke as he sawed his bound hands relentlessly against the rough hawser. He stopped only for the brief time it took Trent to descent from the flight deck and marshal the two Germans manning the machine guns for the task of securing the zeppelin to the roof of Wakefield Tower. As soon as the trio finished fastening the mooring ropes and stepped down onto the roof of the tower, Wyatt resumed his labors.

To his amazement, as soon he did so, the twine binding his arms fell apart. He bent his stiff arms around to inspect the damage done, and found both wrists bloodied and abraded, but not seriously injured. He took a moment to shake out the stiffness, and then crept toward the edge of the platform.

By his reckoning, the only member of Sorensen's gang still aboard the zeppelin was its pilot, Kapitan Doerner. Expert though the man might be with the controls, there was simply no way for him to hold station using the dirigibles ailerons, rudder and power plant. The Sorcerer's entire scheme to loot the Tower hung, not by a thread, but by two thick mooring lines. With no one to prevent him, Wyatt appropriated an iron breaking-bar from the mechanic's tool shed, and worked the lines loose from their grommets.

The zeppelin did not immediately spring into the sky, but only seconds later it began to drift away from the tower. Wyatt however was already hastening to the ladder in order to ascend to the flight deck. Once there, he found Doerner frantically working the controls in order to bring the airship back to the tower. The Boche officer didn't notice Wyatt's presence until the last instant—right before the Wolfpack captain clubbed him in the back of the head with his pry bar.

The controls were quite a bit different than those of his Spad, but through trial and error, Wyatt quickly figured out how to operate the throttle and tilt the ailerons. The towers vanished below the viewing window as the zeppelin coasted forward, rising gently into the sky above the Thames. But Wyatt's elation was short lived.

Over the streets of London, Sorensen's fighter planes had continued to harass citizens and soldiers alike, perpetuating the pandemonium that would divert attention away from the real goal. But each pilot kept a wary eye on the center of their wheel of chaos, waiting for the signal that success had been achieved, and now they had it. The zeppelin was leaving the Tower; it was time to return to their new headquarters in the sky.

As one, the five remaining planes of the Ghost Squadron turned toward the Sturmwolke.

## CHAPTER 10 - LORDS OF THE SKY

**The Wolfpack was** having a bad day—more like a bad week, thought Bull Caine, as he struggled to keep his eyes open. He had flown hundreds of miles, stopping twice to refuel, and fatigue had been his co-pilot for several hours now. The compact sergeant knew he wasn't alone; every one of his fellow flying warriors was fighting a similar battle against heavy eyelids. His wounded shoulder was smarting from the tension and exertion of flying, and he imagined Travis was feeling even worse; the Texan's head wound had started oozing blood the moment he had peeled the bandages off in order to don his helmet, but no force on earth was going to keep either one of them from coming to Wyatt's aid

Bull and Styles were leading the rest of the 44th, a dozen gray Spads bearing the howling wolf insignia and the star of the US Army Air Service in a desperate bid to save their captain and prevent the greatest jewel heist in the history of crime. But Wyatt's note had of necessity been brief, and none of the men in the squadron knew for sure what they were going up against.

With the channel crossing now behind them, the mass formation of warplanes began following the course of the Thames leading inland toward London. The skyline of the city was already visible in the distance and Bull straightened in his seat, realizing that the nearness of their destination likely meant that combat was imminent. The mild-eyed marksman began scanning the sky for any hint of the trouble that lay ahead, and he soon found it: the mid-morning sun was glinting off an enormous silvery-gray shape drifting low across the sky directly above the river.

His finger settled on the stick trigger as he waggled his wings, signaling to the rest of the squadron that he had spotted the enemy.

**"Wyatt!" Sorensen uttered** the name as though it were a curse. He couldn't make out the figure behind the glass of the zeppelin's viewing window, but what other explanation could there be?

"Trent! Leave the loot here and come with me."

"Where are you going?" the British pilot asked nervously.

"I have to get to the Sturmwolke," Sorensen hissed. For the first time since he conceived the scheme, the Sorcerer felt a nagging hint of uncertainty; everything hinged on being able to escape in the zeppelin. "I need you to help me get my plane back in the air."

Trent lowered his bag to the rooftop, but gripped his pistol as if fearing some unexpected treachery. Nonetheless, he followed the Sorcerer back into the tower and down the stairs to the courtyard. Sorensen sprinted ahead to his abandoned Spad, climbing in and prepping the engine as the Englishman lagged behind.

"Hurry up, damn you!"

Trent finally seemed to realize that Sorensen was not abandoning him. He warily stuffed his pistol into his belt and took a station at the propeller. "Contact!"

A mighty heave on the propeller blade started the Hispano turning and Sorensen quickly coaxed it to a throaty roar. Trent fell back as the fighter plane turned a tight circle and burst forward, down the length of the Tower Green toward the Traitor's Gate. The blocked arch loomed closer and closer and it seemed that the Spad's wheels were rooted to the ground, but at the last instant, Sorensen yanked the stick back and the little fighter leapt skyward, climbing into the air above the Thames.

The Sturmwolke lay directly ahead, but out of the corner of his eye he saw, like a gathering of ravens in the distance, a squadron of fighters racing to intercept his fellow air pirates.

**The Wolfpack met** the Ghosts in a storm of lead high above the city. Tracers scorched the sky like lightning bolts as the Spad fighters broke formation and crashed through each other's lines. The Sorcerer's aces had spied the oncoming threat and immediately moved to counter it, even though they were outnumbered by more than two-to-one. The numerical superiority of the Wolfpack did not trouble these hardened veterans in the least; each man had been among the best of the best in their respective air corps, and had built their personal legends on emerging victorious even against long odds.

Their experience and finely honed skill was evident in the first moments of the battle. After the opposing forces passed through each other's lines like football players in a scrimmage, two of the gray Spads were in flames and spiraling out of control toward their doom. The odds were now not quite so stilted against the aces of the Ghost Squadron.

The Wolfpack flyers appeared shaken by the loss of two of their comrades. Several of the biplanes overshot the turn, breaking formation as if they intended to keep flying away from the battle. From the cockpit of his fighter Bull craned his head around, dismayed at the disarray. Half the squadron struggled to regroup, leaving the rest of them—including himself and Styles—dangerously outmatched as they charged back into the fray.

Like knights of old, the pilots lined up and charged each other. Bull put all thoughts of danger from his head and focused instead on directing his fire to deadly effect. One of the Ghost Spads hovered at the edge of his sights, but he withheld fire adjusting his position and waiting for just the right moment to strike. When that moment came, he released only a short burst from his machine guns, but it was enough. The pilot of the enemy plane slumped over his stick and his plane veered out of control, away from the battle.

Bull did not allow the victory to distract him from the greater battle. He quickly scanned the skies again to see the results of the second pass of the skirmish. It was much worse than expected. Three more of the 44th had left the battle; one was winging away, trailing smoke but still somehow aloft, and two others had been blown from the sky. On the other side of the equation, Bull's lone kill represented the only damage to the enemy. The battle was going badly, very badly.

He pulled up even with the lieutenant, their wingtips nearly touching, and shouted across the sky. "We're getting wiped out!"

Styles looked back at him, his face grim but determined. "We've got to work together!"

The sergeant nodded, realizing the truth of the Texan's admonition, but knowing also that the tide of the battle was against them. Then something completely unexpected happened, and Bull's knew his prayers had been answered; off to the East the enormous zeppelin had suddenly become a blazing inferno in the sky.

**Wyatt did not** see his former commanding officer take to wing from the Tower

Green below, but he had an unobstructed view of the incoming squadron of planes and knew, even without the aid of field glasses or telescope, that they were the Spads of the 44th. His message had made it through and his friends had come for him.

But then in an instant his excitement turned to horror as the Ghost Squadron broke off their approach and turned instead to meet the Wolfpack. Wyatt knew his men, knew how well they were trained, but knew also that the men they now faced were the very best in the sky. In the first few moments of the dogfight, it became painfully evident that the Wolfpack were going to need a miracle to win the day.

Wyatt pushed the engine controls to their stops then abandoned the flight deck altogether, leaving the zeppelin to be borne along by the vagaries of wind currents. He hastened down the landing deck, which was now canted at a fifteen-degree angle as the dirigible overhead kept ascending. Leaning into the pitch, Wyatt made his way across the platform and up the slope to the plane moored at the front end of the suspended runway. It was Sorensen's black Albatros.

The wheels were securely locked in place, the only thing that kept it and the other planes from rolling down the deck and plummeting into the river, but Wyatt made no move to release the tie-downs. Instead, he leaned into the cockpit and worked the choke lever in order to get the engine ready for a cold start, and then moved around to rotate the prop. It took three tries to get the Mercedes started, but once he found the right setting for the throttle, the mighty engine purred to life and the biplane began to rock in its moorings as the spinning propeller tried to pull it forward. Wyatt now loosened the tie-downs so that only one wheel remained secure, locked in place with his handy pry bar, to which he had attached a length of rope. Once he was secure in the cockpit, he goosed the throttle and yanked the bar loose.

The plane surged forward, but the cant of the platform also caused it to skid sideways across the deck. The tail struck the wing of another plane, giving Wyatt a jolt, and then the Albatros swung into line, careening down the length of the titled runway with a boost from gravity. The landing deck flashed by in a blur and then the vibration from the rolling wheels ceased as the plane dropped free. Wyatt felt a surge of excitement as he hauled back on the stick and climbed heavenward in a broad loop above the derelict zeppelin. At the top of the arc, he rolled over and swooped toward the Sturmwolke, squeezing the triggers of the fuselage-mounted Spandau machine guns. Bullets tore into the skin of the dirigible, rupturing its hydrogen cells; tracers ignited the escaping gas and before Wyatt even completed his strafing run, the airship was ablaze.

His elation was short-lived however, for an instant later his plane began to rock under the impact of steady machine gun fire from his rear.

**As he returned** to the roof of Wakefield Tower, Allan Trent found the pair of German pilots watching in disbelief as their only means of escape was transformed into a second sun above the Thames. The three would-be air pirates looked to one another in disbelief and then, almost as if reaching a silent psychical agreement, turned for the stairs and fled.

They didn't get far. A contingent of Tower Guard, who had been alerted to the danger by the sound of the dynamite explosion, was waiting for them with guns poised. Trent, realizing that a traitor's fate was the only possible outcome, made a grab for the pistol in his belt, but the Guardsmen's guns spoke first.

**Sorensen was only** a few hundred yards from Sturmwolke when he saw the black Albatros drop from its underbelly, and knew in that instant that he was too late. The Sorcerer's apprentice had ruined everything.

Cursing into the wind, he broke off his approach and followed Wyatt into the sky, but the Albatros had too great a head start and its guns tore into the zeppelin before Sorensen could bring his own to bear. The Sorcerer's face darkened with rage as his dreams for a glorious aerial fortress of crime literally went up in smoke, and his fingers tightened on the stick trigger of his twin Vickers guns. He watched with grim satisfaction as the rounds arced through the sky and smashed into Wyatt's plane, but then the Wolfpack captain, twisted out from under the attack and rolled beneath the Spad.

Sorensen was too canny to allow his one-time comrade in arms to fly circles around him. Immediately as the Albatros vanished from sight, he knew where the counter-attack would come from, and he threw his own plane into an Immelmann turn—almost a mirror image of the reverse Split-S Wyatt had used to escape the attack. As he flew inverted at the top of the turn, the Sorcerer saw his foe several hundred feet below, beginning to climb back toward him, and this time it was Wyatt's guns that were blazing. Sorensen however had expected no less; instead of completing the turn and roll maneuver, he continued into a full loop, driving headlong toward the other plane.

Lead raked his wing as the two planes were, for the space of a few heartbeats, rushing at each other on a collision course, but Sorensen gave as good as he got; his Vickers's lashed into Wyatt's plane, splintering the thin veneer of the wings. And then, as quickly as they had faced off, the two passed again. Sorensen immediately banked in order to come around and he expected Wyatt to do the same, but when he scanned the sky above, the black Albatros was gone.

**Wyatt knew that** he could not hope to outfly the Sorcerer. Tyr Sorensen was the best; had he been so inclined, he could have written the book on aerial combat, and he had taught his protégé only a fraction of what he knew. More than that, he had the natural instincts of a hawk. Recognizing the superiority of his foe, the Wolfpack captain did the only thing he could; he left the battle.

He knew that Sorensen would be looking for him to come around again, so immediately after passing the Spad, he cut throttle and stalled the Albatros. The black biplane nosed down and immediately went into a steep dive, at which point Wyatt flashed unnoticed past the Sorcerer. He let gravity take him faster and faster toward the river below, but then as he drew level with the zeppelin—now a cloud of fire above the Thames—he pulled up on the stick and flew under the hovering conflagration.

The Sturmwolke was in its death throes. Each hydrogen cell that erupted in flames triggered a sympathetic explosion of several more, and as the lighter-than-air gas was consumed in the blaze, the zeppelin began to sink toward the river. Because the fire had started atop the airship, there was nothing to contain the superheated air that might have kept it aloft, and so when only about a third of its hydrogen had either escaped or burned up, the craft plummeted toward the Thames.

Wyatt had been keeping a wary eye on the underbelly of the zep, waiting for something like that to happen, and when it did, he nosed down and dove at a forty-five degree angle toward the water. Although he cleared it by more than a hundred feet, a wave of heat buffeted the Albatros as the Sorcerer's floating airbase plunged past him and crashed noisily into the river.

He did not wait to see if Sorensen was chasing him; he had no intention of returning to single combat with his former mentor. If there was one thing his recent misadventure had taught him, it was that he was not 'Captain Wyatt, Ace of Aces' but rather one of the Wolfpack. And wolves did not hunt alone.

He skimmed along the river, his black Albatros looking like nothing more than a shadow on the water, until he was directly under the raging battle between the Ghost Squadron and the battered remains of the 44th, where he hauled back on the stick and climbed straight up into the fray. As soon as he could differentiate friend from foe, he let lead fly.

One of the ersatz RFC Spads broke up in mid-air before any of the combatants could fix the origin of the fire. The remaining Wolfpack flyers however quickly divined that help was on the way and rallied. The junior pilots took their cue from Styles and Bull, and remembered their training; they were teammates, and the only way to win was to look out for each other. The three remaining Ghosts suddenly found themselves overwhelmed as the Wolfpack attacked in successive waves. Whenever one tried to elude a V-formation of gray Spads, he found himself directly in the line of fire of another group.

In the cockpit of his Spad, Styles heaved a grateful sigh as he watched his squadron pursue and destroy the bogus British warplanes, and then another as a familiar Boche-made warplane drifted into formation alongside him. "Welcome back, sir!" he shouted, flashing a thumb's up. Although he was further back and separated by more than fifty yards, Bull's whoop of joy crackled through air.

Wyatt returned the signal then pulled ahead taking his place at the front of their V-formation. There was still one last bit of business to attend to. With a tilt of his wings, he banked back to the East where the Sorcerer was waiting.

It was a showdown like no other in history; one man, a master of aerial combat and easily better than any three men, fighting against three who together were unstoppable. The Sorcerer met their charge in a frantic display of aerobatics, twisting through the sky so that his Spad seemed to be in three different places at the same time. Each of the Wolfpack felt their planes battered by hot lead and sizzling tracers, while their foe somehow emerged unscathed.

The Sorcerer nevertheless knew that he was outgunned. His bold attack was merely the prelude to the kind of decisive strategy that had earned him his moniker. In the instant before he would have shot through the V-formation of his foes, Sorensen pulled up and shot skyward, into the sun. The abrupt turn caught Wyatt by surprise and he banked left to avoid a collision, and just that quickly, their foe was gone, vanished into the blinding glare overhead and surely waiting for the opportune moment to pounce like a bird of prey.

But the Sorcerer underestimated his foes, or perhaps simply failed to understand the bond the three men shared—a bond that was both friendship and fraternity, but at the same time so much more than that. It was as if the Wolfpack could read each other's thoughts. When their foe turned into the sun, each one knew exactly what to do.

Viewed from above, the three planes—two gray Spads and one black Albatros—formed the points of a triangle, each separated from the next by no more than fifty yards. In this formation, they flew skyward, firing their guns into the sun and filling the sky above with a deadly storm of lead. It was a flurry that would either flush the Sorcerer from hiding or blast him from the sky. Up and up they flew, firing until their ammunition was all but expended and the air was too thin to breathe. At the top of their climb, they split in three different direction, squinting through the lingering fireworks of sun-blindness for their foe, but Sorensen's plane was nowhere in the sky.

The Sorcerer had vanished.

In the cockpit of his Albatros, Wyatt clenched his fists angrily as he turned back to rejoin the rest of the squadron. But as his friends fell in alongside him, he realized that the victory was greater than he imagined. While Tyr Sorensen, defector and would-be sky pirate had seemingly eluded justice, no more would his specter hold sway in their lives. The Wolfpack would never again be haunted by the Sorcerer's Ghost.

**End**

Pulp hero Secret Agent X, the original man of a thousand faces, is about to face his greatest challenge as a diabolical villain prepares to unleash a wave of death. But first he must unlock the mystery of a strange scar on his hand...from a wound he cannot remember. As he follows the trail of clues, the Secret Agent will discover that he has lost more than his memories...

# SECRET AGENT X: THE SCAR

**There were five** of them—five against one—and although none of the men shared any particular characteristics of race or physique, they had one thing in common: they looked tough. These were fighters, hard men and likely hardened criminals, intimately familiar with the use of violence. He knew that he was going to have to fight them and knew also that to lose that fight might well cost him his life. His greatest regret was that he had been discovered before gaining any real insight into the identity of the real villain; no matter the outcome of this fight, his foe would know that Secret Agent X pursued him.

He struck the first blow, feinting forward at the thug directly in front of him, then reversed and thrust backward with his right leg. His judgment was flawless; his heel connected squarely with one of the men, drove the wind from his lungs with a whoosh, and propelled him backward to crash noisily into one of the warehouse's tin walls. In the same smooth motion, he brought the extended foot down on the spot where the stunned man had been standing and delivered a chopping blow to the throat of the man directly to his right. The brute dropped to his knees, gagging and unable to breathe, and just like that, the odds against the lone Agent were reduced to three-to-one. Those were numbers he could deal with.

However, as fast as he had been in taking down the two men most likely to initiate the assault, his actions had left him open to a counter-attack from the front. He tried to get his right arm up to block a punch from one of the men, but was a fraction of a second late. A ham-sized fist caught him just below the sternum and sent him reeling. But instead of collapsing stunned on the warehouse floor, he quickly recovered after retreating only a few steps, and took up a stance used by practitioners of the Oriental fighting arts, his body perfectly balanced, his fists ready.

If the thugs recognized the stance or understood that the man they now faced, despite having the clothes and appearance of a common dock worker, was in fact an expert in jiu-jitsu and a dozen other forms of unarmed combat, they gave no indication. Instead, the three remaining assailants closed ranks and began steadily advancing. The man in the center produced a long fixed-blade knife with which he began slashing the air to intimidate his prey, while the fellow to his right gripped a leather blackjack and thumped it suggestively in his open palm.

The weapons did not greatly concern the Agent. If anything, he knew that the men who wielded them would be overconfident, believing that their arsenal gave them superiority on the battlefield. But the possession of killing tools was not the same as mastery thereof, and by resorting to their use the men had unknowingly betrayed a lack of fighting skill. No, he could handle weapons. What was bothering him was something far less tangible.

In the middle of a fight, with his adrenaline surging and curiously conflicting the physical discipline by which he kept panic at bay, it simply wasn't the time to attempt to sort out mysteries of a more intellectual or philosophical nature. Nevertheless, he was having difficulty keeping his mind in the moment. Like the ticking of a clock, a barely formed thought kept rattling inside his head, diverting his mental faculties from the matter at hand.

The knife slashed closer and the Agent pivoted, turning into that man's weak side to deliver a punch that broke his foe's jaw. He followed through with a kick that swept the goon's legs out from under him, and then spun again to block a strike from the other fellow's bludgeoning instrument. The man had put everything he had into the downward strike and it was a simple thing to redirect his momentum and send him stumbling across the warehouse.

The men no longer resembled the hardened murder squad that had surrounded him mere minutes before. Of the original five, only two were not clutching at some injury, and none of them exhibited the confidence they had earlier manifested. He had broken their spirit; now it was time to end the fight. He returned to his fighting stance and raised his fists again.

And that was when he saw it.

I don't remember that, thought the Agent, staring at the scar on the back of his right hand.

For more years than he could remember, he had been at war with the darkness. Through countless battles he had fought, always victorious, but not always emerging unscathed and his body was a living tapestry of those near misses. Aches and pains that never quite went away, scar tissue from dozens of bullet and knife wounds, and each one told a story, a story he remembered in vivid detail.

But this one he didn't remember.

About an inch long, faintly pink against his tan skin, it ran from the knuckle of his right index finger along the fleshy web toward his thumb. As he stared at it, he realized it was itching furiously.

His world suddenly exploded in blue light and the next clear image he perceived was of two of his assailants advancing toward him, seemingly walking without difficulty on a vertical wall. He knew this to be an illusion; the unseen blow had knocked him to the ground and he was looking at everything sideways. The Agent shook his head in confusion and was rewarded with a splitting pain in his skull.

Itch... itch... itch...

Where did that scar come from?

He struggled to an upright position, bringing the world back into correct focus, but he was too slow. The pair of goons reached him before he could raise a hand in his own defense. A foot lashed out, knocking his supporting arm away. Another kick struck the center of his chest, driving the breath from his lungs, but the kicker paid the price for what he thought would prove to be a debilitating attack. He cursed audibly and hopped away, unable to stand on the foot that delivered the strike; the steel armor the Agent always wore beneath his clothes had broken several of the man's toes.

The Agent backpedaled, trying to put some distance between himself and the gang of bruised, but hardly beaten malcontents. He tried to focus his attention on them as he might pieces on a chessboard: Who would attack next? What were their vulnerabilities? But strategic thinking eluded his grasp, consumed by the fire of an itch and a scar he had not noticed until mere moments before.

He caught a glimpse from the corner one eye of a man hefting a timber, but that image blurred as the rough board swung toward him. His reaction was again too slow by a heartbeat. The makeshift club slammed into his back, and this time he felt the pain immediately.

The men were on him, kicking at his exposed extremities and stomping down on his armored, but nonetheless vulnerable back. The assault was relentless, the agony transcendent. He gratefully embraced the blackness of unconsciousness, but even there he could not escape that nagging itch.

"Someone's coming." The shouted voice was distorted, like a phonograph recording that was winding down. "Let's get out here."

"What about him?"

"Leave him."

The Agent couldn't tell if the assault had ended. The blackness swallowed him whole.

**"Mister! Hey, mister!"**

The Agent awakened with a start and immediately started scratching the scar. It took a few seconds for him to put everything in order, time enough for the pain to return with a vengeance. His vision was doubled, but floating before him was a craggy, unshaven face. He reacted instinctively, scrambling back and raising his hands defensively.

That scar….

"It's okay, mister. Them guys moved off."

He stared back incredulous, uncomprehending, but by degrees his vision and his awareness returned. The man reeked of stale sweat and cheap wine, but his face was unfamiliar; this was not one of the men that had assaulted him. Still, something about the old bum's gaze bothered him. He touched a hand to his face as if feeling for cuts and bruises; there were both aplenty, but what he was really checking for was damage to his disguise. The cosmetic putty still covered the metal pads that he had used to build up his cheekbones, and although he could feel some minor tears in the mask, it was mostly intact; his secret identity was still a secret.

"You need to get to the hospital, mister."

He shook his head.

"I—I can go get some help. The police…"

"No. No police."

The bum seemed relieved.

The Agent got gingerly to his feet. "The men who attacked me. Did you see them?"

"I didn't see nothing, mister. I don't want any trouble."

"I don't want to make any for you." He absently scratched his hand and looked around the warehouse. It was empty. The crates were gone; he had failed. With a heavy sigh, he turned back to the vagrant and extended a hand to the man. Tucked in his palm was a folded five-dollar bill. "Go get yourself a hot meal and warm room, friend. Thanks for your help."

The man gazed at the offering suspiciously—

Is he looking at my scar?

—then took the money and edged away toward the large open doorway. The Agent waited until the fellow was gone, then returned his attention to the place where the crates had been stacked.

He remembered that there had been three of them; three large wooden boxes marked with Chinese pictographic writing that gave little clue as to their contents. His informants had alerted him to the arrival of the shipment, a mysterious and dangerous cargo that had made its way across the world, but no one seemed to know exactly what was inside. He had been told only that the cargo was the property of an Oriental gentleman named Doctor Wu Sun.

The Agent knew all about Wu Sun and yet, like everyone else who had heard of the man, he had to admit that he knew nothing. Wu was an enigma, a living legend of evil. His name was whispered in the darkest depths of the underworld, the mastermind behind the most diabolical criminal schemes. He was said by some to be a puppet master, controlling both governments and crime syndicates from his hidden lair. Others claimed that he did not exist at all, but was a myth perpetuated by a number of different gangs and villains to deflect attention from their own enterprises.

One thing was certain though; if the cargo the Agent had failed to intercept did belong to Wu Sun, then there was big trouble afoot in the city.

He hastened from the warehouse, exiting cautiously through the large doors that opened onto the wharf. He stayed in the shadows, charting a seemingly random path back to the waterfront avenue, watchful for spying eyes that might have remained behind to finish the job the thugs had been forced to abandon. Twice he doubled back on his path, certain that he was being followed, but saw no one. He no longer completely trusted his instincts; his failure against the five thugs, and for that matter the hole in his memory that ought to have explained the strange scar on his hand, filled him with doubt.

In this case however, his instincts were flawless and he was wrong to mistrust them, for after he reached the relative shelter of his sedan and sped away into the night, a rough-looking figure emerged from a darkened alley, still holding a folded five-dollar bill in one hand.

**In the relative** safety of an anonymous apartment, one of many he kept across the city, a very tired and battered Secret Agent settled into a chair positioned in front of a three-way mirror and began to clear away the remains of his latest disguise.

The plastic cosmetic putty concealed large bruises from the battering he had taken earlier, but it wasn't until he had wiped away the last bit of his mask that he saw the full extent of the damage. It went beyond a few cuts and contusions; his mouth was oozing blood and several of his teeth felt loose. He couldn't remember ever suffering such a beating, nor had it ever taken quite so long for him to begin healing. Normally, the aches and pains were quick to fade and the blood from minor scratches would clot and cease weeping from his wounds. The awful truth was that he was feeling even worse now than he had back in that warehouse.

And then there was the scar.

That innocuous looking strip of pink tissue—all that remained of a minor cut or burn—consumed his attention. The mystery of its origin nagged at him like the buzz of a mosquito in his ear. And the itching… he felt like the only relief from the itch might be to claw the scar away with his fingertips.

Through a supreme effort of will, he forced his scratching nails away from the scar and stared at his reflection. The face that confronted him no longer seemed familiar; it might have been simply another disguise. It wasn't just that the features looked unfamiliar, no doubt the effect of spending so much of his life wearing false faces; it didn't feel like his face. The way the skin seemed to puff and sag, the dark circles around his eyes—it was like looking at a vision of how he might look as an old man.

"Pull yourself together," he told his reflection. "Doctor Wu Sun doesn't care how tired you feel."

The admonition sounded as hollow as he felt, but he gamely began applying a new layer of cosmetic putty to his face, covering both his natural visage and the many injuries it had sustained, with a flesh colored disguise.

Without any sort of evidence to guide him to the nefarious villain behind the incident at the warehouse, he knew he was going to have to do some old fashioned legwork to pick up the trail. His best bet, he reckoned, was to start scouring the city's underbelly in order to locate one of the five thugs who had been waiting for him at the warehouse. He knew that he had injured at least two of them seriously enough to warrant professional medical attention, and he knew that these men were not the sort to simply walk into a hospital and wait their turn.

Long years of battling some of the city's most notorious gangsters had allowed the Agent to develop a list of contacts used by those criminals for emergencies. There were more than a dozen different doctors, many of whom had lost their licenses to practice medicine due to some scandal of a personal or professional nature, who now provided their services, at a highly inflated rate, to victims of gunshot and knife wounds who did not desire for their condition to become public knowledge. As soon as his disguise was complete, he hit the streets again, and at his third stop, Morgan's Taxidermy Studio, he hit pay dirt.

When the Agent gained access to the taxidermy studio which fronted the disgraced Dr. Morgan's illicit clinic by a back door, he immediately heard the sound of conversation which, given the lateness of the hour, seemed a pretty good indication that the doctor was in. He crept through the still-life menagerie toward a door marked "OFFICE—PRIVATE" and opened it a crack.

Instead of an office, the Agent beheld a well-equipped examination room occupied by a total of four men—two sprawled unmoving on a table top, one observing, and the other evidently in the process of returning a dislocated knee to its original position. A howl of pain escaped the patient's lips as the joint popped, and the Agent got a good look at the man's face, confirming what he already believed to be true: he had found them.

There would be no battle this time, at least not in the physical sense. At the warehouse, the men had surprised him, but even at that he would have easily bested them if not for the scar....

He reflexively began scratching at the mere thought.

But this time, although he had the advantage of surprise, he would not be relying upon his skills as a martial artist. Simply beating the men into submission wasn't going to get him the information he needed.

He waited until the doctor finished tending to the man with the injured knee before activating one of his knockout gas grenades and slipping it through the door. The colorless, odorless gas dropped the men where they stood in mere seconds. When the agent opened the door, the rush of air from outside the room quickly dissipated the noxious fume allowing him to enter while breathing normally. He knew from experience that he had only about ten minutes before the men would regain consciousness, so he set to work quickly.

The first task was to study the facial features of the injured man and then duplicate them perfectly. It was a tedious job, but years of practice had honed his ability to mimic almost anyone, and as luck would have it, the fellow was a close match in height, build and hair color. Nevertheless, nearly five minutes passed before he completed his disguise. Another minute was spent stripping off the rough fellow's clothes and exchanging them with his own. With a renewed sense of urgency, he grabbed hold of the man, whose face he now wore, by the shoulders and dragged him through the studio and to the back door. By the time he reached a spot about half a block away, the Agent was panting for breath and in a cold sweat.

Must be getting a touch of the flu, he thought as he positioned the other man in the gutter. He placed an empty gin bottle beside the man and then checked his watch. Not much time left, he thought, with a mixture of concern and nausea in his gut. He quickly produced a small hypodermic syringe and injected a large dose into the still unconscious man's thigh, then sprinted back to the doctor's office. Dark spots were swimming across his vision as he stumbled into the room where the three other men were beginning to stir. He barely had time to set the doctor and the uninjured man in seated poses before their eyes fluttered open.

The knockout gas usually left its victims with only a slight sensation of having lost time. Unless someone knew they had been exposed to it, the natural tendency was to dismiss the incident as a mild fainting spell. As the Agent lay back on the exam table, approximating the position the wounded thug had occupied, he heard the thug's comrade attempting to rouse the doctor.

"Hey, doc. Wake up. We ain't payin' you to take a nap."

"What?" murmured Morgan, struggling to open his eyes. "Oh, I'm quite sorry gentleman. It is late after all."

"Just fix up Benny and Snooze so we can be on our way."

Benny or Snooze, the Agent thought. Which one am I?

"I'm afraid your friend Benny won't be going anywhere. That blow bruised his windpipe. I had to perform a tracheotomy—that's the hole in his throat—in order to let him breathe. If you try to take him, he'll almost certainly die."

Well, that answers that. Snooze it is.

"Fine, just take care of him. Snooze, you listening?"

The Agent moaned convincingly, and task made easier by the fact that he now felt genuinely ill. "Doc, my stomach don't feel too good. Can you give me something for it?"

What the heck, he thought, I am in a doctor's office after all.

"I'm not surprised," Morgan offered. "You probably swallowed a lot of blood from that mouth injury. It's a wonder you can talk. Some bismuth should settle your stomach."

The Agent grateful slurped down the chalky pink solution when it was provided. "I feel better already," he lied. In fact, he wasn't sure he would be able to walk without fainting. What's happening to me? I never get this sick.

He absently scratched the scar on his hand as his—or rather Snooze's—unnamed comrade assisted him out of the examination room and toward the now quite familiar back door of the studio. The change to night air once more triggered a cold sweat, but the bismuth had at least made his nausea abate.

"I'll need to keep Benny here for at least a few more days," the doctor explained as he showed them out. "I'm afraid caring for him is going to be quite costly."

"You know who we work for, doc. We're good for it."

"Yes, well Cheng Lo has a reputation for…how should I say it? Ruthlessness?"

Cheng Lo, thought the Agent. Then it is true!

Although no one had ever actually seen Dr. Wu Sun and lived to tell the tale, the accounts of those who had dealt with his lieutenants were in abundance. Some could be dismissed as rumor or false braggadocio, but there were far too many stories identifying a man named Cheng Lo as Wu's most trusted and loyal agent, for them simply to be discounted. Unlike most Oriental gangsters operating around the world, Cheng Lo was not a member of one of the shadowy triads—rather, his operation eschewed the traditional considerations of tribal or racial loyalty. He recruited men from every walk of life, handsomely rewarding success and brutally punishing failure. Some stories suggested that Cheng was infatuated with Wu's exotic but equally diabolical daughter, while others hinted that he might in fact have already married her.

It was said that he was the very image of Dr. Wu Sun.

"I would hate for your employer," the doctor continued, "to decide that your friend is no longer worthy of the measures I have taken."

"You'll get your money, doc." The thug promised irritably, as he and the Agent passed into the back street. "Even if I have to pay for it myself."

"Yes, well I quite wonder if you can afford it."

"Lousy quack," the man murmured when they were out of earshot. "He'll have a tough time spending that money when Cheng Lo get those crates."

The Agent laughed sympathetically as he got into a waiting sedan, but inside his mind was racing. Dr. Wu Sun was planning something diabolical, of that he was sure, but what was his scheme, and when was it going to occur? He surreptitiously glanced down the alley, picking out the motionless form of Snooze. Eventually the thug would recover consciousness and then his disguise would be compromised. He figured he had two hours at best to infiltrate Cheng Lo's organization and find those crates.

So focused was he on the path ahead, the Agent did not see a figure emerge from the shadows and kneel down beside the unconscious man.

**The brief rest** after so much frantic activity helped the Agent throw off some of the fatigue that had earlier plagued him, but he was still tired and sore as he limped from the sedan to the back alley entrance of the Lung Mei Inn, a restaurant located on the cusp of Chinatown.

Presently, the three crates which the Agent had so narrowly missed at the warehouse were now stacked in the pantry area. The two goons remaining goons he had fought were idly smoking and playing dominoes with two young Chinese men, but rose from their game when the door opened.

"Hey, Nails! Snooze! Where's Benny?"

"Benny's hurt pretty bad," explained the man who evidently employed the nom de guerre "Nails."

"Doc'll fix him up though. Have you heard from the boss?"

"You know he doesn't work like that, Nails."

"Yeah, yeah; sealed envelopes with our instructions to be opened only when we finish the jobs. But that didn't take into account that we would be runnin' into trouble at the warehouse. That was Secret Agent X back there."

The man who had been addressing Nails now shrugged. "The boss told us that X might try to mess with us. If he ain't worried about it, then I ain't."

The Agent listened intently as he limped over to a chair, but his downcast eyes were secretly studying the crates. If what the men said was true, then Cheng Lo and Dr. Wu Sun might not even be physically present in the city.

"So we just gotta wait," grumbled Nails. "I hate waiting."

"You and me both brother, but the boss knows what he's doing." The man then turned to the Agent. "Snooze, you don't look so hot. Maybe you should go upstairs and lay down."

The Agent considered the suggestion, but it was doubtful that he would find anything of importance on the premises. "Nah," he grunted. "I gotta better idea. Why don't you guys go out and have some fun. I can watch the goods here. I ain't much good for anything else."

Nails and the other men exchanged a glance. "That don't sound like a half bad idea."

The two Chinese men conversed in rapid-fire fashion in their native tongue, then one of them spoke in halting English. "Our master will not permit us to leave."

Nails shrugged. "Suit yourselves. Snooze, I guess you'll have some company."

The Agent nodded, secretly pleased. With his knockout gas gun, he could easily subdue the two men and then the crates would be his.

Suddenly the relative quiet was shattered by the jangling ring of a telephone. All of the men present looked up in alarm, and the Oriental who had translated for his friend hastened to answer. "Lung Mei Inn," he said into the receiver. A perplexed expression came over his face and then he turned to Nails. "It's for you."

A look of bewilderment, mixed with raw fear, came over the big thug as he took the phone and listened intently. The Chinese man however moved closer to where the Agent was sitting and nodded to his comrade.

The Agent knew, even before the men made their move, that his cover was blown. He reached for the pocket where his gas gun was kept, but an iron grip seized his wrist. Despite his diminutive size, the Chinese man was extraordinarily strong.

Nails whirled around in that instant and looked him square in the face. "Boys, that ain't Snooze. It's him! It's Secret Agent X."

As he struggled helplessly in the grip of first one and then three captors, the Agent racked his brain to understand how his secret had been so quickly discovered. Snooze should not have recovered from the dose of sedative for at least another hour. He had gravely underestimated his enemy, and where Dr. Wu Sun was concerned, that could prove a deadly mistake.

"What do we do with him, Nails?" asked one of the men.

"Tie him up. The boss wants to see him before…" He drew a finger across his throat. "Of course, nothing says we can't rough him up a bit first."

The prospect of further violence did not trouble the Agent as much as the fact that "the boss," no doubt Cheng Lo himself, knew of his investigation. Dr. Wu had covered every angle.

Suddenly the door burst open and a flood of men in blue suits inundated the kitchen. At the exact same moment, several more similarly attired men stormed in from the dining area. "Police! Nobody moves!"

One of the Chinese men either failed to understand the command or simply disregarded it, but before even as he charged the ranks, the policemen swarmed over him, their polished batons flashing. The rest of the gang offered no resistance and raised their hands submissively, but as soon as the struggle with the Oriental ended, Nails sneered: "You coppers have no idea what you've done."

"Maybe you'll enlighten us then," said a voice from behind the blue line. A handsome older man, wearing a dark suit with a rumpled overcoat, stepped through the midst of the officers and circled the room, stopping at last in front of the Agent, who like the others offered no resistance. The detective scrutinized him a moment, and when he spoke again, his eyes did not leave the Agent's face. "Good evening gents, I'm Inspector Burks. One of my undercover men tipped me that something was going on here. I'd say we got here just in time."

The last bit seemed especially directed at the Agent, but the latter merely continued to slump in his chair. The inspector straightened and turned to the man in charge of the raid. "Sergeant, put these men in lock up, but be alert. If they're working for whom I think they are, then the trouble's only getting started." He glanced back at the Agent. "I'll take care of this one."

Nails said nothing more as he and his fellows were cuffed and ushered out, leaving Burks with his lone prisoner and the three mysterious crates. The inspector regarded the Agent for a moment, then positioned a chair directly in front of him and sat down.

"You're lucky my detective picked up your trail. Your life wouldn't have been worth a stale fortune cookie if they'd gotten you out of here."

"I don't know what you're talking about," mumbled the Agent, keeping his head bowed.

"Hmm. You don't look so good, fellow."

I don't feel so good. "Must have been something I ate."

Burks crossed his arms. "Why don't we start with your name?"

"I ain't talking to no one but my lawyer." The Agent straightened in his chair, casually dropping a hand to the pocket where he kept his gas gun.

If Burks noticed the sly move he gave no indication. "Lawyers are for criminals. Are you a criminal?"

The Agent spat out a derisive laugh, but said nothing more. The knockout pistol was mere inches from his hand. Burks however chose that moment to rise from his chair. Without looking away from his captive, he walked over to stand beside the crates.

"Any idea what's in here?"

The Agent's hand closed on the grip of his pistol. "Not a clue."

"Let's have a look then."

Curiosity overcame the Agent's desire to escape. He watched in fascination as the policeman used a large meat cleaver to pry open one of the containers. Rising unsteadily, he crossed over to inspect its contents. Hidden in a nest of packing straw was a sealed glass jug, filled with a clear liquid. Burks hefted it in one hand. "Feels about the right weight to be ordinary water."

"People don't go to all this trouble for ordinary water."

Burks raised an eyebrow at the comment. "So you're feeling a little more conversational?"

The Agent shrugged but said nothing as Burks opened the remaining boxes, revealing two more flasks identical to the first. The inspector lined them up on a counter. "So you've no idea what's in them?"

"None at all." But if Dr. Wu Sun is involved, he thought to himself, scratching his hand, then uncorking them might be as dangerous as opening Pandora's Box.

Burks took hold of two of the jugs, one in each hand. "Grab that last one, if you please."

"What are you doing?"

"I'm taking them to a special police laboratory where we can analyze the contents." He cast a suspicious eye at the Agent. "There are medical facilities there as well."

"I'm fine." The Agent took hold of the remaining jug. There would be plenty of time to get away from Burks later on, after he knew a little more about Cheng Lo's mysterious cargo.

**The laboratory was** located in midtown, on the fourth story of a non-descript office building. There were no signs to give outsiders any hint that the facility behind the locked door was operated by the metropolitan police agency, but that anonymous portal concealed a first rate facility. The Agent was well versed in the physical sciences and immediately recognized several pieces of analytical equipment.

"Just put it on the table," Burks directed, setting his own burden down.

"Looks as though you'll have to wake your scientist up."

"No need," replied the inspector. "I know a thing or two about chemical analysis. Just grab a chair while I get to work."

"I didn't realize that police detectives were trained in science as well as criminology."

Burks turned his back to the Agent, busying himself with one of the flasks. "Oh, you've got know a little bit of everything to do the job these days. Ah, there we go."

He held up a strip of adhesive tape darkened by a few faint smudges.

"What's that?"

"Fingerprints," explained Burks.

Cheng Lo's fingerprints, thought the Agent. Or perhaps the fingerprints of Dr. Wu Sun himself. But then another thought struck him. Burks had lifted the prints from the jug he had carried; the inspector was trying to learn his identity.

He tensed, preparing to subdue Burks and recover the evidence, but he was already too late. The inspector was examining the whorls of his fingertips under a magnifying glass, comparing them to another set on a piece of paper.

"I thought as much," he announced. "A pleasure to make you acquaintance at last, Mr. Hyde."

Something about that name stayed the Agent's hand even as he prepared to wield the gas gun. Hyde. He knew that name, but the memories associated with it were obscured. Just like the scar.

"We've been hoping you would turn up," Burks continued. "Scotland Yard launched an international manhunt when you went missing in Hong Kong."

Hyde… Hong Kong… The memory was so close to the surface that he could almost touch it. Hyde was one of the aliases he had used, it had to be; how else could his fingerprints have been so quickly matched? But, if he had been to Hong Kong, why couldn't he remember anything about it?

"You've had a lot of people worried," Burks continued. "Where exactly have you been for the last two weeks? And how did you end up here?"

Two weeks? Hyde? Yes, I remember now, David Hyde, Inspector for Scotland Yard.

But Hyde was a real person, someone he had impersonated. How then had his fingerprints gotten mixed up with the real Hyde's?

Burks however did not pursue the matter. "Sorry about deceiving you like that, but I had to be sure. Your secret will remain safe with me for as long as you like. In the meantime, let's see what's in these containers."

The Agent forestalled him. "Inspector, I feel it only fair to warn you that those canisters were probably sent here by Dr. Wu Sun, or one of his agents. Opening them could be very dangerous."

"Wu Sun? Surely he's just a myth."

"I wish that were true. But those men you arrested tonight work for Cheng Lo; they told me as much. And if Cheng Lo does exist, then you can bet Dr. Wu Sun exists too. And you can bet that whatever's in those containers is worse than your worst nightmare."

Burks looked at the jugs thoughtfully. "Some kind of poison? An infectious disease perhaps? We'll know soon enough."

He placed one of the containers in a large glass box and sealed its lid. A pair of rubber gloves was attached to one side of the box, allowing him to open the jug without exposing himself to its contents. He deftly drew off several samples of the liquid in test tubes and put a single drop on a microscope slide.

In a matter of minutes he confirmed that there were no biological organisms in the solution. Nor did he detect the presence of anything but the most common mineral elements in what seemed to be ordinary water.

"It can't just be water," the Agent stated emphatically. "There has to be something in it."

"I'll check it for radioactivity." Burks took a Geiger counter from a cabinet and switched it on. The device immediately began to emit a stream of clicks, but when he held it closer to the sample the intensity of the reading did not change. "That's peculiar. There's some radioactivity here, but it doesn't seem to be coming from this solution."

"Something in the lab?"

"We don't store radioactive elements," Burks answered, waving the bulb of the detector around the room. The indicator clicked steadily until he pointed it at the

Agent. "It's you."

He continued sweeping the bulb over the Agent's extremities until the reading peaked directly above his right hand.

It was the scar!

The Agent peered at the mark on his hand, noticing it again as if for the first time. The flesh around scar was now bright red, irritated by his incessant scratching. Burks took him by the wrist and held the hand under a bright lamp.

"Where did you get this wound?"

The Agent pursed his lips together, not so much unwilling to answer as simply unable.

"There's something under the skin. A very thin piece of metal." Burks then looked up with a grave expression. "Your illness; could it be that you've been exposed to a dose of radiation?"

The gravity of the question descended upon him like a death sentence. My god, he thought. I've been poisoned and I don't even remember where or when it happened. But I've a good idea who did it.

"I think someone placed a strip of radioactive material in your hand. You need medical attention."

"It may already be too late for that." The Agent raised his eyes. "We still have no idea what Cheng Lo is up to, and the clock is ticking."

Burks frowned, and then pointed to the containers on the table. "I've run every test possible. Those jugs contain nothing but plain old tap water. Could these be a red herring? An attempt to flush you into the open?"

The Agent gasped. Burks was absolutely right; he kicked himself for not having seen it earlier. "A decoy. The real poison, or whatever he's planning, must be somewhere else. We've got to find it."

"This is a dead end," countered the detective. "Let's think about this rationally."

"Rationally?"

"Let's start with where you've been for the last two weeks. What happened in Hong Kong?"

"Hong Kong." The Agent searched his memory in order to construct a plausible fiction, but his mind was a void. He rubbed his inflamed hand. The itch was maddening enough, but the realization that its cause—some kind of exposure to a radioactive substance that might well kill him—had seemingly been erased from his memory was tortuous. As painful as it was to admit, he was going to need some help to defeat Cheng Lo.

"Inspector, the truth is, I don't know what happened to me. The last two weeks are a blur."

"How is that possible?"

"I think I may have been captured; either by Cheng Lo or by Dr. Wu Sun himself."

"You don't remember anything? How is that possible?"

"There are ways to erase memories; torture, hypnosis, drugs. I've no doubt that Dr. Wu Sun is well versed in all of them."

"That scar on your hand... part of the process?"

The Agent stared at the mark. "I don't know. I don't remember. I've never heard of radiation being used in torture though."

"There's something we're not seeing here. Why would Wu Sun wipe out your memories and then release you? It doesn't make any sense." Burks stared at the Geiger counter thoughtfully, but if it afforded him any inspiration, he did not share it. He set the device on the table. "Is there a way to reverse the process? You mentioned hypnosis; what if we hypnotized you again?"

The Agent swallowed nervously. As much as he wanted to solve the mystery of what had happened, he didn't dare let Burks have access to his subconscious mind. And from that sprang another terrible thought; what had he revealed about himself to the inscrutable Dr. Wu Sun? But Burks was right; if his enemy had gone to the trouble of capturing him, tampering with his memory, and then poisoning him with some kind of radioactive substance, then his own role in Wu Sun's scheme had to be greater than he realized.

"Inspector, there's something I need to tell you." He took a deep breath to still his heart, which was now beating like a trip hammer. "I'm not who you think I am."

Burks eyed him suspiciously. "You're not Inspector David Hyde?"

"No. My real name is not important, but you probably know me better as Secret Agent X."

There it is, out in the open. What will happen now?

"Secret Agent X, is it?" Burks smiled enigmatically. "I figured it was something like that."

But if the detective had more to say, he was struck silent when the lights in the laboratory abruptly winked out. In their place, a red glow emanated from a pair of red light bulbs located near the exit doors.

Burks was on his feet instantly. "Somebody has broken into the building."

His warning was almost too late. The Agent whipped out his gas gun at the exact moment that both doors simultaneously burst open, releasing a swarm of men who were uniformly wearing black garments and masks. They carried no weapons, but if their apparel was any indication, they needed none; these men wore the garb favored by Oriental assassin cults.

The gas gun released a stream of potent anaesthetizing vapor into the midst of the group nearest the Agent and several of the black-suited invaders went down, momentarily impeding the progress of those who had escaped the soporific fume. Spying a window of escape, he turned to the inspector but Burks had already disappeared under a writhing veil of dark cloth.

He knew he had only a split second to decide on a course of action. He could not hope to outfight these men; even under the best of circumstances, it would be a brutal struggle, but weakened as he was by the poisonous radiation, he could not hope to win. If he did not flee, he would most certainly be recaptured or killed, but that meant abandoning the policeman, and that was not something he was willing to do. He had to find a better answer. His eyes flashed about the room looking for that alternative and he caught the ruddy gleam of the emergency lights reflecting from the jugs of water on the counter.

Maybe....

He snatched one of the jugs and held it over his head. "Back off, or I'll smash this!"

It was a gamble. His shouted warning was enough to create a momentary lull in the fighting, but if the assassins knew that the container was a decoy, then all was lost. "I mean it. Cheng Lo won't be pleased if his precious cargo is destroyed."

As if bound to a single consciousness, the assassins began edging toward the doors. Their retreat revealed Burks on hands and knees, stunned but otherwise intact. The Agent moved closer to the detective, but his gaze continued to rove warily between the two groups. "Inspector, are you all right?"

Burks struggled to his feet and looked around the room. "It's a standoff," he declared. "Got any clever ideas?"

"I'm thinking. Grab that other jug. Maybe we can use them as a shield to get out of here."

Burks complied immediately, hefting the container over his head. "Okay, now what?"

The black-clad intruders seemed to echo the question silently with their aloof posture. It was impossible to tell who among them was the leader, yet all seemed to be waiting for some indication of what to do next. The Agent moved closer to Burks, positioning himself at the policeman's back so that all avenues of approach were covered.

"Something tells me this isn't going to hold them off for long. Think we can push past them and get out of here before they decide to rush us?"

"It's worth a try." Burks kept his voice low so that only the two of them could hear what he said next. "I don't fancy smashing these jars, even if they make a try. There's got to be a reason Cheng Lo is pulling out all the stops to recover them."

The Agent glanced at the third jar, now sealed inside the examination box. "What about that one?"

"That one?" Burks replied, now speaking loud enough for everyone to hear. "If they try to open that case to get it out, it will depressurize and spray the contents everywhere. If they're smart, they'll leave well enough alone."

It sounded like a desperate bluff to the Agent's ears, but Burks's tone was confident enough that just maybe the attackers would think twice before trying to retrieve the last jar. With the detective's back pressed against his own, he began making his way toward nearest exit. The invaders regarded him warily, but gave ground clearing a path to the elevator foyer. "We should take the stairs," the he murmured.

"No." Burks was adamant. "Elevator. Trust me."

Against his better judgment, the Agent navigated toward the waiting lift car and after a cursory examination to confirm that no one was hiding in the overhead space, got in. The inspector followed and quickly closed the door, shutting them off from the invading force. He set his burden down and grasped the elevator control handle. To the Agent's surprise, he suddenly felt heavier; the car was ascending.

"Why up?"

Burks flashed a conspiratorial grin. "We'll be leaving by a different door."

Over the noise of the elevator machinery, the shouts of the confounded intruders were audible and the Agent knew that their enemy was already wise to the change in plans. Burks however seemed unperturbed as he eased the car to a stop and threw open the door.

"Quickly," he told the Agent, grasping the jug in one hand and hefting his automatic pistol in the other. "The door to the roof is at the end of the hall."

The black-clad attack force burst from the stairwell before he could take two steps, but they were too far away to impede his escape. The inspector brandished his pistol meaningfully, holding them at bay a few seconds longer. The Agent eased the door open, his gas gun at the ready, but the stairwell leading to the roof was empty.

Burks pushed him across the threshold. "Your gas gun," he shouted. "Shoot down the stairwell."

The Agent understood immediately and fired two blasts from his special pistol into the ascending space. A few of the dark-clothed pursuers had already begun venturing onto the treads, but fell back as the potent vapor cloud rolled toward them. Burks pulled him back and slammed the door shut.

"That will give us a few minutes," the policemen said.

"A few minutes to do what?"

"I've got an idea. Go to the front of the building and watch for them to try climbing the exterior." The inspector delved into the depths of his overcoat and produced a boxy object with a telescoping metal rod attached to its housing. A glimpse of this strange contraption stopped the Agent in his tracks. He knew exactly what it was: a handheld wireless unit, capable of making short-range radio transmissions, but this one was more miniaturized than any design he had ever seen. What surprised him most however was not the compact design, but the fact that Burks possessed it at all.

"I didn't realize that the police department was issuing those."

The inspector merely nodded, as if the statement was a rhetorical observation, and continued working the handset. When he had tuned it to the correct frequency, he turned away and began speaking into the device.

The Agent continued to watch over the side of the building, but his mind refused to simply overlook what he had just seen. He reflected back on the events that had transpired since his capture by the thugs in Chinatown, rewinding his memories as one might turn a film reel backwards. In every frame of that mental movie, he saw something that just didn't fit.

...a gang of black-suited intruders materializing as if from nowhere in a secret unmarked laboratory....

How did they find us so quickly?

...Burks saying: "Nothing more than plain old tap water...."

And I believed him. But what if it's not just water?

...the police raiding the Lung Mei in the nick of time, tipped off by an undercover officer, Burks had said. But how had the detective known in that split second that he was not one of the thugs? How had he known to look in the crates?

Burks knows a lot more about this than he's told me, the Agent thought, and then he recalled something the policeman had said.

"...a red herring...flush you out in the open...."

The scar on his hand itched ferociously.

Radiation poisoning? Just one more thing he's told me, and I accepted it without question.

"Help is on the way," the inspector announced, unaware of the maelstrom that raged in the Agent's fevered mind. "Five minutes. Any sign of them?"

"No," the Agent rasped, struggling to keep his composure. He no longer saw the detective as an ally, but without definitive proof he could not completely resign himself to declaring the man his enemy. If Burks was not in fact in cahoots with the gang of invaders in the building below, then the "help" he had summoned was going to come in handy.

"No," he repeated. "All quiet on this end. But that gas cloud will dissipate before five minutes is up."

"Let's hope they don't figure that out," Burks replied, holding his pistol up.

The Agent turned his eyes back to the street, scanning the dark approaches for villains in the shadows and eagerly watching for the revolving red beacons of police patrol cars, but his attention was fixed on the enigma that churned within him.

What if all of this is some elaborate plot to bring me into the open? How far would Burks go to hunt me down? Could he be in cahoots with Cheng Lo?

And then another thought struck him.

What if that isn't really Inspector Burks?

The realization stabbed through his head like a railroad spike, and a cry of agony ripped past his lips....

**He had been** on the trail of the Chinaman for over a week now, and he had been David Hyde for almost as long. The real Inspector Hyde was dead, murdered by the Chinaman's assassins, wrapped in iron chains and dropped in Kowloon Bay. But the Agent didn't think the Chinaman knew that, and even if he did, a visit from the dead policeman might be just the thing to shake him up.

But it wasn't time to strike just yet. He still wasn't sure what the Chinaman was up to, nor was he absolutely certain that his foe was indeed the diabolical Dr. Wu Sun, or perhaps one of his chief lieutenants. So he watched and waited, stowing away on the freighter as it churned across two oceans to New York. Hidden in the ship's ventilation pipes, he had overheard the Chinaman speaking of a second ship with "the cargo," whatever that was, following behind them and due to make port in a couple days.

Whatever he's planning, the Agent thought, that cargo is the key.

The Chinaman had no intention of lingering on his ship however. A hired towne car arrived to pick him up, and the Agent had to hastily follow in a taxicab.

He had half expected that the sedan would venture into Chinatown, where the villain might easily blend in with his kinsmen, but to his surprise the car bypassed Canal Street and headed onto the Brooklyn Bridge. Once across, they meandered past the brownstones of Brooklyn Heights, until quite without warning, the sedan stopped. The Agent hastily exited the taxi a full block behind the Chinaman, and then lingered in the shadows until his foe entered a building on the corner of Montague Street.

The Agent did not immediately venture into the lion's den however. Instead, he moved out from his hiding place and strolled calmly past the brownstone, as if he was an ordinary New Yorker enjoying an evening walk. From the corner of his eye, he scrutinized the building; it was a unique structure in the neighborhood—the brick edifice was an unnatural crimson hue, and the exterior was decorated with grotesque dragons.

The Chinaman, it seemed, possessed a flair for the theatrical.

The attack came so stealthily that he had no memory of it. One moment he was in the shadows, peering at the brownstone, and the next he was laying supine on a table in a room that looked like it might be the Devil's workshop. He came awake struggling against the thick leather restraints that held him fast. Only when his primal panic subsided did he relax and take in his surroundings.

The room had the musty feel of a cellar. There were no windows, only bare concrete walls, illuminated with an eerie red glow. Directly above him, stretched out across the ceiling was a magnificent and terrible image of a dragon—a stylized wingless Chinese serpentine figure, unlike the rough bas-relief on the exterior of the building. As he studied the mural, he became aware of another presence in his prison.

The Chinaman.

"Welcome to my humble abode, Secret Agent X."

"I'm not…" His denial caught in his throat as the menacing villain nimbly hopped up onto the table, crouching over him like a vulture preparing to feast on his flesh.

"Oh, yes. You are Secret Agent X, and I have been waiting for you."

There was something in the Chinaman's hand—something that glinted in the ruddy glow—but it wasn't until he felt a stab of pain in his arm that he realized what it was. By then, the poisonous injection was already surging through his bloodstream like liquid fire.

The last thing he saw as the agony consumed him was the dragon, writhing in ecstasy above his head....

**"Are you all** right?"

Burks voice snapped him back into the present, but the pain of the memory continued to burn within him. He realized that the inspector was now grasping his shoulder and looming over him, just as the Chinaman had done.

The Chinaman, Cheng Lo, had set a trap for him.

He stared up at Burks, still trying to reconcile the vivid recollection with every-thing that had happened since. The concern on the policeman's face seemed so sincere....

"I'm fine," he managed to say, his voice cracking. He struggled erect once more and grasped the parapet, staring out into the night as if to resume his vigil. In truth, he was fearful of letting the detective see the doubt that lingered in his eyes. Why had he trusted Burks with the secret of his identity?

The inspector however did not pursue the matter. "Look," he said, almost shouting as he pointed to the skyline. "There it is."

The Agent followed the invisible line of the other man's finger and saw a blinking star moving over the rooftops. "An airplane?"

"Better than an airplane," Burks answered with a gleeful grin.

Instead of wings, the approaching aircraft had a pair of horizontal propellers on outriggers, giving it vertical lift while an ordinary prop on its nose pulled it forward through the sky. It was a helicopter, likely the German Focke-wulfe or a prototype based on that design. Unlike an airplane or gyrocopter, the helicopter could land almost vertically, setting down without a runway on a space as small as the span of its rotor blades.

Just as with the portable two-way radio, the appearance of the strange rotor wing aircraft, beating its way through the sky, struck the Agent as completely wrong. He couldn't bring himself to believe that the New York Police Department had access to machines and equipment like that. But Dr. Wu Sun might. As he grappled with the mystery, the helicopter slowed its approach directly overhead and began to descend, whipping up a tempest that seemed powerful enough to blast him from his perch. He imitated Burks's posture, crouching low as the pilot of the flying machine gingerly settled the craft onto the rooftop.

"Come on!" the detective shouted, circling around the helicopter in order to wrap his arms around the frame of the outrigger.

Braving the whirlwind, the Agent approached the craft, but instead of climbing on, he stared accusingly at the man whom he was quite certain was not Inspector Burks after all.

"Who are you?"

Burks's eyes narrowed and there was no doubt that he had heard the accu-satory question over the din. Before he could frame an answer, the door leading back into the building burst open and half a dozen black-clad forms vomited forth onto the tumultuous rooftop.

The inspector acted instinctively, stabbing his gun at them and pulling the trigger.

The Agent gaped in disbelief at what he saw.

Even with the noise of the helicopter's engines, the report of a gunshot should have been audible, but Burks's weapon made no sound. There was no jet of flame as the gun discharged; only a hint of white vapor that was swept away by the rotor wash the moment it left the barrel.

Inspector Burks had a gas gun.

The mere sight of the gun had more of an effect on the onrushing horde than the dose of anaesthetizing gas, which was rendered completely ineffectual by the artificial wind created by the helicopter. The attackers held back for just a second, not realizing that the weapon was powerless to harm them, which gave the Agent just enough time to swing onto the outrigger. The pilot wasted no time in lifting the whirlybird straight up into the night sky.

However, the Agent felt no sense of relief as he watched the intruders on the rooftop fall away beneath his feet. He had escaped them, true, but in so doing he had committed himself to following a man whose weapons and abilities seemed to match his own, and he knew of only one person with the resources to so perfectly imitate him. As the helicopter raced through the chilly night, he could only hold on for dear life and gather his courage for the coming showdown.

It did not even occur to him that he had left the jug of water behind on the rooftop.

**The flight was** interminably long and yet as he clutched the frigid metal skeleton that held one of the upright rotor assemblies in place, the Agent could not help but be awestruck by the beauty of the vast cityscape beneath him. Very few of the weary souls who called the city home ever got see it like this; not a maze of concrete canyons, but rather a forest of monumental trees, twinkling with thousands of tiny stars—a living organism. This was what he had sworn to protect, and what he was prepared to give his life for. He had no idea what Cheng Lo and his inscrutable master had planned for his city, but he swore by all he held holy that he would live to see them fail.

First however, he had to deal with the man pretending to be Inspector Burks—possibly Cheng Lo himself. He still had his own gun, with at least two more doses of the knockout gas, but his biggest advantage would not be his ability to fight—he wasn't sure he possessed the strength for another pitched battle—but rather the fact that his foe was unaware that he had uncovered the scheme.

Who are you fooling? he chided himself. You still don't have a clue what's going on.

Maybe not, but as long as the phony Burks thought he was cooperating, he would have a chance to figure the rest of it out.

Nevertheless, the scope of Wu Sun's grand design was never far from his thoughts as the helicopter brushed across the Manhattan skyline and then ventured out across the Hudson River toward New Jersey. Another fifteen minutes passed before the pilot angled the aircraft toward a brightly lit airfield.

The moment the helicopter touched down "Burks," still carrying the container of water, hastened to his side, wearing an expression of grave concern. "How are you doing?"

The Agent searched the other man's face for any sign of duplicity; if the phony policeman was faking his anxiety for the Agent's health, then he was a masterful actor. "I'll manage," he replied, then as casually as he could, he asked. "So why are we in Jersey?"

"Let's get into the hangar. I think we'll be safe there. Then I'll tell you everything."

He guided the Agent to a small apartment at the back of the enormous Quonset hut where the helicopter was kept when not in use. A pot of coffee was waiting and Burks poured a mug for each of them before settling down in the modest dining area. The Agent took a seat across from him, his hand on the grips of his gas gun beneath the table. To his surprise, Burks placed his own pistol on the tabletop, as if trying to signal his good faith.

"To answer your question, we are in New Jersey because Dr. Wu Sun won't be able to track you here."

The statement caught the Agent off guard. "Care to explain that?"

"That scar on your hand," said Burks. "That's how he's been able to follow your movements in the city. That's how they caught you at the warehouse, again at the restaurant, and then at my lab.

"I couldn't figure out why he would poison you like that, but then the Geiger counter gave me the idea that maybe he's using the radiation to track you."

"That's crazy. He'd have to have Geiger counters all over the city."

Burks nodded. "If it was anyone but Dr. Wu Sun, I'd agree that it sounds… implausible. But there's no denying the fact that you have a strip of radioactive metal in your hand."

The Agent realized that he was unconsciously scratching the scar and forced his hand away. As much as he wanted to disbelieve the other man's suggestion, it did have a ring of truth about it. "Tracking me. Why? Why not just kill me when he had me captive?"

"I think he did it so that you would find me."

"You?"

Burks took a deep breath, and the Agent sensed that the moment had arrived for the critical revelation. Nevertheless, nothing could have prepared him for what he heard the man say next.

"Yes. You see I am Secret Agent X."

**The silence that** followed was uncomfortably long, but somehow when Burks…or X… or whoever he really was spoke again, the Agent felt like still needed a few minutes to digest the statement.

"I know you're thinking: 'How can he be Agent X if I'm Agent X?' Well, there's an explanation... It's a doozy, but if you'll hear me out, you realize that we both want the same thing: to stop Dr. Wu Sun."

"Okay, I'm listening." How are you going to try to twist my brain now? He thought, but didn't say it.

"To begin with, you are David Hyde of Scotland Yard; the fingerprints were a perfect match. I even have a picture of you, and I'm betting that if you remove your disguise, the face will be a match too."

Clever. False documents to back up this madness. But why? What could Cheng Lo hope to gain by convincing me that I'm David Hyde?

"So now you're wondering why you think you are Secret Agent X," the man continued.

"I'm afraid you haven't said anything to convince me otherwise."

"You were captured in Hong Kong; captured by Dr. Wu Sun himself. You know that really happened. You know that he probably tortured you, and you admitted to me earlier that part of your memory has been wiped away. I think that what Wu did to you is even more complicated than that; I believe that he used hypnosis and drugs to convince you that you are me—Secret Agent X, that is—and then turned you loose in New York. The cargo that you've been chasing, these jugs of water, were put out there to lure both of us in. Wu must have known that I would investigate, but he had no way to tell who I was. That's why he used you."

Although the other man's arguments were as counter-intuitive as an assertion that the earth was flat, certain elements of it rang true. "You were at the warehouse; the hobo that frightened those thugs off."

A nod.

"And how did you know to come to the restaurant?"

"I followed you from the warehouse to your apartment and then shadowed you as you checked on those rogue doctors. It wasn't until you disguised yourself as that goon you left in the alley that I realized you weren't just an undercover detective. Theatrical disguises and knockout grenades—that was my turf and I was curious about what you were up to. So I revived your double and managed to get two names from him; The Lung Mei restaurant, and Cheng Lo."

"For the last week, Cheng Lo's name has been on the lips of every thug and low-life in the city. But when I heard him say it, I knew you were walking into a trap. As Inspector Burks, it wasn't too hard to whistle up a squad of policemen to raid the restaurant. When that phone call came in, I knew you'd been made."

"How? How did they know I wasn't that thug, Snooze?"

"I think Cheng Lo was watching his radiation detectors. When he saw that the reading was coming from the same restaurant where his goons were guarding the cargo, he knew that his bogus Secret Agent was closing in."

The Agent resisted the urge to sneer at the implication that he was "bogus." Aside from that particular point of contention however, the idea of Cheng Lo using radiation to follow his movements was an intriguing one. He realized he was scratching the scar again and forced himself to stop.

"There's a problem with your theory. You see, I'm starting to remember what happened. I wasn't captured in Hong Kong. Cheng Lo caught me in Brooklyn, only a few days ago."

The man wearing Inspector Burks's face seemed genuinely surprised. "Did he? You remember that? What else do you remember? How did you escape?"

That stopped him. Even the simple act of trying to dredge up those memories again sent a spear of pain through his head. "I don't..." He sucked in a breath. "I managed to slip out of my bonds and used my spare make-up kit to disguise myself as one of the thugs."

That's what I did, he thought. It has to be; how else could I have escaped?

The other man stroked his chin thoughtfully. "I haven't convinced you that you're not me, have I?"

The simple truth of the matter was that he had not even for a second considered that he might not be Secret Agent X. He knew who he was.

And yet, why am I having such a hard time remembering things? It wasn't just the missing two weeks. He found that he couldn't seem to recall any details about his life. He knew about the apartments throughout the city, but couldn't seem to remember the house he had grown up in, or even what his parents looked like.

It's part of what Cheng Lo did to me.

And he knew that to be true, but what if the villain had in fact done exactly what this man was now claiming? What if he really was David Hyde? What if this is what Cheng Lo wants? What if all of this is an elaborate scheme to destroy who I really am by convincing me that I'm someone else?

"Cheng Lo knows the answer," he said at last. "And I know where to find him."

The man disguised as Burks looked at him with a curious expression. "You can't seriously be thinking of going after him."

"I don't see an alternative. He's planning something big, and I think we can both agree that getting Secret Agent X out of the way is critical to his scheme."

"You are in no shape to go up against him. Even if you were, his radiation detectors would give us away the minute we set foot in the city."

"Not if we cut this piece of metal out."

"Even that might not be enough. The radioactivity has spread throughout your body."

"I have to go," he insisted. "Maybe you're right. Maybe I'm not really a secret agent, but I'll be damned if I'm going to let Cheng Lo get away with what he's done to me. But if that's not a good enough reason, then try this: I know where Cheng Lo's base of operations is. You won't find it without me."

The other man regarded him warily. "You'll be no good to me in a fight."

"Then we won't fight." He managed a wry smile. "We're Secret Agent X, remember? The Men of a Thousand Faces?"

At that the man broke into honest laughter. "You know, it just might work."

**Early twilight was** just beginning to lighten the sky when the sedan, driven—or so it appeared—by Cheng Lo's henchman Nails and carrying his injured comrade crossed the George Washington Bridge and began the long journey south across Manhattan island. The real Nails was still locked up—that much had been confirmed with a phone call to the police—and Secret Agent X's operatives had detained Snooze.

The Agent—he could not quite bring himself to think of himself as David Hyde, even though deep down, he believed that it must be true—had allowed his host to extract the thin radioactive wire from his hand before leaving the hangar. The strange scar that had troubled him was now once more a fresh wound in his skin, but the absence of the thin sliver of metal had brought a degree of physical relief, along with easing his mental anguish. In a very literal sense, Cheng Lo no longer had his hooks in him.

There was only so much that could be done to mask the radiation that had already permeated his flesh, but at the urging of his host—he had taken to calling the man "X"—he had imbibed a great deal of water, to flush at least some of the poison from his body. He was still weak and faintly nauseous, but even X had commented that he looked like he was feeling better.

But I'm not better, he thought. Just as he had come to accept that maybe he wasn't really Secret Agent X, he also knew that the damage Cheng Lo had wrought upon him was both irreversible and fatal. David Hyde might not have died the way he remembered it, but he was nevertheless a dead man walking. At least he would have the satisfaction of seeing his tormentor brought down as well.

The great irony was that, by turning him into an almost perfect duplicate of Secret Agent X, Cheng Lo created the very weapon that would help destroy him.

"Be careful," X had advised him. "We still don't know exactly what Wu's grand design is. We may very well be playing into his hands."

He had no memory of how David Hyde conducted his investigation, but as Secret Agent X, he knew that he worked alone. It was an odd feeling then to not only to trust the man driving the sedan as a partner, but to actually follow his lead. He was curious to see if X would make the same choices he might make.

"We'll circle the block," X said as they left Brooklyn Bridge and made their way toward the Heights neighborhood. The Agent/Hyde had given him a rough street address, though strangely he felt compelled to omit mention of the ornate dragons on the exterior. "Get the lay of the land before we try to go in."

"If they have a watchman at the door, we may be asked for some kind of password."

"I thought about that. It might be better to try to go in a different way?"

"Back door?"

X grinned. "Something like that."

The building was exactly as he remembered it, but somehow in the early dawn, the dragons didn't seem nearly as grotesque as he remembered. X did not slow or even turn his head in the direction of the building; the only indication that he even saw it was a murmured: "So that's the lion's den."

The Agent whispered an affirmative. "That's where he caught me."

X pulled the car to the curb. "Are you sure you can do this?"

"He has to be stopped. And I have to understand what he did to me."

"That's good enough for me. Watch your step in there; there's bound to be some nasty surprises inside that house. Don't hesitate to use the gas gun if things go south."

The Agent held his own familiar pistol—fully recharged and ready for action—up for inspection, then stowed it in a clever pouch sewn into the folds of the pea jacket his host had provided as part of his disguise. The hidden holster was not the only secret hidden by the coarse navy fabric. X had outfitted him with a number of gas bombs and throwing darts tipped with a more potent form of the same anesthetic in the gun, ideal for use in close quarters where the gas might inadvertently blow back in one's own face.

Nothing more was said as they disembarked and began walking down the sidewalk toward their destination. The Agent felt an odd chill as he passed the place where he had once hidden to observe his foe and been captured for his efforts.

To his surprise, X ascended the stoop of the building right next to Cheng Lo's headquarters. He inserted a key into the lock on the front door and applied gentle pressure. There was a faint mechanical clicking as tiny cams on the strange key began rising up and down in a careful sequence, experimentally testing every possible setting for the pins in the lock. After only a few seconds, the key turned and the bolt slid back.

The Agent withheld his inquiries concerning their strategy; he had a pretty good idea what the other man had in mind and as they began ascending the staircase, he knew he had judged correctly.

For the second time that night, the pair found themselves on a rooftop. Like most of the multiple residence apartment houses in the neighborhood, the brownstone had a flat roof and shared common walls with structures on either side, although in this particular case, it was a full story taller than the Dragon building on the corner. The two men crept to the edge and peered over, down onto the roof of Cheng Lo's headquarters.

X took out a pair of binoculars and began scrutinizing their objective. There was just enough light in the sky to illuminate the rooftop without revealing their presence to any early risers on the street below. "Looks clear. But watch your step anyway."

They shinnied over the wall, making the drop without the aid of the grappling hook and line that X had affixed to the parapet; those would serve their purpose later, in the event that they had to make a hasty retreat. Using his mechanical skeleton key again, X unlocked and opened the roof door as cautiously as an expert cat burglar.

The staircase descending into the house was as still as a crypt. Both men strained to catch some sound that might reveal the presence of a living soul within but absolute silence reigned supreme in the Dragon house. With his hand resting on the grip of his gas pistol, X began his tentative journey into the darkened interior, with the Agent close on his heels.

They reached the landing of the top floor without incident, but here too they paused, listening for anything—a murmur of conversation, a sleeper snoring, the tick of a clock or the hum of an electric fan—but heard no sound louder than their own soft breathing. X cautiously tried the doorknob of the first room they came to, and the door swung open to reveal a vacant apartment.

"It would appear Cheng Lo isn't interested in tenants," he murmured to his companion as he closed the door.

"I think we'll find him in the cellar," the Agent whispered. He didn't elaborate, but his suggestion earned a nod, and their explorations resumed.

X tried two more doors before they reached the main floor; both opened onto empty rooms. For his part, the Agent felt his pulse quicken as they drew closer to the place where Cheng Lo had ripped away a part of his soul. Although he had never seen the halls through which they now passed, he knew exactly what he would find below them, and the thought filled him with the full spectrum of anxiety.

"I need to go first," he said abruptly, as X reached for the door leading into the basement.

A flicker of apprehension crossed the other man's features, but he stepped back and gestured for the Agent to take the lead. "I'm right behind you."

That simple assurance filled him with courage. The pounding of his heart began to subside, enabling him to take that first step... and then another... and another.

And then he saw the light.

The eerie red glow—the hue of a cheap neon sign—filled his eyes, triggering a visceral response. He almost faltered, almost turned and fled, but the purity of his quest drove him on. He had sworn to defeat Cheng Lo; he would not fail. Yet, each step that brought him deeper into the violent crimson dungeon, echoed with the grim certainty that he would not only fail in his mission, but that his very presence here would unleash Dr. Wu Sun's evil upon the world. Almost without thinking, he removed the gun from its holster and stabbed it out in front of him, ready to pull the trigger at the first sign of movement.

But there was no one in the cellar.

He stood at the foot of the stairs and gazed on the familiar room. The table where he had been imprisoned sat in the center of the room, still adorned with the leather restraints that had once held him fast. Sitting atop the otherwise empty surface was another familiar object—the glass jug he had left behind on the roof of the laboratory building. Cheng Lo had evidently thought it important enough to retrieve and bring back to his lair, but where were the guards to protect it now?

He scanned every dark corner of the room, looking for black clad assassins or hidden television cameras or trip wires for booby traps, but the cellar was another empty space in an empty building.

"Where are you, Cheng Lo?" he muttered, taking a step toward the table, and then another.

X was close on his heels, walking backward so that his eyes could constantly scan the parts of the room that his partner could not watch. "We're too late."

The Agent stopped directly in front of the table, one hand still gripping the gas gun, as the other reached out to touch the jar of water. Very slowly he looked up at the dragon mural on the ceiling above.

That was when he remembered who he was.

"No," he said, no longer whispering. "We're just in time."

And then he turned and shot his gas gun directly into the face of Secret Agent X.

**"When you see** the Dragon, you will remember," his tormentor had said.

Restrained on the table, consumed by the agony of the procedure, it was impossible to believe that he could ever forget, even for a brief time, this unimaginable experience.

Nevertheless, he knew it would happen exactly that way. Already, the lines between who he had once been and the identity imprinted upon his conscious mind were growing indistinct, blurring together like the pigments in a watercolor painting. He was still in control now, but when the post-hypnotic command took effect, the person he was would fall away, imprisoned in the darkest corners of his mind until....

Until the Dragon. Look for the Dragon.

But even that bit of knowledge was locked away behind yet another trigger.

"When you find the man you seek, then you will remember the dragon. You will remember that the answers lie with the Dragon."

"How will I know when I've found him?" The question came out as a scream; every breath he took was a cry of unbelievable torment.

"You will know. You will see something that unlocks the door, and then you will remember the Dragon."

The man had then placed a hand upon his feverish brow in a strange gesture—strange because it seemed like an act of compassion, as a father might comfort an ailing child. "You are my finest creation," he said. "My heart is filled with pride.

"You shall rest until you see the Dragon once more. Sleep, Cheng Lo, my son."

**Secret Agent X** lay spread-eagled on the table, even as the impostor had once been. He—the Agent, the man who had once almost believed he was David Hyde, but now answered to a different name—regarded his prisoner with amusement as the restrained man's eyes fluttered open.

"David?" X seemed confused. That was understandable. Dr. Wu Sun's plan was beyond the comprehension of a mere mortal like the Secret Agent.

"No," The Agent answered. "I am not David Hyde. You were mistaken."

X tested his bonds as he looked around the cellar; the heavy leather straps did not yield one iota. "You are Cheng Lo," he said simply.

"I am more than Cheng Lo now," the Agent answered.

"How?"

"My Master has perfected the process of transferring the consciousness of one mind into another. Through years of experimentation, he discovered the part of the brain where memories are stored. If the soul does exist, then this is the place where it lives while we are corporeal. It is not an organ or tissue, but rather a fluid, which may be drawn out of one body and injected into another. The brain nevertheless retains much of the knowledge—the instincts and abilities—of its former host, and these are added to the whole. Thus have I become something greater than merely the sum of body and soul."

X regarded him coldly. "And David Hyde? Does his soul live on somewhere else?"

The question stung, yet he could not put his finger on exactly why. "Hyde was our enemy, captured while making a feeble attempt to infiltrate my Master's empire. Even in your own country, spies are executed for their crimes.

"But Hyde was the perfect vessel for the next stage of my Master's plan. He was a man very much like you, Agent X, a master of disguises and an expert at unarmed combat. The Master honored him by using his shell to carry my essence."

"And what about your shell, Cheng Lo? What happened to it?"

The Agent shrugged. He was only revealing the details of the memory transfer to X because early experiments had shown that when a subject was not mentally prepared to undergo the procedure, death from shock was almost inevitable. The disposition of his own shell was not something he cared to share with his enemy, but the truth of the matter was that the young and virile flesh of Cheng Lo had now become a house for a much greater consciousness whose own physical form was all but destroyed.

"I'd say you got the raw end of the deal," X continued. "That body you're in—David Hyde's body—is dying. Surely you can see that. The radiation sickness is spreading, destroying your organs."

"For every great accomplishment, there is also great sacrifice. Enduring this sickness was a small price to pay in order to see my Master's goals come to fruition. Incidentally, you were exactly right about the isotope's purpose. The radiation enabled my Master to pinpoint my location at all times in order to guide me along the path."

"Why go to all the trouble?"

The Agent laughed. "You still don't understand the complexity of the Master's plan. You see, until we walked into this room, I still thought that I was you.

"There is much more to the process of transferring a soul than an injection of fluid. You see, to continue with the analogy, it is necessary to furnish the house before the new tenant can move in. In the case of Inspector Hyde, that meant hours of hypnosis in order to convince him that he was Secret Agent X. Then, when the transfer was complete, I underwent a similar process. My real identity was buried deep beneath the belief that I was Secret Agent X."

"Why? Why imitate me?"

"It was the surest way to draw you out. We could not be certain when, or even if, you would attempt to interfere with our plans to move the virus into the city, but the Master felt certain that you would be drawn to the enigma of someone that was in every way like yourself. And there were other considerations as well."

"What virus?"

"Ah, yes." The Agent lifted the container for inspection. "The Spanish Influenza virus, recovered from victims found frozen on the Kamchatka peninsula. The liquid you tested is indeed ordinary water, but the inert virus samples are hidden in bubbles within the glass itself."

"I don't suppose you're planning to use those samples in order to develop a vaccine."

"Oh, we already have. The Master has a supply adequate to inoculate several thousand individuals."

"While you unleash a plague that will wipe out millions," X snarled angrily.

Once again, the Agent winced involuntarily at the other man's indignation. The plan was perfect. Death and suffering were a part of the human condition, but Dr. Wu Sun's goal would make the world a better place, and the cost in human lives would be small compared to the greater good it would yield. So why did his enemy's diatribes fill him with doubt? He shook his head to clear away the stray thoughts.

"There aren't enough samples in this one container to begin cultivating the new strain, but it will be a simple thing to retrieve the other two jars once…."

"Once you steal my body," X finished.

"As you pointed out, this body is not long for the world. This form was never intended to be anything more than a temporary residence."

X held his stare. "You said something earlier: 'I'll be damned if I'm going to let Cheng Lo get away with what he's done to me.' That was David Hyde talking. There's still a part of him in there, fighting to get out."

The Agent flinched again, but recovered his composure smoothly. "It was necessary to allow that vestige to come to the surface in order to draw you out, but the post-hypnotic command has rendered it quiescent once more."

"I don't think so. There's more to a man than just his memories. You are David Hyde, not Cheng Lo."

The Agent shuddered again, but tore his gaze away from the prisoner. He set the jar on the floor beneath the table and picked up a syringe filled with amber liquid. "I have told you what you need to know in order to prepare you for the next phase of the transfer. There is much work yet to be done before your body can be made ready to house my essence, but no further discussion is required."

"I'm not talking to you Cheng. I'm talking to David Hyde." X drew in a sharp breath. "I'm talking to Secret Agent X. To the man who has sworn to defend the city from villains like Dr. Wu."

Enough.

The denial screamed in his head, but for some reason, his lips did not form the word. He thrust the syringe forward, stabbed the needle into the prisoner's bicep, and depressed the plunger, injecting the solution—a careful balance of sedatives and neurotoxins milked from the venom of scorpions—into Secret Agent X's veins.

Except… he hadn't moved at all. Somewhere between his brain, where the nervous impulses formed, and the muscles of his extremities, the connection had been broken.

I'm Secret Agent X, and I can beat you Cheng Lo.

The words had not been spoken, certainly not by the prisoner strapped to the table, but he heard them nonetheless. The voice, not his own, but still very much the voice of David Hyde, echoed through his head.

No. You don't exist anymore.

You have fashioned the weapon of your own destruction, Cheng Lo.

An invisible war raged within the man as the last remnants of David Hyde and the false, but nonetheless convincing persona of Secret Agent X battled for control of the ravaged body that stood statue still in front of the bound prisoner.

Yet, for all that Dr. Wu Sun did not completely understand the intricate connection between the physical brain, the mind and the soul, he had anticipated that such a conflict might arise.

When you see the Dragon, you will remember. Look to the Dragon, Cheng Lo.

The voice of his master broke through the struggle and the Agent's eyes flicked up to behold the ornate design that stretched across the ceiling. As before, the powerful image triggered the hypnotic command, banishing the displaced personalities to bring Cheng Lo back to the surface.

"Now I shall end this madness," he rasped, raising the syringe.

But the table was empty.

Shocked, he whirled around, looking for his foe, but in that instant a powerful hand seized the injector from his grip and in a single fluid motion, the needle reversed and stabbed into his upper arm. There was a blossom of pain as the contents erupted into the soft muscle tissue, and then a wave of darkness crashed over him.

His last thought as he fell into the void was that he had succeeded. He had beaten Cheng Lo.

**One month later,** Inspector David Hyde made his final journey, returning home to his native country where he was laid to rest. Despite the best efforts of the staff at a private hospital in upstate New York, the radiation poisoning had ravaged his body beyond any hope of recovery. What none of the doctors treating him realized was that David Hyde had already been dead for weeks. Only his ghost—the echo of the man he had been—had remained, lingering only long enough to see his murder avenged.

A New York City police detective escorted the lead-lined coffin to its destination and greeted the Chief Inspector who had been Hyde's superior prior to his disappearance in Hong Kong.

"Ah, Inspector Burks, is it? I'm grateful to you for bringing David home."

The New York detective shook the other man's hand. "It was the least I could do. A pity that the world will never know how much it owes this man."

The Chief Inspector shook his head sadly. "It still boggles my mind. The nefarious Dr. Wu Sun? A plot to unleash a deadly plague? And our man Hyde helping Secret Agent X foil the scheme? It's quite a bit to digest."

The British chief of detectives had not been told the half of it. Not a whisper had been spoken of Wu Sun's attempt to transfer the consciousness of his lieutenant Cheng Lo into Hyde's body. Hyde's friends and surviving family didn't need to know the full extent of the terrors wrought upon the brave policeman, and omitting mention of the whole affair in no way diminished his heroism.

Nevertheless, the war in which Hyde had made the ultimate sacrifice was far from won. Dr. Wu Sun had been beaten, all three of the flasks containing his virus samples had been destroyed and his operation in New York City had been effectively shut down, but the nefarious mastermind was still at large, and his ambitions had not changed one bit. The only difference now was that he had revealed himself to Secret Agent X.

You were right to fear me, X thought as the casket was transferred into a waiting hearse for the final leg of its journey. You have made an enemy, Dr. Wu Sun, and I will not rest until this brave man is avenged.

He laid his hand on the coffin.

"Good bye, my friend. It was my honor to serve with you," he whispered, his voice too low to be heard by the Chief Inspector. "You made a fine Secret Agent X."

**End**

*Doctor Satan, the World's Weirdest Villain, has finally been brought to justice. A fantastic prison, from which escape is impossible, has been built to permanently incarcerate the master of dark science and black magic, but criminologist Ascott Keane remains wary. He knows Doctor Satan will not submit quietly to judgment, but even Keane is caught off-guard when the diabolical villain turns the tables. Caught in a trap of his own devising, can Keane win his freedom, or will he forever remain the Prisoner?*

## DOCTOR SATAN: THE PRISONER

**The history of** civilization is the history of architecture. As nomadic bands of hunters gradually transformed into stationary cultures, the first order of business was to begin constructing permanent dwellings. At first, these were simply utilitarian; any sort of artistic beauty was purely incidental. But later, as the artisans refined their craft and their particular niche in society became more specialized, unique patterns began to emerge, and in time these would become the hallmarks of great civilizations. The designers and builders were no longer limited to the task of creating places for the citizens of their societies to live; they were called upon to create great palaces, temples and even tombs. Some of these would be reckoned Wonders of the World and would endure for centuries, even into the modern age. Of some, nothing but ruins remain, others are remembered only in legend. Yet, of all the many types of structures designed and built by civilizations past and present, the one that is rarely assigned any sort of eminence is the prison.

To be sure, there have been memorable prisons: The Bastille in Paris, which became the flashpoint of the French revolution; Devil's Island off the coast of South America, considered to be one of the harshest and most inescapable prisons on earth; and the Tower of London, which was transformed briefly into a prison for deposed royals awaiting execution, though such was never its primary function. In modern times, the names of penal institutions have wormed their way into the public consciousness: Alcatraz, Sing Sing, Attica, and others. None of these however are known for elegance of design, and for good reason—no one wants to waste beauty on thieves and murderers.

The edifice constructed on Plum Island, just off the northeastern tip of Long Island, New York was a rare exception to that rule. Like any other prison, it was strictly utilitarian, but because form often follows function, the overall aesthetic design was, if not exactly pleasing to the eye, then at the very least a memorable spectacle.

The scheme of this particular prison was a unique marriage of structural integrity and esoteric artifice. If the final product resembled a Gothic cathedral built according to the blueprints of the Temple of Solomon, then it was because that unique floor plan, along with its elaborate décor—pillars inscribed with eldritch symbols, topped with grotesque gargoyles and sphinxes—was necessary in order for the prison to achieve maximum security. If ever a prison could be considered escape-proof, then it was this one, for its walls were designed not merely to foil attempts at scaling over or tunneling under, but also to counter the direst of supernatural attacks. Yet, for all the elaborate measures of design and a considerable investment of public and private money, this prison had been built to house only one man. And much to the frustration of a certain Mr. Ascott Keane, who had advised the chief architect, Arthur Hotchkiss, it was beginning to look as though that man was going to escape final justice once more.

The man—if indeed man he was—for whom the Plum Island facility had been constructed, presently occupied an ordinary lock-up cell at the Riker's Island detention facility operated by the City of New York, awaiting trial for the murder of several wealthy industrialists who had been the target of a fiendish extortion racket. It was only the most recent of his many criminal schemes, carried out not with guns and knives, but with the application of scientific genius and black magic, and was by no means the pinnacle of his reign of terror, but in this particular instance, the perpetrator had been caught more or less red handed, thanks in no small part to the diligence and more importantly, supernatural puissance, of the aforementioned Ascott Keane.

Then something remarkable had happened.

**During the course** of his criminal career, this diabolical genius had been thwarted many times, believed killed almost as often, and once or twice, been subdued and taken into captivity. In the latter instances, he had proved especially difficult to incarcerate; a master of magic, he had little difficulty escaping handcuffs and prison bars. Much to Keane's chagrin, the arresting authorities failed to heed his advice to augment the physical shackles with supernatural ones—powerful incantations to limit the villain's psychical abilities—and another escape seemed almost inevitable. Everyone was quite surprised to learn then, that in the matter of The State of New York vs. Doctor Satan, the defendant, on the advice of his legal counsel, Melvin Torrance, esquire, had appeared at his arraignment to enter a plea of not guilty.

To his dismay, Ascott Keane had been subpoenaed to appear as a hostile witness for the defense, even though he was already on the list for the State as both an expert witness and a participant in the events. When he was called to testify for the prosecution, Torrance refrained from cross-examination beyond the clarification of a few basic facts. In fact, throughout the prosecutorial phase of the trial, Doctor Satan's lawyer did little to defend his client. He allowed assistant district attorney Bill Hammond to make his case without interference.

The case for the defense was concise and delivered with almost surgical precision.

"Mr. Keane," Torrance began, still seated at the defense table, his penetrating blue eyes peering over the tops of his spectacles at a pad of notes he had taken earlier in the trial. "In your previous testimony, you described yourself as a special investigator. Could you enlighten us further as to what makes your investigative process 'special?'"

Keane sensed the pitfall, but saw no way to avoid it without dissembling. "I investigate crimes with other than natural explanations."

"'Other than natural'?" Torrance looked up with a smile, and then moved out from behind his table to approach the witness box. "You have explained to this court in very scientific language, how you believe that my client committed these rather extraordinary crimes; isn't it fair to say that what you are really asking this court to believe is that my client is some kind of sorcerer?"

Keane checked his reaction; deep down he had known this moment would come. The district attorney had gone to great lengths to avoid making use of terms like "black magic" and "sorcery" knowing full well that it would take only a single skeptical juror to see their case fall apart.

"Doctor Satan," Keane replied smoothly, enunciating the villain's chosen sobriquet so as to remind everyone present of the fact that the defendant's very name symbolized things that were both evil and supernatural, "is unquestionably a scientific genius, with access to technologies that are beyond the comprehension of ordinary people like ourselves."

"I'll remind you that you are under oath, sir. Do you believe that my client is a master of black magic?"

Keane bit his lip, and before he realized that any time had passed, the judge directed him to answer the question. "Yes," he said at last. "The skills that Doctor Satan possesses fall into the category of what most people would consider 'black magic.' He used those skills to kill Victor Crenshaw and Paul Chadwick—"

"No further questions," interjected Torrance, but Keane wasn't done.

"Not merely to kill these men, but to turn their blood to acid within their veins, so that they died in horrible, screaming agony, literally bursting apart as their acid blood boiled through their skin—"

A worried look crossed the defense attorney's face and he hastily shouted: "Your honor, I move that this testimony be stricken—"

"—and splattered all over their horrified loved ones."

"Your honor!"

The tapping of the gavel interrupted both men. "Sit down, Mr. Torrance. Your motion is denied. You asked the question, and Mr. Keane answered it. Now if you have no further questions, this witness is excused."

Keane's face felt as red as the defendant's garish costume, but as he passed by his nemesis, he saw that beneath the elaborate crimson mask and black horns, Doctor Satan looked as animated as a tailor's dummy. The villain seemed not to care one whit whether the court found in his favor or not.

**While the question** of Doctor Satan's guilt or innocence remained in doubt in the halls of justice, the situation in the court of public opinion was quite a different story. While some of the more liberal-minded newspaper editors elected to simply follow the events of the trial, the Clarion, one of the city's more sensationalistic tabloids, lead with strident editorials, courtesy of its owner Thomas Fulton, who held back nothing in his indictment of the nefarious villain, and warned the court that if it failed to deliver a guilty verdict in this case, the blood of future victims would be on the hands of everyone involved. In the streets at least, there were few even among those disinclined to believe in magic or absolute evil, who thought that Doctor Satan deserved to go free.

Meanwhile, throughout it all, construction of the Plum Island facility, nicknamed simply "Hell" by its builders, continued apace. If and when the jury returned that guilty verdict, Doctor Satan would find himself its sole occupant.

Keane remained a constant fixture in the courtroom until the closing arguments were given, and lingered in Hammond's office while the jury deliberated. Much to everyone's surprise, the jury was out for only six hours.

"Is that a good sign?" Keane asked the district attorney as soon as the news arrived.

"Hard to say. It's rare for twelve people to agree to anything so quickly. Either our arguments were very persuasive, or Torrance's ploy to discredit our case was."

The two men hastened back to the courtroom where court was called into session for the reading of the verdict. Ascott Keane found himself holding his breath as the judge asked the jury foreman to read aloud their unanimous decision, and when he finally heard the word: "Guilty," he felt as though he might faint from sheer relief.

He could not have known that this strange chapter in New York's legal history was but a prologue for a much greater evil to come.

**Doctor Satan wore** the same striped prison uniform as any other inmate. His red devil costume had been taken away early on, and he was permitted to don it only when making his court appearance, a decision that confounded prosecutors; how could any jury possibly sympathize with a man who openly identified himself with the very essence of evil? It seemed almost as if the notorious villain wanted to be sent away for the rest of his life. He certainly didn't appear to be leaping to his own defense. His jailors could not remember a more lethargic criminal.

When the guards came to fetch him for the final day of his sentencing hearing, he followed along behind them like an automaton, never speaking, never resisting in any way. The young man with the bland face—whose true name still eluded authorities—simply followed along like an obedient dog. The guards escorted him into a secure conference room so that the 'milquetoast master of evil' as some guards had taken to calling him, could meet with his lawyer, possibly for the last time.

When the door clacked shut, Torrance rose from his chair and leaned close to his client. "You have done exceedingly well," he whispered. "Today, you will be freed from your chains of captivity."

The prisoner merely stared back as if deaf, dumb and blind.

**There was not** a person in the city that had not become familiar with the rather ordinary face of the unmasked Doctor Satan; Thomas Fulton had seen to that. The finishing solution on the prisoner's mug shots wasn't yet dry when the newspaper publisher managed to acquire a copy for the front page of the Clarion. Yet, as widely distributed as the paper was, no one recognized the face. It was a visage that slipped as easily from one's memory as the first dream of the night, and if asked to describe him mere minutes after looking at the photograph, an ordinary person would be hard pressed to say anything more than: "He's a man with…dark hair, I think…maybe blond…"

Doctor Satan remained a mystery, even on this, the historic day that would see him locked away for no less than two successive life sentences.

Ascott Keane was particularly troubled by this as he watched the costumed villain climb the steps of the courthouse with his charismatic attorney at his side. Throughout the trial, he had remained poised for action, certain that his arch-nemesis would never allow the scales of conventional justice to tip against him. He could feel the taint of magic in the courtroom—had in fact sensed it every day of the trial—and knew that Doctor Satan was employing the dark arts in some way, but the manifestation remained as elusive as memories of the unmasked prisoner's face.

Early on in the proceedings, Keane had crafted a powerful spell that would, he believed, nullify any other form of magic for several minutes, but he was loath to use it. Once the keyword was uttered, completing the incantation, Doctor Satan would immediately begin seeking a spell to counter it, and Keane had little doubt that the villain would succeed. His nullification chant was a last resort, to be employed if and when Doctor Satan attempted to escape. The criminologist was especially wary today; he did not expect his foe to go quietly.

Court was called into session promptly at 10 o'clock and presiding judge Joseph Prescott wasted no time in addressing the matter at hand.

"Will the defendant please rise?"

The man in the garish costume stood with robotic efficiency, mimicking the movements of his lawyer.

The judge peered down his nose at the villain, making no effort to hide his contempt. "It is a rare thing indeed for a court of justice to hear the case of a monster so completely beyond redemption. I frankly cannot believe that the district attorney did not seek the death penalty against you; I can think of no one more deserving.

"However, on his advice, and the advice of certain members of the community, it has been decided that incarceration is the only suitable punishment."

Keane felt someone tap his shoulder and turned his head just as the judge delivered the final judgment. To his dismay, he found himself staring at the bestial countenance of one of Doctor Satan's chief lieutenants, the "monkey man" Girse.

Girse had been rounded up along with several other lesser members of Doctor Satan's criminal entourage and, as far as Keane knew, was scheduled for his own day in court. There had been no news of an escape.

Even as Keane's jaw dropped in surprise, the beast-man raised a finger to his lips and then in a motion that seemed too dainty for the simian hands, raised what looked like a perfume atomizer and squeezed the bulb. A bitter taste hit Keane's tongue, and he immediately spat the offending substance from his mouth, rising from his seat to sound the alarm.

Every eye in the court turned to him in that instant, but when he tried to cry out, only a gasp of breath escaped his lips. He pointed urgently to Girse, but the seat where the apish thug had been only a moment before was now empty. Over the sudden tumult, Keane could hear the judge, pounding with his gavel and demanding a return to order, but the criminologist knew it was not to be. Doctor Satan was making his move.

His view of the courtroom dissolved in an eruption of brilliant white light. Keane spoke the keyword to complete the null-magic spell, but no sound issued. The chemical in Girse's atomizer had rendered him temporarily mute.

It took only a moment for his eyesight to return, and when it did, he beheld a sight that only the devil himself could have dreamed. A few steps away, Melvin Torrance esquire stood enveloped in a crackling net of blue energy. His eyes were wild with terror, but Keane sensed also confusion; doubtless the attorney could not understand why his client had turned on him.

"Release him!" Keane heard someone shouting through the din, but something about the voice struck him as powerfully as any magical attack. The voice was his own.

He turned his head toward the sound and for a moment thought he was gazing into a mirror. Then the reflection gripped his shoulder and shouted passionately into his face: "Let him go, Doctor Satan!"

At that instant, Torrance's cries reached a fever pitch. The web of energy had begun to tighten around him, burning his skin wherever it touched, insinuating into his mouth and nose and ears. Before the horrified eyes of all present in the courtroom, Doctor Satan's defender began to burn from the inside out. His bones flared as brightly as torchwood, rendering his flesh transparent like an X-ray image, and then were gone—consumed by the unholy fire. The lawyer's structureless form collapsed, smoking and sizzling, on the oak floor.

Keane reeled, disoriented by the sudden violence. He pulled free of his doppelganger's grip and retreated toward the group of uniformed guards, still futilely working his mouth to utter the spell that would render Doctor Satan impotent. To his surprise however, the guards surrounded him and began pummeling him mercilessly with their batons.

"Make way," cried a voice that Keane recognized as his own. "He's still dangerous. Don't let him make any gestures or say anything."

Keane had offered no resistance during the unexpected beating; he had been utterly unprepared for it, and the clubs had left him stunned. Unable even to breathe, he could only turn his eyes toward the figure that now knelt beside him.

You! Suddenly Keane understood. He glanced down and saw the crimson clothing that had replaced his gray suit. No. I'm not Doctor Satan. I'm Ascott Keane. This is an illusion.

The words never left his mouth. As he worked his jaw in vain, one of the guards thrust a balled up handkerchief between his teeth. "None of your black magic, Devil Man."

His reflection leaned over him. "You're going away for a long time. You were a worthy adversary. But this is checkmate."

**The strange potion** that had robbed Ascott Keane of his ability to speak wore off quickly, but the gag in his mouth prevented him from counteracting the spell of illusion that had convinced everyone in the courtroom that he was Doctor Satan. As Keane was bundled into an armored paddy wagon, the full impact of his foe's rather simply ploy began to sink in.

The judgment against Doctor Satan was absolute. The sentence would be carried out promptly and the prisoner would be delivered to his new lodging on Plum Island before the day was out. Keane felt a crushing wave of despair as he considered what this would mean.

He and Hotchkiss had designed the ultimate prison for Doctor Satan; a place from which escape, or for that matter even release, was utterly impossible. Once the cell at the heart of the structure was occupied, the key would quite literally be thrown away. In order to prevent the master criminal from gaining confederates among the prison staff, absolute isolation had been deemed essential. Meals and other limited creature comforts would be delivered through a clever mechanical system. It was the intent of his jailors that Doctor Satan never again see or speak to a living person.

Keane relaxed against his bonds, willing himself into a meditative state. There was a slim possibility that he could get a message out before the prison door slammed shut.

He visualized a wall of darkness, completely separated from the physical world. On one side, there was the ambient light that crept in through the narrow window slits of the armored car and the faint murmur of the wheels on the road and whispers of conversation barely overheard; on the other side, total, absolute nothingness. Keane embraced the void, tuning out all other sensations and completely isolating his astral self from his physical form.

For a moment, he remained there in the truck, observing the shell of his body in the company of the police guards, but he did not linger. The armored vehicle was racing towards its destination and time was of the essence. Incorporeal, he floated up out of the enclosure, passing through the metal sheets as effortlessly as the air itself.

Racing through the firmament swifter than any airplane ever traveled, his astral body began seeking out his familiars—those who would not fail to recognize the subtle influences, which were the limit of his ability to affect the physical world— his Sikh manservant Shakir, and his lovely and spirited secretary Beatrice Dale. He probed the living aura of the city, tasting it, sniffing it, for a hint of their presence, but was filled instead with the dark and bitter presence of the enemy.

Keane projected his essence toward his own residence, hoping to find one or both of his companions there, but as he drew closer, the stink of Doctor Satan grew stronger. The illusion that had allowed Doctor Satan to switch identities with Keane did not extend to the astral plane. If anything, the pervasive evil of his enemy's aura was more obvious to his mind's eye than the flamboyant costume was to the physical; there could be little doubt that Doctor Satan had invaded his own dwelling.

Bravo, Mr. Keane. Satan's telepathic message oozed with sardonic laughter. I would have been disappointed if you had not made this effort. The spell that holds your companions is a simple one, and I don't imagine you will have too much difficulty defeating it. Don't take too long though. Once your body is delivered to that unique little dungeon you built for me, it will be quite difficult for your soul to find its way back.

Keane did not waste time or energy cursing the villain. He recoiled from his enemy's presence and snapped back toward his captive flesh as though his astral body was attached to his physical form with elastic bands. Even so, he was dismayed to see that, during the timeless period he had spent searching for his friends, the police vehicle had made the ferry crossing to Plum Island.

The auras of the police guards stood out in bright contrast to the shadowy space—Keane's soulless form, still looking for all appearances like Doctor Satan—suspended between them as they made the short journey toward the single awe-inspiring structure at the center of the complex. Yet, as swiftly as he had traveled through the astral plane, Keane now found himself mired in quicksand.

He reached out to his waiting flesh, kicking and clawing through the ether, but his journey was that of a mountaineer trying to climb a steep slope of shifting scree. Although the physical structures around him were barely perceptible, the enchantments inscribed up their walls burned brightly, casting a web that had been carefully designed to prevent astral projection. Keane watched in dismay as the two officers carried him over the threshold and into the waiting cell.

Between his spirit and flesh, lay a gauntlet of his own devising. To the naked eye, they appeared merely as statuary figures—grotesque chimera with bestial limbs and faces that were not quite human—but the soul's eye saw something different. Dark shapes, shifting and writhing like shadows, resided in the stone figures. Ancient entities, bound to the effigies like guard dogs chained to a post, emerged at the very scent of a disembodied soul. Keane had placed these guardians here to prevent Doctor Satan from projecting out of the prison, but now it seemed they would prevent him from ever reuniting with his own flesh.

This is going to hurt, he thought.

The guardians ripped into his soul with ferocious glee, but his speed carried him through. The attack left him in tatters, but he continued clinging to the singular goal of survival. Stretching out, holding nothing back, he hurled himself at the final barrier, reaching out with a single tentacle of his soul to grasp even a molecule of his physical being.

The breach was just enough to reverse the polarity of the force opposing him. Now instead being repelled from the prison cell, he found himself sucked into it as if caught in a psychic whirlpool. His soul returned to his body with the severity of a guillotine and a cry of unendurable agony escaped his lips.

The two police guards however heard nothing. They had already left the prisoner in his garish costume behind and closed the door.

**Doctor Satan pondered** the reflection that gazed back at him from the mirror. Ascott Keane was handsome man, dignified in both manner and appearance, and the idea of continuing to masquerade as the criminologist was appealing. There were endless possibilities for further humiliating his adversary by wearing his face and besmirching his name. It was a passing fancy however. The game with Keane was diverting to be sure, but the real victory would come when the city's highest officials realized that the real Doctor Satan had effortlessly eluded them and that they had imprisoned the wrong man in a dungeon from which no release was possible.

He uttered a single word of cessation, ending the illusion, and the face of Ascott Keane dissolved away, to be replaced by his own familiar horned visage. He had missed being himself. He had used the same illusion spell on Torrance, switching places with the lawyer on the occasion of their first meeting. While he had enjoyed both freedom and all the luxuries and comforts afforded a high priced attorney, Torrance had sat in his cell, trapped in unfamiliar flesh and bound by a spell that left him little better than a Haitian voodoo zombie. He had briefly considered allowing the defense lawyer to actually try for an acquittal, but that would have meant enduring months of confinement in a holding cell, and that was simply something he couldn't do.

He turned away from the mirror and strode back into the front room where Beatrice Dale and Shakir sat statue still in the grip of a minor enchantment. "Girse. Get the car and be quick about it. We have much to do."

The ape-like face glanced longingly at the seated pair. "What about them?"

"What about them?" countered the Doctor.

"Well, I thought maybe I could have a little fun…."

"You 'thought'?" Satan's voice frosted the air. "You don't get to think, Girse. Keane's friends yet have a great part to play     in our endeavor. Their ceaseless efforts to locate and secure the release of my enemy will provide me with far more amusement than watching you play Tinkertoys with their extremities."

Girse scratched his bestial head, uncomprehending.

"The car, Girse. Now!"

The ogre jumped as though his feet had suddenly caught fire and hastened from the room. The diabolical Doctor made a casual gesture, lifting the enchantment upon Ascott Keane's closest companions, and then followed after him.

**Keane lay panting** in the darkness for a long time. The physical toll of temporarily separating soul from flesh had been compounded exponentially by the effort of challenging the psychic barriers of the prison cell. As dire as his situation had become, he was simply too exhausted to do anything but sleep. Yet, even his in his dream, he found no solace; the awful immutable reality of his imprisonment hovered over everything.

When he finally regained a measure of strength, he picked himself up and sur-veyed his new home. He was intimately familiar with the prison facility, having worked hand-in-hand with the architect on several details, even supervising on site construction, but now he saw it all in a way he had never expected to: from the eyes of a prisoner.

The cell was a perfect cube, stretching exactly twelve feet between opposing planes. The geometry of the room was just the first of several layers of magical defenses designed to prevent Doctor Satan from using his supernatural abilities to effect an escape either directly or by conspiring with his allies on the outside. Unfortunately for Keane, he had arranged to counter every possible magical attack he could think of; his own skills with light and dark magic would be of little benefit in putting an end to his unjust imprisonment. Furthermore, the prison's eldritch "bars" were only half the story; Arthur Hotchkiss had designed the prison with a fail-safe device; any attempt to undermine the walls, in any place, would trigger the collapse of a massive block of granite that would completely crush the occupant of the cell. It had not been designed to be cruel, but rather to deter any of Doctor Satan's confederates from attempting to tunnel into the cell or blow up the walls. In fact, the walls were unlikely to yield to any sort of breaching device; they were hewn from solid chunks of granite.

Despite the impervious stone walls, certain concessions to prisoner comfort had been made. There was a comfortable bed, hot and cold running water in the lavatory area and a system for delivering hot meals three times a day. Keane peered at the tiny slot through which these meals arrived. It was about eighteen inches wide but just under six inches high, but the real key to the system lay on the other side of the wall. The channel through which the meals arrived was a long, one-way conveyor belt that snaked through several trap doors that would not allow any-thing—a message or an escape plan—to get back to the outside. Keane did not know this particular system as intimately as he knew the spells and enchantments inscribed on the walls, but he knew enough to believe that the meal delivery slot just might hold the key to his escape.

He folded himself into a position called "the lotus" by Hindu yogis, and began to hum an atonal mantra.

**Although it was** a unique and almost monumental project—the sort of thing that would be a feather in the cap of any architect—the prison facility on Plum Island was the last thing on Arthur Hotchkiss's mind as he sat at the desk in his drafting room. He had more than a dozen projects in various stages of development, not the least of which was two enormous office buildings that would ultimately add further character to the New York skyline. His stock was on the rise and there was nothing to be gained, so he believed, by looking backward. In this, he was very much mistaken.

The cheerful voice of his perky secretary piped from the speaker on his desk.

"Your doctor is on the line."

Hotchkiss blinked in confusion. "My doctor," he murmured. "I'm fit as a fiddle. Why would my doctor be calling?"

He picked up the telephone receiver. "Doctor Ernst?"

"No Arthur," was the amused reply. "It's your other doctor."

Hotchkiss's blood turned to ice. "Why are you calling me?"

"Why to congratulate you, of course. Everything went exactly according to plan."

The architect was not fooled by the smooth voice. "I did what you asked. Our deal is done."

The voice on the other end made a tsk-tsk sound. "Arthur, the deal is done when I say it's done. However, I require only one small thing of you, and then indeed, our arrangement will be concluded."

Hotchkiss sighed heavily. "What now?"

"I need the plans, Arthur."

"The plans? For the prison? There's only one copy."

"I realize that. That is why I must have them. Bring them to the Empire State Museum. I will meet you in the Rotunda. Perhaps we can have lunch afterward."

"I can't be seen with you in public."

Sardonic laughter issued from the telephone speaker. "Why Arthur, do I embarrass you? I imagine it would be very embarrassing if the details of our arrangement wound up on Tom Fulton's desk. Come to the Rotunda at noon and bring the plans."

He didn't add "or else" and he didn't need to. Hotchkiss hung up the telephone and checked the wall clock; it was eleven thirty. He sprang up and hastened into the archive where the blueprint of the prison compound was kept. With the plans rolled up and tucked under one arm, he all but ran to the sidewalk where he hailed a cab.

The Empire State Museum was another of his keystone projects, and one that had been languishing due to financial problems prior to his arrangement with "the Doctor." When he had first conceived it, the design would have put the city's other repositories of art and history to shame, but then the original patron of the project had lost everything in the Stock Market crash, leaving Hotchkiss with an unfinished building that no one wanted. Then, seemingly from nowhere, a benefactor had appeared to put the museum project back on track. Now the museum was nearly complete; aside from a few finishing touches, all that really remained was to start bringing in exhibitors. There would be a few more months of growing pains, but once the Empire State Museum opened its doors, Arthur Hotchkiss would become the city's premier architect. Only now did he begin to wonder if the arrangement he had made was, not an answer to his prayers, but a deal with the devil.

He had never actually met his strange benefactor. All arrangements had been handled by telephone or proxies, and his part of the deal involved nothing more than helping Ascott Keane construct a prison from which escape was absolutely impossible—something he would have been happy to do anyway—and making a few minor changes to the design on behalf of his unseen partner.

He arrived at the museum site with five minutes to spare, but fearful of potential reprisals, he all but sprinted into the cavernous interior of the structure, threading the maze—albeit a maze that he knew as well as the back of his hand—through the various galleries to the great central lobby known as The Rotunda.

The museum seemed to be deserted, but Hotchkiss barely noticed; the workmen were probably on their lunch break. Nor did he notice the fact that the Rotunda, which was capped with a glass observation dome, was as dark as midnight. His attention was fixed on the crimson clad figure that stood in the center of the great hall. He resisted an urge to simply throw the roll of blueprints down and run away, and chose instead to affect a supercilious expression as he strode toward the rendezvous.

"So, we meet at last, Doctor Satan."

The crimson figure raised its bowed head and Hotchkiss, despite his best efforts, cowered at the sight. He had always thought the idea of a man wearing a devil costume to be rather absurd, but what his eyes beheld bore as much resemblance to that mental picture as a child's Teddy bear did to a Kodiak grizzly. Doctor Satan wasn't some fop in a pair of red pajamas—he looked like something from Dante's worst nightmare.

It was impossible to tell where the mask left off and Doctor Satan's own human face began. Up close, the red costume seemed more like coarse skin, stretched taut over bestial muscles. Beneath curling ebony horns, the diabolical visage leered with eyes that glowed like fiery coals and his lips curled back in a smile that looked like a mouthful of daggers. "Yes. At last."

A hot wind, reeking of brimstone, washed over the architect and he froze in place. Doctor Satan reached out from beneath his cape—only it wasn't a cape, Hotchkiss saw, but rather folded leathery wings—and despite the fact that more than ten paces separated them, a claw-hand stretched across the distance and snatched the blueprints from the architect's nerveless fingers.

"That concludes our business, Mr. Hotchkiss." The voice was the rumble of a volcano about to erupt. "I have no further use for you."

Hotchkiss stood rooted in place.

Doctor Satan threw back his head in a peal of sulfurous laughter then unfurled his wings.

Hotchkiss fled. He ran like he had never run before, and Doctor Satan's laughter followed close on his heels.

He didn't think about where he was going. He ran down the corridor into the museum, turning left or right at random. The mocking hilarity still rattled inside his head, but at least he had escaped the piercing gaze of those awful eyes....

He rounded a corner and found himself staring down the corridor into the Rotunda where the nightmarish outline of his tormentor now towered. Hotchkiss stumbled to a halt and wheeled around, fleeing the chamber again.

How did I get turned around? He wondered. He didn't remember any junctions that would have caused him to loop back on his path, but perhaps in his panic he had mistakenly done an about-face. He determined not to repeat that mistake, and once the looming figure was out of sight, he paused to get his bearings.

I'm in the north wing. If I keep going straight, I'll come to the North Gallery, which exits onto the greenway.

A hissing sound startled him out of his musings. He whirled to find the corridor behind him filled with a shape that looked like nothing less than a crimson dragon.

The architect again took to flight, but this time he had an objective. He burst into the North Gallery, but to his complete surprise, found only a blank wall where the broad exit doors should have been.

Did we change that? I know I called for an exit there.

With the dragon still creeping along the main corridor, there was no turning back, but his eyes found an alcove on the west wall of the gallery—again, something he didn't remember from the original design—and he hastened toward it, discovering a pair of doors that opened into another grand gallery.

I must have gotten turned around in the Rotunda, he realized. This is the South Gallery, not the North. The South Gallery was close to the main entrance. He needed only navigate through a couple more exhibition halls to find his escape....

Instead of the Reception Lobby, he found himself staring once more into the Rotunda.

How...? There was a scrabbling sound behind him, and he took off running again. He knew this museum like the back if his hand; he just needed to calm down and think clearly. The exit, he was sure, was just around the corner.

**Girse stepped from** his hiding place in the Rotunda and scooped up the roll of blueprints. Hotchkiss lay nearby, twitching as if in the grip of an epileptic seizure. A smile creased the thug's monkey-like face, and then he reached down and deftly plucked a thorn from the architect's neck, careful not to let the needle-sharp bark prick his own flesh. The poison Doctor Satan had cooked up was only supposed to work on its intended victim, but Girse wasn't going to take any chances; he didn't want to share the other man's fate.

Arthur Hotchkiss was going to be running for a long, long time.

**It was difficult** to concentrate in the prison cell. Although barely audible to the human ear, a pair of speakers secreted in the ceiling was constantly broadcasting a recorded cacophony of noise designed to interrupt the sort of meditation that a master of magic would need in order to weave even the simplest of spells. Keane however was not attempting to employ magic, but only a type of mental discipline used by contortionists and escape artists. His chanted mantra allowed his muscles and even his skeleton to relax and become pliable. When he reached the desired state, he simply leaned forward, his movements flowing as though he were a balloon full of water rather than a creature of solid flesh and bone, and began insinuating himself into the slot through which his meals would be delivered.

His arms went in easily, but as the top of his head met the wall, it seemed certain that he would go no further. Remarkably however, he kept pushing forward. His scalp scraped against the edges of the slot, but inch-by-inch his entire head disappeared into the niche, followed by his shoulders and upper torso.

Progress inside the chute was interminably slow. He pulled himself forward with his fingertips, moving no more than an inch per minute. His body filled the confined space, shutting off all light and restricting the flow of air into his lungs, which were already pressed so tight that he could barely draw breath.

Almost an hour after squeezing into the slot, he reached the first of several trap doors. His probing fingers found the back of the metal plate that angled back in his direction. With very little leverage, it was difficult to lift the spring-loaded door and pull it back to allow passage, but he did so and began snaking forward once more. Movement here was even more difficult. His clothes caught on the edge of the trap door and pulled its edge down, painfully arresting his progress. Another hour passed before he cleared the first trap door and was able to move resume his earlier incremental snail's pace. Another agonizing hour passed before he reached the second trap door.

Suddenly, the claustrophobic space was filled with a violent tremor and Keane felt the surface beneath him begin to move. He knew immediately what was happening; it was mealtime and the conveyor belt was bringing his first meal to him. He tried to press himself against the top of the chute, but the friction from below was too great. A few seconds later, something solid came out of the darkness and began pushing against him. He held on as long as he could, but the conveyor belt did not stop until it had pushed him and the covered tray with his lunch all the way to the cell.

Exhausted from the abortive escape attempt, Keane was too tired to even think about eating.

**In all his** years of prosecuting criminals, Bill Hammond had never found a way to cope with what was at times, a paralyzing fear of sending an innocent man to jail. His dedication to justice—to making sure that no innocent ever paid the price for someone else's crime—had not served him well politically; the public at large, like his superiors, often cared more about getting a conviction than they did getting at the truth, but by assiduously checking all the details of every case he prosecuted, Hammond had never lost a night of sleep worrying that he had sent the wrong man up the river. Perhaps that was why Beatrice Dale's telephone call was so unnerving.

"Mr. Keane has vanished," she had said, her voice trembling with panic. "And Shakir believes that Doctor Satan may be behind the disappearance."

"But Doctor Satan is in jail."

"Shakir believes that Doctor Satan may have switched places with Mr. Keane at the courthouse. If he's right, Mr. Keane is trapped in Doctor Satan's prison cell."

Switched places? His first instinct was to scoff, but he had spent too many hours working with Keane on the case against Doctor Satan to so easily dismiss the claim. Once he accepted that it was a possibility, the full impact of Beatrice's plea hit him like a ton of bricks.

*My God! Keane is in that place and there's no way to get him out.*

They had done their job too well, he realized. They had built both a criminal case and a prison cell from which there could be no escape, and now their enemy had turned their righteous efforts against them.

*No. I refuse to accept that. There has to be a way to get him out. Hotchkiss will know how to open the door to that cell.* He picked up the telephone and asked the operator to connect him with the architect. Instead, he got Hotchkiss's perky secretary, who now sounded none too ebullient.

"Mr. Hotchkiss took ill today," she explained, her voice trembling. "No, I don't know if… I mean, when, he'll be back in the office."

It took a while for him to get the whole story out her. After ringing off with her, he called Beatrice Dale back. "I have bad news. Arthur Hotchkiss has had some kind of mental breakdown. He's been committed to a private sanatorium."

He could hear Beatrice relaying the news to Shakir, and then after a moment, she said. "Doctor Satan is behind this."

"I think you might be right. What can we do?"

A different voice came over the line; a male voice that spoke in a sing-song accent. "Hammond Sahib. We must get a message to Keane Sahib in the prison cell."

"He won't be able to respond."

"Nevertheless, he must know that we are working to free him, so that he does not lose hope."

"Yes, you're right of course. I will go out there myself." He replaced the telephone in its cradle and grabbed his jacket, intent on following through on his promise immediately. His hand settled on the doorknob, but before he could he could turn it, the telephone jangled again. With a grimace, he released his hold on the doorknob and returned to his desk.

"Bill Hammond here."

"Bill?" The voice was distant, as if the person speaking was at the distant end of a tunnel, but Hammond recognized the speaker immediately.

"Ascott? Thank goodness. Beatrice is frantic—"

"Help me, Bill."

A chill gripped Hammond. "Where are you, Ascott? Everyone is looking for you?"

"It's so dark here." Keane's voice might have been coming from a crypt. "I can't move."

Hammond's collar suddenly felt too tight and he nervously loosened his neck-tie. "Then it is true. Ascott, we know what Doctor Satan did. We're working to get you out."

"Don't leave me here."

Hammond swallowed. His friend's plea, a plaintive wail from inside a prison cell, descended on him like an accusation of betrayal. "We'll get you out, Ascott—"

"So dark... can't move...."

The prosecutor didn't know what to say. "We'll get you out," he repeated. "Don't lose hope."

Keane's voice continued to issue from the telephone. "Dark...the walls so close...."

Hammond wanted to hang up—wanted to sever the connection that had now drawn him into his own sort of prison cell—but found that he could not. The thought of cutting off Keane's only contact with the outside world seemed like the worst sort of treachery, but that was not the reason he stayed on the line. Hammond could not hang up because the telephone had somehow become affixed to his ear.

The voice, more accusatory now, and sounding nothing at all like Ascott Keane, reverberated inside his head. He tried again to pull the telephone away from his ear, but a sharp pain—as though his ear itself was being torn off—caused him to relent. He glanced down at the object in his hand and realized that something had changed. He could no longer see where his hand gripped the phone; instead, it looked as if the molded polymer had softened and engulfed his fingers, spreading over them like a glove. He tried to release his grip—to drop the telephone—but to no avail; the handset was swallowing him as a snake might swallow its prey.

The panic that came over him was absolute. In an instant, he was reduced to an atavistic creature—human in form only—struggling to get free of the bizarre telephone call the way an animal might chew its leg off to escape a trap. But the harder he struggled, the more intractable the bond became. The dark plastic, rigid and immutable, flowed over him like oil, and wherever it went, it immediately became a shell that permitted no movement whatsoever.

In a matter of seconds, his entire arm was rendered immobile, but that was not the worst of it. Though he could barely feel it, the strange plastic shell was also spreading from the point of contact against his ear, oozing to envelop his head. He could feel it creeping across his scalp, a faint weight, hardly more than that of water, but when he reached up with his free hand, his fingers immediately felt the smooth unyielding hardness of Bakelite.

"So dark...can't move...."

It was only when the plastic shell covered his eyes, sealing him inky blackness, that he began screaming, but by then his ears were likewise covered and he couldn't even hear his own cries.

**No one outside** his small office heard him screaming, but later that night the janitor found him with the telephone still pressed to his ear and his mouth opened in a silent, eternal cry. The custodian shook the district attorney then, fearing the worst, began checking for signs of life. The prosecutor was alive, but nothing anyone could do could rouse him from his catatonic state, nor could any effort pry the telephone from his hand.

Bill Hammond had become a living statue, frozen into premature rigor mortis. In this, he was not greatly different than the hard plastic effigy of himself, posed in exactly the same way, in a tiny diorama on a shelf in an abandoned Victorian manor house on the edge of the Bowery district.

"An amazing invention," Doctor Satan remarked, and then to Girse's confused look added: "The telephone. It almost eliminates the need for human contact. Now if I want to, I can just reach out and touch someone whenever I please."

**Keane gradually regained** both his strength and his appetite, and for a few hours at least, did nothing more strenuous than chew his food. A second meal arrived on the conveyor belt exactly five hours after the first—dinner this time—and he likewise consumed the rather bland fare without really bothering to taste it.

He was by no means resigned to a life of confinement, but at present there was little to be gained by throwing either his physical strength or his supernatural prowess against the prison's formidable defenses. If he was going to escape, it would be through the exercise of his mental faculties. The prison had been designed to foil Doctor Satan's magic and genius, and while Ascott Keane was not quite the equal of the nefarious villain in the first department, he believed his intellect to be superior to that of his nemesis, and that he hoped would prove to be the difference between a temporary stay and a life sentence.

He recalled that the meals were delivered on a strict schedule: Breakfast at 7 o'clock, Lunch at noon and Supper at 5 pm. Thus, between the last meal of the day and the next morning, there would be a 14-hour period when the conveyor belt would be dormant. While that was a long time, he didn't think it was enough to make the exhausting journey through the food chute. Moreover, he knew that the trap doors were not the only perils that lay along that path, and had he paused to consider that earlier, he would not have made the attempt even once. However, the meals and the conveyor belt, which delivered them, represented his only source of outside input and he still believed that, if a solution was to be found it would involve the food delivery system.

He shifted his gaze to the discarded paper trays that had been used to deliver the meals. There was a second slot in the wall near the lavatory area marked for refuse disposal, but Keane had delayed throwing his garbage away. Like everything else, the trays carried the seed of a plan that had not quite germinated.

He finally settled once more into the lotus position, meditating not so much to prepare his body as to awaken his mind. There was a way out of this prison, and he was going to find it.

**Beatrice Dale spent** a sleepless night and most of the next day fretting over the fate of her employer and close friend. It was not the first time she had despaired for his safety. He had battled some of the city's worst criminals, including deadly showdowns with Doctor Satan, and narrowly escaped death more times than she could count. Nevertheless, this time was different. She knew he was alive and in relatively little danger, but it was the terrible fact of his isolation that plagued her. He was alone and probably felt his loved ones had abandoned him. She could not think of a worse fate; even death seemed preferable to a cage.

She had waited by the phone in Keane's mid-town office for Bill Hammond to call back with the news that Keane's release had been effected, or at the very least, that a message had been sent into the cell, assuring the criminologist that he had been forgotten, but when the telephone finally rang, it was not the district attorney.

"Tom Fulton, here. Can I speak with Mr. Keane?"

"Mr. Fulton? From the Clarion?" She made a face. The Clarion was useful for wrapping fish and lining birdcages, and not much else. "I'm sorry, but Mr. Keane is unavailable."

"Unavailable?" Fulton thundered. "Well, I suggest you make him available, missy."

Beatrice resisted the urge to hang up without another word. "Can I give him a message?"

"Just put him on."

"Mr. Keane is not available," she repeated. "And it is not his custom to take telephone interviews with the press."

"Bollocks to that," roared Fulton. "That's the least of my concerns right now. Tell your boss, if he doesn't already know, that his fancy prison hasn't stopped Doctor Satan one bit. He's already gotten to Hotchkiss and Hammond, and who do you think is going to be next on his list? Tell Keane to watch his back, because it's one of us is going to be the next to fall."

Beatrice sat in stunned silence as the newspaperman ranted on. Something had happened to Bill Hammond? She hung up the phone, cutting Fulton off in mid-sentence and rang up the district attorney's office. Although the receptionist did not come right out and say it, Beatrice knew from the other woman's manner and her choice of euphemism that something dire had befallen the one man she had trusted to rescue Ascott Keane.

She rang Keane's apartment and gave Shakir the dire news. Something about the Sikh's manner—his eerie voice and precise way of speaking—helped combat her anxiety.

"We must take action to free Keane Sahib," he said. "Doctor Satan does not count us as a threat to his plans; in this he is very much mistaken."

"Where do we start? Should we go to the prison and try to get a message to Mr. Keane?"

"And what shall we tell him? No, we do not have all the facts. I will begin with a visit to Mr. Hotchkiss in the sanatorium. Perhaps there is something he can tell us after all. You must remain there and wait for more news. Learn what you can about what has happened to Mr. Hammond."

Beatrice knew the tall warrior from India, who shared a strange life-bond with the criminologist, was absolutely right. Doctor Satan, while disguised as Keane, had placed both of them under a strange spell, but curiously had done nothing to harm them. That, she vowed, would be a mistake the villain would soon regret.

**Despite its serene** setting in a lush forested corner of Long Island, the Arkham Retreat and Sanatorium was seldom a peaceful place. A private institution that provided mental health treatment and long term convalescent care to figures of wealth and notoriety, the facility had seen some of the city's best and brightest at their worst and darkest. There was a running joke among the staff that men of wealth and power did everything in a big way, to include fits of insanity. While the Arkham Retreat was no better or worse than similar facilities throughout the state, its doctors and orderlies could be counted on for discretion; they were paid very well to make sure that the outside world never learned of their patients' bizarre afflictions.

Arthur Hotchkiss had proven to be one of the less interesting cases. Although he had only been in the sanatorium for a day, it seemed unlikely that he would join the ranks of men who believed that they were Jesus or Napoleon, pontificating endlessly in the common area, or that he would become what the staff simply called a "Picasso" painting the walls of his padded room with unmentionable substances. The famed architect was very nearly comatose. The only activity in his body was a constant muscle twitch, as though he were running in a dream. What concerned the doctors most about the catatonic Hotchkiss was that his heart rate and blood pressure were extremely high, as though he were indeed engaged in some kind of footrace. Sedatives had not calmed his metabolism one iota, and without constant intravenous supplements, it seemed certain that he would "run" himself to death.

Ascott Keane's manservant, Shakir, gave an inscrutable nod as the doctor explained the architect's condition. The doctor, believing that the physically impressive Sikh must be some kind of tamed savage, tried to keep his vernacular as simple as possible, little realizing the Shakir was a genius with several doctoral degrees, and was in fact, a board certified MD.

Shakir's presence had caused quite a stir among the staff whose first inclination upon seeing the turbaned figure was to assume that he was a patient suffering from the delusion that he was a Maharajah, but when the Sikh had calmly thwarted the efforts of half-a-dozen orderlies intent on putting him in restraints, the stunned doctor had chosen the wiser course of listening to what he had to say.

"Doctor Sahib," Shakir began, addressing the man with the highest honorific. "I believe that Mr. Hotchkiss's condition is the result of an exotic toxin, used in combination with a form of ritual magic. I have seen this before many times."

The doctor nodded, all the while wondering how he was going to get the Sikh's arms into a straightjacket, but then Shakir's next statement put him at ease.

"This is the work of Doctor Satan."

"Doctor Satan? But surely he's in prison. I read about it in the Clarion."

"We were fooled," Shakir said simply. "Doctor Satan is at large, and he seeks revenge against the men who attempted to imprison him. Mr. Hotchkiss was the architect of that prison."

"If it's a poison as you say, then we must find an antidote."

"The poison has already left his body; its effects cannot be reversed. Its only purpose was to open the doors of his mind to Doctor Satan's machinations."

"Dear God."

"Indeed, sahib. Only God can help Mr. Hotchkiss now. But it may be that Mr. Hotchkiss can help another." Shakir took a chair, positioned it alongside the hospital bed and took a seat facing Hotchkiss. "Will you leave us please?"

"I…uh, very well. I'll be just down the hall."

Shakir had ceased listening to the doctor; his attention was now focused on an entirely different plane of existence.

The warrior-saints who followed the path of Sikhism did not dabble in mysticism and magic, but that did not mean that they denied the existence of such uncanny powers, nor were they defenseless against attacks of a supernatural nature. This was especially true for Shakir, who was both a devout student of the Guru Granth Sahib and an associate of Ascott Keane in his unending battle against criminals like Doctor Satan who had chosen to follow the dark path.

For several minutes, Shakir simply meditated, bringing himself into harmony with the Cosmos and the omnipresent divine creator. When he achieved the desired state, he immediately became aware of the wrongness that surrounded Arthur Hotchkiss. In the eye of his mind, it looked like nothing less than a dagger of glowing hot iron driving down out of the Cosmos and into the architect's skull. It was a wedge driven into the door of Hotchkiss's consciousness, allowing Doctor Satan free run of the man's psyche. The torments that villain might inflict were without limit, but Hotchkiss's body would not survive such terrors indefinitely. Shakir, a courageous lion of a man, shrank from the eldritch invasion, but knew that if he was to gain any insight, he would have to master his fear. He extended himself forward, feeling the heat of Doctor Satan's spell as he pushed through into Arthur Hotchkiss's nightmare.

He doesn't recognize the strange open hallway, but knows that it must be one of the architect's works-in-progress. The plaster walls are smooth and unadorned and everywhere there is the dust that workers track to and fro in building sites. He turns in a circle, trying to decide which way to proceed, but the staccato beat of approaching footsteps renders the matter moot.

"Run!" shouts Arthur Hotchkiss, panting and sweating profusely. His own pace is faltering; he stumbles forward exhausted, barely able to lift his legs. "He's right behind me."

"Who?" He knows the answer, but senses it is the right thing to ask.

"Doctor Satan." Hotchkiss grabs Shakir's elbow and drags him along. The Sikh has no difficulty matching the other man's pace.

"Why is he chasing you?"

The architect's eyes are both pleading and frantic. "I don't know. I did what he said. I designed the prison exactly the way he wanted. I brought him the plans— Oh my!"

Shakir glances over a shoulder and sees a looming shape—Hotchkiss's night-mare, crimson, draconian, slavering and breathing acrid sulfur fumes. Then he too is running.

The hall through which they flee opens into a labyrinth of rooms that seem to go nowhere. The architect curses at every seeming dead end, mumbling about how nothing follows the plan. Abruptly they transition into a strange circular room with a vaulted dome high overhead.

"The Rotunda again!" Hotchkiss gasps.

"You designed this building," Shakir cries. "Do you mean to say that you are lost here?"

Even as he says it, he knows that something is not right about this. He cannot remember how he came to this place, but he knows that he should not be here. Nevertheless, the urgency of their plight holds him rooted in the moment like sticky mud. He struggles to remember what it was that brought him here, but the dragon's breath on the back of his neck consumes his attention. If only I could reach Keane Sahib, he thinks, he might be able to rescue us from this labyrinth. But Keane Sahib is....

He remembers that Keane is in the prison cell, and everything clicks into place. The quicksand sloughs away for a flickering instant, but then he feels the architect's hand on his arm, trying once more to drag him away from the monster and at the same time deeper into the nightmare.

He snatches his arm away. The architect stares at him dumbfounded, then throws up his hands and runs away.

The dragon smiles, revealing teeth that look like fiery scimitars. "Intruder. You will share his fate!"

Shakir feels the heat on his face, the brimstone fume scorching his nostrils, but he does not flee. Instead, he grips the haft of his kirpan and draws the ceremonial short sword. When the beast's howl rattles the building to its foundation, he knows he has made the correct choice.

**Keane patiently and** methodically tore the two paper trays into tiny fragments no larger than the nail of his little finger. When he was finished, he scooped up the mound of paper shreds and carried them to the small sink in the corner of the cell, where he began the equally laborious process of soaking the particles in water. The paper softened and swelled, and soon the pile of paper became a great gelatinous mass of pulp, which he carried in both hands back the table.

This was not the best plan he had come up with, but all of the others, which preceded it, were plagued with some particular flaw that had forced him to abandon each one in turn. His problem, he decided after a while, was that he knew the prison and its unique attributes too well; he was too close to the problem to see a solution. The prison cell was like a chess problem of his own creation; he had already explored every possible angle during his work with Arthur Hotchkiss.

He found himself thinking about the classic tales of imprisonment and escape—Dumas's Count of Monte Cristo, Poe's Pit and the Pendulum, even Verne's Mysterious Island. There were no particular parallels in those stories with his present plight, but his reflection helped him to think outside the immediate problem. One thing that he took away from each of the stories was the importance of having an ally. Even the protagonist of Poe's short tale about the tortures of the Spanish Inquisition would have been lost if LaSalle's armies had not taken Toledo at just the right moment.

If Keane was going to escape this "pit" he was going to need outside help; he was going to need to get a message to the outside world.

He began kneading the mass of sodden paper as a baker might a heap of dough. When the mass seemed to be the right consistency, he commenced working it into a shape that resembled a gingerbread man or a child's doll, about twelve inches in height. He gave it a rudimentary face, with holes poked where eyes and mouth would be, but he spent nearly half an hour fashioning crude digits at the end of the figure's stumpy arms. The last thing he did was to carefully inscribe three cryptic symbols into its forehead:

תאמ

The strange symbols were letters from the Hebrew alphabet and the word they formed, Emet, translated as 'truth.' As soon as he finished the final stroke of the third letter, figure began to move.

In the lore of Judaism, certain Rabbis had been able to fashion artificial men out of mud, just as the Creator had fashioned Adam out of the dust of the earth. Unlike Adam, these "uncultivated persons," or golem, did not possess life; they were automatons, mindless servants with no personality, no soul. In another age, people might have called them 'robots.'

Keane's decision to attempt the creation of his own golem was not one arrived at hastily. He had employed various Kabalistic devices in the design of the prison itself and there was every likelihood that this effort would fail.

If it succeeded however, if the golem could make its way up the food delivery chute and carry the message that it was he, Ascott Keane, that had been imprisoned and not Doctor Satan, then at least he would have allies on the outside trying to win his freedom.

If… if… if….

The golem stirred, then abruptly hopped erect as if waking from a bad dream, and began looking around.

"Well, that's a good sign," he murmured, and then in a louder, clearer voice, he said: "Golem, if you can hear me, raise your right hand."

The little paper man-shape bobbed uncertainly for a moment, then lifted its stubby right arm.

"Excellent. Golem, climb into that chute in the wall and make your way outside. Once there, you must tell the guards to contact Bill Hammond. He'll know what to do."

The golem remained motionless and for a moment. Keane wondered if the instructions were perhaps too complicated for the simple simulacrum. He leaned closer.

"Golem, do you understand my instructions?"

The creation of wood-pulp and mysticism seemed to be staring back at him uncomprehendingly. Keane sighed. Evidently the defense spells permitted the creation of the golem, but did not allow him to command it to do anything that might help him escape.

Well, back to the drawing board, he thought. He reached out to wipe away one of the letters on the creature's forehead. The only way to deactivate the golem was to change the word Emet, 'truth,' to Met, the Hebrew word for 'death.'

The golem shied away from his hand, and then without warning, leapt at him. Keane threw up his hands, beating at the strange cardboard creation, even as its featureless round mouth clamped down on his fingers. The golem wasn't made of stiff enough stuff to cause any trauma, but the bite hurt nonetheless. Keane flapped his hand, trying to shake the thing loose, but his agitation only seemed to excite the golem further. He slammed his besieged hand down on the table and gripped the figure with his free hand, trying to pry it free and when that failed, tried instead to rub out the letter on the thing's forehead in order to end the attack permanently.

The golem abruptly released him and scrambled away, intent upon self-preservation. Then, with equal suddenness, it hurled itself at his face. Before Keane could raise a hand in his own defense, the golem closed over his mouth and nose.

Keane's surprised gasp was stifled by a mouthful of wet paper. He tore at the thing with his fingers, ripping away shreds of paper, but the golem did not relent. If anything, it pressed its attack, forcing more of its bulk into his mouth. The criminologist gagged as the mass hit the back of his throat, blocking his airway.

I can't believe this is happening, Keane thought. He had faced death at the hand of his archenemy countless times and emerged alive, and now he was going to be killed by a pasteboard puppet of his own devising. He renewed his counter-attack, biting down on the paper mass and tearing away bigger and bigger chunks. He could feel the prehensile little fingers he had worked so hard to fashion now scratching at his eyes and reaching far up his nostrils to suffocate him.

His lungs were burning as he got the bulk of the thing out of his mouth. The squirming mass in his hands now bore little resemblance to the makeshift man shape he had crafted, but the curious and potent Hebrew letters were still visible, just out of the reach of his clenched fingers. If he let go, even for a second, in order to end the spell that gave the golem its vital force, the thing would no doubt renew its attack. He gazed around the cell, looking for some sort of tool or weapon with which to defeat the creature and then inspiration dawned. There was, he realized, another way to obliterate both the word of power and the golem itself without making himself vulnerable to an attack.

He wrestled the thing toward the corner where the lavatory fixtures were located, and without any hesitation, plunged both hands into the bowl of the commode. The golem struggled in his grip, but its resistance only hastened its dissolution, and after a few moments, there was nothing left of it. Keane removed his hands from the swampy mess and pulled the chain, releasing a torrent of fresh water into the bowl to flush away the remnants of the rebellious little automaton. Frustrated by the failure of his latest effort, Keane slumped against the wall and rested his head on his knees.

A whirring sound filled the room as his breakfast tray rolled down the conveyor belt and was dispensed onto the table, but Keane paid it little heed. It would be some time before he discovered that the tray had brought more than simply nourishment.

**Doctor Satan watched** with amusement as Thomas Fulton hastily fled his luxurious mansion and sought refuge aboard his equally luxurious motor yacht. The arrogant newspaperman actually believed that he was the next name on the diabolical one's agenda of revenge; in fact, Fulton and his newspaper were too valuable a tool to be neutralized. In publicizing the trial and loudly demonizing Doctor Satan in its endless editorials, the Clarion had helped elevate him to legendary status. With the tabloids touting his extraordinary powers, the mere name "Doctor Satan" would be enough to sway the loyalties of the weak minded and strike fear in the hearts of those who might otherwise resist his schemes. The Doctor had no intention of ever repaying Fulton's insults with injury; he kept his eye on the newspaperman only because the latter's paranoia was a source of endless entertainment.

"Enough." He waved his hand across the surface of the mirror basin and the image of the motor yacht chugging out into the Long Island Sound vanished, replaced instead by a vision of the true target of his next attack. An eager smile curled the corners of his mouth as the man came into focus. "Your honor, I must object."

The statement earned a perfunctory chuckle from his henchman Girse. The ape-like man lingered in the corner of the room as his master finished the final preparations for his revenge on Judge Joseph Prescott. Doctor Satan waved his hands over the scrying basin once more, chanting faintly to complete the spell. When he was done, he took a stoppered glass tube from his cloak, uncorked it, and shook its contents—a single sharp thorn, six inches in length—into his palm. He touched the needle-tip of the thorn to the basin, then replaced it in the tube and handed it to the monkey-man.

"When the toxin on this thorn enters the judge's bloodstream, his body will be paralyzed and his mind will belong to me."

"What are you going to do to him?"

"This is my masterpiece, Girse. While Judge Prescott sleeps, a madman will enter his house, murder his family, and devour them like a wild animal."

"Do I get to do that?"

"Oh, no Girse. While you are certainly qualified, I have someone else in mind for the job. Judge Prescott will of course be paralyzed by grief and will hunger for revenge. The murderer will be tried for his crimes and sentenced accordingly, though I imagine there is every possibility that he will be sent to an insane asylum for the rest of his days. Only then will I break the spell and allow Judge Prescott to see that he is the madman—he is the one who killed and devoured his loved ones.

"His suffering will be sublime."

Doctor Satan's laughter chilled the room, but then his mirth abruptly vanished. He peered into the scrying basin, but the image there was a featureless haze. He gestured and uttered an incantation to regain his link with the judge, but the picture in the water remained unchanged. "I'm being blocked. Keane…."

His eyes rolled back as he entered a self-induced trance and allowed his astral essence to rise up above the city. If his arch-nemesis had indeed escaped the inescapable prison on Plum Island, then his psychic presence would be as visible to Doctor Satan as a bonfire burning in the night. He cast his gaze in every direction, but there was no sign of Keane.

Of course not. Keane cannot escape. But who else could block my sight?

His attention now became transfixed on the dark spot in the vast tableau of human auras glistening throughout the city. The shadow covered Prescott's home, blocking his ability to sense both the judge and the identity of the person protecting him.

Very well then, he decided as he drew back into his corporeal form. I shall make this delivery in person. "Girse, we're going for a ride."

**His peers considered** Judge Prescott, a married father of two teen-aged children, to be a modest and temperate man. Eschewing the entitlements often reserved for men of his stature, he chose to live in a simple house in Queens Borough, a short drive from the district courthouse where he presided, rather than residing in a stately Long Island manor like so many others. To his way of thinking, he was a public servant and he wanted to stay in touch with the public he represented. His motives notwithstanding, his choice of living quarters placed him within easy reach of Doctor Satan's machinations.

Doctor Satan peered out from the darkened interior of his limousine at the home of his prey. He had been observing the house for some time, waiting for street traffic to subside enough to allow him to make a surreptitious entry.

His psychic sight was still blocked, but his physical eyes had resolved the mystery of why. Even from a distance, he could see that someone had surrounded the house with a circle of sacred salt. It was a simple mechanism of defense against the supernatural. There were perhaps a dozen adepts within the city who would know of the efficacy of the simple and abundant substance, none of whom were in the same class as himself or Keane, but that was not what concerned the master of evil; what troubled him now was the fact that someone had anticipated his attack against the judge. There was no telling what surprises might be waiting for him inside that house.

It was nearly midnight before he sent Girse out to kick out a breach in the protective circle. The physical disruption of the salt ring did not immediately nullify its supernatural properties, but the fog cleared enough to allow him to probe the interior of the house with his psychic sight. To his dismay, he sensed no human presence at all.

"This is a trap," he murmured when his semi-simian driver returned. "How very interesting."

"Should we leave?"

"Be serious, Girse. Whatever advantage our enemy might have possessed has been lost. We have nothing to fear."

"But if they knew we were coming, they must have moved the judge somewhere else."

"No doubt. But I am curious to see who is behind this little charade. Such displays of temerity cannot be tolerated." He murmured a minor spell and the streetlights nearest to the car winked out, plunging the entire street into darkness. With his crimson cloak wrapped around his tall figure, he emerged from the car and stalked up the walk to the front door. He hesitated imperceptibly as he crossed the break in the salt ring; there was no physical resistance, but he felt a sudden pressure in his mind. Pushing through it, as one might push through a spider's web, he continued forward.

The front door was open, a silent and dangerous invitation which Doctor Satan did not hesitate to accept. He hung a number of spells in the air—offensive and defensive incantations to counter anything his anonymous foe might have to throw at him—but his weapons were not limited those of a supernatural nature. In his right hand, he held three phials of glass: one with a substance similar to magician's flash powder, but strong enough to blind and disorient a room full of men; one with a choking gas similar to mustard gas and just as lethal; and one that created a vapor that could disintegrate any organic substance in a matter of seconds—the master of evil was particularly eager to try out the last one.

The house was unnaturally dark and a flick of the light switch in the foyer did nothing to change this situation; in anticipation of his arrival, his unknown foe had turned off the electricity to the entire house. He readied an illumination spell, but held off employing it as he continued deeper into the house. He paused again at the sound of whispering in the blackness beyond, and then an all too familiar voice reached out to him:

"Good evening, Doctor. What kept you?"

Uncertainty filled the red-robed villain with… something… an emotion that was for Doctor Satan, something like panic. "Keane!"

"You were expecting someone else?" The voice was unmistakably that of the esteemed criminologist.

"I'm disappointed in you Keane. Clearly architecture is not your forte. It seems your 'escape proof' prison wasn't so escape proof after all. Perhaps you should have stuck to less grandiose aspirations." He cocked his head, awaiting the reply in order to fix his foe's location within the house.

"Oh, the prison was perfect. I'd still be there right now if I hadn't discovered your arrangement with Arthur Hotchkiss. Once I realized that you had compromised the design, it wasn't too hard to discover your back door."

The voice was coming from a room off the main hallway and Doctor Satan continued silently forward, with Girse at his heels, to another open door. In the faint illumination of moonlight streaming through a window, he could just make out walls lined with bookshelves, and in the center of the room, a desk with a human figure silhouetted against the backlight.

The master villain quickly reviewed his arsenal of physical and supernatural weapons and poised himself to attack his nemesis.

"Careful about using your dark arts in here," Keane warned. "My assistant has already repaired the protective circle around the house. Any magic you work here will rebound back on you."

"Then maybe I'll just pound you to jelly," growled Girse, taking a step forward, but his master's restraining hand forestalled him.

"Patience, Girse." Doctor Satan turned back to the shadowy figure behind the desk. "I applaud you Keane. You are indeed a masterful gamesman. Tell me this: discovering my 'back door' as you so colorfully call it, was perhaps inevitable, but you must tell me how you managed to unlock it."

There was a perceptible hesitation between the asking and the answering. "It wasn't too terribly difficult to figure out. I know how you think."

What are you up to, Keane? "My keyword was certainly simple enough, but the spell was specific to my voice. My voice only; not even the cleverest imitation would suffice. How did you defeat that?"

"A simple simulation spell, not much different than the illusion you used at the courthouse. It was enough to fool your trigger spell."

"What are you playing at Keane? You know as well as I that your prison negated even the simplest of spells."

"Give me some credit. I knew the prison's supernatural defenses better than anyone; it wasn't that hard to bend the bars enough to say those two words."

"Two words?" Doctor Satan's sinister brow drew into a deep crease.

"'Open Sesame.'"

"But my key word was 'Abaddon.'"

A strange noise filled the room and Doctor Satan knew he had been had.

He cast his illumination spell, filling the room with incandescent brilliance, but the light revealed only how his foe had outwitted him. It was not Ascott Keane that sat behind the desk, but simply a crude man-shape—a scarecrow made of pillows stuffed into a business suit. The voice of Ascott Keane had not come from the effigy's mouth, but had rather had issued from the phonograph speaker mounted squarely on the desktop and connected to the telephone line. A second wire trailed from the telephone receiver and was attached to a radio microphone, transmitting every word that Doctor Satan had spoken to a location some ninety miles away where an amplifying speaker reproduced every note and syllable with perfect clarity.

In that instant, the doors of the cell on Plum Island, swung open with a noise like the grinding of boulders, and Ascott Keane stepped out of the eldritch prison, a free man once more.

"Keane!" Doctor Satan spat his foe's name like it was the foulest of curses.

The criminologist's voice issued once more from the speaker. "You are trapped, Doctor Satan. The police have already moved in to surround the house. Your magic is bound by the salt circle. The game is over and you've lost."

"Oh, no Keane. The game is never over." Satan's eyes flashed dangerously in the dazzling light of his spell. "You haven't trapped me at all. The wonderful thing about the telephone is that it works both ways.

"Manos Ragnarok!"

Because Doctor Satan shouted the word to close the spell that would, even across miles of copper wire, blast Ascott Keane to atoms, he failed to hear the faint click of Keane terminating the connection.

As there was no longer a medium to extend Doctor Satan's words to a place outside the house, the spell instantaneously created a burst of psychic energy with nowhere to go. More potent than the largest military bombshell, the spell raced out across the astral plane, seeking its target... and hit an invisible wall. Because it was a thing of magic, not bound by physical laws, the spell's energy did not dissipate, but instead grew in intensity, doubling and doubling again in order to blast through the barrier.

Doctor Satan's eyes widened in horror as he realized what he had unleashed. "Girse! Quickly, break the circle."

The monkey-man hastened to obey. He stumbled through the house, but as he stepped onto the front porch, a shaft of light transfixed him like a bug on a pin.

"You there! This is the police. Come out with your hands up."

Girse hesitated, shading his eyes against the blinding spotlight. The curving stripe of salt was only a few paces away. He raised his hands and took a step forward. "Don't shoot! I surrender!"

"Halt!"

Girse advanced another step. One more and I'll be able to wipe it out with my foot.

But then the home of the Honorable Judge Joseph Prescott suddenly erupted into a blinding pillar of light that stretched up into the heavens.

The policemen on the scene were temporarily blinded by the event, but when reinforcements arrived on the scene, they found a perfectly circular crater in the ground where the house had been. No trace of Doctor Satan or his henchman was ever found.

**Ascott Keane took** one last look at the Plum Island prison. He had often thought of the place as strangely beautiful, but that was no longer the case. No matter how elaborate and artistic its design, it was a prison and like all prisons, was a dark and terrible place.

More than a month had passed since his accidental incarceration, but the sting of the experience had not quite faded. He still remembered the suffocating despair as one escape attempt after another had been thwarted, and then that transcendent moment when his companions, with the permission of the prison staff had contrived a way to send a telephone line into the cell along with his breakfast tray.

The realization that his friends were aware of his plight and working to liberate him was encouraging enough, but when Shakir had recounted the tale of his visit with Arthur Hotchkiss and revealed the architect's duplicity, Keane had seen his opportunity. He knew that his foe would have created some kind of escape route from the cell to guarantee that the place would never hold him, but was at a loss to discover the means to activate that doorway to freedom. In that moment, he realized that if he was going to get out, he would have to trick Doctor Satan into opening the door himself.

Oddly enough, he had never doubted that the villain would come after Judge Prescott. Shakir and Beatrice had acted as his proxies, both to help the Judge escape undetected and to rig up the device to amplify the telephone signal coming into Prescott's study. When the protective circle of salt was drawn, the game had begun and in the end, it was Doctor Satan's own arrogance that had defeated him.

"Seems a waste," offered a voice at Keane's side.

Keane turned his eyes from the prison to look at the considerably more appealing form of his secretary, Beatrice Dale.

"What if Doctor Satan isn't really dead?" she asked. "If he comes back, can't we still use it to keep him locked up?"

"Unfortunately, he's the only person that prison won't hold. The changes he made to the designs are permanent. If he did come back and we were somehow able to arrest him and lock him up, all he would have to do is say that one word: Abaddon, the name of the Angel of the Abyss, and he'd be able to walk right out. Meanwhile, if anyone else gets locked up by accident, they'll be imprisoned there forever. The prison is too dangerous to be left standing."

As he was speaking, a burly little man wearing a hard hat and overalls approached. "All the charges are set, Mr. Keane. We're ready when you are."

The criminologist nodded and then took Beatrice's hand as they sought refuge behind a hastily erected wall of sandbags. The foreman of the demolition crew handed Keane an oblong box with a t-shaped handle sticking out of it and a pair of wires that spiraled from its underside. "Thought you might like to do the honors."

"Give the word."

The foreman raised a megaphone to his lips and began counting down from ten. When he reached zero, Keane worked the plunger on the device.

A series of muffled thumps reverberated through the ground as dozens of small explosive charges simultaneously detonated throughout the prison complex. The tremor built to a climax as the walls of the grotesquely beautiful structure crumbled into a shapeless mass of rubble.

Keane felt a strange thrill as the dust cloud settled. The chains were finally broken; he was a prisoner no more.

**End**

*Cargo ships are mysteriously disappearing on the high seas. Dozens of men and millions of dollars' worth of cargo have been erased from existence. Despite her concern over the long absence of Secret Agent X, Betty Dale, star reporter of the Daily Herald, cannot resist the lure of adventure and sets out to discover the secret of the shadowy villains known as the Sea Wraiths. Meanwhile, in the City's organized crime underworld, Nazi agents are hatching a plot to turn New York's capos into foot soldiers for the Third Reich, and threatening a quiet peace that has kept the streets free of violence. Will Secret Agent X emerge from hiding to thwart the machinations of Nazi spies? Or will he rescue his beloved Betty Dale from the clutches of the Sea Wraiths?*

# SECRET AGENT X: THE SEA WRAITHS

# PROLOGUE-A STORM IN THE CALM

**The mariner does** not have the luxury of choosing only to practice his craft when conditions are ideal; through fair seas and foul, he must guide his vessel to its destination. But some days are better than most and this morning found the ore carrier Coleridge chugging pleasantly along through an Atlantic ocean that could hardly have been more placid. In the days of sailing ships, these conditions would have been undesirable—no wind meant no movement—but with the advent of the steam boiler, ships no longer had to depend upon a favorable breeze to reach port. Instead, the crew could simply revel in the stillness of the sea's surface, free of the constant rolling from swells and chop.

In his office, just off the bridge of the Coleridge, Captain Orell White plotted the ship's position and made a note in the log. He then hailed Bill Kerns, the radioman on watch, and instructed him to transmit the information to the navigational relay station at Cape Hatteras. His logbook read like a sailor's dream; day after day, the entries were the same—fair weather, calm seas. Aside from a mild tropical depression encountered near Bermuda, the long voyage from the Argentine port of Rio Plata had been blissfully uneventful.

The Coleridge's burden of nearly 10,000 tons of Peruvian zinc ore, was destined for New York harbor, where the cargo would be transferred to barges and shipped up the Erie Canal, ultimately bound for smelting plants in Detroit, Michigan where the refined product would be used in everything from electric battery production to the galvanization of steel—all part of the city's thriving automobile industry. Captain White anticipated a few more days before the vessel reached port and that it would be more than a week before the ship had a new cargo and was ready to set out again for distant shores.

He could not have been more wrong; the Coleridge would never reach its destination.

The first hint of trouble came only a few minutes after the radioman received an acknowledgement from the navigation relay at Cape Hatteras. In a matter of seconds, the brilliant rays of sunlight streaming through the porthole were swallowed up, plunging the captain's office into premature night.

"What the devil?" White murmured, rising to his feet even as the bell sounded, summoning him to the bridge.

The men in the wheelhouse seemed frozen like statues as they gazed out into the sudden roiling darkness. The sea was almost completely obscured by a thick cloud layer, which was itself almost indistinguishable in the total blackness. "Where did this weather come from?" White roared. "Wasn't anyone paying attention? Call Cape Hatteras and check the forecast again."

Jack Hanson, the man at the wheel answered, his voice a quaver of fear. "Sir, I don't think it's weather. It's more like thick smoke?"

"Smoke?" The word heralded dire possibilities. White hastened to the voice tube and rang the engine room. "Jimmy, are we on fire?"

From the bowels of the ship, where daylight—or the inexplicable lack there-of—failed to penetrate, there was only a confused reply. "No, cap'n. Leastwise nothing's burning down here."

"Sir," the radioman shouted. "I can't raise Hatteras. I can't raise anyone. It's like the line is dead."

White felt utterly helpless. Unable to conceive of a course of action, he rushed out of the bridge and onto the open gangway overlooking the heavily laden open cargo holds. A few deckhands were gazing in disbelief out over the bow, into the heart of the strange omnipresent cloud. It was quite evident that the Coleridge itself was not the source of the fume, but the captain nevertheless sniffed at the dark air. The scent was strange, not quite the odor of burning but faintly metallic with a hint of ozone. As he lingered there, the captain felt something like spider webs brush at his exposed cheeks and the skin of his neck.

"Static electricity," he murmured, and glanced up to the aerial mast. As expected, the radio antenna was crackling with St. Elmo's Fire. It wasn't unusual for low clouds to cause static buildup, even thunderstorms, out over the ocean. That at least explained why the radio wasn't working, but how had the cloud overcome them so suddenly and without warning?

It was a mystery indeed, but the sea conditions remained calm. The ionization effect in the atmosphere would probably play havoc with the compass and had already knocked out ship to shore communications, but aside from that, nothing really disastrous had happened. There seemed little alternative but to simply ride it out. Rubbing fitfully at the ephemeral webs of electricity that tickled his face, he was about to step back into the wheelhouse when he felt the Coleridge begin to turn.

"Steady as she goes, Hanson—" White stopped short as he realized that Jim Hanson was no longer manning the rudder. In his place was a hard looking fellow wearing black oilskins and a watch cap. "Where's Hanson?"

He turned to Kerns, but the radioman's seat was empty. White's immediate reaction was confusion; like a man who wakes up in a strange place, he struggled to assign familiarity to a setting that defied comprehension. He stared dully at the unfamiliar man at the wheel, who despite his tough expression seemed more interested in steering the Coleridge ninety-degrees off its northerly course, and then gazed with even more incomprehension at the two shapes that looked almost exactly like men... sleeping men... stretched out on the deck against the far bulkhead.

Why, they are men! He thought to himself. In fact, it was Kerns and Hanson. But why are they sleeping on duty?

And as it finally sank into his head that something very wrong was happening, fireworks exploded before his eyes and he saw no more.

**Because no SOS** was received, nearly six hours passed before the Coast Guard received word that the Coleridge was missing. Search planes were immediately sent off and ships in that part of the sea were directed to begin combing all areas along the route from the ore carrier's last known location. The search lasted for several days, but no trace of the Coleridge was ever found; no debris or oil slicks to indicate that she might have broken up or capsized. The crew of the vessel joined the long list of mariners forever lost at sea, and nothing remained of the Coleridge except a push pin in a map on the wall of the regional Coast Guard command, noting the date and time that the ship went missing.

Some weeks after the incident, a young ensign, freshly posted to the facility commented on the fact that it seemed to be an unlucky year for ships along that route; indeed, more than a dozen commercial vessels had gone missing along a two hundred mile stretch.

"Don't make too much of it," his immediate superior told him. "The sea is a dangerous place and ships go down all the time. You'll learn that soon enough."

The young ensign took the advice to heart, but over the course of the next few weeks, as two more futile search and rescue efforts were launched in the same area and two more pins added to the map, he began to wonder.

**It was a** meeting of the most influential minds in America. The attendees were men of wealth and power; lawmakers and members of the Presidential cabinet rubbed elbows with captains of industry. The agenda was ambitious, but all of those present agreed that the policies they were debating would shape the future of the United States, and quite possibly the entire world.

Ostensibly, the goal of the meeting was the furtherance of the President's economic policy. Not everyone present supported the New Deal plan to stimulate growth and many believed it was the cause of the current recession that now plagued the nation. During the course of the formal meeting, various theories—some reasonable, some radical—were proposed, but for the most part the discussion stayed on point. After the close of business however, in small private discussions, the conversation soon strayed into the arena of foreign policy.

"We cannot continue to ignore the German problem," the Secretary of the Treasury said. "Hitler's ambitions are plainly obvious. He means to rule all of Europe."

"The affairs of Europe are not our concern," argued the director of the Federal Bureau of Investigation. "But even if he does, so what? A unified Europe is just the thing we need against the growing Soviet threat. Marxism is a plague that is even now starting to infect our shores."

"There'll be war in Europe no matter what we do," offered a third man, prompting a low murmur of agreement.

"At the risk of sounding opportunistic," observed steel-magnate Henry Barton, "A European war might be just the thing to bolster our own economy."

"Until we get dragged into it."

"Dragged in, you say?" The Treasurer wagged his head. "We ought to be more aggressive right now in support of Britain. Hitler is a monster. He is exterminating Jews—"

Though no one said a word, several of the men in the group rolled their eyes. The Secretary of the Treasury was himself of Jewish descent, and the plight of the Jews in Europe was known to be one of his pet causes. As if by some unspoken agreement, several of the men began to drift away, making excuses or choosing that moment to refresh their cups at the punchbowl, but the Treasurer forestalled two of the men—the FBI director and one other high government official—drawing them close for a private conversation.

"They are fools," he said. "Hitler is not some benevolent potentate who wishes to become our ally and trading partner. He means to rule the world. Those who do not embrace his vision and become his vassals, he will conquer."

"He won't find America to be an easy conquest," remarked the FBI director.

"You are absolutely right. Which is why we must be ever vigilant. I believe that his agents may already be in place, waiting for the word to strike if we should openly oppose his schemes."

"You mean sabotage?" asked the other man in a low voice.

The Treasurer nodded gravely. "The Secret Service has begun investigating some groups—"

The FBI director bristled at this revelation. "Then you've stepped out of your jurisdiction, Mr. Secretary."

"Let's hear him out," suggested the other man. "What do you need from us?"

The Treasurer gave a grateful sigh. "This peril will grow, and we will only be able to defeat it by combining our efforts. The Secret Service, the Bureau, and…" He nodded to the third man.

The grim face director of the FBI was confused. "I don't understand."

"Nor do I, Mr. Secretary. What are you implying?"

A victorious gleam shone from the cabinet official's eye. "Let me tell you a story, sir, about a very secret, very powerful agency operating within our own government, yet completely outside the authority of its elected officials, outside the law. Unfettered by legal restrictions, the agents of this organization have declared war on criminals who have escaped justice. In every city, they are sweeping up organized crime and thwarting the schemes of the most diabolical villains."

"Some sort of vigilante conspiracy?"

"Perhaps," the Treasurer answered with a wink. "These secret agents are in a unique position to root out the growing threat from Nazi spies. It is time to bring them into the fold. I mean to have control of this agency, to make it a part of the Secret Service."

The FBI director said nothing, but listened intently to every word, carefully watching the facial expressions of the two men, and remembered every detail.

"Why are you telling me…I mean us… about this?" asked the third man.

When the Treasurer spoke again, his voice was low and determined. "I have the President's support... K-9."

The third man drew a sharp breath.

"Oh, yes. I know all about your Secret Agents. Fear not, I have no intention of removing you from your post. You will continue to run the agency, but you will do so under the direction of the Treasury Department; my direction."

The third man, the man who indeed used the code name K-9, was silent for several moments, but when he again spoke, a curious smile creased his face. "If you indeed 'know all about' the Secret Agents, then you would also know that they do not report to me nor do they take orders from anyone. Whether or not they choose to work under your auspices is entirely up to them."

"Is that so? Then sir, I suggest that you arrange for me to meet with these brave men so that I may impress upon them the importance of serving their country."

"Your request is beyond my power. Even if the President himself ordered me to do it, I could not. The identities of the Secret Agents are secret even from me."

"Damn you, sir. This is a matter of national importance. You will cooperate."

K-9 stared back at the cabinet official, seemingly unmoved by the appeal, but then he relented. "There are channels through which I keep in contact," he said in a quiet voice. "I'll see what I can do.

## PART ONE: THE HUNT FOR SECRET AGENT X

## CHAPTER 1-UNFINISHED BUSINESS

**New York had** become a battleground for giants. The titanic struggle had gone on for many years; those found wanting fell by the wayside, vanishing into ignominy, while the strongest—the best and brightest—daily squared off in a competition for the hearts and minds of the citizenry. In a world where the pen was indeed mightier than the sword, the struggle to become the top selling newspaper verged on all-out war.

The tactics used by the champions varied widely. The Clarion appealed to the baser instincts of its readers, filling its pages with salacious gossip, rumor and innuendo, while others, like Jim Anthony's New York Star and The Herald chose the higher ground by offering intelligent and insightful editorials, and made certain that its lighter fare was suitable for reading over Sunday dinner. That is not to say that the reporters of the higher-class tabloids shied away from sensational news. To be sure, many of The Herald's faithful readers had been drawn to that periodical because its journalists were often at the center of the action, and none more so than the plucky blonde reporter, Betty Dale.

Only Betty wasn't feeling very plucky lately, and the assignments rolling her way had, for weeks—even months, now—been the sort of garden-variety stuff typically foisted on female journalists. Her gender was not however at the root of the problem; she had paid her dues and was esteemed by her male peers as one of the best crime reporters in the city, period.

Rather, the simple—she hesitated to call it 'awful'—truth was that all of the news lately was good news. She spent her days following the progress of the mayor's sweeping reforms and Commissioner Foster's overhaul of the police department. Major crime in the city seemed to have ground to a standstill. Worse still, her friend, the mysterious 'Secret Agent X' who was magnetically attracted to trouble and had saved the city countless times, had not been heard from in months; no surprise really, since danger had not reared its ugly head in all that time.

Betty sighed and rolled the page in her typewriter up to review the story she was working on, a fluff piece on a Shakespearian troupe that wanted to start staging free plays in the amphitheater at Central Park.

"You look blue today, Betts."

She raised her eyes to meet the handsome stare of Richard Acer, The Herald's award winning photographer and smiled. "Nothing I should complain about."

"Ah, no news is bad news, is that it?" Acer settled into a chair beside her desk. "I know the feeling. You can only photograph the mayor so many times before it becomes pointless."

Betty sighed. She liked Acer—he was certainly attractive, charming, friendly... everything a girl could want—but she was reluctant to field his admittedly benign advances. Her heart belonged to another, to a man whose face she had never even seen. Still, maybe she had no right to keep a candle burning for Secret Agent X. They were friends, true, but she could never compete with his single-minded determination to rid the world of evildoers.

Acer on the other hand had a lot to offer. Unlike most news photographers who seemed to live hand-to-mouth, he was independently wealthy. Working for The Herald seemed to be more a labor of love than an occupation. He had joined the staff only six months previously, but his resume was impressive; his photographs had appeared in Life, National Geographic, Look and dozens of other national periodicals. Betty had asked him one day over coffee why he had given up the exciting life of world travel to work at a local newspaper.

"The Herald is hardly just so much fish wrapping," he had answered with a gleam in his eye. "It's the most prestigious paper on the East coast. And besides, you work here."

She had laughed politely as she always did. His flirtatious overtures made her uncomfortable, not because she was offended but rather because she felt guilty for enjoying the attention.

She leaned back in her chair and met his steady gaze; his gray eyes, the color of steel, seemed like they could under certain circumstances be hard as granite, but whenever he looked at her, she always felt that they were full of laughter. "So what's the solution, Ace? What can we do to make our job a little more interesting?"

"You could come with me to Charleston."

The invitation caught her off guard and despite her normally cool demeanor she burst into a coughing fit.

"Oh dear," Acer laughed. "I just realized how that must sound. What I meant was, I'm going to the Outer Banks as part of an expedition to find a sunken ship, several of them in fact. You could write the story for my pictures. I know it's a little off your normal beat, but the change of scenery might be just the thing."

Betty quickly regained her composure. "A sunken ship? Is this some kind of hunt for lost Spanish gold?"

"Nothing like that, I'm afraid. A Coast Guard officer contacted one of my old friends at Geographic about a strange spate of ships being lost along the coast. He's catalogued more than a dozen different vessels that vanished without a trace. The ships went down in calm seas, with no distress calls and not so much as a stick of wood has been recovered."

"This sounds like a big story. How come I haven't heard about it until now?"

Acer shrugged. "I don't know. Maybe it's just been waiting for the right reporter to come along and blow it wide open. What do you say?"

Betty tapped her desk, apprehensively. There were a lot of good reasons to go, and the only reason she could even think of for staying... Heck, she hadn't heard word one from Agent X in months; what difference would a few days out of town make? "All right, I'm in. When do we leave?"

Acer smiled broadly. "Thursday afternoon, if you can be ready. I've got some unfinished business to take care of first."

**The Secretary of** the Treasury met with his department heads every Wednesday morning to brief them on upcoming projects and receive reports on current ones. The meetings typically did not last longer than the time it took for the men to finish their coffee and this one was no exception. Immediately following, a few of the men lingered in his lavishly appointed office to discuss unofficial matters. One man however, the Director of the Secret Service, lingered at the back of the room, biding his time until the others left.

The uncharacteristic behavior for the normally charismatic and extroverted career lawman piqued the Secretary's curiosity. "Something on your mind Frank?"

The Secret Service man looked up. "A private matter, Mr. Secretary. Regarding that special project you were interested in."

The Secretary's brows knitted; he didn't recall anything that fit that particular description, but he waved the other man forward, dismissing his other guests. The Director however did not immediately approach, but instead took a position at the door and when the last of the department heads had exited, swiftly threw the privacy bolt.

"I hardly think it's necessary to..." His voice trailed off when he saw that the Secret Serviceman held a gun in his right hand. "What the devil's going on, Frank?"

The director's face was devoid of emotion, but his steel-gray eyes were as intent as a surgeon's scalpel. "The Director wasn't able to make it today."

The Treasurer was dumbfounded. The face belonged to a man he knew well, but the voice was wholly unfamiliar. "Who…?"

"Frank" threw a card down on the desk; a white business card with a single luminous letter: X. "I have an appointment, Mr. Secretary. You requested to speak with me."

"You…I…" The cabinet official realized he was sputtering and sank resignedly into his chair. "I had heard that your lot were masters of disguise, but I had no idea. I trust you haven't hurt my Secret Service Director."

"He'll wake up in a few hours embarrassed that he overslept." The Secret Agent lowered his automatic and took a seat opposite the other man. "My time is however limited, Mr. Secretary. You called for me, I'm here; get to the point."

"Didn't K-9 explain it to you?"

"Who?"

Hidden behind his clever make-up, X's face was unreadable and the other man could not tell whether his inquiry was from sincere ignorance, or if the man was merely being facetious. "I'll speak plainly then. Our country has become the battlefield for a new war, a clandestine war.

"Espionage agents from Nazi Germany have already infiltrated our communities; sleeper agents and saboteurs, waiting for the moment when we commit to supporting England and declare open hostilities on their Fatherland. And believe me, that moment is closer than you might think—"

"So?"

The Treasurer nearly choked in disbelief. "Good God, man. You're an agent of the United States government! A sworn defender of the Constitution—"

"You know nothing about who I am or what I do, Mr. Secretary. With all due respect sir, I don't work for you and I have no intention of following your orders or prosecuting your agenda."

"But… it's war, man. America's enemies are on our hearths."

"America's enemies," the Agent rolled the word on his tongue as if it were a new and not altogether pleasant taste in his mouth. "I fought in the last war against America's enemies. When it was over, our side imposed a peace that chopped Europe into pieces, strangled Germany and made it possible for a man like Hitler to rise to power. Who is the real enemy then: the evil man, or those whose wrongheaded policies made certain that he would seize power?"

The Secretary was stunned, but he quickly remembered who he was. "Whether you agree with the policies of America's elected officials or not, you are her sworn servant, and by the authority of the President, you will follow my orders."

"America has more enemies than you believe, Mr. Secretary—hardened criminals, gangsters, madmen with unbelievable technology at their disposal, wealthy autocrats who believe they are above the law—and for nearly a decade, I have been fighting them. I am still fighting them every day, sir, and I will not abandon that fight to play your spy games. Good day, sir." The Agent stood and turned for the door.

"Stop right there!" the Treasurer blustered. "I'll call for help... I'll... HELP! ASSASSIN!"

The Agent whirled with his gun drawn and before the cabinet secretary could stifle his cries, the trigger was pulled. Yet, there was no report of a bullet being fired. Instead, a spray of vaporized anesthetizing gas blasted across the room and struck him full in the face. The Secretary of the Treasury collapsed unconscious into his chair.

**Secret Agent X** muttered a curse under his breath. Already, the sound of inquiries was penetrating the thick polished wood of the Treasurer's office. There would be no leaving by that route. Even as he contemplated his options, the voice on the other side became more demanding and then the person began to use force against the door.

With a little more time, he might have been able to use his expertise with theatrical make-up to exchange places with the stunned Secretary and foist some plausible fiction upon the Secret Service bodyguards, but he correctly guessed that only seconds remained before those selfsame protectors of the government's highest officials came smashing through. It was time to go.

One of the benefits of being the head of the vast Department of the Treasury was an office with a view, and the broad window that looked out over the street now presented itself as the best escape route for the Secret Agent. He didn't hesitate. Pushing the slumped figure of the slumbering Secretary from his chair, the Agent plucked up the heavy upholstered furnishing and hurled it at the glass. To his dismay, it rebounded from the inch-thick panes and bounced back at him.

Suddenly the door burst open and two black-suited Secret Service guards burst in, guns drawn. They caught a glimpse of X with what looked like an automatic pistol in his hand standing over the supine form of the Treasurer, and deduced the obvious: director of their agency or no, the man in front of them needed to go down.

X did the only thing he could; he raised his special gas pistol toward the guards, who in turn fired their weapons point-blank.

One round missed him completely, striking the heavy window pane to accomplish what the Agent had failed to do with brute force; the glass fractured away from the point of impact in a large crack that ran from the top sill to the sash. Another good whack would have the window open completely.

The second bullet however, did not miss.

The .38 caliber slug punched into the center of the Agent's chest, blasting him back and into the damaged window. The glass burst outward in two enormous sheets that went sailing out over the concrete walk below, frightening and scattering a few pedestrians out of the path of danger. X followed close behind.

**In a small** apartment above a storefront four city blocks away from the Treasury

Building, a weary man sat hunched over a desk, listening intently to the sounds issuing from a pair of headphone speakers. For a week now, every word uttered in the office of the Secretary of the Treasury had been overheard by a listening device hidden in the telephone, and subsequently transmitted to this location where an endless rotation of FBI agents monitored the line round the clock, whether the office's occupant was in or not.

The agent had followed the earlier meeting with bored attentiveness. The political machine of the nation's capital interested him only insofar as it affected his paycheck, but using this apartment to spy on the mark was a lot better than some of the places he had holed up in the past. It was only when the meeting broke up that he sat a little straighter and started paying heed to every word. When he heard someone say "special project" he stiffened.

"Wes!" He stage whispered unnecessarily, then shouted louder: "Agent Greaves, wake up!"

The man to whom he spoke was startled from his nap at the sound, but quickly became lucid and hastened over to pick up a second set of headphones. Greaves was younger than his compatriot, but the handsome G-man had not let a little thing like youth stand in the way of his ambitions. Wesley Greaves had advanced through the Bureau like a wildfire; he was fit, fast, deadly with a handgun, and most importantly, possessed a razor sharp intellect. It was whispered in the halls of the Justice Department that he was the Director's wunderkind, and for good reason— he was the best. The fact that he had been assigned this particular stakeout was an indication of just how important it was.

Greaves listened for only a moment before exclaiming. "This is it! Keep listening; I'm going to get over there."

The youthful G-man snatched up his jacket to cover the shoulder holster rig and dashed from the room, leaping down the stairs in a few quick bounds. Out on the street, he flung himself behind the wheel of an intentionally non-descript Ford sedan. Less than sixty seconds after his declaration, he tore from the curb and raced toward the Treasury Building.

He arrived just in time to see a man come crashing through a second story window.

**The Secret Agent** did not fall to the sidewalk. One outflung hand managed to snare the decorative façade beneath the window ledge and arrested his fall… at least until his full weight whipped around and he smashed into the side of the ornate building. The impact stung, though not quite as much as the lead slug that had hammered into his manganese-steel bulletproof vest hard enough to drive the wind from his sails. His face, or rather the mask of plastic putty and prosthetic plates, scraped against the marble as his tenuous handhold failed and he started sliding down the vertical surface.

He scrabbled for a hold but his foot struck a ledge before his hands found anything helpful and he bounced away from the wall out into space. Instead of smashing uncontrolled into the pavement though, he twisted in midair, and landed on his feet as gracefully as a cat.

The two Secret Service guards appeared in the window an instant later, once more brandishing their guns and shouting threats. The Agent scanned the street in either direction, looking for the best route to freedom, but before he could take a step, a car screeched to a halt in the middle of the street and a young man wearing a gray suit leapt out, likewise armed to cut off that avenue of escape.

"Federal agent," the newcomer cried. "Don't move."

The Agent did not hesitate. Whirling in place, he sprinted in the opposite direction. Something struck him in square in the middle of the back, simultaneous with the report of a pistol shot, but his armor reduced the lethal impact to nothing more than a sharp shove. More bullets scorched the air around him, but none found their mark and thankfully, none struck bystanders who were now likewise darting for cover.

Nevertheless, X realized to his chagrin that he was imperiling innocents by the simple fact of his presence. It was only a matter of time before a stray round from these well-intentioned lawmen found a living target, be it an unwary civilian or a vulnerable part of his own body. Instead of continuing to flee away from the scene, the Agent did something he hoped would confound his pursuers: he ducked around the corner of the building and made a dash for its entrance.

The gunfire ceased, but the G-man on the street immediately gave chase, alternately giving the command for the fugitive to stop and telling others to impede the Agent's progress. Neither supplication was heeded; no one wanted to risk getting in the way of the fleeing man that they imagined to be some kind of crazed criminal. X vaulted over the head-high wrought iron fence that surrounded the courtyard entrance to the Treasury building and crashed through the tall hedge wall beyond. The brushy branches further dislodged parts of his disguise, so that when he broke out of the barrier of arborvitaes, onlookers saw what they took to be a horribly disfigured man shambling toward them. Cries of alarm and dismay went up and followed the Agent as he hastened toward the broad marble stairs leading into the building.

A moment later, the FBI agent followed suit, scrambling over the fence and plowing through the hedge, still waving his pistol. "Which way?" he panted to the nearest stunned spectator. The man wordlessly pointed to the entrance and the G-man did not break stride as he steered in the same direction. The Agent would be trapped now; Wesley Greaves was going to get his man.

Inside however, the situation was very different. The noise and chaos had not penetrated the thick walls and the people standing in the entrance foyer did not register surprise until they saw the pistol in the FBI man's grip. "Federal officer," he explained in answer to their worried and questioning glances. "The man that just came through here…where did he go?"

He expected a unanimous round of finger pointing, but instead there was only dull silence. The man nearest to him, a uniformed guard, finally spoke. "Uh, what man?"

Confounded, Greaves hastily described the man he had seen fall from the outside window—hair color, build, clothes, and when that failed, even admitted that the man might have looked like the Director of the Secret Service—but the perplexed expressions did not change.

The guard shook his head. "Sorry, mister, but nobody's come through those doors in quite a while."

**As Agent Greaves** of the FBI grilled the people in the entrance lobby, trying to determine the whereabouts of the fugitive, the man he was looking for strolled calmly down the sidewalk away from the Treasury Building. Had anyone cared to notice, they would have seen a rather ordinary looking man with wavy brown hair wearing spectacles and a tweed sport coat; a man who looked nothing like the head of the Secret Service.

Secret Agent X still had his disguise; he had peeled the false face and wig off and stuffed it into a pocket at the threshold of the imposing edifice. At the same time, he had stripped off his suit jacket and hastily turned it inside out. Instead of the silk lining one would normally expect on such a garment, the reverse of the coat was a herringbone tweed pattern. No one saw him make the hasty alterations to his appearance and no one gave him a second glance as he strolled down the long walk to the gate leading out of the courtyard.

**Jim Hobart leaned** back in his plush upholstered chair and stretched his legs beneath the surface of the expensive cherry-wood desk. He had just signed the last of the payroll checks for the detectives and staff of Hobart Investigations, more than fifty people in all, loyal to their employer not merely because of the considerable salary he paid, but because they knew he was a good man who would always take care of their needs. Rewarding that loyalty was a source of no little pride to the former policeman turned very successful private detective.

Nevertheless, the redheaded, freckle-faced Hobart was acutely aware that as the success of his investigative empire increased, the actual amount of time he spent doing the job he loved diminished. He was more a manager now than a private detective, and though the change had happened gradually, sometimes he felt the difference as acutely as if a part of his body was missing.

Often when he was in this mood, all it would take to set him back on an even keel was a glance at the photograph in the frame on his desktop: his lovely wife Leanne, who was now only a couple months away from making him the father of a bouncing baby boy… at least he hoped it was a boy; the nursery in their modest house in Queens was already decorated with baseball players and airplanes for Jim jr. As an expectant parent, he knew that maybe it was time to think about settling down a bit, leaving the rough work on the streets to the younger detectives. Yet, for some reason, that argument seemed less and less convincing with each deskbound day.

The trilling of the telephone stirred him from the doldrums. "Yes, Maggie?"

"Call from Mr. A.J. Martin," the switchboard operator supplied in a conspiratorial stage whisper.

Hobart immediately felt his pulse quicken with a tingle of adrenaline. A.J. Martin was one of his major clients—no, strike that, the mysterious and reclusive newspaperman Mr. Martin was his premier client, and had been almost since the inception of his agency. Martin had kept him busy investigating various cases during the formative period when he was just a former—at the time, actually disgraced—flatfoot looking to solve crimes for hire. Without the newspaperman's support, Hobart Investigations most surely would not have grown to such glorious proportions.

Yet, despite the fact that Martin sent him a monthly check to keep him on retainer, there had been no call for his services from that quarter in more than half a year, and Hobart had a pretty good idea why. He was too good a detective not to see that there was some kind of link between Mr. A.J. Martin and the mysterious Secret Agent X.

"Mr. Martin, Jim Hobart here. Always a pleasure to hear from you."

"Jim!" The voice on the other end was slightly scratchy, as if the call was perhaps being placed from somewhere both out of doors and outside the city. "Sorry but I've no time for chitchat. I need you to look into something for me. I need you to do it personally; trust no one, understand?"

"Not even my own detectives?"

"I'm afraid not. Not yet at any rate."

Hobart frowned into the telephone handset, but it was a frown of deep thought, not disappointment. Inwardly, he was elated at the prospect of solo work, beating the street for leads, despite the fact that his client was advocating the worst kind of paranoia. "What's the gig?"

"I need you to make discreet but thorough inquiries into the likelihood of foreign saboteurs operating on American soil."

"Foreign saboteurs? In New York?"

"Not just New York, Jim; the entire seacoast. There's rumors of Nazi sleeper agents—do you know that term?"

"Sure. Undercover agents who live and work in the community, doing nothing until they receive a code word or somesuch to put them in action."

"That's right," Martin replied. "I'll be straight with you Jim; this one is going to be tough, but I need to know if the rumors are true. Can you handle it?"

Hobart did not have to even consider the request before answering affirmatively.

## CHAPTER 2 - THE NEW BOSS

**City and police** officials were quick to declare that it was their tireless efforts that had curtailed the rising influence of organized crime in the city. Among the citizenry, this was largely believed to be the case, though there was some debate over coffee cups and water coolers as to the role played by the city's own vigilante, Secret Agent X; some believed that is was he and not the police that had cured the disease of crime, others labeled him a master criminal and contended that his apparent absence from the scene was the reason why criminal activity was on the ebb. It was even rumored that the police had captured him and kept the arrest a secret in order to prevent his supporters from attributing him martyr status.

In truth, the defanging of the criminal element owed more to the repealing of the Volstead act and the 18th Amendment than anything else. Bootleg liquor had been a main pillar of criminal activity during the years of Prohibition, and the re-legalization of spirits had forced the mobsters to fall back on their traditional sources of income: racketeering and other illicit vices such as the narcotics trade, gambling and prostitution. Yet, even those activities had shown a marked decrease and the real credit for that belonged not to the crime fighters, but to the city's top criminal, crime boss Aldo Novelli.

Unlike many Mafiosi, Novelli did not live the high life, cavorting in nightclubs or gallivanting about town in chauffeured sedans. A quiet, reserved figure, he was more often to be found at a back table in the Napoli eatery on Canal Street than in the Stardust Lounge. He had gained his title as Don of Dons, not through violence and treachery, but rather by earning the loyalty of his lieutenants, men who like himself, were honorable and interested in the advancement of the community. A moral and religious man, at least insofar as any crime lord could be so considered, Novelli disdained violence and vice, and encouraged members of his organization to pursue legitimate concerns such as construction and importing of trade goods. There was strife to be sure, and the list of Novelli's enemies grew daily as disenchanted and ambitious underlings sought a return to the old ways, but the Don's faithful supporters valued the peace and tolerated no rivalry to their leader.

On this particular Wednesday night, Novelli was entertaining several of the men he believed most likely to attempt a coup, in hopes of averting a war between the factions. The heavyset widower sat calmly at his table, listening rather than talking, as the debate raged around him.

"If we don't take control of the old business," Jack Scorza was saying, "someone else will."

"We've outgrown the old business," countered Luigi Petrona, one of Novelli's chief supporters. "We're respectable now and we should stay that way."

"There will always be people who want drugs, men who want whores." Scorza was on his feet. "It's a gold mine and it's ours for the taking. If we don't take it, someone will move in on us. It's already happening. Instead of trying to shut these places down, we could be collecting from them—"

"Do you want to raise your children in a city full of dope pushers? Do you want your daughters working in those brothels?"

Novelli raised his hands, interrupting his lieutenant. "Sit down, both of you."

Scorza sank glowering into his seat but did not challenge the Don. A low murmur circulated around the table, but no further arguments were voiced.

"Mr. Scorza is right," Novelli said, his deep voice silencing even the whisperers. "It is the nature of people to sin and if we do not supply them with the means and opportunity to do so, someone else will. However gentleman, as the guardians of our community, we have to consider what our obligations are."

"We ain't cops," Scorza muttered.

"No, we aren't. The police are constrained by the very law they are sworn to uphold. Worse, because they are merely men, they are easily seduced into corruption. We cannot always trust that the police will keep our streets safe for our children. The responsibility then falls upon our shoulders."

Scorza did not answer, but his sneer spoke louder than anything he might have said. Seeing that he had failed to win his point with the hotheaded young capo, the Don turned to the rest of the group. "Please consider what I have said, gentlemen. We have won peace and prosperity for our people, but the battle to keep it never ends. If we choose the easy way—the old way—we condemn our neighbors and ourselves to war without end."

He signaled the waiters to bring out drinks and cigars and then retired from to a private room, where he was joined by Petrona.

"Watch out for Scorza, boss. He wants your job and your head."

Novelli puffed on his cigar and nodded. "There will always be someone like him, Lou. That's why I prefer to have him here, at my table, where I can see him."

"Yeah, I guess it's harder to stick a knife in someone's back when you're sitting in front of him."

"'Keep your friends close, and your enemies closer.'"

Petrona laughed. "That's good, boss. But I think Scorza is gonna make a move soon."

"Hmm. He needs more support first. But keep an eye on him, anyway."

"Gotcha boss." Petrona winked.

Novelli sighed. "We've created something great here Lou, but nothing great can endure if good men don't fight to preserve it. The war is far from over. In fact, the greatest battles lay yet ahead."

The crime boss could not know how prophetic those words would prove to be.

**Betty Dale stepped** down from the train into a humid but agreeable late summer Charleston day. Acer, ever the gentleman, set down their luggage and extended a firm hand to the female journalist as she disembarked. Betty was surprised at the pleasant feelings his touch evoked; the decision to accompany the photographer was proving to be a very good one.

"I'll hire us a car," Acer said. "We can retire to our rooms and unpack. No sense in going right to work."

They hadn't discussed work much at all during the overnight train trip from

New York to Charleston, and Betty more than once found herself forgetting the very reason for their journey. However, she had been a reporter too long to let the mystery of the lost ships stray too far from her thoughts.

Prior to leaving, she had done a little digging of her own into the story, and what she discovered made her wonder further about the seeming lack of general interest in the disappearances. Thousands, perhaps even millions of dollars' worth of cargo had been lost, to say nothing of the dozens of sailors who were now listed as "lost at sea, presumed dead." Nevertheless, there was a rational explanation for the chasm between the tragedies and public awareness; the ships were, more often than not flying the flags of foreign countries and their crews were the driftwood of society, men without families or ties to the community.

A call to the Coast Guard ultimately put her in touch with Ensign William Barlowe, the man who seemed to know the most about the vanished ships. He had compiled what he believed to be a comprehensive list of vessels, crews and cargos—it was impossible to know with certainty if he had got them all—and even included weather reports for the days and times when the sinkings occurred, but what he could not supply was an explanation, if indeed there was one.

"For all we know, it may very well be a case of coincidence and bad luck," Barlowe had said, though his tone showed a lack of conviction.

Betty's research had not ended there. She knew next to nothing about ships or sea trade, so the days in between Acer's invitation and their departure were spent at the public library, reading everything she could about modern maritime history.

She told Acer of her findings that night as they shared a late meal in the hotel's restaurant. "Do you know what is the greatest threat to ocean-going vessels in the modern age?"

"Hmm." Her companion seemed distracted. "Icebergs?"

"Not hardly. The last time that there was a rash of ships lost, the cause was German U-boats."

"U-boats?" The handsome photographer raised an eyebrow. "Well, that would certainly be a sensational story, if true."

"I don't mean to suggest that there's a new submarine menace out there." Somehow, his reply made her feel foolish for even thinking that there might be a human cause.

As if noting her embarrassment, Acer quickly back-pedaled. "We can't dismiss the possibility, though. But consider, when a torpedo sinks a ship, there's debris, wreckage, oil slicks. The searchers found nothing of that sort."

"That would also be true if the ships encountered sudden bad weather or a giant wave."

"Very true," Acer observed, steepling his fingers as he stared across the table at her. "Betty, there's something I've been wanting to tell you, for some time now."

She nodded, but her mind was still wrapped around the mystery. "I wonder if perhaps we're looking at this the wrong way. Everyone assumes that the ships went down. What if there's another explanation? Maybe the ships did meet with some misadventure, but not the one we think."

"You know that I care deeply for you," he continued, seemingly oblivious to her musings. "But there's something about me you don't know. I'm not who you think—"

"Pirates!"

Acer sat upright, surprised by the outburst. "Excuse me?"

"Long before German submarines, there were other villains who roved the seas looking for ships to plunder. Some of them lived right here on the Carolina coast."

Acer pondered the suggestion. "You think that a modern day Captain Kidd is now the scourge of the high seas? The pirates of old were after treasure—silver, gold, tea—anything that could be easily converted into hard cash. What would a buccaneer want with a ship full of copper ore? He couldn't hope to just sail a captured freighter into port and unload; as soon as he did, the game would be up."

"It's not as difficult as you might think. A fresh coat of paint, a new name and a new crew, and you're back in business. It could even be a massive insurance scam."

"Interesting. It certainly bears looking into."

Betty nodded eagerly. "I'll start looking into it first thing in the morning. By the way, what were you saying a moment ago?"

Acer flashed a tight smile. "It was nothing."

**Agent Wesley Greaves** picked the strange pistol out of the evidence box and held it up for inspection. At first glance, it looked like an ordinary automatic, but the resemblance was purely superficial. The pistol, unintentionally left behind at the crime scene, was not machined from blocks of gunmetal as would be the case with a firearm, but was rather a hollow construct of thin plates. One of those plates had been loosened, exposing the inner workings of the device, and according to the report of the technician who had opened it, doing so had triggered the release of the pressurized contents inside; an anesthetizing gas of unknown composition that had knocked the technician out cold for several hours.

The gas gun and the technician's report, like everything else associated with the strange attack on the Secretary of the Treasury, had been delivered to Greaves's office following several days of intense political wrangling. The Director of the FBI had successfully lobbied to assume control of the investigation, much to the chagrin of the Secret Service, who had already suffered a black eye for their failure to prevent the attack in the first place. The Treasurer and his subordinates had complied with the executive order transferring jurisdiction over the case to the Justice Department, but that was the extent of their cooperation. Greaves was neither surprised nor disappointed; he already had all the information he needed. The knockout gun and use of top-notch theatrical disguises identified the culprit as effectively as a fingerprint.

Greaves put down the pistol and picked up the telephone. In a matter of minutes, he was connected to the New York City police department.

"Inspector Burks," he said by way of introduction. "I'm Agent Wesley Greaves of the Federal Bureau of Investigation."

There was an uncomfortable pause. "What can I do for you, Agent Greaves?"

"I understand that you are the expert on the vigilante known as Secret Agent X."

"So?"

Greaves smiled into the telephone receiver. City cops were often reluctant to cooperate with federal authorities, imagining that the G-men were trying to horn in on their territory. "Inspector, we are investigating a crime in the nation's capital and our preliminary evidence seems to implicate the same man that your city newspapers have identified as Agent X. I'm not trying to take your case away from you, but if this X fellow is operating across state lines, that makes it a federal matter. Now, there are two ways we can do this: we can work together and just maybe bring this guy to justice, or I can serve you with a federal subpoena and take complete control of the investigation. It's up to you."

Burks growled into his ear. "What do you want to know?"

"I've read all the news articles; the public seems to think X is a hero, like Robin Hood or Zorro. You don't agree?"

"When somebody shows up every time there's trouble, you start to wonder if maybe he's not the cause of the trouble."

"The same might be said for the police."

"Hah! The police are sworn to uphold the law; Agent X shows complete disregard for the authority of the police and the letter of the law. He has impersonated police officials on countless occasions, which by itself is enough to warrant his arrest."

Greaves nodded absently. "I'm more interested in understanding what it is that he hopes to accomplish. According to the articles I've read, he has stopped a number of criminal schemes."

"Of course," rumbled Burks. "He puts his rivals out of business."

"I wonder if that's really what's going on." Greaves thought about the conversation between X and the Secretary of the Treasury; the disguised X had flatly refused the Treasurer's request to employ his talents in defense of the nation. He could think of only one explanation for that. "We think this Secret Agent may be involved in some kind of un-American activities."

"I can't think of anything more un-American than crime."

"How about espionage?"

"Espionage?" Burks seemed honestly surprised. "Well, I haven't seen anything to indicate that. To tell you the truth, we haven't seen much of Agent X in the last few months. If he is behind some crime in DC, then he may indeed have moved on to new criminal horizons."

"Inspector, I feel it only fair to warn you that the FBI is now assuming control of the hunt for Secret Agent X. I hope we can count on the full cooperation of your department."

"Do I have a choice?"

Greaves smile was without humor. "No, sir. Not really."

**The patrons of** Gustav's Gasthaus immediately pegged Hobart as an outsider, and not just because of his fiery red hair. Although the little public house was one of dozens in the city, its clientele was mostly limited to a few familiar regulars; it was not the kind of place that appeared in tourist guides. The investigator returned the stares of the men lined up at the bar and, undeterred by their unveiled suspicion, took a seat beside them.

"Can I have a pint of yer foinest ale my good man?" he asked in the thickest brogue he could manage.

"No ale," the barman said in a flat voice.

"Och, ale, beer, whatever you're callin' it's foine by me."

The other man scowled then moved off, presumably to fill the order. Hobart tapped on bar and smiled to the other dour-faced customers. "Evenin'. I was supposed to meet a fella' named Johann here tonight. Name ring a bell?"

He received only scowls by way of answer. With a shrug, he turned to the flag-on of beer the barkeep had placed before him and took a long draught. He lingered there only long enough to imbibe the beverage, and then pushed away, extravagantly tossing a dollar bill beside the empty stein. "A foine brew, my good man. If you see Johann, tell him his money's still good with Seamus O'Grady."

Ignoring the other man's grunt, Hobart strolled from the tavern and headed down the block. Gustav's was the fourth such establishment he had visited in the predominately German neighborhood, and each time the reaction was the same. Hobart was neither surprised nor disappointed though. The goal of these visits was to observe and gather information, but if there was a criminal element in the neighborhood, it was a good bet that someone would want know more about Seamus O'Grady and his business with the mysterious Johann.

The seeds he had scattered took root more quickly than he'd hoped. As he rounded a corner, he found three burly men—he recognized them from the Gasthaus—blocking his path. "Bless me," he said loudly, inwardly steeling himself lest the encounter turn violent. "Did Johann send you fellas?"

"What do you want here, O'Grady?"

"Och. If you're from Johann, then you already know what I'm after."

"We don't know any 'Johann.' Now answer the question."

Hobart smiled. "Well, I'm not particular. Seamus O'Grady is in the import and export business. I buy goods—the kind of goods that are hard to come by, mind you—and see them on their way to my brothers fightin' for the Republican cause. Sometimes I move a little product on the side for some extra spending cash, if you catch my meaning."

The spokesman for the group continued to eye him cautiously. "A gun runner."

"Oh, aye, I've been called that."

"He's a copper," snarled another of the men.

"I'm no lawman," Hobart remarked with a conspiratorial wink. "Though I've a friend or two on the police force; helps to grease the wheels of commerce. Now, if you fellas are looking to acquire some of my merchandise, I'd be happy to oblige. Otherwise, I'd appreciate if you'd allow me to be on my way."

The men exchanged a nervous glance. Hobart knew this was the moment of truth; if he pressed too hard, the men would panic and the opportunity would be lost. He let his invitation hang for a moment then moved as it to continue on his way.

"O'Grady," called the spokesman. "Tomorrow night, behind Gustav's. Come alone and bring samples. Maybe we can do business."

## CHAPTER 3-X MARKS THE SPOT

**Bart Fannow was** a rough man, which was fortunate for he was in a rough business. The polite name for his rough trade was "marine salvage," but the men with whom he worked, and more often than not competed, had little use for politeness. He was a treasure hunter, plain and simple.

The treasures he sought were many and varied. Cumulatively, he had spent years looking for the lost trove of Edward Teach—more popularly known as Blackbeard the Pirate—along the Carolina coast, but the wealth of the legendary buccaneer had proved no less elusive for Fannow than for the thousands of other fortune seekers who combed land and sea for the lost treasure. Hopes and dreams did not pay the bills and maintaining his salvage ship, the Black Spot, required him to use his skills and talents for more mundane tasks, such as recovering the cargo of ships lost to storms and other misadventures.

Fannow was busy making last minute preparations aboard the Black Spot when Betty Dale and Richard Acer arrived on the dock. Normally, the surly skipper had little use for spectators, but this pair was paying handsomely for the privilege of watching him work, and even a modern pirate like Fannow was not immune to the allure of fame.

Acer made a point of running interference for his lovely companion, but Betty was not intimidated by the leering crew of the salvage vessel; she had dealt with more than a few unsavory characters in her years with The Herald, and knew how to use her feminine wiles to both hold the rough bunch at bay and get them to do what she wanted. Nevertheless, Fannow was quick to move his fares to relative seclusion of the Black Spot's bridge.

Betty wasted no time in pumping Fannow for information. "Captain, can you tell us how you plan to find the missing ships?"

"My pleasure, little lady." He directed their attention to a nautical map spread out on a tabletop. "This chart has the position of all the known wrecks along the coast. What we're going to do is run a search pattern back and forth across the area until we find something that isn't supposed to be there."

"It's pretty deep out there. How will you know when you've found it?"

"Well, it's a mite technical, but we'll use our sonar to look for irregularities in the sea floor and then we can lower our magnetometer to see if it's a shipwreck."

"Sounds like looking for a needle in a haystack," Acer remarked.

Fannow grinned, revealing teeth stained by tobacco. "If it was easy, everyone would be doing it. But these modern ships are big and their metal hulls make our job that much easier. I'll warn you though, it's a long, painstaking process and there's no guarantee we'll find anything."

Betty looked at the chart thoughtfully. "What are the chances of finding any of the ships?"

"Well, they're out there, aren't they? More than a dozen ships… it's not a matter of a little needle in a haystack, but several very big needles."

"And what if they aren't there at all?"

Fannow's eyes narrowed suspiciously. "What do you mean?"

"Maybe the ships weren't sunk, but taken by modern pirates or insurance scam artists."

"Missy, these ships met with bad luck, nothing more."

The captain's tone was firm, but Betty could not help but notice that her suggestion had touched a nerve. Captain Fannow knew more than he was letting on.

**Jack Scorza had** not earned his place in the ranks of New York's criminal underworld by being a law-abiding citizen. No matter what Boss Novelli said, they were criminals and gangsters, and breaking the law was their bread and butter.

Novelli's vision for a more legitimate presence in the community had not put Scorza's rackets completely out of business, but it had forced him to go even deeper underground. Where once his gambling clubs had operated almost in plain sight, protected by generous bribes to the cops, now the betting parlors were concealed from view by clever facades, not unlike the speakeasies of the Prohibition era. To further the illusion, the false fronts were not merely so much camouflage, but had to be fully operational businesses in their own right.

Chang's Laundry was just such an endeavor. The inscrutable Chinaman who ran the business actually turned a nice profit, but that was chump change compared to the take from the casino in the sub-basement. Each night, the relatively small betting floor was packed tight with New Yorkers who were all too happy to buy a drink for Lady Luck, and more often than not, walk out empty handed. Although the casino was now empty of patrons, the stale odor of cigarettes hung in the air like a pall. Scorza lit one of his own as he reviewed the previous night's earnings from behind the bar.

"Just couldn't resist, could ya, Jack?"

Scorza's hand flashed to the butt of his holstered automatic, but his bodyguard had already drawn a bead on the intruder. The latter spread his hands in a show of surrender.

"What the hell are you doin' here, Lou?"

Petrona smiled disarmingly. "Trying my luck, Jack old man. Don't worry, I ain't gonna rat you out to the boss. If you want to get your hands dirty, that's none of my business."

"If it's none of your business," Scorza replied, folding his arms over his chest, "then answer the damn question. What the hell are you doing here?"

Petrona kept his hands up as he approached his fellow gangster. "I'm just delivering an invitation. There's gonna be a big meeting tonight to discuss the future of our enterprise. I know how concerned you are about that."

"I don't need to hear another speech about how we're all supposed to be upstanding members of the community."

"Oh, it won't be that, I promise." Petrona sat across the bar from Scorza and slowly reached into his jacket for a cigarette. "There's something big coming, Jack."

"Something big?"

"For men who aren't afraid to take chances and make hard decisions, it will be a chance to take control in a big way—to be kings of the city. Does that sound like something you'd be interested in?"

Scorza was skeptical. "That doesn't sound like Novelli's style."

Petrona blew a cloud into the air and studied the whorls of smoke as they briefly coalesced into bizarre shapes, before making his reply in an ominous voice. "Who said anything about Novelli?"

**If Betty had** entertained fantasies of high-seas adventure, the realities of maritime search and salvage quickly disabused her of the notion. Once the Black Spot was under way, the only thing worse than the tedium of shipboard routine was the pitching of the deck under a constant twelve-foot swell. Betty endured both for a few hours, but as the vessel began running the prescribed search pattern, she retreated to her cabin.

Her attempts at note taking were thwarted by the undulations of the vessel; the mere act of reading was enough to induce nausea. It mattered little though since there was very little to report, and if her suspicions were true, the expedition would return to port empty handed. Resigning herself to inactivity, she laid back on her bunk and tried to take a nap.

A knock roused her from her restless slumber. It was Acer.

"Hey, Betts… oh, you look a little green around the gills."

She managed a wan smile. "Guess this city girl doesn't have sea legs. What have you been up to?"

"I've been photographing the crew at work. Interesting I suppose, but nothing that's going to win me any awards. Feel up for a stroll around the deck?"

"Ugh."

Acer grinned and held out a hand. "Come on, the salt air will do you good."

Her reluctance—and to some degree her seasickness—vanished as soon as she felt his firm grip. Holding his hand no longer felt strange or awkward; instead, it gave her a little thrill.

Aside from the rolling swells, the conditions were fair; the sun shone from a cloudless sky, but a light breeze kept her cool. Acer led the way to the bow of the ship where the blue-gray Atlantic seemed to stretch out forever.

"It's beautiful," she sighed, unconsciously squeezing his hand.

"We might not have much of a story to tell, but at least we're... What's that?"

Betty followed the direction of his glance. There was, quite literally, a dark cloud on the horizon. "Where did that come from?"

The cloud was low, like a fog bank rolling just above the wave tops, and being born on the breeze directly toward them. The vapors were impenetrably black and Betty's first impression was that it was more smoke than cloud. "That doesn't look natural."

Acer made no attempt to hide his concern. "Let's go find Fannow."

The Black Spot was not a large vessel, but the bulkheads of the superstructure hid the bridge from their view as they hastened aft. They had only gone a few steps when a clanking sound drew their attention to a grappling hook that had just dropped over the gunwale. Another just like it leapt into the air from just beyond the low rail and dropped with a metallic thunk a few feet further along.

"We're being boarded!" Betty gasped. Even as she said the words, they sounded ridiculous in her ears; this was the twentieth century, for goodness sake, not the Spanish Main.

Acer rushed to look over the side. "Betty, quick! Warn the captain!"

At that instant, a burly arm reached up from beyond the railing and hauled its host over the side. Acer struck a fighting pose and attacked before the man could gain his feet.

Despite Acer's admonition and her own primal instinct to flee, Betty remained rooted in place. It was not terror's grip that held her, but rather her fascination with the photographer as he transformed from mild mannered journalist into someone very much like... Could it be?

Acer launched into a flurry of punches that drove the boarder back against the gunwale. He might have succeeded in knocking the pirate back into the sea but for the intervention of another man clambering onto the Black Spot. The second intruder delivered a roundhouse that staggered Acer back and gave the first man time to recover his wits. In a flash, both men were on him.

Betty started forward, her concern for her friend's life overriding even her own primitive fear. She howled like a banshee of legend, flailing her fists at the exposed back of one man, but to her surprise, the attacker was already staggering back from Acer. The photographer was still on his feet, crouched low to keep his balance, and directing his blows with expert precision. He caught a glimpse of the blonde reporter, now disheveled from tussling with one of the villains, and flashed her a wink. Betty however simply stared back in amazement, not at his fighting skills, but at the strange flap of skin that now hung from one cheek, exposing a thin metal prosthetic pad.

The strange revelatory moment passed and Acer's attention was once more consumed by the brawny pair of intruders. This time, Betty did not interfere, nor was there a need to. The handsome photographer—if in fact that was what he was—quickly dispatched the already battered pirates, and hoisted them over the side.

When he had finished with them, all she could say was: "Your face is, uh, coming off."

Acer's eyes widened in something like embarrassment and he put his fingers to the loose layer of theatrical make-up and attempted to press it back into place. "Well, I guess my secret is out."

She gave his shoulder a squeeze. "Your secret has always been safe with me."

Acer returned her smile, but then his face hardened and he was strictly business. "That black cloud is getting closer. Something tells me it's no coincidence that the cloud and those clowns showed up at exactly the same moment."

"How did they get here?"

A glance over the side revealed the answer. Floating alongside the Black Spot, tethered by the two lines that were attached to the grapnels and bumping against the vessel's hull, was something that looked like a cross between a convertible roadster and a manta ray.

"It's some kind of mini-sub," Acer observed. "And there's a good chance it's not the only one. Come on, let's tell the captain."

"The captain already knows, Secret Agent X."

Betty and her companion turned to find Fannow and his crew blocking their way. The salvage operator's expression was hard, but not as hard as the cold metal of the revolver in his hand.

The dark cloud settled over the ship with unnatural swiftness; even before the knots binding Betty's wrists were pulled tight, the vessel was shrouded in premature night.

Although the circumstances were dire, Betty felt no fear. She had seen her friend Secret Agent X get out of scrapes that were infinitely more perilous than this, and had helped him thwart villains far more resourceful than this bunch of pirates. Nevertheless, the appearance of the ominous cloud and the boarders who had arrived in the curious mini-sub left her with little doubt that Captain Fannow was nothing more than hired muscle.

"X," she whispered, as soon as the crewmen binding him had finished their work and moved off to attend to other duties. Fannow remained nearby, training a gun on the Agent, but his attention was focused on something happening out in the ocean.

"Don't worry, Betty. I'll get us out of this."

"I'm not worried. But what do you think is going on?"

The man she had known as Richard Acer strained to look over the gunwale. "That mini-sub wasn't alone. There's a whole fleet of them headed this way."

"What about this cloud?" She sniffed. "It smells funny, almost like rusty metal."

"I have a feeling we'll get a chance to ask about that soon."

Fannow swung his attention back to them with a snarl. "Shut up, you."

The captive was unbowed. "What's going on here, Fannow? Who are you working for?"

Fannow spat a gob of tobacco juice over the rail. "It's none of your business, but you'll find out in a few minutes anyway. Until then, keep your yap shut!"

"Or what? You'll shoot me? Something tells me you're being paid to deliver us alive."

"You're right about that, mate. Paid handsomely. But that doesn't mean I can't smash up that face of yours…" Inspiration dawned on the skipper's dull face and he took a step forward. "Or for that matter see what's under it. I've always wondered what the famous Secret Agent X really looks like."

Betty gasped as Fannow gripped the loose piece of plastic skin dangling from her companions face and peeled it away to reveal his true countenance. For a fleeting moment, she considered averting her gaze, allowing her old friend to preserve the secret of his identity, if only from her. She did not however; her curiosity got the better of her and she did not ever blink as the mask was torn away.

He did not look that much different than the man she knew as Richard Acer. The disguise had been little more than a couple of pads to make his cheeks seem fuller, giving the illusion of added years. He was as handsome as he had always been, perhaps even more so, now that Betty no longer felt torn between loyalty to X and attraction to Acer. His defiant gaze was riveted on Fannow, but he caught her staring and winked. Despite their urgent situation, Betty was suffused with hope.

"Well done, Mr. Fannow," came a new voice.

Betty reflexively swung her eyes toward the speaker and saw a group of men wearing black oilskins, identical to the attire worn by the pair of boarders that X had tossed back over the side, striding up the deck. The newcomers advanced and began speaking in hushed tones with the crew of the salvage ship.

"You were right, Betty," Acer observed in a cold voice. "It would seem that pirates still roam the high seas. I think we're looking at the explanation for the missing ships."

"But why?" Betty asked. "And why didn't any of the ships radio for help?"

"The answer to your first question, I'm sure, is the same as it was for Blackbeard and Captain Kidd: simple greed. As to your second, unless I miss my guess, that black cloud is creating some kind of electrical interference that fouls up radio signals. Once the ships are cut off, the pirates can board at their leisure, seize control and sail the ship to a port of their choosing."

Betty pondered the suggestion; she saw only one flaw in her friend's logic. "If Fannow is working with the pirates, why did they use the black cloud to approach his ship?"

"Good question. I can only surmise that they were afraid you or I might somehow get a message off. Or perhaps they didn't trust Captain Fannow." He raised his voice loud enough to be heard by the renegade skipper. "What do you think, Fannow? Do your new partners trust you?"

The skipper's expression was a mixture of guilt and arrogance. "Shut up. You're dead meat and you don't even know it."

Acer smiled defiantly. "Something tells me that you're in a lot more danger right now than we are. Haven't you ever heard the saying that there's no honor among thieves?"

The leader of the boarding party laughed aloud at the comment. "How true, Agent X, though I'm afraid you have done me a grave injustice in calling me a thief."

"The shoe fits," Betty remarked.

"It must seem that way." The man frowned theatrically. "Ah, but where are my manners? My name is Smith—"

"Sure it is."

"Come now, Miss Dale. You are now my guest; please try to behave as one."

"A guest may take their leave whenever they please," observed Acer. "Will we have that privilege? Why don't you just call a spade a spade; we're your hostages."

Smith sighed. "If you insist. Either way, you are coming with me."

"Not until you're square with me," Fannow interjected, emphatically.

"Ah, yes." Smith turned to one of his minions. "Give Mr. Fannow his gold."

The salvage captain stiffened as if expecting treachery, but none was forthcoming. Instead, the oilskin clad boarder signaled to two more of his comrades who in turn began manhandling a large and obviously heavy suitcase onto the aft deck of the Black Spot. Fannow nervously ambled back to inspect the contents and despite the shroud of darkness enveloping the vessel, his face lit up. "A pleasure doing business with you, Mr. Smith. They're all yours."

Betty opened her mouth to hurl a final insult at the modern day pirate, but before a single word could escape, a firm hand clamped over her face. She gasped, involuntarily drawing in a heavy dose of vapor from the ether soaked rag in her captor's grip, and everything in her world began to spin crazily and faded slowly to nothing.

**The intruders left** the Black Spot as swiftly and silently as they had arrived. Mr. Smith quickly settled into the control seat of his manta-like mini-sub and slid the heavy transparent cover into place in preparation for submerged travel.

"Well done," commented the man in the second seat. "A nearly perfect execution."

"Nearly, mein herr? I thought everything went exactly as planned."

"The captain's curiosity may jeopardize our security. Will he be able to resist telling the world that he has seen the face of Secret Agent X? I think not. Sink his ship immediately, while the cloud persists. Leave no survivors."

"It will be done, mein herr." Smith knew better than to question his passenger. He toggled the control switch to fill the ballast tanks and the sea quickly swallowed the craft. The black submarine hummed as its screws churned to life, and under the deft touch of its pilot, the undersea vessel circled around beneath the hull of the salvage ship until it was presented with a broadside target. Without hesitation, he released two small torpedoes, then peeled away to escape the concussions from the underwater detonations. The blast slapped the small craft, jostling its occupants in their seats, but did no real damage. The same could not be said for the Black Spot.

The salvage vessel's death came swiftly. The sea poured into the gaping holes in its hull, which weakened by the force of the explosions split into three pieces as is heeled over and slid beneath the swells. Smith brought his craft around for a single pass to scan for survivors but saw only debris floating on the surface. If any her crew succeeded in abandoning the doomed ship, they were sucked down by the cavitations and sped along to the same fate.

"Mark the location," the passenger commented. "And send back a salvage team for the gold. It won't be of any use to the good Captain Fannow."

## CHAPTER 4-UNDER THE GUNS

**Jim Hobart was** understandably anxious as he threaded his sedan into the narrow alley behind the tavern, but his concern had less to do with the approaching rendezvous with the men he believed might be spies for a foreign power than with the simple fact that he was transporting a small arsenal of illegal guns. For the former policeman, the idea of breaking the law, even in the interest of exposing a greater crime, left him ill at ease. But gaining the trust of these criminals required him to lay aside some of his inhibitions; if ever the end justified the means, it was here and now.

He pulled the sedan in close to the building and got out. One of the men from the group he had spoken with earlier was waiting. "What you got, O'Grady?"

"And top of the evenin' to you too my foine man," Hobart answered with a roguish grin. He opened the sedan's boot to reveal several firearms laid out for inspection. "I wasn't sure what you'd be wantin', so I brought a little bit of everythin'. Most of my customers like this one, the Thompson submachine gun, but for my money, a single well placed shot is more effective than spraying a whole drumfull of bullets. This here is the M-1 Garand rifle, semi-automatic, gas-operated, air-cooled; the perfect weapon for the infantryman—"

"Is this all you brought?" the man asked, peevishly. "I thought you wanted to do business with us?"

"Well sir, not knowing what you need them for, I thought a general sampling would do the trick. If you could perhaps give me some idea—"

"Never mind. Get in, we're going for a drive."

Hobart's instincts immediately sounded an alarm, but there was little he could do to take control of the situation. Gripping the wheel, he steeled his nerves for whatever lay ahead. The other man got into the passenger seat and grunted out a series of directions that took them well away from the German neighborhood and to the Brooklyn docks. Even at this late hour, the docks were alive with activity, but Hobart was ordered to pass by the busy longshoremen. Their destination lay in a section of the waterfront that had fallen into disuse and was, to all appearances, utterly abandoned.

"Stop here," the man growled as the sedan pulled up in front of a dark warehouse. "Flash your headlights two times."

Hobart complied, noting as he did, that the streets around the building were deserted; not a soul was in evidence. To his surprise however, the large bay doors of the warehouse began to swing open like the maw of some great shadow beast.

"Drive inside."

The red-headed detective swallowed down his trepidation and did as instructed. As the sedan slid into the cavernous enclosure, a group of men wearing the standard garb of laborers issued from the dark recesses and surrounded the vehicle. The passenger got out and greeted them in coarse-sounding German. He then leaned back inside and addressed Hobart. "Get out."

Hobart did as instructed, careful not to look any of the men square in the eye. There was nothing to be gained by a show of resistance. One of the men briskly searched him, immediately uncovering a forty-five caliber semi-automatic in the waistband of his trousers.

"What's this?"

"I'm an arms dealer," Hobart confessed. "You don't think I'd go out without using some of me own wares, do ye?"

The searcher snarled and pocketed the pistol. Hobart frowned at being deprived of his sidearm, but was secretly pleased that the impromptu frisking had not revealed the snub-nosed .38 in an ankle holster. "I'll be wantin' that back, boyo."

"Hehe. Sure."

"Enough chatter," intoned the first man—the one that had escorted him to the docks. "Our guests are due any minute. Get the guns from the boot. There's not much, but it will have to do."

The investigator didn't like the sound of that one bit, but decided to stay in character a little longer. "Ah, a little test fire, is it?"

"Shut up. Dieter, put our friend somewhere out of the way."

The man that had searched him frowned. "Why not just—?"

"'Cause I'm in charge, dumkopf. We have to be quiet, get it?"

"Ja," grumbled Dieter. He grabbed Hobart's arm and without further commentary steered his captive away from the sedan.

The detective's heart was pounding now. He had no illusions about the fate that lay in store and his mind was racing to plan an escape. Nevertheless, for all the danger he was now facing, he realized that he had failed to uncover anything more than criminal activity.

"Och," he blurted hastily. "You're missing a grand opportunity, fellas. There's not another arms dealer in the city who'll sell to Nazis, you know."

The leader of the group did not deign to answer, but at his shoulder, Dieter snarled: "We've already got all the guns we need, you dumb Mick."

Aha, thought Hobart. So it is true. Now I just have to figure out how to get out of here with my skin.

The rest of the group added Hobart's contraband weapons to their own arsenal before dispersing to various points throughout the warehouse. From the niche where Dieter now kept him under guard with his own .45, the investigator saw two men still standing in the open: the man that had brought him here, and a nattily dressed fellow who looked tougher than all the others combined.

"You know what to do?"

The man in the suit nodded, assuredly. "Leave it to me, Karl."

Even from a distance, Hobart recognized the second man; it was Luigi Petrona, a noteworthy figure in the city's underworld. Before he could fully digest the significance of this, the warehouse was abruptly filled with light as a car pulled inside, followed by several more. Hobart's curiosity quickly supplanted his trepidation; he had stumbled into something big.

The scene on the warehouse floor unfolded quickly. The occupants of the small parade of cars emerged like spiders, eager to pounce on some unwary insect trapped in a web. The investigator recognized several more faces; all of them notorious mob bosses—a veritable Who's Who of organized crime in Gotham—and each one accompanied by two or more tough-looking young men who openly brandished Tommy-guns and pistols. The bodyguards eyed one another suspiciously as the assembly moved toward the center where Petrona and the German, Karl, now waited, bait for the trap.

"What's this about, Lou?" Hobart recognized the deep rumbling voice of Boss Aldo Novelli, the legendary kingpin that had single-handedly reformed the Mafia.

"Boss, glad you could make it. I see everyone's here." Petrona's grin was as slick and sincere as a snake-oil salesman. He took a step back and pitched his voice loud enough for all to hear, "Gentleman, I'm sure you wondering why I brought you all here—why we didn't just have this little meeting on more familiar turf. Well, there's a good reason for that and I'll tell you about it in just a minute."

"Who's this guy?" inquired one of the Mafiosi—Jack Scorza, if Hobart was not mistaken—jabbing a thumb in Karl's direction.

"I was just getting to that, Jack. But first, I want to tell you all about a little business proposition.

"Fellas, we run the city. Make no mistake about it; nothing happens here unless we say so. With that kind of power comes the responsibility to protect our people and our turf." Petrona nodded to Novelli. "You've done great things for us and the city, Boss. We couldn't have got this far with out you.

"But no matter how respectable we become, we're always wanted men; criminals, operating outside the law. I'm here to tell you that it doesn't have to be that way anymore."

Scorza sneered. "You brought me here for this?"

"Hear me out, Jack." Petrona offered a placating smile and held up a hand. "I know what you're thinking; we've had to make so many sacrifices to earn even a little bit of respectability. And some of us—" He winked at Scorza—"haven't really given up the old ways at all.

"I'm talking about something completely different, though. A whole New Order of things, where we are the kings of the city; not hiding in the shadows and the back rooms anymore."

Novelli shook his head sadly. "Lou, after all we've done together… I can't believe you are so quick to embrace these delusions of grandeur."

Petrona continued, ignoring the barb. "The city—all of America, in fact—is headed for a change; a big change. Those of us who see it coming will be in the best position to seize power when that day finally arrives, and believe me friends, it's close.

"The man at my side is Karl Heissler, an envoy of sorts representing the interests of the German Third Reich…"

Hobart sucked in an involuntary breath, as did several of the mobsters at the center of the warehouse.

"A damned Nazi spy!" raged one of the capos.

"Not a spy," replied Heissler. "I am as American as any of you, and I want what's best for America. And what's best for America, my friends, is change."

"The Nazis are no better than Il Duce's fascista. Our brothers are fighting against them in Sicily, and now you expect us to join with them?"

"Mussolini fights what he fears," answered Heissler, evenly. "And he is right to fear your kinsman, for they are strong and have the will of the people. My Fuehrer sees the potential in you men. He cannot mind the day-to-day affairs of an empire that spans the ocean; for that he needs strong and capable governors who have already proven their ability. In every city on the East coast, men like yourselves have accepted this grand privilege. Join our crusade now, and I promise that you will, quite literally, be kings of this city."

"Basta!"

The thunderous declaration seemed to rattle the tin walls of the immense warehouse. Every eye turned to Novelli who now stood directly in front of his wayward lieutenant.

"I cannot believe you have listened to this man's lies, Petrona." He faced off with Heissler. "You are going to overthrow America, are you? And how, pray tell, will you accomplish that? With a handful of treacherous wiseguys?"

The German's smile was a blade spreading across his face. "I'm sure you'll understand that the details of the plan are not something we can share with those who do not embrace this vision."

"You've already said too much." Novelli turned away in disgust and headed for his car.

"Does he speak for the rest of you?" Heissler asked.

The mob boss stopped in his tracks and slowly turned to look at the group. His eyes searched the men's faces—each one well known, yet somehow in this moment, completely unknowable. The mobsters themselves seemed unsure of what to do, but gradually, as if moved by an invisible current, they began to gravitate—some to Petrona, some to Novelli.

In his hiding place, Hobart's heart felt like a lump of lead in his chest. This is exactly what they wanted, he thought. Winnow out the ones who will never work for the Nazis and... oh, no!

As if in response to his mental turmoil, Dieter's attention—and more importantly the barrel of the automatic—shifted away from Hobart and toward the scene unfolding a few yards away. Though he was helpless to prevent what was sure to be a bloodbath, in that moment, stretched like taffy into infinity, he saw his chance to get away.

His captor may have outweighed him by a good forty pounds, but Hobart was a veteran of the New York Police Department, and had learned a thing or two about taking down rowdies twice his size. The important thing was the gun....

On the floor before him, and from the shadows at the perimeter of the building, a flutter of gunmetal being readied for lethal action broke the stillness. The crime boss sensed it; it was evident in his eyes as he suddenly broke for the relative cover afforded by his sedan. His bodyguard moved in slow motion, vacillating between loyalty and fear—fight or flight—and in that fateful moment became more a target than a combatant. Dieter stabbed the automatic in the direction of the meeting, drawing a bead perhaps on Novelli himself. His finger tensed and grew tight on the trigger, and then with what seemed like an almost painful effort, the steel lever began to rock back....

Hobart hammered his bunched fists into a point at the base of Dieter's skull. He held nothing back and the blow instantly paralyzed the German saboteur. The gun fell impotently from fingers that were now spread out as if genuflecting, and Hobart deftly caught the weapon before it could clatter to the ground.

His decisive action might have prevented Dieter from claiming the kill shot, but there was little he could do to prevent the other snipers from firing fatal rounds at the mob boss and his loyal lieutenants. Thunder roared in the tin walled enclosure as Thompsons and Garands lashed out at the unsuspecting mobsters. Hobart caught a glimpse of Novelli twisting under the impact of dozens of rounds and sprawling headlong mere inches from his idle sedan, which was likewise now riddled with bullet holes.

Hobart threw himself to the rough concrete floor and began crawling on his belly out toward the loose circle of cars. The battle was an assault on his senses.

His ears were already ringing from the explosive concussions of near-constant gunfire. The air above his head was humming as bullets split the air, and smoke and dust formed a noxious miasma that burned in his throat. He did not look up to assess which faction was emerging victorious, though it wasn't hard to guess; the ambushing Nazi agents had the dual advantages of surprise and concealment even before the first shot was fired, but the support of roughly half of the mobsters assembled—those who had chosen to stand with Petrona against Boss Novelli— added superiority of numbers to the equation. With Novelli dead in the first salvo, the surviving loyal members of his coterie were demoralized, fighting only to save their own skins.

The red-haired detective scrambled underneath one of the parked sedans, where he paused to gather his wits and plan his next move. The gunfire was slacking off as the victorious group laid aside their submachine guns and began a more traditional exchange of pot shots from the relative safety of cover. Hobart ignored the occasional report as he did the cries of the wounded who lay in the killing zone, and focused instead on the large door leading out to the street. The path to escape was still shrouded in darkness; the only illumination in the warehouse had been from the headlights of the various automobiles, some of which had been shot out in the skirmish, and all of those were directed away from the exit. The threshold and freedom lay only about twenty-five yards from where he hid, a distance he could cover in a couple seconds, but it would be two seconds where he would be fully exposed to the guns of both groups.

"Well, it's not as if there's an alternative," he grumbled, summoning up his courage.

He scooted his prone form to the rear edge of the sedan's undercarriage and waited for the combatants to exchange one more round of gunfire before springing erect and making his mad dash.

Somebody must have noticed, because he got no more than three steps before a shout went up and muzzles erupted in his direction. He felt bullets tugging the air all around and something slapped his upper right arm but he did not slow down or even cast a glance to see how bad the wound was. With his great strides, he needed only a couple more steps...not even one more second...to escape the battlefield.

Natural darkness enfolded him as he crossed beneath the high lintel and caught his first breath of air not poisoned by the stench of cordite. His legs continued pumping, but his heart was already singing the song of freedom.

Made it!

But then something slammed into his back and he went sprawling.

## CHAPTER 5-BEHIND THE MASK

**For a long** time, Betty drifted close to the surface of consciousness, but always it remained just out of reach. Occasionally, her eyes would flutter open—or at least she believed them to be open—but all that she saw before sinking back into somnolence was utter, immeasurable darkness.

It was her own shivering that brought her fully awake, how long after her abduction she could not say. She sat bolt upright as memories rushed into the void like ocean waves into a footprint on the sand. Her teeth were chattering from the frigid environment, and although someone had spread a coarse wool blanket over her, it had fallen away at some point during her slumber. Still shivering, she snatched it up and wrapped it around her torso. Only then did she take in her surroundings.

She could think of no better way to describe the room than to call it a prison cell. Roughly cubic in dimensions, there was only one door, set directly in the center of one wall, and one bare light bulb, hanging from the ceiling overhead, which did little to illuminate the black walls of the cell. The only furnishings in the room were two thin mattresses, situated opposite the door. Betty sat on one, huddled beneath her blanket, and a similarly wrapped form occupied the second. She let out a squeak of relief as she realized who the occupant of the other mat was.

"X!" She knelt over him, pulling back the coverlet to reveal his now familiar face. What she saw caused her moment of elation to wilt.

The man she knew as both Agent X and Richard Acer had been beaten severely. Dark bruises colored his cheeks and a ragged weal was visible around his neck, as if someone had tried to throttle him and stopped just short of his death.

"X," she said again in a more subdued tone. "Wake up, X."

His eyes fluttered once, then he started, twisting away from the glare of the overhead light and throwing his hands up to protect himself from an imagined threat.

"X, it's me. Betty Dale."

But her pleas seemed to fall on deaf ears. He shrank away from her. "Stay back."

Chagrined, she complied, drawing back to her own mattress while her friend's wild eyes darted about the interior of the cell.

"What is this place?"

"I was hopin' you could tell me, X."

His gaze fixed on her. "Why do you keep calling me that?"

The question hit her like a slap. Why would he ask her that? "Because… That's what you call yourself. Secret Agent X."

His eyebrows came together in a frown of deep concern. "I… What's my name? My real name?"

"I don't know," she replied, her heart suddenly feeling as cold and heavy as the air in the room. "Oh, geez X. You've got amnesia."

He shook his head as if her statement was irrelevant. "You know me. You must know my name. It's…it's right on the tip of my tongue. If you could just tell me, I'd know it if I heard it."

"But X, no one knows your name, leastwise I don't think anyone knows." The plea in his eyes made her hazard a guess. "Is it Richard? Is Richard Acer your real name?"

"You only know me as Secret Agent X? I can't believe that I would have kept the secret from you." He frowned again, but then extended a hand to brush a stray blond ringlet away from her face. His fingers then alit on her cheek. "I feel a connection to you; I feel that we are very close."

"Oh, yes X. We are. I think you must be my best friend in the whole world. You remember, don't you?"

His hand lingered a moment longer, the touch somehow electric, but the spark was not enough. "I don't remember anything. I have no idea where we are or how we got here."

"Well, I can help you with the last part." She briefly related the events leading up to their capture by the strange submariners.

"Why don't I remember any of this?"

"They knocked me out with ether or something. When I woke up, we were both in here, but they must have separated us at some point. You look pretty beat up. They might have…"

The word tortured caught in her throat, but he seemed to understand. "They must have injected me with a truth serum. Sometimes those drugs can block memories."

"You remembered that," she remarked.

He nodded. "The drugs inhibit the part of the brain that houses our identity, but the skills we learn—everything from how to walk and talk to complex systems of knowledge—remain available. Wouldn't do much good to make a person forget how to speak English if you wanted information from them, would it?"

"I guess not. Do you know what they wanted from you?"

His frown returned. "I don't remember that either. I have no way of knowing if they made me talk or not. Betty, you have to help me remember; I can feel the memories right there, like a bubble waiting to burst. Help me remember who I am?"

His plea wrenched at her heart. "Oh, X. I simply don't know. I know that you are brave and noble, and that you always stand up for justice and help the oppressed. I know that you can look like anyone you want to, and I know that you've saved my skin, and probably everyone in the city as well, more times than I can count."

"A name," he groaned. "Tell me my name Betty, please!"

"I just don't know, X. Gosh, how I wish I did."

Suddenly the door exploded inward with a clang of metal on metal and two men in dark uniforms rushed in, followed by a third who brandished some kind of carbine; Betty thought it looked like a machine gun. X hopped to his feet, striking a fighter's stance and faced off, but the two unarmed men simply moved to either side of him and let the man with the gun handle the situation.

"Back off, or the first shot goes through your little girlfriend."

X lowered his hands, but his face remained hard as iron. "What do you want?"

"Come along peacefully and nothing happens to the girl."

The agent turned to her. "Don't worry, Betty. I'll think of something."

A wan smile fluttered across her lips. "You always do."

But as the three guards marched him through the door, leaving her alone in the cold cell, she could only huddle under the blanket and hope.

Mr. Smith watched the entire scene unfold through a view port cleverly disguised as an air vent. As the door to the cell slammed shut, he likewise closed the cover on his peephole and turned to his superior. "I fear we may have taken away too much of 'Secret Agent X's memory," he said with a wry grin.

The other man did not look pleased. "We must have information about the Agent's network. It is critical to our plan."

"What should we do?"

The man took a deep breath and let it out in a heavy sigh. "After another lengthy—and perhaps a little more bloody—session of interrogation, we will put them together once more. Perhaps something will come to her mind while she waits alone in the darkness."

"Darkness?"

The man offered a cold, cruel smile. "Oh, yes. By all means, turn out the lights on Miss Dale."

**Jim Hobart struggled** to draw a breath as he was roughly hauled to his feet and dragged away from the warehouse entrance. The suddenness with which he had been brought down and the impact with the ground, which had driven the wind from his lungs left him feeling dislocated and vulnerable. Vulnerable indeed to both the bullets that still sizzled through the air of the warehouse and to the dark stranger that now pulled him away from the battle scene.

"Stop!" he managed to gasp after they had gone half a block. There seemed to be no sign of pursuit.

"Not a chance." The deep voice was very familiar. "If they're not already after us, then it's just a matter of time before they start."

Hobart panted a few times, and through a few more steps, then managed to croak out a single word. "Novelli?"

The other man pulled him into an alley, out of direct line of sight from the warehouse entrance, and allowed him a rest break. "Heh, that's right."

"You were shot; I saw it with my own eyes."

"Yeah? They got you too, kid, but you're still on your feet."

"I guess so," Hobart answered, unconvinced. "Why did you save me?"

The mob boss looked him up and down. "You ain't one of my guys. So when I saw you running, I wondered to myself: 'Why's this guy trying to escape?' Something told me you weren't working with Petrona or those Nazis."

"You're right about that."

"So anyways, I figured helping you out was the best way to get some answers."
Novelli glanced around the corner, back toward the warehouse, now shrouded in
eerie silence. "Let's get moving. I know a place where we can get patched up, and
you can tell me what's what."

Hobart nodded and they moved off briskly, traveling away from the docks and
hiked a few blocks deeper into the city. Every step away from the scene of the
bloody massacre made the young detective feel a little better, but when the mob
boss ushered him into a dark brownstone apartment some two miles from the
waterfront, his apprehension returned. "Maybe I should just catch a cab…"

The saturnine Don fixed him with a steely gaze. "I think we want the same
thing, kid, but it's up to you."

Hobart glanced into the dark room beyond. "Are you sure it's safe here?"

"Pretty sure. Petrona doesn't know about this place, none of them do." Novelli stepped inside and held the door open. "Come on. At least let me patch up that
arm."

At that, the red-haired investigator looked down and realized that he had for
some time kept his left hand clasped over the aching wound in his right arm. His
fingers, like his coat sleeve, were sticky with blood. He nodded and followed the
larger man inside. With the door securely locked, the two men moved through the
apartment to the kitchen where a light was finally turned on.

Novelli gestured to a table. "Have a seat. Let me get you something to drink; it
might help dull the pain. What's your poison?"

"Whatever you're having," Hobart grunted, prying his fingers away from his
arm. He wrestled out of his ruined tweed jacket and then peeled away the cloth
fabric of his shirt to expose the wound. Despite the pain and swelling, the bullet
had done little more than crease his arm; there appeared to be no damage to the
deep muscle tissue.

Novelli set two tumblers on the tabletop then pulled a chair alongside his guest
in order to begin ministering to the young man's injury. The detective took a
grateful sip of the substance—a heady sweet whiskey—and then glanced at his
benefactor. "What about you? I know you took a round or two back there."

"Believe it or not, kid, I got lucky tonight." He considered his words and
laughed derisively. "Lucky? Ha! Months of work to put an end to the gang wars,
and in a single night, it's all gone."

"Not all gone. They didn't get you."

"They might as well have." Novelli began mopping Hobart's wound with an
antiseptic soaked cloth. "What's your story kid? What were you doing there?"

"I suppose there's no harm in telling you. I'm James Hobart, a private investigator."

"A private dick? How'd you get mixed up in all this?"

"I was retained by… well, I probably shouldn't tell you that… Suffice it to say,
I was hired to look into the possibility that foreign saboteurs might be active on

American soil."

"Heh, I'd say you hit pay dirt. Nazi spies, can you believe it?"

"If I hadn't seen it with my own eyes," Hobart agreed. "But what I can't figure out is what they're after. Why set the gangsters, if you'll pardon the expression, at each other's throats?"

"That's the sixty-four dollar question." Novelli snugged a bandage into place on his arm. "All done, kid. Stay out of gunfights for a week or two and you'll be good as new."

"Thanks, I'll do my best. What about you?"

Novelli sighed and sat back in his chair. "I'm gonna have to lay low for a while. But I'm not completely on my own, and I am not gonna let that rat Petrona get away with this."

Hobart nodded then got to his feet. "Well, be careful Mr. Novelli. I can't say I approve of what you are, but you seem like a good man."

"Thanks kid. Believe it or not, I think we both want the same thing."

The Don guided him back through the dark house to the front door where Hobart, wearing a grimace of pain, nonetheless shook his host's hand. "Good luck."

"You too, kid. And tell your boss that he should give you a little extra for hazard pay."

Hobart chuckled dutifully then exited the apartment, eager to get back to the relative safety of his own flat, and even more so to make a full report to Mr. A.J. Martin. What had once seemed a ludicrous notion, namely that Nazi sleeper agents were at work in the city, had been proved dangerously true. Worse still, they had already struck the first blow in a diabolical scheme to control organized crime in the city.

But to what end? wondered Hobart as he hiked down the dark street.

It was the same question that perplexed the man who watched the red-haired investigator from the shadows of the darkened brownstone apartment. When Hobart was no longer visible, he moved back inside and took a seat before a large three-way vanity mirror. He studied his reflection for a long time, noting with grim amusement the craggy worry lines that creased his forehead.

"Well Aldo, we gave it a good go. Pity it didn't work out."

**Although she did** not sleep, nightmares visited Betty in the absolute darkness of her cell. Against a backdrop of unnatural night, the cinema of her imagination played an unending montage of terror, waking dreams in which her friend, Secret Agent X, was subjected to unspeakable tortures. How long she endured these torments of her own devising, she could not say. The void was utterly unchanging, without sight or sound. She tried talking, just to hear something other than the chattering of her own teeth, but her words were like stones cast into a bottomless pit.

When the light bulb overhead did eventually blink on, its glare was like the brilliance of the sun, and Betty shrank beneath her blanket as if the illumination might burn her skin. But even before her eyes could adjust to the light, the sound of something being dragged across the floor prompted her to peek out from her shelter. She could just make out the silhouettes of two men dragging a third between them. The unconscious man was dropped unceremoniously on the second mattress and the pair of captors hastened from the room.

"X? Are you okay?" Even as she asked the question, she was kneeling beside him, his hand clasped in hers. She was still squinting against the brilliance of the overhead light, but even through the blur, she could see dark bruises and a ragged weal on his cheek. One of his eyes was black and swollen and his lips were oozing blood. Nevertheless, his eyelids fluttered open and he gazed up at her.

"Betty? You… look good."

Before she could even contemplate how to respond to that comment, the door flew open again. One of the men she had seen earlier entered and placed a tray, with a bowl of water and a towel, on the floor. Another man—Mr. Smith, the apparent leader of the pirate gang—stepped past the orderly and approached to within a few steps of Betty and the agent.

"I request the pleasure of your company at breakfast."

Betty couldn't believe her ears. "You're insane. You've beaten him nearly to death, and you think we're going to eat with you?"

"Actually, the invitation was for you alone, Miss Dale. I am satisfied that you are not a witting accomplice in the schemes of Secret Agent X."

"Well you can take a flying leap for all I care. I wouldn't eat with you if I was starving to death."

Smith offered a humorless smile. "Come now, Miss Dale. Surely you are curious about this place, and about who I am. This is your chance to interview me; imagine the scoop."

"As if you have any intention of letting me go."

"Miss Dale, my invitation stands. I shall have one of my men return in five minutes for your answer."

Betty jumped to her feet and took a step toward the other man, surprising him with her ferocity. "I can give you my answer right now," she said, fury rising into her throat.

"Betty…" The sound of the agent's voice, a barely audible croak, instantly defused the building explosion. "You should go."

Smith took that as his cue to leave and vanished through the door before Betty could say another word. She knelt again at the agent's side. "I won't leave you."

"Listen to me. I need you to be my eyes and ears. Remember everything he says and pay attention to everything he shows you. This might be our chance to figure out what he's up to and just maybe how to escape."

Betty bit her lip nervously. "I don't know if I can do it, X."

He smiled up at her, and a bead of blood oozed from his split lip. "You can, Betty. I believe in you."

Betty felt as though her heart might break, and indeed, it might very well have literally done so if, in that moment, she had learned the truth about her companion.

## CHAPTER 6—IN THE LION'S DEN

**A hot cup** of coffee was waiting for Inspector John Burks as he entered the scene of what newshounds were already calling "the Midnight Massacre." Unfortunately, the hand that proffered the steaming beverage belonged to the last person on earth that Burks wanted to talk to.

"Agent Greaves," he muttered, and though he said nothing more, the implicit question was: What are you doing here?

Greaves tended his best disarming smile. "Don't worry about me, Inspector. I am just a curious lawman, watching New York's finest at work. I have no intention of interfering."

"See that you don't," Burks growled. "Thanks for the coffee."

It was only their second meeting face to face. Greaves had stopped by the Inspector's office the previous afternoon in order to read the police department's exhaustive file on Secret Agent X. Few words had been exchanged and it was plainly evident that Burks did not want the G-man meddling in local police business. Policemen were notoriously territorial and typically resisted ceding their jurisdiction to federal officers, so even though Greaves had full legal authority to do whatever he pleased, he often found it helpful to play nice—at least at the outset. A cup of coffee didn't cost very much, but it might yield enormous dividends of trust and cooperation.

"I was still reading the Agent X file when the call came in," he explained. "Quite a gruesome scene."

Burks took a sip from the coffee as he strode into the center of the warehouse, getting his first glimpse of the slaughter. Gruesome didn't begin to describe it. The floor was sticky with drying blood—gallons of it, by the look—which had flowed from eight different victims who now lay contorted in their death throes along the east wall of the warehouse.

"Back before I ever joined the Bureau, I read stories about shoot-outs like this: Dillinger, or Bonnie and Clyde, shot up like Swiss cheese. Nothing can prepare you for seeing the real thing though."

"Agent Greaves, aren't you supposed to be hunting Secret Agent X?"

The young G-man smiled again. "It occurred to me that he might have had a hand in this."

Burks harrumphed. "If you'd read those files, you'd know that he rarely uses firearms."

"Ah, yes. His infamous knock-out gas gun; we retrieved it from the crime scene in Washington."

"We've captured one or two along the way as well. He always makes a new one. This kind of wanton violence isn't his style."

Greaves was pleased that the Inspector was finally talking to him and decided not to press the matter. "Any idea who these victims are?"

"As a matter of fact, we've identified several; mobsters, one and all. There had been a standing truce between the different mob factions, but I'd say that's over now."

"I wonder what set it off?"

Burks gestured to the corpses with his coffee cup. "There's a lot we can learn from them. But it's the ones that aren't here who can probably tell us the whole story."

"Meaning?"

"These men were all loyal to Aldo Novelli, so whoever knocked these guys off is probably gunning for their boss as well."

"So I expect you'll be paying him a visit soon? Mind if I tag along?"

The inspector fixed him with a frown. "Already losing interest in the hunt for X?"

"I actually did read the files, Inspector; they were quite instructive. Secret Agent X has a habit of sticking his nose into this sort of situation. I'm betting he will end up coming to us."

**Jack Scorza had** not slept at all since the fateful meeting at the warehouse, and despite his best attempts to drown the images of horror and betrayal in hard liquor, he was still haunted by the clamor of gunfire. He had hastened from the aftermath of Petrona's bold move against Novelli, seeking refuge at his casino, fearful of any possible retribution from the faction loyal to the crime boss.

If there's any left, he thought mordantly. Indeed, Petrona had planned his strike perfectly. Novelli had been taken completely by surprise. Yet, despite Scorza's own ambitions against the Don, he was not altogether pleased at the turn of events. Too bad that being on the winning side means getting in bed with those Nazis. Sometimes it's better to go with the devil you know.

He downed another slug of whiskey and settled into his desk chair.

"Heavy thoughts, Jack?"

Scorza froze in his chair as the voice—a deep baritone that could only be coming from the grave—enveloped him in icy tendrils of fear. He started from his seat, but the voice along with an iron grip on his shoulder, held him fast.

"Don't even think about it." The voice was unquestionably Novelli's. But how can that be? Novelli is dead.

"How did you get in here? My guards—"

"I'd say that's the least of your worries, Jack. I thought about killing you the moment you walked in here, but unlike Luigi, I've got respect for the old ways. But if you so much as twitch, I'll send you straight to hell."

"Sure, boss. Not a muscle. You know I had nothing to do with it, right? It was all Luigi's idea. None of us knew he was gonna betray you."

"Really? I didn't see you jumping to my defense last night."

"It was survival, boss. He had the drop on you and if I'd stood up for you, I'd be dead right now." Scorza winced as he said it, knowing that the switch in allegiance had merely postponed his fate.

"So you'd rather be a Nazi stooge?"

The question surprised the gangster. Why did Novelli care about that? "Of course not. I don't think any of us want that."

"What happened afterward? After the shooting stopped?"

"That other guy—the Nazi—talked for a while about what we should do next."

"And that was what?" Novelli pressed.

"Wait. Get organized and be ready for the next phase. He didn't say what that was."

"That's all you know?"

"I swear it, boss."

"Then I guess you're of no further use to me."

Too late, Scorza realized his mistake. "Wait—"

The mobster slumped in his seat, but there had been no gunshot. The only wound he had suffered was a tiny pinprick on the back of his exposed neck; an injection of a fast acting anesthetic, which when coupled with the alcohol already in his system would leave him unconscious for the better part of the morning.

A few minutes later however, Jack Scorza walked past the bodyguards stationed outside his private office. "Gonna go for a walk boys. Hold down the fort while I'm gone."

**Secret Agent X** ducked into an alley behind the Chinese laundry that fronted Scorza's casino and quickly peeled off the disguise. That Scorza was not part of the conspiracy came as something of a relief; it was bad enough that his most loyal lieutenant had completely fooled him. Then again, who could have anticipated that foreign spies would attempt to seize control of the New York underworld?

The betrayal was a bitter pill to swallow, not because he had ever really trusted Petrona, but because it represented the total destruction of months of hard work. It had been his boldest undertaking, and success had seemed almost within reach; the mob was reforming itself and gang violence had almost entirely ceased. Now it was all in ruins.

It had been a long and strange journey. He had not intended to assume the identity of the number one crime boss in the city, but when Novelli—the real Aldo Novelli—had begun taking strides to legitimize the powerful underworld organization and turn it into a force for positive change in the city, the Agent had begun working to support that noble endeavor. At first he did so indirectly, feeding Novelli information about his enemies both within and without. Later, in the guise of a philanthropist who shared that vision, he had begun working directly with the widowed Sicilian Mafia don to bring that grand vision to fruition.

Then fate had struck a blow. While the two men were vacationing away from the city, developing strategies for the next phase of the plan, Novelli had suffered a debilitating stroke. Not willing to let the vision suffer the same paralysis that left the Don a bed-ridden invalid, the Agent acted quickly by assuming Novelli's identity. For nearly six months, he had lived in Novelli's house, worn his clothes and managed his affairs, without arousing the suspicion of his subordinates. The alter-ego had consumed every waking hour, but the dividend it had paid was worth the sacrifice: an end to organized crime in the city.

But now something much worse than the mob had sunk its teeth into the Big Apple.

X returned to his specially modified sedan—a vehicle that he had used but rarely during the sixth months in which he had posed as Novelli—and drove a few blocks to a plumbing supply store that doubled as Luigi Petrona's personal headquarters. During the time in which Petrona had served as his right-hand man, the Agent had carefully observed the man's habits; he always went out for a cup of coffee and a newspaper at 9:30 every day. Like clockwork, exactly five minutes after X pulled up, the new reigning king of organized crime stepped out onto the sidewalk. X waited until the mobster turned the corner before exiting his car.

His suit and topcoat were enough like the garments typically worn by Petrona to survive a casual inspection, and the mask of cosmetic putty that had reshaped his face was so perfect as to make such scrutiny unlikely. Nevertheless, he moved briskly, always aware that the clock was ticking.

One of Petrona's men, sitting behind the sales counter, looked up as he entered and his face registered surprise at the boss' early return.

"Forgot something," the Agent muttered, without breaking stride. He heard the man grunt in acknowledgement and settle back onto his stool. The Agent closed the office door firmly and went to work.

He moved through the office like a whirlwind, yet strangely when he finished searching a drawer or a stack of papers, everything was returned to exactly the place it had been before. In less than five minutes, he had thoroughly combed the room, even rifling the contents of the small wall safe hidden behind a picture from the Brown & Bigelow "Dogs Playing Poker" series. Yet, through it all, he found nothing to link Petrona to the group of spies that had helped orchestrate the massacre at the warehouse.

He checked his wristwatch. Petrona wouldn't return for another ten minutes or so, but there was always a chance that the guard who doubled as a salesman for the plumbing shop might get curious and come calling. He settled into Petrona's desk chair and tried to imagine the double-crossing Mafioso making the call to his Nazi counterpart.

His gaze fell upon a business card tucked in the corner of a desk blotter. He had noticed it earlier; the simple block letters read: "Carl Harris, Butcher and Seller of Fine Meats" along with an address on Canarsie Street and a telephone number.

"Carl Harris. Karl Heissler?" The Agent rose from the chair and pocketed the card. He wasn't going to find anything else in the office to incriminate Petrona, but his intuition told him that he had already found what he was looking for. He picked up a determined stride as he passed through the office door, nodded to the guard and headed for the exit. Then the telephone jangled, breaking through the still, musty air of the shop like a brick through a window.

"Sal's Plumbing... boss?"

The Agent quickened his step even as the dull-witted guard wrestled with the fact that his employer was in two places at once. The man on the other end of the phone call however was much quicker on his feet. X didn't hear that side of the conversation, but before he reached the exit, the guard was shouting: "Hey you! Stop!"

X bolted for the door and threw it open. If he could make it around the corner, it would take him only a moment to rip off the disguise and shed the overcoat, and if that wasn't enough to fool the guard, well there was always his gas-gun....

"Ah, Mr. Petrona. We were just about to pay you a visit."

The Agent halted so abruptly that he almost careened forward into the small knot of men that now barred his path—not Mafia enforcers, but members of the New York Police Department, led by a very familiar face.

"Inspector Burks," he replied, mimicking Petrona's voice perfectly. "What a pleasant surprise."

The policeman's brow furrowed. "You know me?"

The Agent affected an innocent expression. "Only from the funny papers, Inspector."

The door to the plumbing store abruptly flew open again as the guard prepared to give chase to his boss' impostor. To his credit, he had not drawn a weapon yet, or the sudden standoff might have ended badly. Instead, he simply froze in his tracks as a half-dozen of New York's finest drew their sidearms.

"Back inside sonny," warned a well-dressed young man at Burks's side. The Agent almost did a double take; this was the G-man that had nearly thwarted his escape from the Treasury Building a few days previously. It was an uncomfortable coincidence.

"It's okay Sal," the Agent added, winking at the befuddled watchman. He had no idea if the man's name was Sal, but the fellow gave no indication otherwise; he simply shrank back inside the store, probably to inform the real mobster of this development. X watched the man for a minute, and then turned back to the policemen. "What's this all about? Am I under arrest or somethin'?"

"Should you be?" countered Burks, evenly.

"Haha. You're pretty funny, copper."

But Burks wasn't smiling. "Let me tell you a funny story then, Luigi. Last night, eight of your slime ball wiseguys got themselves blown all full of holes in a warehouse in Brooklyn. I guess you got lucky and missed the party. Or maybe there's some other explanation?"

The Agent chose his words carefully. As much as he wanted to incriminate Petrona, any confession he might offer would certainly be nullified once the police realized the deception; they would just as surely jump to the conclusion that X himself was behind the atrocity. "That's horrible. Who was killed?"

"You mean you don't already know?" Burks listed the victims—every one of them a loyal supporter of Novelli's reforms, a fact which had not escaped the inspector's notice. "Seems like there's two men who ought to have been on this list as well; you and Boss Novelli, and he's gone missing."

"You think whoever did this is going to come gunnin' for me next?"

The question caught the policeman off guard. "That's one theory. I have a few others I'd like to run past you, if you've no objection."

"Objection? You tell me that there's a killer out there who might be coming after me, and you want to chit-chat?"

"I don't think you'll be in any danger at the precinct house."

The Agent resisted the urge to smile. Still, it was best not to seem too eager. "Are you arresting me?"

"Do I need to?"

The Agent forced a cynical laugh. "You got nothing on me, Inspector. I'll come along, sure."

"You got a piece on you?"

The Agent affected a wounded expression. "It's for personal protection."

"You're under my protection now. Hand it over. You can have it back when you leave the station house."

Feigning reluctance, X passed over his gas gun. Although it was the original prototype and not as effective as the newer model he had lost in the office of the Secretary of the Treasury, it was outwardly indistinguishable from an ordinary automatic pistol. Burks dropped it into one of the spacious pockets of his overcoat without more than a glance to insure that the safety was down. He gestured to an unmarked black sedan.

As the Agent got in, he fished out a silver cigarette case from one pocket. "Mind if I smoke?"

**Agent Wesley Greaves** heard the sound of insistent honking and opened his eyes. On the opposite side of the bench-style seat in the rear of the sedan, Inspector Burks lay slumped against the window, unconscious, as was the officer behind the steering wheel. The vehicle was no longer running, and had evidently come to a stop at a traffic signal. Greaves started when he realized that someone was missing.

"Inspector, wake up! He's gone."

Burks stirred then sat upright with a jolt. He glanced around the interior, and then patted the pocket of his coat. The pistol was gone. The vilest of oaths passed from his lips.

"What happened?"

Burks fixed the G-man with a scowl. "You were looking for Secret Agent X; well, he just got away from us."

## CHAPTER 7-SPY HUNTER

**As promised, one** of Smith's black-uniformed goons returned to collect Betty. Remembering her companion's instructions, she made no attempt at resistance, but straightened her disheveled clothing and followed meekly along. As soon as she was gone, the man that she knew as Richard Acer and believed to be Secret Agent X, sprang up from his mattress and hastened through the cell door. Betty and her minder had already turned a corner, but their footsteps were audible. Acer hastened along, staying just out of sight.

His name was not really Acer, but in identifying him as Secret Agent X, Betty had not been too far off the mark. He was indeed a secret agent, as well as a saboteur and sometimes assassin, and like the famed New York vigilante, was a master of disguise and he himself alone knew his true identity.

His allegiances were similarly mysterious, but for some years now he had been exclusively in the service of the Third Reich. His successes on their behalf had earned him a position of leadership in this current endeavor that placed him second only to die Stahlhand—the Steel Hand—an American of German ancestry who was secretly masterminding the entire operation. Piracy on the high seas was merely the tip of the iceberg.

Stahlhand's wealth and power supported a vast network of spies and more importantly, influenced governments and police agencies to look the other way. In the diabolical mind of the Steel Hand, there was only one threat to his grand enterprise that had not been mitigated: Secret Agent X.

Months of investigation had failed to yield up any clues as to the real identity of the Man of a Thousand Faces, but it had revealed a unique relationship between the Agent and a female reporter working for The Herald. The spy, known to his Nazi allies as Karo-As—the Ace of Spades—for his practice of leaving that card as his signature, became Richard Acer, award-winning photographer and went to work for The Herald.

For several weeks, he merely observed the lovely blonde journalist, looking for some hint of an ongoing tryst, or at the very least a clandestine friendship between Betty and the Secret Agent. He had surreptitiously planted listening devices in her telephone and routinely followed her home from work, but there was no sign of anyone at all in Betty Dale's life. As he became more and more convinced that Betty might not know Secret Agent X as well as the Steel Hand believed, Acer began to gently insinuate himself into the void that the Agent ought to have occupied. With casual but leading questions, he learned quite a bit about his quarry. He ascertained that neither Betty, nor anyone living, had ever beheld the Agent's true face. More importantly, he drew an admission from the girl that she was indeed enamored with the mysterious vigilante. From these observations, a plan took shape—a plan that he had executed to the letter, but all to no avail. Betty Dale did not know who Agent X was.

Acer felt a grudging admiration for his unknown foe. He perceived X as a man so wholly devoted to his mission that even the love of a beautiful woman was not enough to get him to lower his mask. Like X, Acer had no intention of revealing his true name or face to anyone, but his motivations were somewhat more mercenary.

All of which left Acer back where he had started nearly six months before. His only hope of success lay in continuing to probe Betty's memory for some clue that might help him expose X before Stahlhand launched his masterstroke: Erste Welle.

First Wave.

Ahead of him by a dozen or so paces, he heard Smith announce: "Ah, Miss Dale. You look a bit worse for wear. I shall see to it that you are immediately given better quarters."

"Forget it, chum. I'm not going anywhere without X."

"Your loyalty is touching. And in this case, it serves you well. I will see to it that you have neighboring suites, along with fresh clothing and toilet facilities."

"I'd rather you just let us go," Betty answered, saucily.

Acer crept forward, stealing onto a balcony staircase that arched above the spacious dining room. He had been here many times and the majesty of the place's architecture no longer awed him, but it remained impressive nonetheless. Unlike the cell and the corridor leading to it, which had not been improved beyond the addition of a coat of paint to prevent rust, the dining hall was just one of the elaborately appointed rooms in the complex. Rich velvet wallpaper and cherry wood furniture made the place seem like something from a resort hotel. Yet, the distinguishing feature of the hall was the wall that stretched high above the balcony on which he now hid; a wall of blackness so total that it seemed as insubstantial as a shadow.

Smith's mien was sad. "I'm afraid that will not be possible, at least not for a while. You will have to endure the luxuries of the Lorelei a little while longer."

"Lorelei?"

"Ah, but I forget myself. You were unconscious when you were brought aboard, so all this is a mystery to you. Let me explain… or better yet, let me show you."

He guided her around the large dining table and under the balcony arch until they were at arm's length from the dark wall. "Wolf," he said, calling to the man that had escorted Betty. "Let's illuminate our world for Miss Dale."

The wall abruptly changed colors and began glowing with a murky green light. Betty gasped as she realized that she was looking through a window, and that the landscape beyond the window—now lit up by four very large electric lamps—was in fact entirely submerged.

"We're underwater! It's like something out of Jules Verne."

Smith smiled proudly. "I think Mr. Verne would be very impressed. But the Lorelei is no mere undersea boat. It is a vast complex—a sea base, if you will—that can sustain hundreds, perhaps even one or two thousand souls for an indefinite period of time."

"You mean without coming to the surface?" Despite the fact that she was his prisoner, Betty's journalistic curiosity was now ablaze. "How deep are we?"

"Lorelei can move about beneath the waves or on the surface, as needed, but this place, only about a hundred fathoms deep on a submerged mountain range in the middle of the Atlantic, is adequate for all our operations."

"A hundred fathoms! That's six hundred feet. I didn't think anyone had ever been that deep."

"The Lorelei represents an astonishing range of first accomplishments, Miss Dale."

Betty shook her head in amazement. "Who is behind all this?"

"Ah, that is something I cannot reveal to you. Suffice it to say, there is a man of great wealth and vision who has made all of this possible; a man very much like the character in Verne's novel." He made a clicking sound with his tongue and several men attired as waiters began shuttling platters to the table. "We can discuss this further over our meal."

Betty took another long look through the giant window, marveling at the seascape beyond, and then realized that she was rather hungry after all.

**The dose of** knockout gas in the special cigarettes was only enough to render the occupants of the police vehicle unconscious for a few minutes, but that was more than enough time for Secret Agent X to calmly exit and blend in with the other pedestrians on the sidewalk. He was nearly two blocks away before the traffic signal changed and outraged drivers began sounding out their ire at the unexpected traffic jam.

The Agent ducked into an alley to remove his disguise and reverse the lining of his overcoat. He donned a Gatsby cap and a pair of round spectacles, and when he emerged from the recess, he looked nothing at all like Luigi Petrona.

As curious as he was to know what had brought the FBI man up from Washington, the Agent had more pressing business. He continued at a brisk pace until the sign for Sal's Plumbing Shop came into view. A sign announcing: "Closed Today" hung in the display window. He kept walking.

In addition to searching Petrona's office, X had also taken the time to plant a small radio transmitter inside the mobster's own box radio. The device ran on battery power and had a very weak signal, but it was strong enough for X to pick it up from his parking spot half a block away. He settled in behind the wheel of his sedan and switched on his radio receiver. Petrona's voice, strident with worry, filled his ears.

"—right here in my own office!"

There was a pause, and the Agent realized that the gangster was talking on the telephone, no doubt to the nefarious Karl Heissler.

"I don't think so. I don't have anything here that would tie me to you anyway."

X's lips twitched in a smile. Petrona had probably memorized the other man's telephone number and forgotten about the business card. He kept listening, but quickly realized that the part of the conversation he could not hear was probably much more revealing. He started the engine and headed for Canarsie Street. After a couple blocks, the signal from Petrona's office faded to static. He pushed the sedan as fast as he dared, navigating the city like a veteran taxicab driver. Speed was essential; his foes would waste no time in covering their tracks.

He made it across town in less than fifteen minutes, pulling the sedan to the curb half a block away, even as he had done at Petrona's place. This time however, there was no need to even leave the car. From his vantage point, he had a perfect view of a telescoping aerial antenna rising from the roof of the butcher's shop. He immediately changed the band on his radio receiver to pick up short wave transmissions and began twisting the tuner until the distinctive sound of Morse code beeps was audible. His radio was equipped with a special device, which used a thin strip of magnetized tape to make an audio recording of the signal, but he also began mentally translating what he heard. After a few seconds, he realized that he was listening to a coded message and abandoned the effort, trusting the tape machine to at least produce a perfect duplicate copy.

The beeps continued for a good ten minutes before the airwaves went silent. There was no longer any doubt now that Carl Harris, butcher, was indeed Karl Heissler, enemy spy. The burning question now was: what were foreign agents planning that involved taking control of the New York mob?

It was a riddle he would not be able to solve on his own. He furiously scribbled out a list of questions and instructions on a sheet of notepaper and stuffed it into an envelope, along with the spool of tape from his radio-recorder. Leaving the sedan parked in view of the butcher's store, he hiked to a nearby bus station and placed the envelope in one of the lockers, after which he hunted down a telephone booth and placed a call.

"This is Acme Parcel Service," he said as soon as a connection was established. "I have a package for you and I want to verify your address." He gave the number of the locker and the street on which the bus station was located. "Is that correct?"

The voice on the other end came back almost immediately. "No sir. We've moved to 730 Marigold Lane."

"Thank you," the Agent replied and hung up the phone.

His answers, at least insofar as Harvey Bates, the director of his vast intelligence network could supply them, would be ready at seven thirty p.m. at a newspaper kiosk a few blocks away from the bus station—one of dozens of drop sites throughout the city designated by a variety of code names. There was nothing to do now but keep an eye on Heissler's operation and wait.

**Acer was waiting** in his new stateroom when Betty returned, though he had in fact followed along behind her through the entire tour of the Lorelei, wearing a different face and the uniform common to the crewmembers. What he had not done was eat, and his stomach now rumbled audibly as he lay on a bed that was a good deal more comfortable than the mattress in the brig. His self-imposed fast was merely part of his disguise and a calculated move to garner sympathy from Betty.

"X?" she called, entering the room tentatively. "How are you doing?"

He opened his eyes and beckoned to her. "Betty. I'm feeling a little better."

"Is your memory...?"

"Bits and pieces," he answered with a faint smile.

"I brought some food." She hastened to his side and extended a platter that was heaped with flatbread and various delicacies, most of which were the bounty of the deep. "You won't believe where we are. This whole place is a giant submarine."

He feigned surprise. "Are you certain?"

"I saw it with my own eyes." She quickly began relating the facts Smith had doled out. "It's all run off electricity. Somehow, these guys found a way to generate electricity directly from seawater, and they use it to power everything. They grow plants in water using sun lamps, and collect seafood right out of the ocean. They even have a way of replenishing the air they breathe."

"Electricity," Acer mumbled, chewing a crust of bread. He already knew all of this, but continued to play his part in the drama. "That explains a lot. Think about the cargoes of the ships that vanished—metal ores especially zinc and copper. They would need those elements to build batteries to store all of the power they generate."

Betty was impressed with his powers of perception; little imagining that it had all been explained to him months before. "That's right. They have these little submarines—we saw them on the Black Spot, remember?—they call them 'Wraiths.' There's a whole fleet of them. They've been using them to sneak up on ships, then they spread this cloud of iron dust in the air to foul up the ship-to-shore radio signal."

"What happened to the crews?" It was a question he felt certain X would ask.

"They're still here. Most of them have volunteered to become permanent crewmembers. The rest are, well, prisoners like us."

It was a plausible fiction and Acer did not challenge it. In reality, the surviving members of the pirated vessels—and not all of the crews had survived the taking of their ships—were slave laborers in the darkest parts of the Lorelei, places that had not been on Smith's tour. The smelting and refining of all the metal ore was a laborious and dangerous process, especially in the close environs of the Lorelei. Every one of the captured ships had all been refitted and sold for a hefty profit.

"Good work, Betty. Now all we have to do is figure out a way to escape." He saw the glimmer of hope in her eyes and matched it, but the gleam in his gaze was not one of hope but of triumph. She was completely in his power.

Suddenly, the door burst open and the two guards rushed in to subdue him. He threw a punch at one, knocking the man back, but his comrade blocked a second strike and flattened him with a ham-sized fist. Though the attack was in reality staged in order to further fool Betty into trusting him, none of the combatants was pulling their punches; it didn't just have to look real, it had to be real. His ears ringing, Acer let himself be dragged from the room, as the blond reporter's protests were ignored. It wasn't until the door was locked firmly behind him that he straightened and began walking unassisted.

"What the devil did you do that for?" he said as he entered Smith's quarters.

"Apparently die Stahlhand was right about this X fellow." His second-in-command handed him a piece of paper with a typed message. "What can we do now? Our plan hinged upon getting Miss Dale to reveal his true identity."

Acer read the message a second time then handed it back to Smith. "All is not lost, my friend. Miss Dale may still be of some use to us. I believe it is time for the sea to give up one of its dead."

## *CHAPTER 8-BOMBSHELL*

**All throughout the** day, X watched for signs of activity in the nest of spies, but saw nothing more that the ordinary day-to-day business of a meat seller. There had been no further radio transmissions, nor any indication that enemy agents were using the place as a base of operations. At six p.m. a man wearing a bloodstained apron—not Heissler, but possibly one of his gun-toting thugs—appeared in the window just long enough to turn the "Open" sign over. The Agent remained where he was, unnoticed behind special glass that was slightly more reflective than ordinary automobile windows. Another uneventful hour passed, and as twilight enveloped the skyline it became apparent that the interior of the store was dark.

The Agent swore under his breath. The Nazi spies had utilized a concealed exit to leave the building. They had correctly assumed that he might track them down and had in all likelihood, abandoned this post and moved out in secret.

Leaving the car behind once more, he strolled down the street right in front of the store, stealing a surreptitious glance at the window to confirm his suspicion; all was dark and still beyond the glass. He kept walking.

He reached the newsstand designated "Marigold" at exactly half past seven, and calmly slipped a copy of the late edition of The Herald from the bottom of the stack. He paid the unsuspecting clerk and moved off with the tabloid tucked under one arm. Despite his burning curiosity, he did not so much as glance at the newspaper until he reached the relative shelter of a Horn & Hadart automat. With a pastry and a cup of coffee, he looked no different than any other New Yorker, enjoying a snack as he perused the newspaper, but the article that held his attention did not appear in any other copies of The Herald.

The page that held the information he required seemed no different than the rest of the printed matter; it was designed to hold up to the closest scrutiny. But the articles contained therein had been cleverly rewritten to include certain words—the substance of the report from Harvey Bates's researchers—and reprinted so as to be indistinguishable from the original. The Agent knew exactly which words to read: the first word of the first sentence; the second word of the second; and so forth, starting anew with each paragraph. He casually sipped his coffee as he read the information, keeping his face expressionless despite the fact that all the news was bad.

The transmission he had recorded had been coded using an Enigma encryption machine, virtually impossible to crack. The Enigma device worked like a simple numerical substation cipher: A=1, B=2 etc. but for every successive letter in the coded message, the values changed according to a unique combination of settings. The only way to decipher the message would be to find the machine that had been used to send and receive, provided of course that the code operator had not since changed the settings.

All that was known about Carl Harris was that he was sole proprietor of the butchery bearing his name; no historical information could be found in the usual sources. Karl Heissler on the other hand, was a name shared by a dozen or so Americans and recent immigrants, none of whom were known or believed to be Nazi sympathizers.

Although Bates promised to continue working on both the Enigma code— there was always a chance of randomly hitting the correct combination using one of the Agency's own machines—and to track down every single Karl Heissler in the country, X knew that any developments would probably come too late to be of help. He had to do something to break the deadlock.

He downed the last of his coffee and was folding the paper in preparation to toss it in the trashcan when the headline on the front page caught his eye.

"No!"

While he had been reading the dire report from Bates, his expression had not changed one iota, but now, as his eyes rapidly scanned the columns of The Herald's lead story, he began to visibly tremble. His knuckles were as white as the newspulp as he held the paper with a grip so fierce that it almost tore in two. The headline continued to taunt him with its bold declaration:

Two of The Herald's Finest, Lost at Sea—Betty Dale and Richard Acer Presumed Dead.

"Betty!"

The cashier and other customers glanced up at his outburst then just as quickly looked away in embarrassment as they saw tears streaming from the man's eyes.

*Betty! How did this happen? How did I let this happen? I was so wrapped up in trying to fight this war that I never saw that you were in danger.*

"Presumed dead," he murmured, reading the words again. *Then she might be* alive; there's still hope.

But the Nazis are planning something—some diabolical masterstroke against America.

"I can't…" The words were inaudible, catching on the lump of grief in his throat. *I can't do both. I can't find Betty and stop the Nazis. I'm just one man.*

*I'm going to need help.*

Still gripping the paper before him as though he held a venomous snake at arm's length, he exited the diner and hastened to the nearest phone booth. When the familiar voice at the other end greeted him, he cleared his throat and began speaking in a different voice.

"Jim, A.J. Martin here. Sorry to call you at home, but it's urgent."

"Mr. Martin! I've been trying to reach you all day. I left several messages with your secretary."

"I haven't been in the office in a while."

"Well, I've got some news for you. There's Nazis working in the city, all right. I don't know what they're up to yet, but believe me, it's nothing good."

The Agent grimaced into the phone handset. "Good work, Jim. But I need you to back off that job for a little while. Something else has come up."

"Name it, boss."

X quickly recounted the facts about the missing ships, including but not stressing the latest victim, a salvage vessel called the Black Spot. He made no specific mention of Betty Dale, not because he feared that Hobart might deduce a connection, but because he feared his voice might crack if he spoke her name.

"I want you to go down there and find out what happened to those ships. This is first priority Jim. Put all your resources into this; I'll pay double the normal rate."

"You don't need to do that, Mr. Martin."

"You've more than earned it Jim. Just bring me back some answers… and if you can, survivors."

*Bring her back to me, Jim.*

After he hung up, X lingered in the phone booth, staring into the darkness. He had hoped that putting Hobart on the case would alleviate some of the turmoil that now gripped his gut, but it was not to be. For nearly two decades he had sublimated the part of himself that desired nothing more than the most basic of human needs—stability, companionship… love—and he had not even realized it until the news of Betty's disappearance drove a nail into the thick skin of his resolve and unleashed the pent up torrent of emotion.

"Focus on the mission," he whispered to the night. "You know what you have to do."

Gathering his courage, he forced himself to think of nothing but the next step in his investigation. Deciphering the short-wave transmission was critical and that meant finding the code machine that had been used to produce it. If he failed….

He slowed his pace as he drew even with the darkened store front of the butcher's shop and paused there, kneeling as if to tie his shoe. Traffic on the street was light and the sidewalks were mostly deserted. No one seemed to be paying any attention to either the shop or to him, but he knew better than to underestimate his foes. The Nazi agents were professionals, trained in the arts of secrecy; if they were conducting surveillance on Harris's business front, he would never realize it. On a tightrope, balanced between urgency and prudence, the Agent was forced to choose the path of greater risk.

With a set of locksmith's tools, he was able to unlock the front door as easily as if he possessed a key, and within a space of no more than thirty seconds, he was inside with the door secured behind him. Using a small handheld lamp, covered with a red lens to conceal its light from outside observers, he scanned the interior room and hastened behind the refrigerated front counter and into the back room. The façade was perfect; nothing he had seen suggested that the building was anything but a legitimate business. If he had not seen the shortwave antenna and recorded the coded transmission, he might have believed himself mistaken in his conclusions. He kept searching.

He finally found what he was looking for in the back of the walk-in freezer. His scrupulous scrutiny showed that one section of shelving was not bolted to the floor or ceiling like the others, and it took only a few more minutes of searching to locate the latch mechanism that caused the false wall to swing out to reveal an ordinary wooden door. A satisfied smile touched his lips and the thrill of discovery helped assuage the bitter helplessness he had felt earlier. Nevertheless, he remained cautious as he confronted the door, listening for several minutes before experimentally twisting the doorknob.

The latch turned without a sound and the door swung inward without resistance. The Agent opened it slowly, all his senses attuned to the unknown that lay beyond. A sliver of darkness, a deeper hue than the area illuminated by the red glow of his lamp, appeared between the door and its jamb and a rush of air, slightly warmer than the frosty atmosphere that spilled over from the freezer, fluttered against his face, but there was no sound at all from within the room.

Except for a single metallic click.

In an instant, the Agent knew he'd been set up. The Nazis had expected him to pay a visit and had rigged the door with a booby trap. He didn't know exactly what kind of trap they had used. Would he get a double-barrel shotgun blast in the face? Or would it be some kind of explosive designed not only to kill an intruder but also erase every last trace of their presence. He reckoned the latter much more likely but the point was moot regardless. Whatever it was had already been triggered and his chances of surviving to learn the truth about it seemed to lie somewhere between slim and none.

**The explosion shattered** windows three blocks from its source and rattled rooftops and nerves alike in the New York neighborhood. A beat cop two streets over was knocked off his feet, but quickly regained his senses and placed a call to his precinct reporting the evident disaster. Not surprisingly, other concerned citizens had already made similar calls to the police station, reporting everything from a cataclysmic thunder strike to the end of the world.

Police cruisers and fire trucks were quickly dispatched to the scene, but the operator took the further step of contacting the central police command. It was in this fashion that Agent Wesley Greaves, who had virtually pitched his tent at police headquarters, monitoring the radios and switchboards for any suspicious activity that might reveal the hand of Secret Agent X, learned of the explosion mere minutes after it occurred. He placed a call to Inspector Burks, interrupting the hard working chief detective's dinner, and then caught a ride to the site of the devastating blast.

The fire trucks had formed a cordon around the destroyed building and were in the process of evacuating the handful of residences that had been compromised by the explosive force. Other than a few cuts from flying glass, there appeared to be no injuries or deaths to bystanders, but the three-story building that had been the focal point of the detonation was a complete ruin; if anyone had been present within at the time of the explosion, it was doubtful that they could have survived.

As the G-man surveyed the wreckage, Inspector Burks arrived on the scene. "Agent Greaves," he called from a distance. "Do you look for Secret Agent X every time there is a mishap in my city?"

The young man smiled. "Are explosions like this commonplace in your city, Inspector?"

Burks harrumphed, but gave no further comment. Instead, he veered away from the G-man and approached the fire marshal who was already beginning his investigation into the event.

"This isn't your typical gas explosion, Inspector. Notice how there is almost no fire damage? If this was from say a leaky furnace line, the fire would still be burning. No question in my mind that someone used high explosives— nitroglycerine or dynamite, if I had to hazard a guess."

Greaves was close enough to hear the discussion but withheld voicing his own opinion. Whether Burks wanted to admit it or not, the sudden reappearance of Secret Agent X had triggered a new crime wave and odds were good that if he wasn't the cause of the explosion, sooner or later he'd be showing up to stick his nose in where it didn't belong. The G-man scrupulously observed the crowd of bystanders, memorizing a few faces; men of average height or taller who seemed unusually interested in what was happening beyond the barricades.

"Hey, we've got someone!"

Greaves and Burks both turned to the source of the cry, a fireman who was sifting through the rubble looking for survivors. Picking their way through the precarious debris field, they reached the spot just as the rescuer levered a heavy section of wall off the victim's inert form. The FBI agent could clearly discern that it was a man, laying face down, unmoving and covered in dust. Though there were no outward signs of injury, the fireman soon confirmed their worst fears with a grim shake of his head.

"He's a goner. Probably suffocated."

"Let's turn him over," Greaves urged.

Working together, the group of investigators and rescuers lifted the corpse and placed it in a supine position on a portable litter in order to transport him away from the scene. Greaves however forestalled the fireman as he was about to spread a blanket over the body.

"Look at his face." To emphasize his point, he pinched a loose flap of something that looked exactly like skin that had detached from the man's chin. Underneath there was an ugly bruise, but the wound was not seeping.

"This is some kind of putty," Greaves announced.

The two representatives of the fire department exchanged a confused glance, but Burks came alive with unexpected enthusiasm. "The devil, you say! Agent Greaves, my hat is off to you."

"Search him; every pocket, every nook and cranny."

The doctor who had arrived in the ambulance was aghast as the two men began none too gently frisking the dead man, but his disdain turned to surprise as the inspection soon uncovered a host of curiosities.

"This is his gas gun," Burks announces, holding up the pistol.

"There's some residue on his neck tie," observed Greaves. He touched it and then smelled and tasted the powdery substance. "It smells faintly of ether. His knockout gas, I'll wager."

"Here's his accursed cigarette case."

"Inspector, look here. He's wearing some sort of armor plate underneath his clothes."

"For all the good it did him," observed the fireman who was now quite excited. "This is Secret Agent X, isn't it?"

"That remains to be seen," hedged Greaves, but the elation in his expression gave lie to the words.

"Can we get rid of the disguise?" asked Burks. "I've been hunting this rogue too long not to get a look at his ugly mug."

"The honor is yours, Inspector. Let's see the man behind the mask."

Burks leaned over the lifeless form and began eagerly rubbing and peeling away the layers of the disguise. His initial elation however quickly gave way to a confused sort of recognition, and then in a gasp of horror he pulled the blanket over the man's face. His own countenance was pale, as if he had seen a ghost. "I don't believe it."

"You know this man?" Greaves asked.

The inspector glanced at the firemen. "Can you excuse us for a moment."

The two rescue workers were clearly upset at being denied a chance to gaze on the face of the legendary Secret Agent, but they grudgingly cleared off, leaving Burks and Greaves alone.

"Well?"

Burks pulled the blanket back to reveal the battered visage. "I would never have guessed it was him in a million years," he said gravely. "Yes, I know him, or rather I should say I knew him, years ago. His name is—"

## CHAPTER 9-TURNING POINT

**For the third** time in less than twenty-four hours, Agent Wesley Greaves read the file on the man now believed to be Secret Agent X, and as before he was stunned by the revelations contained therein.

The man had been a hero of the Great War. He had served behind enemy lines, escaped a brutal prison camp, and received the nation's highest decorations. Following that conflict, he had continued to live a life of high adventure and philanthropy in far-flung places. How then had this paragon of virtue become the infamous criminal master of disguise?

*Unless I've got it all wrong,* thought the G-man. *What if Agent X isn't the criminal we've made him out to be?*

Thus far, the news of Secret Agent X's demise had been kept from the public and only Greaves and Burks had actually seen his face. For the inspector, the triumph was bittersweet; although X had been his constant foil for more than a decade, the revelation of his identity felt like a betrayal. The New York police detective had not balked at the idea of keeping the matter secret from the masses. Greaves however had his own reasons for secrecy.

"Think about it," he had said the night before. "Agent X didn't plant that bomb in order to blow himself up. There's something going on here and he was only a part of it."

"You've got your man, Greaves. You can't continue meddling in city affairs."

"Forget about jurisdiction for a minute. Look at the facts. In two days' time, there have been two major incidents and Agent X put in an appearance at both. That can't be a coincidence. We know the mob was involved in the warehouse shootings but what about this place? A butcher's shop? There's a connection somewhere and Agent X knew what it was."

Burks had looked back askance. "So what are you suggesting?"

"Whoever planted that bomb will be watching to see what happened. For all we know, it might have been a trap designed to kill Agent X. Right now, we're the only ones who know he's dead; as far as the rest of the world is concerned, Agent X is still alive. If we play our cards right, we just might be able to use that knowledge to smoke out the perpetrators."

Now that Greaves knew a little more about the man behind the mask, he was even more certain of the scenario he had described to the inspector; Agent X— more vigilante than villain—had indeed stumbled into some kind of viper's nest and his enemies in the underworld had fought back in a big way.

*Damn the man,* Greaves thought, reflecting back on the conversation he had overheard in the Treasury secretary's office. Maybe X wasn't a foreign spy, but by being a loner and a rogue, he was exactly the kind of champion the country didn't need. By excluding legitimate authorities from his battle against what he perceived to be evil, X had now guaranteed his foes' success. The man of a thousand faces had taken whatever knowledge he possessed about his killers with him to the grave.

The young G-man rose from the desk and tucked the file under one arm as he strode from the office. He met Burks in a waiting car and together the two men made the short trip to the morgue where the post-mortem examination on Secret Agent X was going to be performed.

Neither of the law officers was squeamish about being in the presence of the dead. If anything, the sterile environment of the morgue as a far better place to meet the recently departed than a gruesome bloodstained crime scene. Nevertheless, the sight of Secret Agent X, laid out on the dissection table in the chilly room, made both men feel a little ill at ease.

"Let's get this started," Burks muttered to the pathologist

The man in the white lab coat nodded then took a position beside the cadaver. "As you know Inspector, we're establishing the cause of death as 'suffocation.' This procedure is merely a formality."

"I'm curious to know if there are any indications that he might have been unconscious before the explosion," Greaves intoned. "It's possible someone overpowered him and then left him to die in the blast."

"There are bruises around the face, which would be consistent with injuries sustained in the explosion. It's possible he got those wounds in a struggle, but unlikely. In any event, he was alive when that happened; you can tell by bruise patterns."

"Look for signs of a blow to the skull. Someone might have cracked him with a pistol butt or a blackjack."

The doctor shrugged and then tilted the corpse's head in order to closely inspect the cranium. As he did, his expression changed to one of bewilderment. "What's this?"

Burks groaned aloud. "What have you got, doc?"

The pathologist pointed to a faint line near the cadaver's ear. He selected a scalpel from his tray of instruments and wedged the blade into the nearly imperceptible crack. The skin peeled away from the sharp edge... only it wasn't skin.

"Another mask," Greaves hissed through his teeth.

Burks seemed about to explode with rage, but then his expression changed as suddenly as if someone had thrown a switch. "So it wasn't him after all. Agent X was just pretending to be him, no doubt planning to discredit a citizen who is beyond reproach. Keep peeling, doc. Let's get a look at the real face of Secret Agent X."

"What I don't understand," intoned Greaves as the doctor began separating mask from flesh, "is how we can see the bruises through the make up."

"This isn't ordinary theater make-up," answered the pathologist. "It's a translucent layer that changes the shape of the face but the natural skin tones are still visible."

"Fiendishly clever." Burks's eyes were dancing as inch by inch, the true face of his nemesis was revealed. But with more than half of the man's countenance exposed, it became evident that the face beneath was not as familiar as the mask.

"Recognize him?" asked the G-man.

"Never seen this fellow before in my life," said Burks, chagrinned.

"It looks like we'll have to this the old fashioned way: comparing fingerprints and mug shots. Let's get some photographs before you continue cutting, doc."

The police inspector eyed his younger counterpart. "Why do I get the feeling that you aren't done looking for Secret Agent X?"

"We still don't know what he was doing last night. This last mask seems to have been a good deal more permanent than the other one. I think it might be a good idea to find out why he chose that particular face. Perhaps the man he was impersonating can shed some light on the mystery."

**Only the clock** measured the passage of time in the eternally benighted depths that enveloped the Lorelei. When the overhead light in Betty's suite was turned off, the darkness was absolute; a void that sucked her very life essence. She left the light on, even while she slept.

More than twenty-four hours passed, but Acer did not return. Hunger forced the reporter from her sanctuary, but when she ventured through the doorway, there was no sign of the guards that had earlier been posted to watch over her. She followed the familiar route to the dining hall where the galley staff was more than happy to prepare a meal for her, but as hungry as she was, there was another need that was even more immediate.

"I want to see Mr. Smith."

The chef agreed to summon him, but insisted that she eat. Famished, she relented and was well into the third course of her meal when the Lorelei's chief of operations arrived.

"Miss Dale, you are well I trust?"

"I am not," she answered around a mouthful of succulent swordfish steak. "Where is X—I mean, Mr. Acer?"

One corner of Smith's mouth twitched. "Call him whatever you wish, Miss Dale; he has no secrets from us anymore."

"Then you won't mind letting him go."

"Miss Dale, I'm afraid that simply won't be possible. You see, this man X, to whom you are so devoted, has escaped."

Betty gasped and almost choked on her food. She washed the morsel down with a sip of white wine. "Escaped? I don't believe you."

"It's true. He overpowered his guard and managed to commandeer one of the Wraiths."

"Then he'll be back," Betty answered, confidently. "You can count on it."

The other man drummed his fingers on the tabletop, thoughtfully. "It's a possibility we have considered. The Wraiths are not what you would call long-range vessels, but it is conceivable that he may be able to rendezvous with a ship. But even if he reaches the mainland, it is unlikely that he will be able to find this place again. In truth, I doubt he will even try."

"Then you don't know him very well."

"I submit that it is you who does not know him. He made no attempt whatsoever to find you. He has abandoned you, Miss Dale."

Betty was about to offer further protest, but something about Smith's insistence stopped her. She had not reason to believe him; for all she knew, this was another trick. "Then why don't you let me go?"

Smith's tapping fingers stopped abruptly. "Let you go?"

"Sure. You only brought me here because I was with X… Acer. Now that he's gone, there's no reason for you to keep me."

"I'm afraid you've seen too much for us to let you go, but fear not. No harm will come to you while you are a guest of the Lorelei."

"If X makes it back, your secret will be out anyway."

"Hmmm. You make a good argument Miss Dale. The truth is, I have been wondering what to do with you."

Betty flashed her most winning smile. "I'm a journalist. Let me tell your story."

"My story?"

"The Lorelei! It's a marvel of science. Let me tell the story, and I'll make you seem like a heroic explorer of the deep, instead of a ruthless pirate."

"You would do this?"

"Well, if you were to release me, it would go a long way toward establishing your intentions as benevolent."

Smith chuckled. "Very clever, Miss Dale. I'll make a deal with you, then. It has always been my plan to reveal the Lorelei to the world, and that day is nearly here. Here is my counter-proposal: Stay with us here on the Lorelei a little longer, and then, when the time is right, you will have the exclusive."

Betty smiled again, but not because of Smith's offer. She was certain that the man was lying to her about Agent X's escape, and if she played her cards right, she just might be able to find her friend and then, borrowing a page from Smith's script, use one of the Wraiths to escape. "Well then, I'll need a pen and paper. I'm going to tell the world all about the Lorelei, then I'm going to need to start taking notes."

**With a single** telephone call, Inspector Burks was able to find the address for the man whose face Secret Agent X had been wearing—an address that wasn't listed in the Manhattan telephone directory. A short drive brought the two law officers to the uptown neighborhood where the subject of their search resided.

"You said this guy was rich," Greaves said as they walked toward the stoop of the brownstone dwelling. "I expected something more ostentatious."

"I confess that I don't know a lot about him. He has a reputation for philanthropy. Perhaps he doesn't want to advertise his wealth to freeloaders."

Burks rang the doorbell. The sound of chimes was audible through the door which, after a few moments swung open to reveal a taller than average man with wavy brown hair, wearing a long bathrobe. A towel was wrapped, like a cravat, around his neck. Except for the lack of facial disfiguration, the man's face was exactly the same as the mask worn by the corpse that had been pulled from the scene of the explosion. The man's movements were stiff, as though walking was very painful and beads of sweat were visible on his brow.

"Can I help you?" he asked in a gravelly voice.

"Forgive the intrusion sir," Burks began, diplomatically. "I am Inspector Burks of the NYPD, and this is Agent Greaves of the FBI."

Most men, even the innocent, immediately begin to fidget when confronted with law enforcement officials, but this man simply regarded his visitors with guarded curiosity. "Forgive me for keeping you on the doorstep Inspector, but I'm afraid I'm a bit under the weather."

"You look as though you've been run over by a truck." Burks almost choked as Greaves made the rather impolite observation, but the householder appeared unperturbed.

"A truck called malaria; a little souvenir of my journeys abroad. Don't worry though, you can't get it from casual..." The man broke off in fit of coughing and both of the visitors unconsciously took a step back. After a moment, the spasm passed and the man faced them again. "What can I do for you gentlemen?"

Burks held out a photograph. The lawman had expedited the development process, with the result that the glossy surface was still sticky to the touch. "Do you recognize him?"

The man took the print and studied it for a moment. "I'm sorry Inspector. He doesn't look at all familiar."

"Look again," Greaves supplied. "This is very important."

"If I'm not mistaken, that's a photograph of a dead man. Would I be correct in surmising that you are unable to make a positive identification?"

"I'm afraid so."

He studied it a moment longer then handed it back to the inspector. "I wish I could be of more help."

"Do you have any idea why this man would want to impersonate you?"

"Impersonate me?" The man appeared genuinely surprised, but before he could offer further comment, a second paroxysm overcame him and he leaned against the doorpost coughing and shaking violently.

Burks shuffled his feet as if he was about to leave, but Greaves was not so easily thrown off the hunt. When their host regained his composure, he pressed the question. "I tell you this in strictest confidence sir; we believe that this man is Secret Agent X. He was found tonight at the scene of an explosion, wearing your face, so I ask again: do you have any idea who he is, or why he was trying to impersonate you?"

The man pressed his lips together. "I am not extraordinarily wealthy, Agent Greaves, but it is conceivable that this scoundrel might have thought to assume my identity for the purpose of monetary gain. Perhaps he meant to withdraw money from my bank account or secure a loan in my name. Due to my relapse, I am a virtual prisoner here."

The two law officers exchanged a glance. It was a plausible enough scenario even if it didn't fit together with the other pieces of the puzzle, but Greaves wasn't willing to admit defeat just yet. "Are you acquainted with a man named Luigi Petrona? Or Aldo Novelli? Or anyone in the city's criminal underworld?"

"Agent Greaves!" said Burks, sharply. "That's quite enough. I will not allow you to impugn this man's reputation with such questions." He turned to the man in the doorway. "Forgive our intrusion, sir. If you think of anything at all that might help our investigation, please contact me directly."

"No apology necessary, Inspector, Agent Greaves. You're only doing your duty. I am grateful that you brought this matter to my attention. As soon as I am able, I will consult with my financier to verify that nothing untoward has happened to my accounts."

Burks nodded. "A wise course of action. Good day, sir."

The man smiled but did not offer a handshake as the two visitors bade their good-byes. Instead, he retreated inside and firmly closed the door. Only then did he sag in place as if overcome with exhaustion. Leaning against a wall for support, he hobbled into the front room and sank wearily into a chair. After a few minutes, he gathered enough strength to reach for the telephone on the side table and dialed a number. After a few rings, a wary voice answered: "Medical examiner's office."

"It's me."

"Ah," sighed the man on the other end. "Did it work?"

"The FBI man is still trying to figure it out, but as far as they're concerned, Secret Agent X has crossed into the hereafter. You're a miracle worker, doc."

"Ha! If anyone worked miracles, it was you. That job of make-up was flawless. I couldn't tell the difference, even up close."

Beneath a similar mask of cosmetics—which served not to disguise his face but to hide several garish bruises—Secret Agent X smiled. "It was fortunate that the make-up kit in the heel of my shoe was sufficient for the task, but it wouldn't have mattered one bit if you hadn't caught on to the fact that I was still alive. For that matter, I was doubly lucky that you happened to moonlight for Harvey Bates's agency."

"Harvey recruited me years ago as a special consultant, and even though I was never sure, I had a feeling the work I did was helping your cause." The pathologist laughed. "It was a lucky night all around, X. The dose of anesthetic gas you received when those ampoules broke would have killed an ordinary man, but then I guess you're not exactly ordinary. Instead of dying, you went into a deep death-like sleep. If I hadn't checked your pulse one last time, that would still be you laying on my slab with all your insides taken out, weighed and catalogued."

"Perish the thought. So who was my unlucky stand-in?"

"Citizen John Doe. We get a few of them every week; poor lost souls whose minds have been addled by disease or drink and who wander the streets until exposure finally claims them. We try to track them down with fingerprints and so forth, but most are never identified and end up buried in Potter's Field."

"A pity we'll never know his name."

"As far as the police are concerned, his name is Secret Agent X. You are officially dead, and it might be a good idea if you stayed that way."

"The thought had occurred to me," the Agent sighed.

"You nearly died tonight." The doctor's voice was somber. "You've done more for the city than any man, but maybe the fates are trying to tell you something: It's time to think about retiring. Let Secret Agent X rest in peace. Rejoin the world as yourself."

The words, coming from a man who was virtually a stranger, cut more deeply than he had expected. In all the years of his battle against criminal elements, the one thing that he had never had was a confidant—someone who could speak to the man behind the masks. If someone had said those words to him a few weeks or even a few days ago, Betty might still be alive....

He shook his head at the thought, wincing as pain shot through his bruised and battered body. Nothing he could do now would bring Betty back. But there were other lives at stake, lives that would certainly be lost if he renounced Secret Agent X and tried to settle into the comfortable routine of an ordinary life.

"I'll give it some thought," he said at length. "Meanwhile, there's one more favor I need to ask of you, doc. It's a big one."

"Anything to help."

"You're the keeper of my trust now; the only person alive who knows my true name, my true face."

"I will take the secret to the grave," the doctor promised.

"It may come to that," the Agent replied. "But that's not exactly what I had in mind."

**Jon Mullins's luck** was about to change.

The stout Boston whaleboat fisherman had been plagued with nothing but ill fortune for several weeks. It had been a long time since he had been able pull in a catch sufficient to meet his expenses, and that did not take into account the extra money spent repairing the outboard which had suffered a badly fouled carburetor or replacing nets that had been hopelessly tangled in some uncharted obstruction on the sea floor or the repairs to his hull after an inadvertent collision with another boat in the harbor.

Thus far, this day was proving no different than most. He had netted a few hundred pounds of various fish, but even if he got a decent price for his catch, he would still be adding a little more red ink to his ledger. But that was always the way of the fisherman and Mullins knew that eventually the pendulum would swing the other way—and if it didn't, well, he could always sell the whaler to pay off his debts and take a job in the city. As Mullins finished reeling in the last of his nets and turned the prow toward the distant harbor lights, he could scarcely have imagined that there was one more catch waiting for him, one that would elevate him to the status of local hero.

With the setting sun in his eyes, he was almost on top of the floating object before he saw it. He immediately idled the outboard and cautiously peered over the side of his little boat to see if it was worth hauling aboard. It appeared to be nothing more than a large piece of floating wood but to his amazement, when he snagged it with his gaff hook, he discovered the figure of a man clinging to one edge.

"Help me," croaked the castaway.

Mullins did not hesitate. He hastily dragged the man from his precarious perch as though sharks were circling. In the waning daylight, the man's sun burnt visage was almost indistinguishable.

"You're all right now, fella," the fisherman said, fetching his canteen and splashing fresh water onto the salt-encrusted face. "Are you from a shipwreck?"

The rescued man licked at the moisture that trickled onto his lips. "Black Spot," he croaked. "Been floating for days."

"You're safe now. Are there any other survivors?"

The drifting gray eyes suddenly snapped forward, locking Mullins in a fierce stare. "Betty! She's alive. I know she is!"

## *PART TWO: AGENT OUT OF PLACE*

## *CHAPTER 10-DISTANT SHORES*

**Commander Miles Messervie** shuffled uncomfortably in his new chair. He didn't like it one bit; not the chair, not the desk, not the office...not the new job. He belonged in the field, not trapped here pushing paper and counting beans for the service. But this was his reward for exposing and ultimately destroying a Nazi foothold in Ireland; with his cover blown, he had been promoted from field operative to Chief of Operations for the Special Intelligence Service. Now he had an important position, a plush office and a pretty young secretary with an improbable name.

At least there are a few benefits to being in the office, he though, picking up and ornate Meerschaum pipe and a tin of his special tobacco blend. After a few puffs, his St. James street headquarters was filled with aromatic blue smoke.

A crackle from the intercom on his desk interrupted his reverie. "Sir, the American is here."

"Send him in, Miss Tuppence."

There was a sigh from the girl, who had already grown tired of his little jokes about her name. "Right away, sir."

Messervie settled back into his chair and continued to puff on his pipe as the man from the Colonies opened his door and strode toward the desk. He studied the American's appearance and movements as he might size up a new player at the whist table. The fellow was young but moved with the efficiency and confidence that bordered on arrogance. He walked forward until he was almost touching the desk and extended a hand.

"How do you do, sir? I am Agent Wesley Greaves of the American Federal Bureau of Investigation."

Messervie offered a guarded smile, as he accepted the handclasp, but did not rise from his chair. "Yes, Greaves, I've checked your bona fides as a matter of course. You are a credit to your organization. Please have a seat."

Greaves smiled and settled into one of the matching chairs positioned carefully a few paces away so that anyone seated there would be fully exposed to Messervie's scrutiny. Greaves did not appear nonplussed by the arrangement but simply folded his hands in his lap, waiting for a cue to begin speaking.

"Well Greaves, what can the Ministry of Defence do for you?"

Both men were well aware that the FBI agent had already submitted his request in writing, but Greaves showed no exasperation at the question. "As you may know, I have been tracking a fellow who uses the pseudonym Secret Agent X—a vigilante who had been operating primarily in New York City."

"Had, you say? Past tense?"

"Yes. He was killed under rather strange circumstances, and although we have his body, we have yet to arrive at a positive identification. The New York police are continuing to investigate that angle, but I am more interested in finding the person responsible for his death. You see, there is compelling evidence to suggest that German saboteurs may have set the bomb that killed him."

"Ah, the Hun is at work across the pond."

Greaves nodded. "It appears that way. Agent X may have been working to unmask them, but whatever he knew about their grand design has gone with him to the grave."

"And you want to know what they're up to, is that it?"

"The Nazis are certainly a menace, but my government is not in a position to openly confront them. Nor do we have sufficient intelligence operatives in place to even begin infiltrating their ranks. I aim to do exactly that, but in order to make my way into Germany, I may need a little help from you."

Messervie knocked the dottle from the bowl of his pipe and set it aside. "I shall be frank with you, Greaves. I'm not enthusiastic about the idea of including an outsider, even someone with your training and talents, in our operations."

The G-man smiled forbearingly. "Commander, I've no wish to put your men at risk. If you can put me on the ground in France, I can do the rest without any further involvement from your department."

"Can you now?"

"I speak excellent French and passable German. Some years ago, I vacationed in France and am sufficiently familiar with the geography of the region."

Messervie harrumphed and clamped the pipe stem in his teeth. "And are you a trained counter-intelligence operator?"

"I have done extensive undercover work with the Bureau. I'm not boasting when I say that I think I can handle it."

The chief of operations stared at him a few moments longer, and then began to chuckle. "Far be it from me to stand in your way." He tapped the button on the intercom. "Miss Ha'penny. Send for Lieutenant Tanner."

"Right away," growled the pretty young woman in a voice that was none too pretty.

"Tanner is one of my best men," explained Messervie. "A genius at managing logistics. I've no doubt he'll one day sit in this chair. If anyone can get you behind enemy lines, it's Tanner."

"I'm grateful for your help, sir. If I can ever repay the favor…"

Messervie began tamping fresh tobacco into his pipe, but his stare never wavered. "Oh, I think that quite unlikely Greaves. I doubt very much that you will be returning from this fool's errand."

**Inspector Burks rushed** from his office as soon as he received the call from Detective Malvern, and with sirens shrieking, reached the brownstone neighborhood less than fifteen minutes later. Constant radio communication with the detective guided him to a location only half a block from the subject who was simply strolling down the sidewalk. Burks exited the police cruiser and rendezvoused with Malvern who was tailing the man in an unmarked sedan.

"Need some back up, Inspector?"

"Let's not spook him," Burks replied. "Keep your distance; I'll take care of this."

With that, the police inspector launched into a trot that quickly closed the distance on the walking man. When he was only a few steps away, he called out and the man turned to greet him.

"Ah, Inspector…Burks was it?"

Burks hid his struggle to catch his breath behind a smile. "Indeed, sir. You have a gift for remembering names?"

The man smiled. "Well, you and that fellow from the FBI are the only visitors I've had of late."

"You seem to be recuperating."

"For the present. I fear that I will suffer relapses for the rest of my days, but the symptoms are manageable." He scrutinized the policeman. "It's good of you to check on me, but something tells me that you are not here simply to inquire after my health."

Burks smile slipped a notch. He had not actually considered what he would say. Agent Greaves had asked him to maintain surveillance on the man, but in his haste he had not thought through the whys and wherefores. "Ah, you might say that. Truthfully, we are still trying to get to the bottom of why someone wanted to impersonate you."

"I see. Well, by all means, continue."

"You haven't had any…ah, contact with suspicious persons?"

"None at all. Rest assured, I will call you immediately if anything unusual happens. That being said, I may be heading out of town soon. This business has left me rather ill at ease with remaining in the city."

Burks face fell. "I see. Where are you off to then?"

"I have a house upstate. However, I will only be there until I can finalize my plans for the Botswana expedition."

"Botswana? In Africa?"

The man nodded, showing animation for the first time. "Oh, yes. The Geographic Society is sponsoring a search for King Solomon's Mines. It should be quite an adventure."

"Sir, I have no legal authority to hold you here, but I beg you to reconsider. You are linked, however involuntarily, to a criminal scheme. You may even be the intended victim of this plot."

"All the more reason to make myself scarce. I'm sorry Inspector, but my mind is made up. This expedition has been two years in the planning; I'm not about to back out now."

Burks mind raced to find some argument to persuade the man to stay, but he knew the battle was already lost. "If you go," he stammered, "we won't be able to protect you."

"Protect me? Secret Agent X is dead, is he not?"

"Yes, it certainly appears that way."

"Then I don't see where there's any danger. Worry not, Inspector. When I get where I'm going, I'll be in more peril than you can possibly imagine."

As he walked away, content with the caliber of his performance, the pathologist had no idea how prophetic his words would prove to be for the man he had so perfectly impersonated.

**Invisible in the** inky black of night, the water of the English Channel churned like the brew in a witch's cauldron. The storm clouds that whipped the sea into a frenzy hid the scant light from the quarter moon, creating a zone of total, unyielding darkness. No ship's lights pierced the shadow veil; even absent the threat of Kriegsmarine Unterseeboots cruising beneath the surface like sharks, no ship's captain would have dared to make the channel crossing under such circumstances. Nor did anyone on either shore dare to show a naked light. The night was absolute… impenetrable.

Almost.

Hidden from the sight of any hypothetical observer, six warplanes skimmed above the turbulent surface, the frothy white tipped swells never less than a hundred feet below the underbellies of the sleek fighter craft. The men that piloted these winged stallions were professionals, the best of the best, but even that was no guarantee of safety or success, given the nightmarish nature of their mission this night.

"We'll be flying in low," the American flyer Captain Lance Star had explained in the pre-flight briefing. "Jerry's radar beams sweep the sky, so we'll stay down near the water. I'll warn you: it's going to be hairy."

Hairy did not begin to describe it. Flying virtually blind, the squadron's pilots were engaged in a non-stop wrestling match with their controls, fighting against sudden bursts of wind and downdrafts that threatened to rip them from the sky. Using instruments alone, they could not even be sure of whether they were staying with the group, or when they were veering too close to each other. Radio silence was imperative.

None of the pilots witnessed the gust of wind that abruptly hammered into Bobby "Reb" Nash's Mustang, and no one saw the plane flown by their obnoxious but lovable comrade in arms suddenly slam into the churning water of the channel and break into a thousand pieces. No one would ever know exactly how he had perished that night, but only that one more brave man had been lost in the cause.

The lead plane, flown by Star himself, was slightly larger than the accompanying escort fighters. Unlike the single seat Mustangs, this plane had been modified to carry a payload or in special circumstances, people. On this night, two passengers were huddled in the cargo/bomb bay, clinging to web straps as the benighted aircraft heaved and lurched across the English Channel. Yet, as dire as their present situation seemed, both men knew that this was the easy part of their journey.

"We're coming up on the Dover cliffs," Star shouted, his voice crackling over the intercom. "Get ready. You're only going to get one chance at this."

The two men might have nodded to each other—it was impossible to tell in the darkness—and then both released their handholds and scooted to the middle of the compartment, spreading themselves flat in order to avoid being thrown about as the daredevil pilot made his final run at the continental coast.

The German soldiers manning the anti-aircraft batteries along the coast had almost no warning as the Sky Rangers seemingly erupted from the sea. Their radar screens, which had showed only a chaotic pattern of clouds, suddenly came alive with five hard contacts directly overhead, and an alarm was immediately sounded. Spotlights stabbed into the gloom, searching for targets, even as anti-aircraft guns began to thunder.

The men in the cargo hold felt the concussion of shells bursting all around, but no fragments of shrapnel found their way through the skin of Star's plane. Other members of the squadron did not fare quite as well; two planes took slight damage from flak, but remained airworthy. It was only then that Star broke radio silence, shouting: "Let 'em have it, boys!"

The five remaining Sky Rangers, in perfect unison, dove from the sky like raptors and unleashed a torrent of machine gun fire into the midst of the nearest AA batteries. The spotlights exploded in the opening salvo, lowering once more the protective curtain of darkness on the unfolding drama. Similarly, one of the big guns fell silent as slugs from Star's wing-mounted guns tore into the gun crew. And then, as suddenly as it had begun, the attack was over. The Sky Rangers passed through the hell storm and were over the rural countryside of France.

"On three!" called Star, and the men in the hold knew exactly what he meant. "One... two... three!"

As soon as the word passed his lips, Star hit the button that released the bomb bay doors. The floor beneath the two passengers dropped in a sickening instant and they were snatched away by the relatively still air through which the plane relentlessly flew. At the controls, Star counted to thirty then turned the aircraft sharply. The rest of the squadron followed suit and soon all five planes were racing headlong toward the breach their first attack had created in the enemy's air defense network. Despite the fact that the anti-aircraft guns were inoperative, the brave Sky Rangers knew that German Messerschmitt Bf-109 fighters were probably already in the air and racing to intercept them.

The thirty seconds was critical, not for the sake of the planes, but for the two men who had bailed out into the night sky. Although they were completely indistinguishable against the velvet darkness, when the clock had ticked away half a minute, an enormous mushroom of silk blossomed into view above each of the men, snapping them out of their free fall. Although several pairs of eyes were scanning the dark night for some sign of the planes' return, no one saw the parachutes as they descended silently onto the French countryside and since the radar screens clearly indicated that none of the five planes had gone down, it never occurred to anyone that the attack might be anything other than a simple hit and run assault to test German defenses.

The winds aloft above the French countryside were considerably calmer than the tempest that raged out over the water, but the two parachutists were nevertheless swept away by the unseen currents and by the time they landed, were separated by nearly half a mile. Both men had rehearsed what to do in just such a circumstance and immediately went to work. In a matter of minutes, their parachutes were buried in the loamy soil and the two men were jogging toward a pre-designated rally point—a stand of trees at the foot of a hill nearly two miles west of their respective landing sites.

The first man to arrive found a place of concealment in the trees and waited, keeping a careful watch for enemy patrols. A few minutes later, he heard the soft huffing sounds of a lone figure approaching his location. He remained in his hide, watching to be sure that the silhouette now barely visible in the darkness did indeed belong to the other parachutist, and that the man was not being followed.

When he was certain that nothing unusual was happening, he hissed: "Lightning!"

The walking man reflexively ducked into the shadows, but then immediately gave the agreed upon counter-sign: "Blizzard."

The first man stepped out of his hiding place. "Over here, Tanner."

The man from the Special Intelligence Service smiled at his companion. "Well done, Mr. Greaves. You're now a paratrooper!"

"It was quite an experience," the other man replied politely. "I rather hope it's the most exciting thing that happens tonight."

Tanner laughed. "Exciting or not, we have quite a hike ahead of us."

The other man—one of two who claimed to be Agent Wesley Greaves of the FBI—nodded, but before he set off at a trot behind Tanner, he took a last look around and breathed in deeply the night air.

He had misled Tanner back at the airfield in Britain, feigning apprehension about the prospect of parachuting from an airplane. In fact, he had done more than his share of sky diving, and had even once bailed out of a stricken Sopwith Camel, not far from the very spot where he now stood.

It was an odd feeling being here again. The familiar and unique smells brought back the memories in a rush. He had lived an entire lifetime here; had fought and almost died many times in the French countryside. In all the years that had followed, he had never once even considered returning here. In truth, although this place had forged him, he was no longer the young idealistic soldier that had crossed the ocean to fight for freedom; he was something else now.

He was Secret Agent X.

## *CHAPTER 11-WAR MISSION*

**"This is as** far as I go," stated Tanner when they were within sight of the village that was their destination. "Do you remember what to do?"

The Agent nodded. Everything had been thoroughly and repeatedly explained before he had ever boarded the plane, but he understood Tanner's last minute jitters. He was about to make contact with a cell of the Maquis, French resistance fighters, and that meeting would be fraught with danger to everyone involved. Informants and double agents were everywhere. The Maquisards would be extremely cautious, almost to the point of paranoia, and the slightest misunderstanding might have fatal consequences. Yet, for all the inherent peril of the situation, X was calm. This meeting might be taking place in a country that he had not seen in two decades, but at its heart it was no different than what he did almost every day and night of his life; he was a chameleon, and whether he was in the concrete jungles of New York or the forests of France, he could blend in completely with his surroundings.

Remote though the village was, he immediately saw the evidence that this place was occupied territory. The town was surrounded by a makeshift fence of wire, with fortified gates and guard posts where the main road passed through. From his vantage in the tree line, the Agent could easily distinguish a roving patrol—a single German soldier wearing a heavy blue greatcoat, with two Alsatian shepherd dogs straining at their leashes. Getting through the fence would pose little problem, X reckoned, but the dogs would require a little more finesse.

When the patrol was about a hundred yards past his location, he raised a thumb and forefinger to his lips, positioned a very precise distance apart, and whistled through the gap. The tone of the whistle was barely audible, even to the Agent himself, but the dogs responded immediately to the low sound by standing stock-still.

The puzzled dog handler shook the leash in an attempt to get them to move, but they remained frozen in place and only then did it occur to the man that they might be responding to something. With the leash wrapped around his wrist, he brought his rifle up and began peering into the darkness beyond the barrier, focusing his attention in the direction the dogs seemed to be staring.

The Agent carefully lifted the barbed wire and squirmed underneath. He stayed low, crawling until he reached a place of concealment well away from the perimeter. When he was satisfied that no one had witnessed his infiltration, he whistled again, releasing the dogs from their stupor. The pair of Alsatians immediately resumed walking as if nothing had happened, and although the guard remained perplexed and wary, the patrol continued onward. The entire disruption had taken no more than thirty seconds.

X lingered in the shadows only long enough to strip off the black coveralls he had worn both to protect his clothing from the rush of air while parachuting and to camouflage his movement during the long trek to the village. The overgarment, a gift of the SIS Quartermaster's section, was ingeniously designed so that it could be reversed and folded into a simple cloth traveler's bag; it even had pouches for common toilet articles. The Agent had of course added a few of his own touches to the mix.

Beneath the coveralls, he wore the simple garb of a rural French laborer, but the clothes alone would not suffice to disguise his presence. Unlike the cities of the world, where it was easy for a new face to get lost in the crowd, the residents of this village would immediately peg him as a stranger and regard him with suspicion. He would undoubtedly be asked to explain his presence and his story would be dissected in excruciating detail. With his traveling bag slung over one shoulder, he moved through an alley between two buildings and onto the main street.

His destination was the largest structure in the town, a two-story edifice built of stone that had probably been standing when Joan of Arc led a different generation of French resistance fighters against a foreign invader centuries before. Pushing through the heavy plank door, he entered into a smoky, dimly lit common area where a dozen or so patrons were sipping spiced wine and engaging in muted conversation. As expected, his entrance did not go unnoticed, but he ignored the stares and moved to the bar where he settled with affected weariness onto a stool.

"You are a stranger."

Though the comment was offered in French, the Agent effortlessly understood and answered in the same tongue as easily as if both he and the other person were speaking English. "Yes, I have come from Lyon looking for—"

The words abruptly left him as he caught a glimpse of his interrogator. He had known that it was a woman speaking—a woman with a throaty, sensual voice, and all the more so as it formed the almost lyrical syllables of the regional dialect—but when he saw her face, he simply froze.

His first thought was of Betty Dale. It was a complete incongruity, for the woman neither looked nor sounded like the blonde reporter from New York City. Other than perhaps being about the same age as Betty, the Frenchwoman, petite with jet black hair cut in a wedge that seemed completely inappropriate to the rural setting, might almost be described as her complete opposite. Nevertheless, something about the young woman behind the bar made him think about his lost friend—about the woman that he now realized he should have confessed to loving more than life itself—and the thought filled him with anguish.

"Work?" she finished, raising an eyebrow.

"Yes." The word was out before he could stop himself. Her monosyllabic inquiry had been in English and he had answered in kind.

Damn.

The woman evinced no surprise, but smoothly transitioned back to French. "You can work for your lodging and meals if you like. I have no rooms left, but there is a cot in the cellar. Come with me; I will show you."

"Wait." It was all happening too fast. He had no idea whether the barmaid was one of the Maquisards or an enemy informant, but either way the situation was slipping out of his control.

She leaned close. "I know what you are, stranger; you couldn't have been more obvious. Don't worry. We are on the same side."

"I think you have me confused with someone else."

"Do I? Aren't you Monsieur Wren?"

The Agent felt a degree of relief. "Wren" was the recognition code Tanner had told him to use in order to identify the resistance leader. "That is my name. I'm afraid you have me at a disadvantage Mademoiselle."

Her lips twitched in what was almost a smile. "You may call me Lara. Please, follow me. There is much to be done."

"Lara. That's a lovely name."

She shrugged. "It is a code name."

The Agent couldn't resist a chuckle. "A lovely code name, then. It certainly puts mine to shame."

**The first thing** the Agent became aware of upon descending into the dark environs of the inn's cellar, was that he and Lara were not alone. Barely perceptible in the shadows, he could just make out the forms of half a dozen rough looking men. Although he watched them from the corner of his eye, he kept his attention focused on Lara's back until she rounded a table and took a position directly across from him. Using a long wooden match, she lit a kerosene lamp and beckoned him to sit.

"You're arrival could not have come at a better time," she said, taking out a paper file folder and spreading its contents, three black and white surveillance photographs of a man wearing the uniform of a Wehrmacht officer, out for his inspection. "His name is Oberst Otto Hahn, the senior Abwehr officer in the region. He is staying the night in the house of the mayor. Tomorrow he leaves for Paris. We will only have one chance."

"One chance for what?"

She gazed back at him as if he were a dullard. "To kill him, of course."

Aware that he was under intense scrutiny, X fought to control his expression. "I believe there has been some misunderstanding. I am not here as an assassin."

"No? Then why are you here?"

"I have to get to Berlin on a matter of the greatest urgency. I was told that you could help me."

"Then you are correct. There has been a misunderstanding, and it is on your part. We are not here to do your bidding, spy." The last word was filled with contempt, an accusation. "We report what we see to your government and help rescue your pilots when they are shot down. In return, it is you who do our bidding. I would have thought that you understood this."

"I would have thought so too," the Agent murmured to himself. Messervie and Tanner had said nothing about the Maquis expecting him to act as an assassin on their behalf. "You know where Hahn is and where he's going, what do you need me for?"

"His death cannot be traced to the people of this village. The Nazis will exact a terrible revenge if they have even the slightest suspicion that we are operating here."

X recognized immediately that they were at an impasse. Given enough time, he knew he would have little difficulty making his own way across France and Germany, but time was something he didn't have. The Europe he knew had doubtless changed in twenty years and his unfamiliarity with the new landscape might spell disaster to his mission. The simple truth was that he needed the help of these resistance fighters. Maybe there was a way to turn this to his advantage.

"If I do this for you, then you must agree to help me get to Berlin. Deal?"

Lara scowled. "Berlin is hundreds of kilometers inside Germany. In case you hadn't noticed, we are French. The Germans do not let us simply walk across the border just because they have overrun our country."

He picked up one of the photographs. "Then maybe there's a solution to both our problems."

**Leutnant Heinrich Halle** stood patiently alongside the elegant gray Maybach SW 38 Town Car, waiting for his superior to join him. Oberst Hahn was a disciplined man who believed in setting an exacting itinerary and sticking to it. Halle knew that the senior officer of the Abwehr—Germany's defensive intelligence agency— would not deviate from his schedule one iota, no matter how robust the breakfast laid out by the mayor's wife. He checked his watch one last time, then without even looking reached for the handle of the rear door. In the same moment that it swung noiselessly open on well-oiled hinges, Hahn passed through the front door of the residence and strode toward the vehicle.

Halle snapped a smart salute—the traditional salute of the Heer, the German Army, rather than the Heil Hitler—which Hahn returned without missing a beat. "Good morning, Heinrich. You slept well?"

"Well enough."

"Good. It would be a shame if you fell asleep while driving and made me late to Paris."

Halle smiled at the old joke they often shared. He had been working for Hahn for the better part of a year and took great pride in his abilities as both as a driver and an aide-de-camp. With the Abwehr officer safely ensconced in the spacious rear passenger area, Halle slid in behind the steering wheel and started the 140 horsepower engine. Despite its reserve of power, the Maybach's power plant was as quiet as a purring kitten.

The luxury car certainly looked out of place in the rural village where the horse drawn wagons still outnumbered motorized trucks, and more than a few stares followed the vehicle as it moved smoothly along the cobble-paved main street. Halle much preferred to drive the Maybach on the autobahns of the Fatherland, where the long stretches of macadam allowed the car to reach its full potential, but for all its drawbacks, the French countryside was also a beautiful place for a drive.

A figure stepped into the roadway directly in his path and shook him from his musings. His first impulse was to accelerate and force the loiterer to get out of the way, but a second glance revealed that the man was wearing the same uniform as he—the man attempting to block his path was a fellow German officer.

Hahn looked up when he felt the vehicle braking. "What is this?"

"I will find out, Oberst." He left the car idling and stepped out to greet the officer, whom he immediately recognized as the commander of the detachment assigned to the village.

The officer raised his hand in the Heil Hitler salute, which elicited a frown of distaste from Halle as he returned it. Most of Germany's military forces were denied the dubious privilege of joining the National Socialist Party and the Heil salute felt like an insult to their proud warrior heritage. This man was evidently one of the few whose loyalty to the Fuehrer was fanatically absolute. "Herr Leutnant, it is imperative that I speak with the Oberst. There is a grave threat to his safety."

"Threats to the safety of the Oberst are my job, herr."

"Nein, I must speak to him. The information I have is for his ears alone."

Halle frowned, but before he could say another word, Hahn was out of the vehicle, tapping his wristwatch. "Heinrich, we must be on our way."

The garrison commander pushed past Halle and made a beeline for Hahn. "Herr Oberst, I must speak with you. It is a matter of grave urgency."

Hahn blew out his breath impatiently. "I am a busy man, Herr Oberstleutnant."

"I would not have interrupted your tour if this were not a matter of the gravest urgency."

"If you would simply tell us the nature of this threat," Halle intoned, "then we might be persuaded to change our schedule."

"Ja, that is what I wish to show you. Bitte, Herr Oberst, it will require only a moment of your time."

"Very well." Hahn strode forward and fell into step behind the officer.

"Where are you going?" asked Halle as the two men moved off the street and into an alley that was still shrouded in shadows, despite the hour.

"This will only take a moment," the junior officer promised, "but it is for your eyes only. It is a matter for the Abwehr."

Even as he said it, the officer disappeared from Halle's view, along with the man he was charged to protect. He took a step toward the alley, but Hahn's voice barked out: "Stay where you are, Leutnant. I will return shortly."

Halle sagged in resignation, but nonetheless cocked his ear toward the mouth of the alley. He could hear a discussion in low tones, and caught an occasional word, but the subject of the conversation was lost to him. True to his promise however, Hahn emerged after only about two minutes, pausing only long enough to wave and thank the other officer who evidently had elected to remain in the shadows.

"Quickly Leutnant," Hahn said, climbing into his seat. "To the inn."

Halle was stunned. His superior never did anything on the spur of the moment. Whatever the information that the Oberstleutnant had given him, it was enough for the Abwehr officer to drastically alter his lifetime habits. Halle quickly turned the Maybach around and drove directly to the two-story structure advertised as a traveler's rest. Hahn was out of the car almost before it stopped and his driver had to rush to secure the vehicle and get inside to protect the senior officer.

Hahn paid little attention to the younger lieutenant. Instead, he strode into the dimly lit common area as though he were the guest of honor, making an entrance to a grand ballroom. His eyes swept the room and then locked onto a petite figure with short dark hair that stared back aghast.

"Greetings mademoiselle," the Oberst said in heavily accented French as he stalked toward her. "A little bird has told me that you have been asking after my welfare."

The woman's eyes seemed to grow wider, an expression of complete surprise not quite masking the raw fear she felt at being confronted by one of the hated German invaders. "You must be mistaken, Herr Oberst."

"Oh, I don't think so," Hahn leaned close until his face was only inches from her and whispered the final accusation: "Lara."

"You," she gasped under her breath.

"Me," the Agent whispered, his voice pitched so low that no one else could hear it. Then he straightened and raised his voice—once more a perfect mimicry of Oberst Hahn's manner of speech—for the benefit of the awestruck spectators. "I would like you show you something, mademoiselle. This way, if you please."

The French woman seemed paralyzed, but the man masquerading as a German officer grasped her elbow and steered her toward the exit where his assistant was standing. "Leutnant, please start the car."

Halle obeyed and a few minutes later, the Maybach was once again threading through the village. The Agent stopped him again at almost exactly the same place where the officer had earlier intercepted them.

"Wait here, Leutnant." The Agent guided Lara out of the vehicle and led her into the alley. It was only here, away from the eyes and ears of possible informants, that he resumed speaking to the woman in a normal voice. He pointed to a large footlocker that now rested alongside one of the buildings. "Look inside."

A befuddled Lara complied, but when the lid was thrown back, she gasped in disbelief. Inside the chest lay the slumped figure of Oberst Otto Hahn. "How…?"

"I disguised myself as the garrison commander and intercepted Hahn as he was about to leave. I'll leave it to you to take care of him."

Lara looked again and her eyes flashed angrily. "He's still alive. You were supposed to kill him."

The Agent frowned. "It wasn't necessary to kill him. You said it yourself; he's a senior officer of the Abwehr. He's more valuable to your cause alive."

"That was not your decision to make."

"It became my decision when you involved me. Look, as far as everyone else is concerned, he is alive and well. As Hahn, I can easily make my own way to Berlin without arousing any suspicions. Meanwhile, you can deliver him to British Intelligence for interrogation. Everyone wins."

Lara was breathing through flared nostrils, struggling to control her rage—a rage the Agent could not quite comprehend. Then her expression abruptly changed. "My apologies, Monsieur Wren. Of course you are correct. You see, our loathing for these invaders sometimes overcomes our sense of what is for the greater good. You have upheld your part of our arrangement, and now I shall honor your request and help you reach Berlin."

"I appreciate the offer, but I think I can manage on my own." He turned and moved toward the street.

"Wait. What will you tell the driver?"

That stopped him. He was going to have a hard enough time explaining his actions to the Leutnant. Dragging Lara out of the inn and then leaving her in the alley was sure to arouse the man's suspicions.

"I know all about Hahn. I can help you perfect your disguise."

"And how will I explain you?"

"German officers often take mistresses. Hahn is no exception."

"A mistress?" The Agent smiled. "Well, I think I can manage to impersonate a German officer. We'll have to see how well you can do in your role."

## CHAPTER 12—CITIES OF LIGHT AND DARKNESS

**It had been** ages since he'd seen the streets of Paris, and as the Maybach cruised into the sprawling city that was at once both eclectic and modern, but also very much a bastion of the Old World, the Agent felt a pang of nostalgia. When he had left this place two score years ago, he had believed that the fighting was finally done; that his war had indeed been a "war to end all wars." But even as the invaders yielded the ground they had captured, the seeds of the next great World War had begun to germinate. The so-called Peace of Versailles had left Germany both disenchanted and financially ruined; a fertile environment for the insane ideology of the National Socialist party to grow like a poisonous fungus.

But Paris—ah, that was different. No matter which army claimed the ground as its own, the City of Lights was an eternal place, fixed in an ever-changing universe.

When Hitler's armies had swept across France, killing more than 90,000 French soldiers and citizens and completely exhausting the resources of his army, De Gaulle had made the bitter decision to surrender Paris without a fight. The timeless city, he reckoned was more important than the petty squabbles of nations, and so the majesty and beauty of Europe's greatest metropolis was unscathed; an island paradise in a turbulent sea of conflict. Although it meant that the swastika now flew over her skyline, the Agent reckoned De Gaulle had made the right choice.

To perpetuate the ruse that she was his mistress, Lara sat with him in the rear of the Maybach, embracing and exchanging syrupy expressions of affection. The amorous words were for the driver's benefit, but when Lara whispered in his ear, as she did frequently, she spoke only of Hahn and the agency he represented. Halle discreetly kept his eyes on the road, asking no questions of his superior officer.

When the Eiffel Tower became visible in the distance, X loudly asked: "Where do you want to stay tonight, darling?"

Lara smiled. "I've always wanted to stay at the Ritz."

"Leutnant, you heard the fraulein."

"Right away, sir." There was a hint of disappointment in Halle's tone, but he steered well clear of disrespect, leading the Agent to wonder if the driver wasn't simply a little jealous. He certainly had a right to be; Lara was naturally lovely, but when she made the effort to look less like a barmaid—to say nothing of a resistance fighter—and more like a lady of class, the effect was magical. Sitting with her during the long drive had been at once a thrilling and disconcerting experience. Thrilling, because the mere presence of such a lovely woman, her touch and the feel of her warm breath in his ear as she whispered, had reawakened the vital man within. Disconcerting for exactly the same reason.

He had freely chosen this path, but it had never been his intention to live the life of a monk. Yet somehow it had happened. He had always imagined that one day he would retire from fighting criminals and madmen bent on destroying his city, in order to settle down and have a normal life with Betty....

The mere thought of her opened a wound in his heart, and filled him with guilt—guilt for having failed to save her, for having passed up so many chances to openly declare that he loved her, and worst of all, for actually enjoying Lara's company.

What have I become? he thought. I don't even recognize myself anymore.

One facet of his soul was determined to carry a torch for Betty. She was only missing, after all. Perhaps Jim Hobart's search would pay off, and the sea would give her back to him. But another part of him, a part now speaking much louder than he ever would have believed, was crying for him to learn from his past mistakes. Losing Betty was unmistakably tragic, but the real tragedy was that he had failed to do what his heart wanted. He had passed up a chance at one of those inalienable rights—the right to pursue happiness.

And if another chance came along, what then?

He knew that he and Lara were simply two ships, passing in the night. As soon as he had the information he sought, he would be returning to the United States, while the beautiful Maquisard would return to her village and continue her struggle against the Nazi invaders. Their respective paths would lead them into harm's way, and there was a very good chance that the Grim Reaper would catch up with one or both of them along the way. And then, there would only be the regret of another lost chance at a fleeting moment of happiness.

He pushed his musings to the back of his mind as the Maybach rolled up to the front of the Ritz. In keeping with his disguise, the Agent imperiously ordered the concierge to look after his "lady friend," his car and his driver, in that order. Once ensconced in the relative safety of his suite, he locked the door and collapsed on the bed, where he was asleep the moment his head hit the pillow.

He awoke to something soft brushing against his hair. He opened his eyes to find Lara, seated on the edge of the mattress, caressing his face with her fingertips.

"Good afternoon," she said with a wry smile.

He stared back at her, still trying rising from sleep's embrace, and gradually realized that she now looked very different. Gone were the rough clothes of a rural French innkeeper, and in their place was a stunning evening gown of crushed crimson velvet. Her hair had been expertly coiffed to accentuate her high cheekbones and doe-shaped faced.

"Yes," he finally replied. "It is."

"This disguise is really quite extraordinary. Even this close, I cannot tell the difference. How did you manage it from just a few photographs?"

"Years of practice," he replied, straightening. "What time is it?"

"Almost time for supper. You are going to show me a night on the town, Herr Oberst, aren't you?"

"Just one of the sacrifices I will have to make in order to make this disguise appear more convincing."

Sacrifice or no, he had little difficulty fulfilling his promise. After an elegant dinner in the hotel's dining room, he escorted her along the Champs Elysees. Upon returning to the hotel, the danced for nearly two hours in the ballroom, and when it was all said and done, neither could remember what, if anything, they had discussed.

It was as if they had both taken a holiday from their lives—a vacation from war and strife.

It was well after midnight when they returned to their suite, and only when the door closed did X reluctantly put an end to the charade. "You can have the bed," he announced. "I'll make do in the sitting room."

Lara had not yet let go of his hand and she seemed reluctant to do so. She peered up into his steel-colored eyes. "A remarkable disguise," she said, echoing her earlier sentiment. "But I think I'd rather see more of the man behind the mask."

He held her gaze, his eyes giving no hint of the war within, but for every ounce of desire that he felt for this woman, there was an equal part of guilt for having failed the one woman who meant the world to him.

"Lara." He impulsively leaned forward and kissed her forehead. "Good night."

Her eyes lingered on him, and behind them her face seemed to shift randomly through emotions. She was both impressed by his chivalry and confused by the rejection; angered at a perceived insult and disappointed at having failed to successfully win his attention. After a moment, she gently tugged her hand free. "Good night," she replied, with just a hint of insincerity. "Sleep well."

Later, stretched out on a divan in the sitting room, Secret Agent X would have hours to ponder whether the beautiful woman in the other room was having as much trouble fulfilling her parting words as he.

**The morning found** them once more in Maybach, cruising along the roads toward the mountain passes leading into Germany. If Halle noticed that their displays of affection seemed a little more forced than they had on the previous day, he gave no indication, but both X and Lara were very much aware of the fact that they had something had changed between them.

Blame Paris, the Agent thought, gazing back at the City of Lights.

If Paris was an island removed from the sea of war, then the waters to the east were especially stormy. Although open hostilities had ended, the landscape bore the scars of recent combat and as the road took them closer to Germany, the signs of a military presence increased dramatically. Conversation and even the attempt of maintaining the illusion of a romantic tryst fell by the wayside as they crossed the border and motored toward Frankfurt on the Main River, their next stop on the road to Berlin.

There was no repeat of the previous night's romantic adventures. The Main was not the Seine, and Frankfurt, already a target of British bombing raids was nothing like Paris. Yet the change in the atmosphere between the Agent and Lara had little to do with geography. They ate a quiet dinner in the dining room of their hotel and quickly retired to their room, where X once more surrendered the comfortable bed to his companion.

They set out early the next morning, following the central autobahn, a word that literally meant "automobiles only," as it snaked across the scenic heart of Germany. Traffic was sparse, allowing Halle to indulge his passion for driving fast. The Maybach devoured the miles between the two cities, bringing them to their destination early that afternoon.

"I must speak with Admiral Canaris," the Agent announced. "Take my friend to my flat and then return to Abwehr headquarters to wait for me."

Halle answered affirmatively, while Lara looked at him sidelong, but said nothing. He recalled that she had asked him about his plans at some point during their private moments together, and that his answer had been vague, not because he did not wish to share that information with her, but rather because at the time, he wasn't sure exactly how he was going to proceed and her presence had been distracting enough to keep him from strategizing. The long road trip however had given him plenty of time to remedy that. Although he didn't know exactly what he was looking for, he had a pretty good idea of how to begin the search.

Halle expertly navigated to the heart of the city that had become the crown jewel of the Reich. Through an effort, X kept his expression neutral as they passed by spectacular examples of Nazi architecture—monumental edifices designed to inspire absolute loyalty and devotion to the Reich. In the midst of this sprawling governmental and military complex was the Supreme Headquarters of the Oberkommando der Wehrmacht, the High Command of Armed Forces, which encompassed all of Germany's military assets on land, at sea, and in the air, and right next to this was the head office of the Abwehr.

The Agent exited the Maybach without adding anything to his earlier instructions and stalked toward the main entrance of the headquarters building as if he knew exactly where he was going.

Beneath the brim of his cap, his eyes were flitting back and forth, catching every detail of his environment, registering faces, uniforms and even badges of rank. As he passed through the doors into the building's luxurious reception area, he took the further step of creating a mental blueprint of the office complex, a map that unfortunately still had a lot of question marks. There were two hallways leading deeper into the maze just behind the reception desk, but there was no indication of what might lay in either direction. Suppressing the impulse to explore, he simply approached the front desk and addressed the receptionist. "I must see

Admiral Canaris immediately."

The receptionist, a woman wearing the uniform of a Kriegsmarine yeoman, simply blinked at him.

He frowned haughtily. "Would you please inform him that I am on my way?"

"Ja wohl, herr Oberst."

He remained there, pretending to study the framed portrait on the wall behind her, but his peripheral gaze was fixed on the switchboard, noting the extension she connected to in order to relay his message. The label gave him a rough idea of what floor and office number the head of the Abwehr occupied.

"The Admiral awaits you, Herr Oberst."

He did not thank the yeoman, but simply turned on his heel and stalked off down the hall to the left. Once away from the scrutiny of eyes in the lobby, he was free to roam, but he had no intention of delaying his appointment. Using the brass number plaques on each door, he quickly navigated to a corner office marked not only with a number, but with the legend: Wilhelm Canaris, Admiral.

The Admiral's personal secretary waved him on into the private inner office where he at last laid eyes on Oberst Otto Hahn's superior officer and the man he hoped would help him uncover the truth about Nazi intrigues on American soil. He snapped to attention in front of Canaris's desk and announced himself with a brisk "Sieg, Heil."

The silver-haired Admiral gazed back, the corner of his mouth curling ever so slightly into a smile. "Why so formal today, Otto?"

"My apologies Herr Admiral," the Agent answered, smoothly dropping his salute and settling into a chair. "It is the weight of the information I have been carrying that distracts me."

"Ah, yes. A matter of some urgency."

"I believe it may be." X chose his next words carefully. "My agents have intercepted information concerning the operation in New York City."

Canaris seemed genuinely surprised. "There are no Abwehr operations in the United States."

"That was my understanding as well." He kept his face neutral, hiding his disappointment. He had hoped to resolve the matter here, in the headquarters of German Intelligence, but evidently the source of the plot lay elsewhere.

"The damned Schutzstaffel," mumbled the Admiral. "They do as they please, wherever they please. So now they are working in America. Interesting. What else did your agents learn about this rogue endeavor?"

Schutzstaffel—the elite Nazi security organization, thought the Agent. That will prove a tough nut to crack. But in the subtext of Canaris's comment, he saw something else. There was a rivalry between the Abwehr and the SS, something that went far deeper than mere competition. The SS was fanatically loyal to Hitler and the Nazi cause, whereas Abwehr was an extension of the military and looked out for what was in the best interest of Germany. He thought back to the rival factions within the New York gangs and realized that here too he was operating in a minefield where a single misstep might expose him as an impersonator. He had already erred, he realized, by using the Nazi salute; Canaris was not wearing the lapel pin of a party member, and likely harbored contempt for the radical political group that had hijacked his nation's destiny.

Drawing himself back to the discussion in hand, he replied: "Our spies, or rather those loyal to the SS it seems, are infiltrating criminal organizations in New York. There is talk of an impending event which will change the structure of power not only in the city, but in all of the United States."

"This is a bold play." Canaris's expression hardened into granite and he stood, grasping a walking stick capped with a silver eagle, and paced around the room. He was a small man, the Agent noted, with a faint limp. "But overthrowing the American government? Himmler could not marshal the resources for an invasion without my knowledge."

The Agent kept silent, curious to see what else the Admiral would reveal. After a moment however, the latter returned to his chair. "Excellent work, Otto. We will proceed cautiously."

"It may be too late for that, sir. The information I have received suggests that, whatever it is they are planning, will begin sooner rather than later." The Agent drummed his fingers thoughtfully on his thigh. "Where would the information about this operation be kept?"

"SS headquarters. Certainly, Reichsfuehrer Himmler would have a copy, but that does us no good. I cannot openly question Himmler."

A curious smile crossed the lips of the man pretending to be Oberst Halle. "Admiral, leave that to me."

## *CHAPTER 13-THE FACE OF EVIL*

**Shortly after nine** o'clock the next morning, a motorcade escorting a single staff car, flagged with the unique standard of Germany's highest official, arrived at a top secret location known as 'the Wolf's Den'—a hardened bunker from which the Fuehrer managed the day to day affairs of his campaigns in Europe. Eight men, all wearing expressions as hard as the armor on the vehicles in the motorcade from which the emerged, entered the bunker scrupulously searching every corner of the complex for anything that might threaten the life of the man they were sworn to protect. These men, the elite best of the Waffen SS were Hitler's hand-picked bodyguards and their loyalty was considered beyond question; not so with everyone else in military service. The Fuehrer had already survived numerous assassination attempts, many engineered from within his inner circle of advisors.

When their comprehensive sweep of the bunker was complete, the leader of Nazi Germany got out of his car and confidently made his way to the lavishly appointed office at the heart of the complex. There, he spent nearly an hour reviewing written reports and issuing directives to his key commanders. At approximately half past ten, he rose from his ornate desk and entered the luxurious adjoining bathroom. When he returned to his desk a few minutes later, his aides noted that his attitude seemed different, but they were accustomed to his abrupt mood shifts and gave little thought to the change.

"I want to see everything we have on the American project," he declared.

The aides knew nothing of such a project, but this too did not concern them greatly; much of the war plan was compartmentalized and the more secretive the project, the more likely it was that only those at the highest echelon would have any knowledge. When one of the aides explained this, as diplomatically as possible, the Fuehrer snapped: "Get me the Reichsfuehrer."

Again, the aides followed these orders without question. A telephone connection was quickly established and a few minutes later, the Fuehrer was speaking with head of the SS. "I wish to review the plans for the American project."

The voice on the other end was ambivalent. "We were going to discuss it this afternoon, as you requested."

"I wish to see the information now," the Fuehrer snapped.

"Very well. I will be there shortly."

The Fuehrer hung up without another word and dismissed his aides from the office. Forty-five minutes passed before a harried and frustrated Reichsfuehrer arrived at the Wolf's Den carrying a slim portfolio under one arm, where he found his superior's desk piled with war planning documents. The Fuehrer did not look up.

"Leave it. I will return it to you later."

Behind his round-framed spectacles, the Reichsfuehrer's eyes were beady points of frustration, but he pursed his lips and said only: "Ja wohl."

He set the leather folder on the desk, then smartly turned on one jack-booted heel and strode toward the exit door, but as his hand touched the latch, the sound of another door exploding open stopped him in his tracks. He whirled toward the source of the disturbance and stared in disbelief as a man—dressed only in his underwear—shambled from an adjoining room. Yet, it was not the man's attire that stunned the Reichsfuehrer into paralysis, but rather the fact that the figure emerging from the private bathroom was, in every way except for his lack of clothing, the spitting image of the man behind the desk.

The Fuehrer—the one in uniform—reacted first. He threw something onto the carpeted floor at the Reichsfeuhrer's feet. There was a muted popping sound as the small capsule burst, releasing a puff of white vapor. The head of the SS opened his mouth to sound the alarm, but the anaesthetizing gas silenced his cries before they could be uttered and he collapsed in a heap in front of the door. In the same smooth motion, the man wearing the face and uniform of the leader of Germany produced a second gas ampoule and hurled it at his doppelganger. The fume did its job quickly, reducing the man once more to a state of unconsciousness… but not in time to prevent him from screaming a single word that was the same in English as it was in his native tongue:

"Imposter!"

**Secret Agent X** muttered a very American curse as he stared at the prone form of Adolf Hitler. The dose of intravenous sedative he had given the Fuehrer should have kept the man out of commission for another two hours, allowing him plenty of time to photograph the files and then conceal himself once more until nightfall when he could make a surreptitious escape with no one the wiser. Now that plan was out the window.

He didn't know how long it would take for the aides in the outer office to investigate the outburst, but such a reaction seemed inevitable. The situation was eerily reminiscent of what had happened in the office at the Treasury Building in Washington DC, but this time there was no window through which to escape. There was only one way out of the Wolf's Den. He scooped up the portfolio and strode purposefully to the door, pausing only long enough to pull the Reichsfuehrer out of the way. The SS bodyguards were waiting for him on the other side. Their expressions were concerned, but none of them were impudent enough to ask outright concerning the commotion.

"The Reichsfuehrer is not to be disturbed," he instructed, closing the door firmly. Then, without another word of explanation, he started walking. The SS men immediately fell into step with him, and one of them hastened ahead, trying to anticipate the needs of the man he was sworn to protect.

X's mind was racing as he marched through the corridor toward the exit. The gas in the ampoules would not keep the men in the office out for very long and it was only a matter of time before a general alarm was sounded. If he didn't shake his escort before that happened, capture or death was almost a certainty.

What he did not know, what he could not have known, was that Adolf Hitler received daily doses of the drug Pervitin, a stimulant designed to combat depression that had the undesirable side-effect of altering the Fuehrer's metabolism. The amphetamine had caused his body to throw off the effects of the sedative, and by the same token, combated the effects of the anaesthetizing gas more quickly than expected. X had not yet reached the outer door of the bunker when a still dazed Hitler emerged from the office.

As the first shouts began echoing down the hallway, the Agent broke into a run. He pushed past the SS retinue and burst into the sheltered parking area where the Reichsfuehrer's sedan sat idling. Himmler's driver snapped to attention when he saw the familiar mustached visage, but instead of returning the Heil salute, the Agent pushed him aside and jumped behind the steering wheel.

Even as he sped away, a swarm of SS officers erupted from the mouth of the bunker, firing their pistols without hesitation at the retreating staff car. Bullets plinked ineffectually off the heavy armor plating, but the noise of the shots was enough to draw the attention of bystanders to the fact that something was very much amiss.

X put the pedal to the floor, but the response from the engine was sluggish; the vehicle had been designed with safety and security in mind, not speed, and all the armor plating concealed beneath its fenders made it heavier than an average motor car. The speedometer needle crept higher with agonizing slowness, but gradually inertia began to do its work and the lumbering juggernaut built up a head of steam, smashing through the gates of the military compound and bursting onto one of the city's primary arteries.

Traffic was light, owing to the urban environment and a program of fuel conservation, but what few cars that were on the road hastily swerved to the side when they caught sight of the Reichsfuehrer's standard snapping briskly on the front fenders. The broad way opened before him like the Biblical sea, clearing a path not only for his escape, but also for the three cars filled with SS men that were now hot on his heels.

The Agent muttered another oath. Ordinarily, his disguises had the effect of allowing him to blend in, to go unnoticed whether at high profile cocktail parties or clandestine criminal meeting, but the face he now wore and the car he was driving was having the opposite effect. I have to get rid of both, he realized. The sooner the better.

Before he could put this resolution into action however, the pursuit vehicles made their move. Lighter and more agile than the armored limousine, they shot forward like rockets. The Agent saw their approach in the fender-mounted mirror, and divined their intent: they were going to try to get ahead of him and box him in. A grim smile touched his disguised lips; he knew how to play that game too.

He steered to the far left, driving into oncoming traffic, what little of it there was, putting the passenger side—the left side—close to the sidewalk in order to close off that avenue of approach. This had the unfortunate effect of leaving the rest of the boulevard wide open for his pursuers to make their move on his right side, but like a master chess player shaping the battlefield, the Agent knew exactly what he was doing.

The lead SS vehicle took the bait and charged ahead along his right flank, pulling even with the armored staff car in a matter of mere seconds. The black sedan was filled with uniformed Nazis, and as it pulled alongside, those on the left side began brandishing their pistols and hurling demands for the Agent to surrender.

The Agent waited until the other vehicle was directly beside him, then tapped the brakes for a second, allowing the sedan to charge past him. Before the other driver could react accordingly, he stomped the gas pedal once more and steered sharply to the right, aiming the hood ornament of the limousine at the rear left tire of the sedan.

The impact of the collision shuddered through the car as the back end of the black sedan was blasted aside by the irresistible force of the lumbering limousine. The SS vehicle seemed to pirouette on its front wheels, spinning completely around as it caromed uncontrollably to the left hand sidewalk. The doors of the car burst open and some of the uniformed Nazi elite spilled onto the street tumbling into the path of the two remaining sedans, who hastily swerved and braked to avoid running over their comrades; the sickening crunch of bones under tires and the screams of onlookers indicated that they were not entirely successful in doing so.

The staff car however shrugged off the minor collision. The Agent straightened the wheel, retaking the center of the road, and punched the accelerator once more. His maneuver had bought him a few precious moments, but he knew that the Nazis would not be put off his scent for long, and it was only a matter of time before other forces—additional SS troops or the local constabulary—joined the hunt. His momentary advantage was a commodity that would perish if he did not invest it quickly.

With one hand he stripped off the mask that had given him the face that would one day be regarded as the very visage of evil itself. Though it pained him to do so, he also removed the secondary disguise that lay underneath—the face of Oberst Hahn—to expose his true countenance; Hahn's face might not be as instantly recognizable, but he dared not let the SS catch a glimpse of him as the Abwehr officer. To do so would not only close the easiest door of escape from the city, but also endanger Lara, who was presently sheltered in Hahn's flat.

He was not about to show his naked face to the enemy however. From the shapeless flesh-colored mass of his discarded disguises, he extracted bits of ersatz facial hair, still sticky with spirit gum, which he pressed onto his chin to create a hasty goatee beard, with enough left over to create a pair of bushy eyebrow. A few pieces of cosmetic putty, as malleable as modeling clay, changed the shape of his nose into a patrician beak, and the final touch—a pair of clear spectacles which he kept handy for just such an occasion—gave him the look of a surly professor. With the removal of the gaudy rack of medals and ribbons, the scarlet and black swastika armband, and the bright brass buttons, the Fuehrer's dress uniform looked enough like an ordinary brown business suit to avoid drawing too much attention, but that counted for little as long as Himmler's standard fluttered from the fenders of the limousine. Getting rid of that liability, X determined, was the next course of action. He was scanning the road ahead looking for a good place to ditch the staff car, when he spied a sign bearing the legend: "Zoologischer Garten Berlin," and a wry smile touched his lips.

The Agent pushed the staff car's engine into the red, spearing ahead toward his new destination. Ahead loomed a junction with a similar sign and an arrow pointing to the right, but his foot never touched the brake pedal. Instead, he eased off the accelerator and cranked the steering wheel right. The rolling juggernaut skidded sideways and was on the verge of spinning completely around, but X's deft touch on the wheel kept the limousine on track with only a negligible decrease in speed.

The built-up urban landscape abruptly transitioned into the greenery of a parkland as he drew closer and closer to the Zoologischer Garten—the Berlin Zoo, the oldest such institution in all of Europe. X steered toward the verdant open margin that surrounded the fenced menagerie. No obstacle was sufficient to impede the heavy limousine. The front wheels rolled easily over the curb and the bumper plowed through a sculpted topiary wall in an explosion of soil and shrubbery. The wheels sank into the loamy earth, throwing up a spray of dirt, but the staff car's momentum kept it moving forward.

The Agent kept a light grip on the steering wheel, trying to weave around pedestrian park-goers who now scattered in a frenzied panic, but control was an illusory concept. He wrestled the car toward a low hillock, abandoned by picnickers in the early moments of his noisy arrival, geared down, and punched the accelerator again, squeezing out every bit of speed he could manage.

The vehicle crested the hill, revealing the wrought iron fence that bordered the zoo and in the foreground, a narrow brook that crossed his path. A few visitors roamed along the edge of the stream, but the area directly ahead was clear. He would never have a better opportunity than this. He shifted into neutral, letting the downhill slope and gravity impel the car instead of the engine, and then worked the door lever.

There was no way to adequately prepare—physically or mentally—for what he knew would come next. Without allowing himself to think too much about what he was doing, he coiled himself like a spring and, with one hand clutching the portfolio, leapt from the car as it careened down the hill. In the instant before he hit, he stretched his limbs out and shifted his body weight in the direction of travel so that he would roll upon impact.

The turf was far more forgiving a surface than the macadam of a roadway, but nothing could change the fact that his body was moving at a speed of roughly thirty miles an hour when it slammed into the ground. The effect was something like being assaulted with sledgehammers, albeit hammers that had been padded with pillows. Pain bloomed all over his body as he rolled headlong down the slope. His world was a blur of green grass and blue sky, swirling together as he tumbled from one jolting impact to the next. He heard, but did not see, the limousine crash noisily into the brook in a hiss of steam; his view of the world continued to spin for several seconds after his actual motion ceased.

Secret Agent X lay still as long as he dared, waiting both for the return of his equilibrium and for the arrival of the tidal wave of pain that he knew from experience would slam into him as soon as the adrenaline began to dissipate. He was acutely aware that he was still the object of an intense manhunt, and knew that he had to get moving again. After only a few moments, he rolled onto hands and knees and tried to stand, but a sudden jolt of pain—a burning spear point of agony—stabbed through his chest and he collapsed involuntarily.

It had been more than two decades since a piece of German shrapnel had pierced his body, nearly taking his life. By nothing less than a miracle he had survived, but the wound had left him with an X-shaped scar near his heart, and a fierce blossom of pain that periodically—and unpredictably—left him all but incapacitated. He had learned ways to protect his heart and strengthen the surrounding muscle tissues, but the wound nevertheless became aggravated during times of intense physical stress. During the six months he had spent impersonating Aldo Novelli, the injury had remained quiescent and he had almost forgotten about it altogether, but the events of recent days—not the least of which was barely surviving the bomb blast at Carl Harris's butcher shop—had undone the recuperative effects of the passage of time. When he had first began his career as Secret Agent X, he had believed that the nearly fatal wound would someday finish him off, causing him to collapse in the middle of a hand-to-hand battle with thugs or betraying him during some deep cover operation; now it seemed, his long delayed appointment with the Reaper had finally come.

Two black sedans struggled over the hilltop, following an all too obvious trail, and then began rolling down the slope directly toward the place where Secret Agent X lay, writhing on the grass like a bug on a pin.

## CHAPTER 14-KING OF THE BEASTS

**The Agent struggled** against the invisible bonds of the old injury, trying to will his paralyzed body into motion. It seemed a futile effort; the two cars bearing Hitler's personal bodyguards rolled ominously toward him and would be on him long before he found the strength to take any sort of action in his own defense, but not for a moment did he resign himself to giving up without a fight.

To his complete amazement, the vehicles swerved to avoid striking him and continued down the hill toward the wreck of the staff car. The SS guards had looked right at him, but because he no longer resembled the man they were sworn to protect, they had assumed that he was but a random victim of their prey's destructive driving.

It was, he knew, only another brief reprieve. When the Nazis found the detritus of his original disguise in wreckage of Himmler's limousine, one of them was bound to remember the man in the brown suit lying stunned on the hillside. Nevertheless, the simple fact that he had narrowly escaped discovery, if only for a few moments, supplied the necessary impetus to get him moving once more. The scar on his chest burned as though the piece of German steel had never been removed, but he fought through the pain and got to his feet, shambling over the crest of the hill just as the SS troops disembarked their vehicles.

Once eclipsed from their sight, he veered back toward the zoo, where he hoped to lose himself in the crowd. Already, several more official cars were arriving on the scene, disgorging a small army of uniformed officers—both SS and municipal police—to supplement the small group on the other side of the hillock. He did not dare to hope that the Nazis would simply give up; if anything, throwing them off the scent was likely to prompt his foes to cast a wider net, conceivably cordoning off several city blocks in order to find the man that had not only penetrated into the very lair of their leader, but in so doing, badly embarrassed the men sworn to protect him.

Through a monumental effort, he managed to walk without giving any outward indication of the pain that wracked his body. He affected a disinterested saunter—the pace dictated more by the limitations of his body, than by a desire to avoid attracting attention—and reached one of the entrance gates to the zoological gardens just as the SS began rounding up witnesses in the adjoining park. Their next move, he reckoned, would be to secure the zoo and begin scrupulously searching every person therein. The Zoo Station, one of the city's most noteworthy mass transit hubs, loomed tantalizingly close, but by the same token, he knew that all rail passengers would also become targets of scrutiny. No matter how cleverly he disguised himself, the almost unlimited resources of his enemy would ferret him out the moment he tried to leave the area. As he moved deeper into the maze of animal habitats however, the desperation that had plagued him during his flight began to evaporate; his mastery of cosmetic masks might not suffice to save him, but he had other skills and abilities with which his enemy did not reckon.

Police agents had already begun filtering into the grounds by the time he reached his destination—the lion compound—but thankfully the area he sought was sparsely occupied, and after waiting only a few minutes, his opportunity came. When no one was looking, he slipped over the barrier and descended into the broad concrete moat that separated the habitat of the ferocious felines from the viewing public.

Despite long years of captivity and close interaction with humans on a daily basis, the pride of lions on display had not forgotten that they were instinctively predators. The great cats—predominantly the females—stirred from their restless midday sloth and began prowling closer to the edge of the moat as the now sodden Secret Agent ascended the rusty iron rungs of the safety ladder. Beneath their golden pelts, their muscles rippled as they tensed in preparation to pounce on a hapless victim.

Then something remarkable happened. The lions stood frozen in place, staring into the Agent's eyes as if trying to comprehend a deep mystery, and then for no apparent reason, turned away and returned to their earlier somnolent posture. The cats ignored him completely as he stole into their compound and found concealment within the artificial cave that served as a shelter for the beasts.

Although he rarely had opportunity to use it, Secret Agent X possessed the unique ability to hypnotize most animals simply by gazing into their eyes. It was a remarkable gift that he had discovered and refined during a youthful sojourn to the Orient, but other than the occasional guard dog, there were few animals to mesmerize in the urban jungle where he primarily operated. In the moment he spotted the signs for the city's zoo, the seed of this plan had begun to sprout; he knew that he would never be able to outrun the SS, but by hiding in a place that his foes would almost certainly never look, he was confident that he could outwait them.

Completely concealed from the viewing area, the Agent's first course of action was to simply relax. The throbbing ache in his chest had not yet relented, and the bruises he had sustained while bailing out of the car had now added their own dull noise to the symphony of his suffering, but he was no stranger to pain. Just as his mentors in Asia had schooled him in the use of his gift with animals, so too had they taught him meditative techniques to sublimate pain and quicken the healing process. After about fifteen minutes of quiet, motionless reflection, the roar of his many hurts softened to a faint murmur.

The leather portfolio—the very thing that had brought him quite literally into the lion's den—lay innocently on his lap, and for the first time since acquiring it, he gave into his burning curiosity and opened the clasp. The first page was marked with numerous warnings about the secrecy of the information contained therein, but the Agent's eyes were drawn to the two words in the very center: Erste Welle—First Wave.

His mind began churning over the implications contained in that simple pairing of words. Based on what he had already deduced about Nazi operations in America, the intent of the operation was glaringly evident: it was a plan for the invasion of the United States.

However, as he began thumbing through the document, laboriously translating the cumbersome German into English, he realized that Erste Welle was something much more terrible.

## *CHAPTER 15-THE TRAP*

**He had set** out from the Berlin apartment home of Oberst Otto Hahn unnoticed, as stealthily as a ghost, and almost twenty-four hours from that moment, Secret Agent X returned in exactly the same way. No one in the building took note of his approach, and the lithe form of the Maquisard fighter he knew only as "Lara" did not stir beneath the blanket as he crept in through the upstairs window. Yet, despite the fact that only a single day had elapsed between his going and coming back, the man that now stood in the shadows felt as though the Atlas's burden had shifted onto his own shoulders. He sank wearily into a corner chair and tried to set aside, if only for the balance of the night, the wearisome weight of the knowledge he now carried. At some point in the long night, the gentle rise and fall of Lara's breast beneath her coverlet lulled him into a deep dreamless sleep.

He awoke to the feel of something cold and hard pressing against his cheek. His eyes fluttered open and the first thing he saw was Lara, wrapped in the blanket, barely visible in the pre-dawn twilight. What he couldn't see, but nevertheless knew was there, was the gun she held to his face.

"Who are you?" she asked in a low, threatening tone.

"It's me."

The gun barrel did not move. "How can I be sure? I don't even know what you really look like?"

X almost laughed at the comment. As his mind came awake, he recalled that he had not removed the hasty disguise created during the car chase earlier the previous day. "Believe it or not, Lara, sometimes I forget what I really look like."

When he said her name, the pressure against his cheek eased a fraction. "So you know my name."

"Yes, and you know me only as Wren. Now, what else do I have to do to convince you?"

At that, she removed the gun and leaned close so that he could see her face in the darkness. "Kiss me. I'll know if it's you."

"But we haven't kissed before. You'll have nothing to compare to."

A shadow of disappointment flickered in her eyes but then she straightened. "I guess it really is you. Did you find what you were looking for?"

He thought about the contents of the portfolio, which he had destroyed after making a photographic duplicate. The film record of Erste Welle was now hidden in a secret compartment in the heel of his shoe, but the knowledge of what it would mean for America—for the whole world, really—burned in his brain like an open wound. "I did," he answered simply. "I need to get back as soon as possible."

"We can leave at first light, but...."

"Yes?"

"Something has happened. The entire city is being searched and there are checkpoints at every road leading out. We will be under intense scrutiny when we leave."

The Agent winced; in violating the Fuehrer's sanctum, he had stirred up a hornet's nest. "We'll leave the same way we came in; Oberst Hahn and his mistress."

She nodded, her expression now strictly business, and turned away to begin making preparations for departure, while X began the laborious process of creating a new mask in the image of the Abwehr officer.

Though he was reluctant to do so, he summoned Leutnant Halle to resume his duties as driver, and placed a telephone call to Admiral Canaris's office, informing the intelligence service's chief of his intent to return to France. Establishing a trail of legitimacy would be crucial to getting past the checkpoints at the edge of the city, but he wondered if even that would suffice. Among other things, the Erste Welle project had specifically identified Secret Agent X as an enemy to be reckoned with, and now the Nazis would know for certain who it was that had penetrated to the very heart of their empire. A perfect disguise, the uniform of a senior officer, expertly forged documents...all of those were tricks they would be expecting now that they knew he was in their midst.

Halle arrived with the car shortly after sunrise and their journey commenced immediately. Like Lara, the driver knew of the checkpoints and made mention of the fact that there would be a considerable delay. X, aware that anything he said might arouse the German's suspicions, made a disparaging comment about the SS, which seemed to please the lieutenant.

As they took their place in the line of cars departing the city, the Agent made perfunctory complaints about the delay, while inwardly he fought back a rising wave of anxiety. Only by maintain perfect control—by convincing the soldiers manning the checkpoint that he was exactly who he claimed to be and merited no further scrutiny—would he escape the trap they had set for him. Two long hours ticked by with agonizing slowness as the troops at the checkpoint extensively questioned and searched every person in every vehicle. And then, it was their turn.

The officer in charge saluted him as he got out and offered a disingenuous apology for having to subject someone of superior rank to the indignity of a search. The man's eyes were steady as he spoke, never leaving the Agent's face, and watched for the slightest sign of deceit. X kept his own gaze a cold and firm as steel.

"You are only doing your duty," he said, with equal sincerity. "Now, if you please, dispense with the pleasantries and carry out your orders so that I can be on my way."

The officer regarded him suspiciously and seemed on the verge of making an accusation, a tactic he fully expected as part of their game—one of the tricks employed by policemen all over the world, secret or otherwise, was to confront a person with an unfounded accusation, just to see how they would react—but then a strange grin broke across the man's face. "You may return to your car, mein herr."

The Agent was stunned into momentary silence. "That's it?"

"Of course. You are a trusted officer of our intelligence service, are you not? I would not dream of molesting you." And then he smiled again. "However, your French whore is another matter."

Here then was the trap. How would a German officer react? Would he be offended at the open insult to Lara's honor? Or would he treat her disdainfully, as a chattel? "Do what you must," he finally said. "But try not leave any marks. She is a good mistress."

The officer laughed sardonically, and then gestured to the soldiers in his command. The Agent calmly returned to vehicle, not glancing over at his companion as she was led away. For nearly fifteen minutes, he sat there, not speaking to Halle, not knowing what Lara would say if subjected to intense interrogation techniques, or even…torture.

And then without and sort of warning, Lara returned. Despite an angry scowl, she looked none the worse for wear, but she said nothing as she got in on the opposite side of the car.

The officer leaned close to the Agent's open window. "You are a lucky man, mein herr. Enjoy your trip to Paris."

**They drove almost** non-stop across Germany. Halle seemed to understand that he was eager to return Lara to her hometown, even if he did not quite comprehend why, and thought nothing of trading off driving duties with the man he believed to be his superior, whenever they stopped for fuel or food. They did not stop for sleep as they had during the trip to Berlin, but continued driving through the night. The reached Paris in the early hours of the following morning, but did not stop, not even for breakfast.

Early on, Lara had whispered a few words to him, assuring him that nothing untoward had happened during the search and interrogation at the checkpoint. She had not dared go into detail, not with Halle present, but her tone was calm and confident. He should have felt relief at having escaped the trap set by his enemies, but instead his apprehension was replaced by a different kind of anxiety—the fear that he would be too late to thwart the Nazis diabolical scheme to destabilize the American government. The details of the plan roiled in his conscious mind like a gathering storm; strange names: Die Stahlhand, Karo As—code names only, the Erste Welle document did not reveal the true identities of these foreign espionage agents—and the key to it all, Lorelei.

It was a race now. The plan did not specify a timeline for implementing Erste Welle, but because the Nazis knew that their enemies were aware of their intentions, they would most certainly strike quickly. Every hour spent in transit, every moment that prevented him from revealing what he knew and devising a strategy to thwart the destructive attack, burned in his gut like an accusation of failure.

With Paris behind them, the Agent now gave thought to the delicate matter of returning to friendly shores. He had originally counted on Lara's compatriots in the resistance movement to arrange for travel back to Britain, but there simply wasn't time to make the long journey across the rural northern countryside and into the politically neutral nations that bordered occupied territory—the route most often used by Allied pilots shot down over France. The urgency of his mission would necessitate a much greater level of risk.

X was taking his turn behind the wheel when they rolled up on Lara's village, late that afternoon. With Halle dozing in the backseat, he simply drove the sedan to the travelers' inn where he had made his first encounter with the lovely Maquisard.

"You must find a way to contact the British intelligence service," he whispered as they got out of the vehicle. "Let them know that it is imperative that they arrange to pick me up as soon as possible."

"You're leaving," she replied, a hint of disappointment in her voice. "Just like that?"

In spite of the rightness of his intentions, he felt guilty for having used her as nothing more than a pawn in his game. "Lara, it's what I have to do. Many live are at stake."

"It's a war. Lives are always at stake."

"If the Nazis succeed in this plan, it may ensure their victory. I can't let that happen."

She regarded him with a strange expression; disappointment, but something else too that he could not quite read. "Very well. You must continue to be Oberst Hahn for now. Return to the mayor's house where he was staying. Then tonight, when everyone is sleeping, come to the inn as the man I first met."

"Can you arrange passage out of here?"

"Tonight," she promised, "I will speed you on your way."

**At the appointed** hour, Secret Agent X, once more wearing the face of FBI Agent Wesley Greaves, made his way through the shadows to the place where he had first become acquainted with the lovely dark-haired Lara. It was difficult to believe that, after so many encounters with danger, he had come full circle in less than a week's time, but here he was, right back where he had started, the mission very nearly accomplished.

Lara had slipped effortlessly back into her role as barmaid, though he wondered what stories she would tell the patrons of her whirlwind adventures in Paris and Berlin, and what sort of gossip would haunt her in the days and weeks to come. When she saw him, she gave an eager smile, and then gestured with her eyes in the direction of the cellar door and removed her apron.

Lara's cell of fighters were once more gathered in the basement of the inn, nervously awaiting the presence of their leader and her guest. Few words were exchanged when she arrived, and no time was wasted in setting out for a destination that was—to the Agent at least—a complete mystery. A lesser mystery was solved immediately however—the problem of how to leave the fenced perimeter of the village unnoticed by the German garrison—when two of the Maquisards removed a section of the wall mounted wine rack to reveal a narrow tunnel opening. Without further ado, Lara lit a single stubby candle and proceeded into the dark cut in the earth.

The journey through the long claustrophobic passage took nearly fifteen minutes—if his pace count was correct, X reckoned it to be more than half a mile long, a considerable and dangerous undertaking for the resistance fighters—and when they finally emerged, the village was completely eclipsed by a stand of trees. Now moving in total darkness, the group continued trekking along a game trail until they reached a clearing. Lara signaled for the group to wait there, and then disappeared into the thicket.

The trap was sprung with such alarming suddenness that even the Agent was taken completely by surprise. Perhaps it was the cumulative effects of several exhausting days, or maybe just the false sense of having left the most dangerous part of the journey behind…whatever the reason, he had let his guard down and is finely honed instincts failed to alert him to the danger.

Without any sort of warning, the meadow was flooded with brilliance. Blinding illumination burst out in an incandescent circle, surrounding the small group. Caught unaware though he was, X's finely tuned reflexes caused him to react instantaneously; he threw himself flat on the ground, shading his eyes as he dove for cover, even before his mind had fully processed what was occurring.

The lights were artificial, emanating from battery operated handheld torches—handheld, the Agent knew with certainty, by an unknown enemy. An enemy that must already have captured Lara, he thought with a sick feeling.

The resistance fighters were slower to react, but only by a fraction of a second, and the conclusions they reached were the same. To a man, they shaded their eyes with one hand, while raising their guns in the other. To an even greater degree than the Agent, they knew what this peril represented. Going down in a blaze of gunfire was certainly preferable to the fate that would await them if they were taken alive, but blinded as they were, their shots be wasted in the impenetrable dark spaces between the light. Unarmed, but for his few remaining gas grenades, the Agent did not have that luxury. A shot was fired—by whom, it was impossible to say—and the dam burst.

The clearing was suddenly filled with thunder. Three of the resistance fighters were cut down in the first salvo, one of them falling close enough to where X lay that the latter could see his eyes, wide open, but forevermore sightless. The Agent however did not return the dead man's stare; his gaze was rested on the rifle that lay discarded beside the man.

Through the ringing in his ears, he became aware of the fact that the exchange of gunfire had ceased. A quick glance confirmed his worst suspicion: all of the Maquisards were down, dead or seriously wounded. X scanned the carnage quickly, but his eyes returned to the fallen firearm, perhaps two paces from where he lay. Though he had all but foresworn the use of lethal weapons in his crusade against crime in New York, he had no illusions about the gravity of this situation. Nor did he believe for a moment that he would get out of this trap alive. Focusing his courage into a course of action, he mentally choreographed the minimum number of motions required to reach the weapon and begin firing back at the unseen enemy.

He was within a hair's breadth of making his move when a figure brandishing a smoking handgun emerged from the tree line. The Agent however barely noticed the pistol.

"Lara?" It was not the realization of her treachery that left him unable to do aught else but speak; rather, it was incredulity at his own failure to have recognized it during the course of their time together. Had her guise and guile been so perfect then? Or had he intentionally blinded himself to the warning signs that ought to have alerted him to the danger?

The circle of torchlight closed inward as several more individuals, likewise armed with pistols that stank of burned cordite, joined her. They wore no uniforms, but their dress and carriage was not that of the French rural farmers that lay dead all around; these men were Germans, almost certainly SS agents.

"Do not move," she instructed, staring at him down the length of the gun barrel so there would be no question where the bullet would go if fired. "Not a muscle, Secret Agent X."

He sagged, seemingly in defeat, certainly in resignation of the fact that for the moment at least, he was her prisoner. Nevertheless, while he drew breath, he was not beaten; already the sting of her betrayal was fading, as his imperative to survive began to assert itself. "I was wondering when you'd show your true colors."

"Liar." Her tone was almost mocking…almost. There was something in her voice, in her eyes…an enigma that could not quite be explained away with any of the labels he associated with the crowing of a triumphant victor.

Suddenly the thunder of gunfire again ripped the night asunder, but this time it was the overcoated Nazi agents that went down under a hail of accurate fire—submachine guns by the sound of it. Geysers of blood sprayed bright scarlet in the last instant before the flashlights were dropped to the ground, but in that final moment, the Agent saw Lara's slim figure likewise blossom with deadly crimson flowers. Her silhouette was visible against the diffuse light of discarded torches. She lay only a few feet away, her face twisted in agony.

A second time the guns went silent, but through the roar of blood rushing and the ringing in his ears the Agent barely noticed. He crawled closer to Lara, unconsciously staying low lest the fusillade resume, and moved with an odd sort of sympathy, brushed a bit of dirt from her cheek.

"You could have taken me anytime; why did you wait?"

Her agonized stare locked with his, her face a twisted mask of pain and emotion. "Don't you know?" It was the last thing she ever said.

"Greaves?" A familiar voice shouted in a stage whisper. It was Tanner, the man from MI-6.

"I'm here," the Agent called, staying down and waving a hand until the sound of approaching footsteps indicated that the area was more or less secure. He got to his feet slowly, and saw in the eerie glow of randomly placed a scene of carnage more terrible than anything his eyes had beheld since…since the last war.

The living were outnumbered by the dead. Only two other men walked among more than a dozen corpses; one of them was Tanner but the identity of the second yielded yet another stunning revelation, just when X would have believed himself beyond his capacity for being surprised.

"Oberst Hahn?"

The Abwehr officer, now dressed in civilian clothes, inclined his head by way of greeting, but said nothing. Like Tanner, he cradled a compact machine pistol in his arms, scanning warily for some foe that their assault might have missed.

"Sorry to have waited to the last minute there, old chap." Tanner laid a hand on his shoulder. "Are you hurt?"

"You knew all along, didn't you? You knew she was working for them."

Tanner sighed. "We knew there was an SS operative working in this cell, but we weren't sure who it was. Otto here has been working for us, getting messages to and from a sympathetic official in his service—"

"Admiral Canaris." The Agent realized aloud. "The SS knew that Hahn was working with you; that's why Lara ordered me to kill him."

"Lucky thing you didn't. Nevertheless, his cover is blown."

"You used me to flush her out." It wasn't an accusation; just as with Lara's treachery, the thing that stung the most was his own failure to have seen the web of puppet strings controlling his actions. He had thought to use the British Intelligence Service and the Maquis to his own ends, and instead he had ended up the pawn in a game that even now, he barely understood.

*None of that matters. Let them have their war; I've got to stop Erste Welle.*

Tanner did not answer his question directly. "It's a complicated affair. I'll explain it all when we're safely on our way, but just now we've got to be moving. We've got a plane to catch."

The Agent nodded. "You're right. Let's go home."

But as he left the clearing and the bodies of the fallen behind, Lara's parting question lingered in his mind: *Don't you know?*

He thought that maybe he did know, and that knowledge would haunt him to the end of his days.

## PART THREE: THE SEA WRAITHS

## CHAPTER 16-THE SURVIVOR'S TALE

**It had taken** Jim Hobart the better part of a week to put together the facts—such as they were—regarding the mysterious disappearances at sea. The first and easiest step had been to follow up on the front-page story concerning the most recent tragedy in which two of The Herald's reporters had evidently perished. Hobart had met Betty Dale once or twice and he felt a pang of grief at the thought of her resting in a watery grave. Yet, for all that the news item tugged at the heartstrings of its readers, it offered precious little information about the phenomenon which had led to Miss Dale's untimely demise.

From Betty's editor at The Herald, he had ascertained a few more details about the disappearances. He discovered that Betty and Acer, the photographer, had been in contact with a Coast Guard officer in South Carolina. A call to Ensign Barlowe of the US Coast Guard had given him his first real look at the scope of the crisis; the number of ships lost along that particular section of the coast numbered nearly twenty in the space of less than a year, and with the exception of the salvage vessel chartered by Acer and Betty Dale, the lost ships were ore carriers and freighters with cargo ranging into the millions of dollars. Hobart wondered, much as Barlowe and Betty Dale before, how the loss of so many ships, cargoes and lives had gone unnoticed by the rest of the world.

The most recent disaster, which had claimed the two journalists, had changed that trend. Ensign Barlowe was no longer carrying on his investigations as a hobby;

rather, he now had the full support of his chain of command, along with the cutter Vigilant, to delve into the mystery. It had not taken a great deal of arm-twisting to get a berth on the Vigilant, and so five days after taking the new case, Hobart was going to sea. After a brief tour of the ship, he was led to the ship's wardroom to meet with Barlowe.

The Ensign was much younger than Hobart had expected; he looked barely twenty years old, with wispy blonde hair and a rangy build that seemed ill suited to the life of a sailor. Yet, for all his physical immaturity, this young man had been the only one in his organization to grasp that the missing ships might be more than just a matter of misfortune on the high seas; there was more to Ensign Barlowe, Hobart decided, than met the eye.

"Mr. Hobart, welcome aboard." Barlowe shook his hand effusively. "Can I get you anything? Some food? The coffee here is…" He shook his head sadly.

"Nothing, thank you. If it's all the same, I'd like to get right to the business at hand."

"I will brief you of course before we cast off, but I'm expecting one more passenger first—ah, I believe he's arriving now."

Hobart turned to see a handsome dark-haired young man, attired in a crisp black business suit. The newcomer's expressionless eyes swept the room, lingering on each face just long enough to memorize the features, and then he approached the table. The ensign exchanged a handshake with the man then turned to Hobart.

"Mr. Hobart, this is Agent Wesley Greaves of the Federal Bureau of Investigation. He'll be coming along for the ride."

The G-man cast another appraising glance at the red-haired detective. "What's your affiliation, Mr. Hobart?"

Though there was nothing overtly supercilious about the tone of the question, Hobart felt as though he had just been insulted. "Not that it's any of your concern, Agent Greaves, but I am working on behalf of Mr. A.J. Martin, the newspaperman."

"Never heard of him. So you're a reporter?"

"Ah, not exactly."

"Gentlemen," Barlowe interposed, "there will be plenty of time to get acquainted once we're underway. Before we cast off however, I wanted to apprise you of an exciting new development in this mystery."

The Coast Guardsman paused as if waiting for one of the men to make an inquiry, and simultaneously both men did so. "Development?" they asked, almost in perfect unison.

"Indeed. It seems that a survivor has been found!"

**With each day** that passed, the sting of the memory of the treacherous attack at the Brooklyn warehouse abated more and more, to the extent that Jack Scorza had almost put the whole affair out of his mind. The world that he occupied was a violent place, and violent upheavals were par for the course, but as the Vaudeville performers often opined: "The show must go on." Petrona might have taken control of the mob, but thus far he had been content to let the capos run their respective enterprises without interference, which was actually a welcome change from the way things had been under Novelli. Getting back to business as usual seemed like the best way of putting the whole tragic affair behind him.

He got in late, as he often did following a busy Saturday night at the casino. The house was quiet—his wife had long ago abandoned the idea of waiting up for him—but he was still wound up from the excitement of helping the City's upstanding citizens part with their hard-earned money. Lingering in the front room of his palatial Manhattan town house, he poured a drink and fished out his cigarette case. Before he could flick open his lighter however, a flame appeared in front of his face. He started for his gun, but the sudden feel of steel against the back of his neck stayed his hand.

"Go on and light up, Jack. The condemned man always gets a last smoke."

The familiar voice destroyed the fragile façade of normalcy like brick through a plate glass window. Novelli! "So you decided to come back and off me, huh?"

"Why not? You're still dancing to Luigi's tune, aren't you?"

"Business is where you find it." Scorza did his best to remain defiant, but the cigarette nevertheless fell unlit from his quivering lips. "I don't see you making any move to bring him down."

"You need to open your eyes, Jack. Luigi's about to make his move, and when he does, he's going to order you and the others to betray America to the Nazis."

"It'll never happen."

"Oh, it will. It will happen like this. Something is going to happen—something big and destructive—and the city will collapse into anarchy. Petrona and his Nazi buddies have it all worked out. The police will be overwhelmed; there will be riots, looting—chaos everywhere. That's when Luigi will give the order for the bosses to begin taking control of the city, supported by a small army of Nazis who will show up just in time to establish law and order. The survivors will welcome them, little realizing that the whole thing is a carefully planned invasion."

"That's crazy. Destroy the city? Luigi would never do that." But even as he said it, Scorza thought about Petrona's words at the warehouse meeting—he had promised to make them all kings in some kind of new order of things.

"The question is: would you let him do it?"

The hand holding the lighter abruptly vanished and the gun barrel moved away from his neck. The mobster turned slowly to face his captor, his hands held out submissively. He swallowed down his fear and answered truthfully. "I've worked too hard for what I got. Destroy the city? Not a chance."

"That's all I want from you, Jack. Tell the others what I've told you…as many as you think will listen. When Luigi and the Nazis make their move, it will be up to you to stop him."

"How do I know that this ain't some crazy scheme you've concocted for us to bump him off so you can take back your old job?"

Novelli pocketed the automatic with a cryptic smile. "I'm giving up my criminal ways, Jack. After today, you won't see me again."

"Then who's gonna run the city?"

"I'm sure you fellows will work something out." Novelli backed away, never taking his eyes off Scorza, just in case.

"Hey, Boss. One more thing."

The heavyset former gangster paused at the front door. "Yes?"

"You said these Nazis are gonna do something really bad, try to destroy the city or something? How are we gonna stop them?"

"I'm going to stop them Jack," he answered, his face evincing relief. "But it's nice to know that you're finally on my side."

And with that, the man calling himself Aldo Novelli stepped through the doorway, never to be seen again.

**Agent Wesley Greaves** watched with great interest as the motor launch bearing Richard Acer, sole known survivor of the wreck of The Black Spot, approached the Coast Guard cutter. During the ocean cruise up the Atlantic coast—a journey that had ironically brought him back to New York City—the G-man had pondered what he would find upon meeting Acer; would the castaway photographer be able to lead him to Miss Betty Dale?

It was Betty Dale that had brought him to Charleston in the first place, Betty Dale, the star reporter of The Herald, who seemed to have a unique relationship with Secret Agent X. Inspector Burks had admitted as much and yet the seasoned law enforcement veteran had never followed up on the connection. Greaves biggest regret was he had come to New York too late to arrest Miss Betty Dale for aiding and abetting a fugitive.

Now that Agent X was dead, the mystery of his identity was no longer a matter of great urgency, but Greaves was not yet ready to let the case die along with its chief suspect. X could not have acted completely on his own; there had to be others—hadn't his own chief at the Bureau intimated that there was a network of Secret Agents operating in the shadows? With luck, Richard Acer would lead him to Betty Dale, and Betty would unlock the door on that Agency.

Acer did not look like a man who had been adrift for several days in the Atlantic Ocean. The only lingering indication of his ordeal was hair bleached nearly white that framed a complexion that was an almost ruddy shade of bronze. He was thin, but not gaunt, and seemed to have fully recovered his health. Greaves continued watching as Ensign Barlowe welcomed the man aboard, and was only peripherally aware of his fellow passenger, the red-haired fellow who claimed to be working for some newspaper man—for some reason, Greaves felt he should look into Hobart's background a little more, but that would have to wait until he was back on dry land.

Barlowe, recognizing that everyone was eager to begin the search for the missing salvage vessel, bade good-bye to his counterparts on the motorized launch and then escorted Acer to his berth as the cutter began maneuvering onto its new heading. He wasted little time in getting the photographer to the wardroom where the latter began to tell his tale.

"I'm not quite sure where to begin," Acer said. He stared at both of the ship's guests; a long hard gaze that scrutinized every detail of their faces. The inspection went on for an uncomfortably long period of time, but then Acer's steely eyes relented and he resumed speaking. "I know it's going to sound unbelievable in this day and age, but our ship was attacked by pirates."

Greaves listened in amazement as the photographer told a tale of being waylaid by a force of men who came out of the sea in strange miniature submarines. It was a vivid story, told with an eye for the sort of physical details one would expect from a man who made his living capturing evocative images on film. He described the pirates with astonishing clarity—their swarthy skin, their crude clothing, even the intaglio of tattoos that marked their arms and faces. The pirates took Betty Dale hostage and then left Acer along with the rest of the crew to die aboard the sinking vessel. Although the photographer had been swept under the waves by the cavitation of the hull as it slipped beneath the surface, he had managed to struggle back from his watery grave. For days thereafter, he had drifted—both literally, in the grip of sea currents, and figuratively, as his traumatized consciousness floated inexorably into a state of delusion. At one point, or so he said, he had befriended a shark that had been circling for hours. Their ensuing conversation would have been humorous to the listeners, had it not been a testament to the madness that had overcome him as he faced the very real specter of his imminent demise.

When he finished, Greaves and Hobart asked the same question simultaneously: "Do you know where they took Betty Dale?"

Acer seemed to ponder this question. "I'm no mariner, but I think I can estimate our location based on the length of time we traveled from Charleston. Those mini-subs couldn't have gone too far on their own power, so the pirates either have a base ship or operate from a nearby island."

"We know the last radioed coordinates of the Black Spot," supplied Barlowe. "We've thoroughly searched that area in every direction many times, but it's as good a starting point as any."

"At least we finally have something concrete to go on," Hobart observed.

"I believe Betty Dale is still alive," said Acer, seemingly out of the blue. "I know we can find her."

Wesley Greaves nodded thoughtfully at the comment, but failed to notice that the photographer was once more carefully studying his reaction.

## CHAPTER 17-LIGHTNING STRIKE

**The aged-brick** edifice that housed the Colonial Research Foundation helped convey the impression that the business of the men and women who worked within had something to do with American history. This was partly true; the researchers did not have the task of digging into history, but rather it was their job to collect and archive information from numerous and diverse contemporary sources. In short, they were gathering the most comprehensive record of current events—information that would indeed one day be part of the historical record. What none of the employees of the Colonial Research Foundation—save for the one man in charge of it all—understood was that their tireless efforts contributed to history in another way. The Foundation was in reality, the backbone of Secret Agent X's network.

The head of the institute, Harvey Bates, was alone in the quaint old building, burning the midnight oil. He sat hunched over a desk, laboriously studying a sheaf of papers in the glow of a desk lamp. The hulking Bates, who looked more like a bare-knuckle brawler than the administrator of a vast intelligence agency, was scrupulously reviewing the photographic reproduction of the plans his nameless employer had recovered from Nazi headquarters in Berlin only a few days before.

In an unusual face-to-face meeting, X had brought his number one man up to speed on the events of that journey, which had culminated with a near epic flight from the United Kingdom to the Agent's private airfield in New Jersey. The reason for the Agent's candor lay in the urgency of the situation; the speed with which he had returned from overseas was nothing when held against what he would have to do now to prevent the operation known as Erste Welle from being carried out. So that there would be no confusion about what he should do with the information, Secret Agent X had decided to break his custom of encoded communication in order to give Bates his marching orders personally.

"On this film," the Agent—wearing the guise of Mr. A.J. Martin—had explained, "you will find one of the most terrible acts of violence ever conceived. When you read it, your first impulse will be to give this directly to the highest authority, to the President himself. However, I must implore you to wait—to give me a chance to stop it—because even the mere existence of this plan is an act of war, and war is something…" The Agent had paused then and sighed wearily. "I have to try to stop this from becoming a war."

Bates had nodded. Never in his years of working for the man whose name and face were a complete mystery had there been cause to question him. "How long should I wait?"

"Give me three days. It will take them that long at least to move to the final phase of the plan. God help us all if I'm wrong about that."

"Three days then," Bates had assured him. "You have my word."

Now however, now that he understood just what Erste Welle was, Bates found himself questioning that promise. The scheme was indeed an act of war and open hostility seemed the only recourse against an enemy that would conceive of such a terror. I promised him three days, Bates thought. The day after tomorrow. Dare I wait that long?

He rubbed his eyes wearily then resumed studying the document. It had taken him this long just to translate the particulars, but because of his oath to the Agent, he had not dared enlist the help of an interpreter. The bulk of the plan was now recorded in his nearly illegible scrawl in a stenographer's notebook, and what was left seemed mostly to address certain logistical matters. One page however had caught his attention. It was a list of times and dates, followed by a strange numeric code. Something about that sequence of number struck him as familiar, but it wasn't until he translated the heading at the top of the page that he grasped their significance.

He had found the appendix detailing predetermined contact times for all the agents involved in executing the operation, along with the master key for synchronizing their Enigma encryption machines. In a flush of excitement, he tore the page from his notebook, and then hastened off to the code-breaking department where the Foundation kept its own Enigma machine.

Perhaps he couldn't take action directly against the invasion force now marshaling on the hidden Nazi sea base, but there was nothing to prevent him from tracking down their allies at work in the city.

**To all appearances,** Richard Acer kept to himself during the long ocean voyage along the coast to the coordinates where the Coast Guard vessel would begin its search. In fact, Acer was never far from his fellow passengers. He kept both Hobart and Agent Greaves under constant surveillance. When they left to go to the wardroom for a meal, he stole into their cabins and expertly searched their belongings, looking for the tell-tale make-up kit or knockout gas gun that would indicate which of the men was Secret Agent X. Thus far, his investigations had yielded nothing, and time was running out.

All the pieces were set; the operation had taken place in total secrecy and the only facet of the grand design that had not gone off as planned was the capture of Secret Agent X. Acer was quite certain that X was now within his grasp. He suspected Hobart simply because it seemed unlikely that the Agent would choose an FBI agent as his cover, but either man was a good candidate. Nevertheless, Acer couldn't help wondering if their exhaustive efforts to flush out the anonymous vigilante had not inadvertently drawn him closer to discovering their scheme.

"Mr. Acer?"

The disguised spy jumped a little at the sound of the voice. He was a difficult man to sneak up on, but somehow the G-man had managed to do exactly that, catching him as he stood at the top of the stairs leading from the bridge down to the main deck.

"Agent Greaves, isn't it? What can I do for you?"

Greaves leaned against the rail, positioning himself close enough to study Acer's expression carefully in the darkness. "I was hoping to talk to you a little about Miss Dale?"

Aha! Acer affected a sad manner to hide his elation. "That is a difficult subject. I hope that Betty is yet alive, but I fear the worst."

"I realize that, sir. I've no wish to cause you further suffering, but learning more about Miss Dale is in fact my primary reason for being here."

I'll bet it is. "I don't follow you, Agent Greaves. Is Miss Dale being investigated by the Bureau?"

Greaves expression gave nothing away. "How well did you know her?"

Acer decided to answer with the truth. Agent X would probably already know the facts; deception might only arouse suspicion. "I've worked at the newspaper for about six months, now. I guess I met Betty shortly after I started there."

"That's not what I asked."

The ersatz photographer raised an eyebrow. Was that a hint of jealousy in Greaves voice? Had the fish taken the bait? "I guess the truthful answer is, I didn't know her quite as well as I would have liked. I think maybe we were getting closer though, there at the end."

Greaves face was unreadable. "You were becoming romantically involved with her?"

"That's a rather personal question. I can't see how it matters now."

"It pertains to my investigation, sir."

Acer frowned. "And what exactly are you investigating? If you want my cooperation, then I must insist that you be more forthcoming."

"Very well," Greaves sighed. "As a resident of New York, you are no doubt familiar with the vigilante known as Secret Agent X."

Acer offered a patronizing smile. "Oh, yes. Everyone in the city knows that bedtime story."

"Bedtime story? So you don't believe he really exists?"

"The crime fighting man of a thousand faces? Surely it is the product of too many impressionable minds under the influence of those awful pulp magazines. Some kind of mass hysteria."

"I understand Miss Dale made quite a career of writing about him."

Acer decided to press the issue. "Is that what this is about? Are you investigating Secret Agent X?"

"As a matter of fact, I am. Miss Dale was known to have a relationship with him; it's a matter of public record."

Suddenly Acer was no longer sure of his conclusions. If Greaves was Agent X, driven here by his concern for Betty Dale, what did he gain by publicizing the fact? "I'm afraid I don't know anything about that Agent Greaves."

"I guess I'll just have to ask her when we find her."

"I've complete faith that you'll get your chance, very soon." Acer smiled again for he had just seen something in the darkness that Greaves had not. Shadowy figures, swathed in battle fatigues the color of deepest night, were swarming over the deck rails.

Greaves must have caught the shift in his gaze, for he turned involuntarily just as a knot of men advanced on their position. To his credit, as he whipped out his pistol and took aim, he did not suffer even a single paralyzing second of disbelief

The disbelief came a moment later when a hand, as hard and flat as the blade of a broadsword, chopped into his wrist causing the gun to go spinning across the deck. Greaves whirled to face his attacker, but this time his incredulity left him defenseless. Acer, still grinning like a madman, delivered a second blow that sent the G-man sprawling.

**Because the attack** came in the night, the watch officers aboard the cutter did not immediately discern the presence of the black cloud that heralded the arrival of the Sea Wraiths. The first hint of trouble came when the ship-to-shore radio began to crackle noisily, the result of an electrical build up on the aerial antenna, but by the time the sailor manning that station realized that it was more than just a random static charge, the attackers had already mounted their attack.

They did not use ordinary guns. Their weapons both looked and produced results like something from a space fantasy. When the triggers were pulled, a jolt of electricity arced from the muzzle to the target, instantly rendering the victim unconscious. The discharge carried enough voltage to stop a weak heart, but the Coast Guardsmen were fit young men and fortunately, not a soul perished in the raid. Nevertheless, in a matter of minutes, every soul aboard the ship—save for the attackers and the treacherous master of disguise, Karo As—lay senseless where they had fallen.

One of the intruders hailed Acer. "Permission to come aboard."

The phony photographer frowned. "A little late for that, Mr. Smith. You were to wait for me to give the signal that I had positively identified Secret Agent X."

"We can no longer afford to wait. The Fuehrer himself has given the order for Erste Welle to be launched tomorrow morning."

"Why so soon?"

"It seems our fears concerning Secret Agent X were well-founded. He has penetrated the defenses of the Fatherland and captured a copy of the plans for Erste Welle."

Acer's brow furrowed. "When did this take place?"

"Four days ago."

"Four days! Why was I not told sooner?"

"The news only reached the Lorelei this afternoon."

His mind turned over this revelation. He had been so certain the one of the two passengers, Greaves or Hobart, was really Secret Agent X. But if his quarry knew about First Wave—knew that the very landscape of America was about to change—would he still care about hunting down his floozy? He glanced down at the motionless form of the FBI agent. "Take him to back to Lorelei. There's another passenger, a red head named Hobart, take him as well."

"And the rest of the crew? Do we add them to the labor force?"

"No. Their presence would be counterproductive. Better to simply let them all go down with the ship. Set the charges for fifteen minutes. That should give us plenty of time to get clear."

It took the intruders only five minutes to make their exit, leaving them plenty of time to cut loose, descend into the inky blackness and put some distance between themselves and the doomed vessel. When the explosion finally came, they felt it only as a thump that shuddered through the hulls of their Wraiths.

Acer allowed himself a grim smile as he imagined the ship heeling over in the darkness and sinking slowly to the bottom of the Atlantic. The Coast Guardsmen were but the first of thousands who would fall when First Wave crashed into America.

## CHAPTER 18–THE PLAN IS REVEALED

**Although the Sea** Wraiths were outfitted with view ports, there was very little to see beneath the ocean's surface. The depths swallowed up the even the intensely powerful spotlights that beamed from the bow of each minisub. Navigation was possible only by homing in on the steady pinging sound that issued from the seabase a hundred fathoms down and more than thirty nautical miles distant. It was only in the last few hundred feet of the journey that the Lorelei became visible through the portholes

With a pair of connected domes, suspended above the ocean floor by eight enormous articulated legs, the seabase resembled an enormous spider, silently poised to pounce on unsuspecting prey. The effect was especially unnerving to the crew of the Wraiths as the only way to gain access to the base was by piloting into the narrow gap between the bottom of the sea and the belly of the beast.

Unlike a squadron of airplanes, the Sea Wraiths did not, or rather could not, maintain any sort of formation when traveling between destinations. Following the breadcrumb trail of sonar pings was an imperfect science and invariably it took a while for the subs—twenty of them in all—to find their way back and rise into the well-lit moon pool in the Lorelei's larger dome. This night was no exception; more than an hour passed between the arrival of the first Wraith and the last, with more than thirty long minutes passing between the arrival of the main group and the very last craft. Smith breathed a sigh of relief when Sea Wraith number six—carrying Wolf Hauser and Erich Mensch finally bubbled into view.

"Wolf," he yelled, hiding his concern behind mock ire. "What kept you?"

The other man merely shrugged, and then helped his counterpart climb drowsily from the manta-shaped submarine.

"Better stop by the galley and get a cup of coffee," Smith called down. "It's going to be a busy night."

He turned away from the Wraith launch bay and almost collided with Betty Dale. He did not make an effort to conceal his impatience with her. Not for the first time did he regret the "deal" which had given her, but for a few noteworthy exceptions, free run of his sea base. "Miss Dale. What are you doing here?"

The beautiful blonde journalist flashed her most disarming smile. "I wanted to see what all the commotion was about. Was that German you were speaking just now?"

"You must have misheard me," Smith replied smoothly. He was grateful that Acer had already removed the two prisoners to the brig. "In any event, I must insist that you return to your quarters and remain there. The crew has much to do tonight; I can't have you distracting them with your questions."

"Then just answer one question," she insisted. "What's going on that's so special?"

"I will answer that question, Miss Dale. Tomorrow morning, the Lorelei will be revealed to the world. You're going home."

**Betty had only** just returned to her stateroom when a firm knock sounded at the door. She did not hasten to answer; something big was going down on the Lorelei tonight—something that, despite her best efforts, she had not been able to uncover during the period of her captivity.

Even tonight, she had gleaned a few more clues to the mystery. Mr. Smith had most definitely been speaking German to the men in the Wraith bay; it was not the first time she had caught members of the crew speaking in that tongue, and while there might be any number of innocent explanations, she favored the simplest— the Lorelei was a German operation, likely a German military operation, and its attacks on cargo ships weren't just acts of piracy, they were acts of war.

She braced herself for a confrontation as she threw open the door. "Oh, hello Wolf."

The crewman, who had on occasion been her minder and escort, stared back with a strange expression; his eyes—his steel gray eyes, but Wolf has blue eyes, and I've seen those eyes before—seemed to be on the verge of exploding into tears.

The visitor raised a trembling finger to his lips, signaling her to silence, then drew two intersecting lines in the air. X.

Despite his warning, a squeak of joy escaped Betty's lips as she threw her arms around him, hugging him as though she were afraid to ever let go. His strong arms returned the embrace with equal fervor, and then to her complete surprise and delight, he kissed her.

It was not an affectionate peck, the sort of thing reserved for dear friends and blood relations; no, this was an act of unrestrained passion, and Betty felt herself melting in the glorious glow of his touch.

When the moment passed and they both came up for air, she leaned close to his ear and whispered: "I knew you would come back."

He held her for a moment longer as if considering how to respond. "Betty, there's a lot to do and not much time. Is there somewhere we can talk? I'm sure they'll have eavesdropping devices all over your room."

She nodded then shook free of his embrace long enough to scoop up her notebook before cautiously ducking out into the corridor. "Follow me."

X stayed back a few steps to give the impression that he and Betty were not together, but there was little need for it. The entire section of the Lorelei seemed to be deserted. She led him through the empty galley and into the large pantry behind the cooking area. As soon as they were safe behind the closed door, the reunion resumed and they embraced as fervently as castaways clinging to life preservers.

"Oh, Betty," he whispered. "I thought I would never see you again."

"I knew you'd come back," she repeated. "I never doubted it for a second."

He kissed her again and then held her at arm's length, staring into her eyes. "Betty, something terrible is about to happen. The Nazis are planning to use this base as a stepping off point to an invasion."

She nodded, more in comprehension than agreement. "I knew it was something like that. But as big as this place is, I don't see how they could have enough troops aboard to manage an all-out attack."

"The troops are already on American soil, but they aren't German soldiers. The Nazis have made an alliance with several criminal gangs up and down the East coast." He caught her look of confusion and continued. "This won't be a military invasion. In fact, it's been planned to look like a mission of mercy.

"Tomorrow morning, a gigantic tidal wave is going to sweep over the Eastern seaboard, causing destruction like nothing ever seen before. In the chaos that follows, the criminal gangs will quickly take charge, establishing their own sort of law and order. The Nazis will of course be quick to offer assistance, and the gangs will welcome them with open arms. At the very least, a German-American alliance will be forged; worst case, Nazi occupation of America's major cities—New York, Washington DC. Either way, Britain will have no choice but to surrender."

Betty shook her head in disbelief. "It's too horrible to imagine. But how can they know that this tidal wave is going to strike?"

"Don't you see? They're going to trigger it. Nazi scientists have spent months mapping seismic faults on the seafloor and have pinpointed the areas of greatest instability. The Lorelei sits directly on a sort of seismic keystone. They've packed the area with enough high explosives to trigger a massive undersea landslide that will create a wall of water fifty feet high, moving at nearly two hundred miles an hour toward the East coast." He took her hands in his and smiled reassuringly. "But we're not going to let that happen, are we?"

She brightened instantly. "What's the plan?"

"We have to destroy this base." No sense in sugarcoating it, he thought. She gave a grim little nod, prompting him to continue. "I've got an idea of how to do that, but there's a problem. Two prisoners were brought in tonight; one of them is Jim Hobart. Additionally, I overhead mention of a 'labor force;' my guess is, it's a slave labor force."

"Smith told me that the crews of the ships they captured were either released or volunteered to stay, but I had a feeling he was lying to me."

"We need to determine where they are and free them. But then there's the problem of getting everyone out of here before we blow the place."

She snapped her fingers and then opened her notebook to reveal a detailed floor plan of the Lorelei. Several sections were marked with question marks, but the schematic was surprisingly comprehensive. "Right here," she said, pointing to an area in the center of the larger dome. "These are the life boats. Only they're not boats in the general sense; more like… escape pods, I guess you could call them. There's enough room for in each one for twenty people."

"Good girl, Betty." He scrutinized her hasty blueprint, studying the areas that she had been unable to explore, which included the entire smaller domed section. "This is probably the area where we'll find the rest of the prisoners. Any idea where they might have taken them?"

"Probably our old cell."

X noted the implicit mention of some past, shared experience, and recalled her earlier comment. There was no time to pursue the matter though. He straightened and guided her toward the door. "Unfortunately, rescuing everyone is going to have to be our second priority. Whatever else happens, we must not allow the Nazis to launch this wave."

"What do you want me to do?"

"If you can, try to ascertain exactly where the prisoners are. You'll recognize one of them: Jim Hobart, the private investigator. Then get back to your room and wait for me."

**They parted ways** right there, with X following her blueprint to carry out his mission of sabotage. For her part, Betty made her way back through all of the Lorelei's common areas. For the most part, they were deserted; the crew of the sea base was clearly in a heightened state of activity, which meant that no one paid much attention to her. When she reached the corridor leading to the brig however, she found something entirely new in her experience aboard the Lorelei: a pair of guards, armed with strange looking pistols.

"Sorry, Miss Dale, but this area is now off limits. You need to return to your stateroom."

She flashed her best smile to hide her disappointment. "Sure thing."

Hopefully X is having better luck than me, she thought as she made her way back to her quarters. There was nothing to do now but wait.

The gentle knock on her door caught her by surprise. Surely it was too soon for the Agent to have accomplished his goals, but the rapping sound was nothing like the firm signal Smith and his minions used when paying her a visit. She approached warily and opened the door.

"Betty, thank goodness you're safe! I came back as soon as I could."

She thought she was ready for anything, but one look at the familiar visage of Richard Acer turned her world upside down. And as he gazed back at her, reading her reaction, he saw it too, and his entreating, honest expression changed into something much, much different.

Karo As dropped the charade in a heartbeat. "He's here isn't he?"

He roughly grabbed her arm, his fingers squeezing tight enough to draw a whimper of pain as he dragged her from the room. Her best efforts to wrestle free of his grasp were futile and when she tried beating her fists against him, he answered with a backhand blow that left her stunned, but even that physical pain was nothing against the sting of his betrayal.

How could I have been so wrong? Why didn't I see through his act?

He dragged her past the pair of armed guards and threw her into the prison cell they had once shared—back when she had believed him to be the greatest love of her life. The room now played host to two more prisoners: a pair of men, stripped to their underwear and secured with heavy leather restraints to devices that looked something like dental examination chairs. She recognized one of the men instantly; she had seen his fiery red hair and freckled countenance numerous times in her years on the crime beat: Jim Hobart, former police officer turned private detective. Both men bore the mark of a brutal interrogation and they greeted her appearance with a mixture of joy and dread—they were pleased to see that she was alive, but disheartened that she now shared their fate.

Smith was also in the room, his shirt removed and his muscles glistening with a sheen of sweat from his sadistic exertions. He stared at Acer in confusion, wondering why the deadly master of disguise had chosen to reveal his true allegiance to Betty Dale in this way.

"He's here," Acer grated. "Secret Agent X is here."

Smith glanced at the pair of prisoners. "Not one of these?"

"No, damn him. He must have been masquerading as one of the crewmen on the Coast Guard ship. Have your men search every inch of the Lorelei. We must find him before..." He trailed off as realization dawned and then without another word, dashed from the cell.

**Karo As, the** Ace of Spades, Germany's master spy, knew exactly what Secret Agent X would do, because in the same situation, it was what he would do. He sprinted through the corridors, arriving in the Wraith launch bay less than a minute later, where his suspicions were immediately confirmed.

One of the Sea Wraiths was missing. Secret Agent X had already left the Lorelei, intent on foiling the launch of Erste Welle.

Without a moment's hesitation, Acer sprang into the open cockpit of the nearest Wraith and engaged its controls. The time for his long delayed showdown with his nemesis had come.

## *CHAPTER 19-BATTLE OF THE SEA WRAITHS*

**It hadn't taken** the Agent all that long to figure out how to operate the manta-shaped minisub. The controls were simplistic, much like the stick and pedal configuration of the Sopwith Camels he had flown during the Great War, and the liquid environment was much more forgiving that the open sky. The trickiest part was maintaining the right amount of ballast to keep the small craft from either floating to the surface or plummeting to the bottom, but even that was a fairly simple system to learn. After more than a week of being on the run, constantly changing identities in order to unmask the Erste Welle conspiracy, the simple act of "flying" was strangely soothing; there was no trickery here—no disguises, no chance of being unmasked or betrayed by an imagined ally—just man and machine, working together in seamless harmony.

His joy at finding Betty, alive and safe, albeit a prisoner, had helped to heal the wound of Lara's betrayal, but in some ways it had opened another. When he had learned of Richard Acer's seemingly miraculous rescue back in New York, he had immediately smelled a rat; the information recovered from Berlin had indicated that the Lorelei was responsible for the disappearance of more than a dozen ships along the East Coast and the photographer's tale didn't have the ring of truth. He had of course nursed a flickering hope that Betty might yet be alive, but it was not his love for the spunky reporter that had prompted him to masquerade as a Coast Guardsman in order to slip about the Vigilant, practically under Acer's nose. Stopping Erste Welle was always the primary mission.

The fact that Betty had somehow been caught up in the whole affair under-scored a deeper problem; his enemies had used her in an unsuccessful bid to flush him into the open. The very fact of his fondness for her had put her life in jeopardy, and had caused him to risk Jim Hobart's safety as well.

I can't live in both worlds. Friends, lovers, family…those are the things I will-ingly sacrificed when I took up this life.

There had never been any doubt in his mind that Acer would return to the Lorelei, and so when the Sea Wraiths had made their move, he had been primed for action. Mere minutes after the attack had begun, he had subdued one of the invaders and disguised himself with the man's face and clothes. From there, it had been a relatively easy thing to wait for the Nazis to wrap up their operations and depart. One of his gas-cigarettes had rendered his fellow Wraith passenger uncon-scious long enough for him to see to a few details aboard the ship, not the least of which was presenting Ensign Barlowe with a prisoner, before following the sonar trail back to the Lorelei. By the time the other man had awakened from his stupor, blissfully unaware that he had been drugged, X had already mastered the minisub's controls.

While navigating between two distant points could be accomplished simply by following the sonar pings, the task that now lay before him would require him to see what he was doing and make very precise maneuvers. Fortunately, the powerful spotlight that shone from the Wraiths bow was more than adequate to illuminate the thick bundle of cables that sprouted from a connection on the seabase, and pointed the way directly to his destination.

The science behind Erste Welle was mind-boggling; in order to create the landslide that would trigger the giant wave, it would exact placement of explosive charges with very precise yields, detonated in a very specific sequence. The slightest error in any one of those facets of the plan would produce unpredictable results. Nevertheless, as complicated as the scheme was, all the divergent branches came together in a single nerve cluster in the control room aboard the Lorelei. The wires that would send electrical impulses to the blasting caps on the charges buried along a short section of the seismic fissure all came together in a single cable that ran along the ocean floor, pointing the way more effectively than any road map. In the beam of his spotlight, the black insulation sheathing the line stood out in stark relief to the ever-present gray silt. Accompanied by the atonal hum of the Wraith's electric motor, the Agent raced toward the largest bomb in existence.

In addition to the systems, which regulated attitude, course and speed, the Wraith's control panel featured switches to launch a pair of outboard-mounted torpedoes and a joystick lever that operated a manipulator arm. It was this latter feature of the minisub that the agent now found most useful as he went to work on the first of several bomb placements. The devices were composed of two hundred pound bricks of amatol—a chemical mixture of ammonium nitrate and trinitrotoluene. Amatol was a powerful explosive, much more so than TNT alone, but the addition of ammonium nitrate to the mix made it extremely susceptible to spoilage by moisture, a fact which the Agent was quick to exploit by using the manipulator arm to rip open the thick layer of beeswax that had been used to waterproof the substance. He knew he was racing against the clock. If the Nazis even suspected that he was attempting to disarm their weapon, they might detonate it ahead of schedule; every bundle of amatol he ruined would reduce the destructive force of Erste Welle, hopefully sparing countless lives. By the time he left the first site, more than a score of amatol bricks lay broken apart, their deadly crystals rendered as harmless as the silt with which they now mixed.

As soon as he engaged the propulsion unit, a high-pitched shriek filled the small cabin. He immediately recognized it as the sound of pressurized air escaping into the water, and craned his head around to see if one of the Wraith's oxygen canisters had ruptured, but what he saw was something much worse.

The same reflexes that had saved his life during countless high-flying dogfights during the war saved him again. He revved the electric motor to full capacity and stomped hard on the right rudder, steering the minisub into a tight corkscrew turn. The oblong metallic object that had created the noise shot past his view port, trailing a stream of air bubbles, and buried itself in the sea floor a hundred yards away. In the instant that it did so, a bulge appeared at the point of impact, and the Agent braced himself for what would come next.

The explosive yield of the torpedo was a mere firecracker compared to the amatol packages, but in the unforgiving environment a hundred fathoms below the surface, a firecracker packed a lot of punch. The energy traveled undiminished through the water and hammered into the Sea Wraith, causing it to tumble end over end like a flipped coin. X could only hold on for dear life and pray that the minisub would not spring a leak. A couple notches further down on his list of worries was the fact that whomever had fired that torpedo at him had at least one more just like it.

After what seemed an eternity of being tossed about, the Agent felt the Wraith begin to stabilize its course. He switched off the searchlight, and cut his speed to half as he continued turning a tight circle. Through the view port, he caught a glimpse of his attacker's light, a pinpoint no brighter than a star in the night sky, before it also winked out, leaving him buried in darkness. He immediately threw the throttle control into reverse and straightened the rudder. He held this course for ten seconds then switched off the propulsion until, adding silence to the funereal blackness.

He drained the ballast tanks, and although there was no sense of motion, he knew that the craft was rising toward the surface. He then angled the dive planes in adjust the sub's attitude until he felt himself hanging face down against the safety belt. He waited a few moments longer, and then switched on the searchlight.

He scanned the tableau framed in the cone of brilliance for the black truncated disc shape of his foe's Wraith, but the illumination revealed only an endless expanse of gray silt. He feathered the controls, throwing the beam of light back and forth to catch a glimpse of the enemy that now hunted him. Nothing.

He switched off the light again but instead of the expected curtain of night, he became aware of a second source of illumination spilling in through the portholes. He looked up, even though his instincts screamed that doing so was a mistake— that he should instead activate the propulsion motor and take evasive action...any kind of action—but in that instant, his reflexes won out, and in the back of his mind, he knew why. He had underestimated his foe and he was probably going to pay for that mistake with his life, but he wanted to at least catch a glimpse of the blade as it fell.

He thought he would see metal glinting in the light as the second torpedo raced toward him, but once again he was mistaken. There was no torpedo; only a second Sea Wraith hanging in the midst of the dark water, no more than fifty yards distant. The water magnified everything, amplifying every detail, and he had no difficulty distinguishing the face framed in the view port. The man—he knew him only as Richard Acer, but also knew that was certainly not his real name—smiled, and then held something up against the thick glass pane. It was a standard playing card, and although he could not make out the tiny letter in the corner, the suit was unmistakable; an enormous black spade filled the center of the card. The Ace of Spades.

Karo As.

The gauntlet had been thrown. The light abruptly winked out again, as he knew it would, and X seized the reprieve. He flooded the ballast tanks and threw the motor to full ahead. He understood now that his opponent would not fire his remaining torpedo until he was certain of a killing shot, but this knowledge offered little comfort; in this arena, Karo As held the upper hand.

He found himself second-guessing every decision. His foe would anticipate his every move therefore he would have to act unpredictably.

Instead of leveling out and skimming the bottom as he had intended, he cut the propellers and cranked the rudder over. The ballast and forward momentum continued the minisub's downward journey, but now the nose of the craft was oriented toward the surface. He strained his eyes to catch a glimpse of the other Wraith, but seeing nothing, engaged the motor once more. The electric propulsion system strained against the weight of the filled ballast tanks and while his descent slowed almost to a standstill, the craft did not reverse direction. One finger hovered above the torpedo launch control while another remained poised to flush the ballast tanks and create positive buoyancy on a moment's notice. His only thought was to simply keep moving yet even this realized was a flawed strategy. He could not continue running and dodging forever; his batteries and oxygen supply were limited. His enemy knew this as well. It was time to come up with a better plan.

He toggled the light, flashing the beam for an instant and switching it off even before his eyes could register the image. He then dumped the ballast and as the Wraith shot forward he threw it into the aquatic equivalent of an Immelmann turn—a half loop that ended with the manta-shaped craft turned around and upside-down, except instead of simply turning one hundred eighty degrees, he angled off the left weaving back and forth, seemingly at random intervals. He spun the sub around, flashing the light once more, scanning for his foe.

Karo As saw him first.

The torpedo, propelled by a burst of compressed air, hissed through the water trailing bubbles that glittered golden in the yellow beam of his searchlight. He wrestled with the controls, but the liquid medium did not permit the kind of rapid evasive maneuvers that had saved his life countless times in the skies over Europe. The projectile grew larger, eclipsing his view of the vessel that had launched it, and this time he knew it would not miss. But then the body of the torpedo scraped across the outer hull of the Wraith, occluding the view port in a storm of bubbles, and he realized that he had been spared by mere inches. He was almost right.

The next few moments were an indescribable cacophony of noise and motion. Although the underwater missile had not detonated during its glancing contact with the sub, the vibration had damaged the fuze mechanism, causing it to activate a few seconds later. The first detonation, distant though it was, had tossed the Agent's craft about like so much chaff in the wind, but this one was practically on his doorstep.

The energy of the blast reverberated through every fiber of his being—like a full-body haymaker punch from a heavyweight champion. He felt as though his organs might burst, that blood must be streaming from his ears and eyes, and in the center of his chest, the old wound exploded with scarlet agony. For an immeasurable length of time, he hovered on the edge of unconsciousness, but the pain kept him from slipping into the void; it was his only assurance that he yet lived.

Then a new sensation was added to terrible symphony, a bitter icy cold. In the dark interior, he could not see the cause, but through the ringing in his ears he could make the sibilant hiss of water spraying into the cockpit and splashing all over his battered body.

His foe's searchlight stabbed through the view port, growing larger as Karo As moved in to administer the coup de grace. The German spy had no more torpedoes to fire, but he didn't need them to finish off the wounded Wraith. The manipulator arm unfurled from its underbelly like the talons of a raptor, reaching out to eviscerate its prey.

The Agent reacted without thinking, summoning the last of his waning strength to jam the motor controls to full ahead. There was a grinding noise as the damaged propellers began to spin, but the little submarine grudgingly began to move forward. The opposing Wraith abruptly tried to veer off, but the maneuver had taken the victorious spy unaware and he was a fraction of a second too slow.

The two Wraiths collided in a shriek of metal. The manipulator arm of Karo As's craft snapped off at the joint and the ragged remnant stabbed through the wing-like extension of the Agent's damaged minisub. The impact spun both ships around crazily, but every move made by one man to regain control was countered by an opposite action on the part of the other.

In the gloom, X saw the bottom rushing up and knew that his battered vessel would probably not survive that final crash into the ocean floor. The combined weight of the inextricably joined submarines and the weight of a hundred fathoms of water had sealed his fate. He flushed out the ballast tanks, but it wasn't enough. The propulsion unit whined in protest, but failed to change their doomed course. There was only one switch he hadn't yet tried and although it seemed like an act of sheer futility, he reached out and fired the torpedoes.

## *CHAPTER 20-FINAL WAVE*

**The pool bubbled** like a witch's cauldron, signaling the return of the Sea Wraiths, but what broke the surface looked more like a sculptor's nightmare. The minisubs were twisted together like gladiators that had pierced each other through with their knives, and then continued to grapple until locked together forever by rigor mortis.

Mr. Smith and a contingent of guards armed with electric stun pistols ringed the pool waiting to see if the man that emerged would be friend or foe. The fact that both men were masters of disguise, their true faces a mystery to everyone, had not escaped his notice, and so when he saw the familiar visage of Richard Acer emerge from the cockpit of the Wraith that showed the least amount of damage, he and his men remained wary.

Acer reaction to the tense reception committee was outwardly ambivalent.

"You might want to advise the men against discharging those pistols this close to the pool."

Smith's mouth twitched a little, but he neither frowned nor smiled. "If you are who you appear to be, mein herr, then there is no need to discharge them at all."

Acer did not reply as he climbed onto the wreckage of the second Wraith and pulled the release handle. A torrent of water spilled forth and with it, a body. Acer caught the motionless form by the collar and dragged it onto the gangplank.

"Is he dead?" Smith asked.

Acer peered down at the supine figure. The man's face was no longer recognizable—the cosmetic putty had begun to dissolve in water, creating the impression that his face was melting. Acer grabbed a handful of the malleable substance and pulled it away to reveal a handsome face that was tinged blue. "Mr. Smith, meet Secret Agent X."

Smith moved out onto the walkway to look at the face of the enemy. "He's alive, but appears to be suffering from hypothermia. We'll warm him up in the infirmary. I'm sure the Fuehrer will be quite pleased to get reacquainted with him."

Acer nodded then leaned over and tucked something into the motionless man's fist; it was his signature—the Ace of Spades. Yet, as he watched two burly crew man drag his fallen enemy away, the master of disguise did not fail to notice that Smith and his men were still on their guard. He understood their paranoia; everything would be sorted out once the prisoner regained consciousness. "We should celebrate, Mr. Smith. The last obstacle to the success of Erste Welle has finally been removed."

This evoked a smile from Smith. "Excellent idea. Join me for champagne in the salon. We'll toast your victory over Agent X and our conquest of America."

**The prisoner awoke** shivering in a hospital bed. He glanced around, immediately noting the restraints that held his wrists and ankles fast, and the pair of guards that watched his every move. Despite the fact that his muscles were twitching with spasms as his body temperature gradually and painfully returned to normal, one thought occupied his mind: escape.

His captors had removed his clothing, but the secrets at his disposal were not limited to what could be stored in his pockets.

His shivering concealed his purpose from the guards. Hidden from their view, he contorted his hand in such a way that his long fingers were able to touch the inside of his wrist just above the leather strap that bound him. There, concealed beneath a flap of skin-colored adhesive tape was the blade of a surgeon's scalpel. He had the strap cut nearly through before one of the guard's noticed.

The man started across the room, forcing him to drop the blade and resort to brute force. A single violent wrench finished the work begun with the scalpel's edge and he wrestled his hand free just as the guard came into his reach. He snared the fellow's shirt and yanked him forward, slamming his forehead into the guard's temple. He saw stars for a moment, but retained the wherewithal to seize the electric pistol from the man's senseless grip and fire it across the room at his uncomprehending comrade. A crackle of energy scorched the air, filling the small room with the smell of ozone as the second man went down.

Still shivering, he wrestled with the buckles on the remaining straps and then began rummaging through the drawers to find something to wear, and was ultimately forced to strip one of the guards of his black uniform. Armed with the stun pistol, he crept from the infirmary. He could only pray that he wasn't too late.

**The battle of** the Sea Wraiths had not ended on the ocean floor.

When Agent X's torpedoes had exploded directly beneath the descending submarines, the resulting shockwave and the eruption of gases created a bubble that propelled the inter-locked craft upward.

The occupants of both machines were violently tossed about, but buoyancy and inertia now manned the controls. With his ballast tanks empty, X's Wraith lifted the pair all the way to the surface.

The fractured hull of the Agent's sub groaned and creaked as the weight of thousands of tons of water sloughed away. Cracks appeared in the view ports, but miraculously the craft held together and the torrent of icy water actually abated.

When the Sea Wraiths finally broke the surface, bursting from the waves like a misshapen Leviathan, the men inside wasted no time in rejoining the battle, but this time it was purely physical combat. Though battered and bruised, they exploded from the cockpits on their conjoined vessels and met head on, grappling on the uneven surface of the Wraiths' decks as they bobbed and undulated in the swells.

There could be no retreat; there was nowhere to hide in order to recover and regroup. Only one could emerge victorious; it was a test of skill and will, and in the end, the man with the most to lose found the will to win.

**Karo As had** no memory of what happened after that. Even now as he stole through the corridors of the Lorelei, aware that his own comrades in arms would certainly attempt to take him prisoner once more before ascertaining his true identity, he could not comprehend why his archenemy had spared his life. It was, he vowed, a decision that Secret Agent X would not live to regret.

**X knew his** latest disguise would not endure Smith's scrutiny. He knew nothing of the two men's prior relationship, did not know if there were recognition codes or shared experiences Smith would quiz him about in order to ascertain his true identity. Nor was there time to waste in testing his prowess as a chameleon. As soon as they reached the relative shelter of the salon, he made his move. The gas ampoules put Smith and his guards down before a single hand could be raised against him.

Armed with one of the shock pistols, he raced to Betty's stateroom—empty!

He cautiously unfolded the sodden page on which the journalist had inscribed her blueprint of the Lorelei and fixed the location of the brig. Even if his worst fear, namely that Betty had been caught and detained, was unfounded, it still made sense that she would be in the detention area, attempting to free Hobart and Greaves.

Contact with the crew was unavoidable, but thankfully the men milling about in the corridors recognized him only as Acer—or Karo As—and simply greeted him as they would any superior officer. He returned their salutes without stopping, but upon reaching the brig, he abandoned the charade. As the guards posted outside the door snapped to attention, he shot them point blank with the electrified pistol. Even before their unconscious forms slumped to the deck, he burst through the door and discharged the weapon at the three black-uniformed men who warded the prisoners.

Jim Hobart and FBI Agent Wesley Greaves gaped in disbelief from their prison bonds, but the remaining person in the room caught one look at his face and erupted like a fireball. Betty sprang from her chair and crossed the room in two steps. Instead of the grateful embrace the Agent expected however, the blonde journalist threw a right cross that rattled his teeth.

He caught her hand before a second punch landed. "Betty! It's me!"

Even the familiar sound of his voice was not enough to convince her that he was anyone but the treacherous Richard Acer. She struggled against him, beating at his arm with her free hand.

In desperation he tore open his shirt, exposing the scar that crossed his heart. "Betty, look! It's me, X!" He pressed her hand to the old wound so that she could feel for herself that it was a thing of flesh and tissue and not some clever theatrical appliqué.

More than the fact of the scar itself, his simple entreaty reached through her rage and broke down her defenses. The touch of her beloved one's flesh beneath her hand was like a jolt from one of the stun pistols. "It is you," she whispered and then flashed a wan smile. "We gotta think up some kind of password."

He nodded. "Plenty of time for that once we're far away from here."

Greaves cleared his throat. "Secret Agent X. Back from the dead, I see. And not a moment too soon."

"You can't keep a good man down, Agent Greaves." The Agent hastened to free the G-man from his bonds, then tossed him a pistol appropriated from one of the guards. "I trust you've figured out that I am one of the good guys."

"I'll reserve judgment on that until we're out of this mess."

X nodded then loosed Hobart's bonds. The redheaded detective was grinning uncontrollably as he stared at the disguised crime fighter, but the Agent gave no indication of familiarity.

Disguised with ill-fitting uniforms stripped off the guards—Betty's long blond curls were tucked up in a knit watch cap—they lined up at the door. "We've got to free the rest of the prisoners and get to the lifeboats," the Agent said when the electrified guns had been distributed. "We're going to have to fight our way there, make no mistake, but the element of surprise is with us, and once we free those captured sailors, we'll have numbers on our side too. Ready?"

Three heads nodded.

"Then let's go."

There was no attempt at subterfuge. They sprinted through the corridors, shooting their weapons at anyone who crossed their path. X led, with Betty pointing the way through the labyrinthine corridors to the passage that led into the smaller domed section.

There were guards posted there as well, but because no general alarm had yet sounded, they went down under a barrage of artificial lightning before they even realized that the group of four approaching them were not members of the crew. X worked the electronic lock and the enormous metal door blocking their path slid aside.

It was like opening the door on Hell.

The second dome resembled the heart of a subterranean volcano. The fiery glow and acrid stink of molten metal suffused the place, but it was the haggard forms of the prisoners, visibly brutalized by their task masters as they labored night and day to refine the pirated ore, that truly resembled something from Dante's Inferno.

Yet, in the moment that the first of the guards went down twitching after a blast from the Agent's pistol, a little bit of life returned to their eyes. As the distracted overseers turned their attention to the small group of intruders, the slave laborers grabbed anything that might function as a weapon and turned on their masters.

The fight was brutally swift.

More than thirty men—a handful really of all those that had been considered lost with their ore carriers—still survived and readily followed their liberators back into the Lorelei's larger dome, eager to see the sky once more. The noisy mob surprised no one, but the crewmembers that noticed their approach fled without a fight.

Betty led the group straight to the highest deck, where a series of circular hatches permitted access to the escape pods.

"Everybody in," the Agent shouted. As soon as one lifeboat was filled, he closed the outer hatch, while the man inside sealed the inner door and activated the release mechanism. The remainder of the group filed into a second pod until only X, Hobart, Greaves and Betty remained.

"Get in there," he instructed.

"What about you?" countered Betty.

"I still have a job to do. But don't worry. I'll see you on the surface."

The private investigator and the G-man complied immediately, perhaps not understanding the peril into which their rescuer would be rushing, but Betty lingered.

"X…"

He silenced her with a kiss. "Betty, don't worry about me. I always come back."

Before she realized what was happening, he maneuvered her into the lifeboat and sealed the hatch.

Acer—Karo As—found Smith and several of the guards sprawled unconscious in the salon and hastened to rouse them. Smith came awake with a curse on his lips.

"No time for that," Karo As replied. "Every moment we delay increases our chances of failure. You must launch Erste Welle now!"

Smith struggled to his feet. "Ja. To the control room!"

"I will hunt him down, but do not wait for me. Activate the device immediately."

Both men left the lounge at a run, but went their separate ways the moment they crossed the threshold. Unlike the spy, Smith had a fixed destination in mind—the control hub for the entire sea base—and reached it in a matter of minutes.

He burst through to door, surprising the watch crew, and began shouting orders. "Cast off all moorings and prepare to surface. We are commencing Erste Welle immediately."

"But commander," protested one of his officers. "It is yet eight hours before our scheduled—"

"Do as you are instructed or I will shoot you myself!"

"Ja wohl."

The crew members immediately set to their tasks, flipping switches and pushing buttons on their control boards in order to flush out the Lorelei's massive ballast tanks and reverse the augurs that tipped its spider-like support appendages in order to free them from the thick layer of sucking sediment.

"Deploying main propulsion units and maneuvering thrusters now," announced the officer of the watch.

Suddenly a light began to flash on one of the panels they were not manning. Smith leaned past his men and read the legend printed beneath the blinking bulb. Someone had just activated one of the lifeboats. A moment later, a second light began blinking.

Smith breathed another curse, but then returned his attention to the task at hand. No matter if they try to escape, he thought. We will be on the surface soon enough, and then they will be easy targets for the Sea Wraiths.

**Secret Agent X,** alone once more, backtracked until he found the familiar central corridor that led to the launch bay. Confusion reigned aboard the Lorelei as the crew rushed frantically to ready the massive sea base for its journey to the surface. Murmured talk of the slave revolt and launch of the lifeboats was already spreading among the crew, and no one gave him a second glance.

A tremor shuddered through the deck plates as the Lorelei began struggling to shake off months of idleness in order to rise to the surface. X knew that this was the precursor to the detonation of the bombs placed in the seismic fissure—the launch of Erste Welle. If the Lorelei was underwater when those explosions occurred, the shock wave would smash the entire sea base like a tin can crushed under the wheels of truck. All of which meant he had mere minutes to finish what he had started earlier, and he quickened his pace accordingly, slowing down only when he reached the entrance to the Wraith launch pool. He peeked around the bulkhead, scanning the area for signs of enemy presence, and seeing nothing, moved inside.

"That's a nice face."

The familiar voice froze him in his tracks and he raised the shock pistol, searching for its source.

"It used to be mine," Karo As continued, a disembodied presence, speaking from the shadows. "But then it was only ever just a mask. You and I, we don't have faces of our own anymore. No faces—no loved ones to welcome us home, no lives of our own.

"That poor wretch, Betty Dale, actually believes that someday you will carry her off to a fairytale castle, but we both know better. Our fate is to die as lonely men."

"I'd be happy to speed you on your way," answered the Agent, the words pushing through his clenched teeth. He backed up until he was against one massive steel bulkhead, and then began edging along its length, peering into all the hidden spaces between the rows of idle Sea Wraiths.

"Ah, you already had your chance to do that. But then again, killing isn't your way, is it? You lack the stomach for it."

Something about the pitch of Karo As's voice as he spoke the last sentence warned the Agent that an attack was imminent and he threw himself flat on the deck just as a tendril of electricity scorched the air where he had been standing. He rolled and brought his own pistol up, firing blindly, but his target had already retreated from view. He lay there for a moment, breathing hard and waiting for his foe to make a second appearance. Before that could happen, another tremor shuddered through the deck.

"Do you know what that is?" Karo As taunted. "The Lorelei will be on the surface soon, and then all that you know will be swept away. Of course, you will be dead long before the wave reaches its target."

He's stalling, the Agent realized. He knows that if he can keep me here just a few minutes longer, there will be no way for me to stop Erste Welle.

With that simple realization, he knew what he had to do. Without wasting another breath to exchange verbal barbs with his foe, he leapt onto the gangplank and sprinted for the nearest Wraith.

There was a crackle of electricity as Karo As snapped off a desperate shot, but X was out of the limited range of the weapon and the energy pulse dissipated harmlessly before it ever touched him. In that moment, he dove into the cockpit of the minisub and pulled the canopy into place.

With one hand he worked the clamp that would seal him in and keep him safe from the crushing pressure of the deep; with the other, he flooded the ballast tanks and then engaged the motor.

The Wraith dropped like a stone and was immersed in dark water. The only illumination came from the launch bay above, where he knew that his foe would also be hastening to deploy a minisub in order to come after him.

He wasn't about to let that happen.

As he dropped into the narrow gap between the Lorelei's underbelly and the sea floor, he reversed the propulsion motor and angled the nose up so that he was facing the opening to the launch bay.

Karo As had been wrong about one thing. His decision to use non-lethal weapons in his war on crime in New York had nothing to do with his ability to stomach violence. Sometimes there were better solutions to a problem than killing someone....

And sometimes, that was the only solution.

Twin streaks of silver, followed by a rush of bubbles, shot from beneath the wings of his Sea Wraith and raced toward the large square opening overhead. It was a short journey.

The torpedoes exploded simultaneously, filling the launch bay with light. The shock wave pounded X's retreating sub mercilessly, but most of the explosive force went up, into the open air of the launch bay, annihilating everything.

X did not linger to survey the damage. It would take more than the small explosive charges in the warheads of the torpedoes to put the Lorelei out of commission. Spinning his Wraith around, he switched on the light and picked up the thread of cable that connected the sea base to the amatol charges that would trigger Erste Welle.

In that instant, a groaning sound resonated through the body of the little sub. In the side porthole, he saw a massive cloud of silt rising up from the ocean floor behind him and knew it could mean only one thing: Lorelei was rising. He had run out of time.

The giant spider-shaped base seemed to float up out of the nebulous sediment, trailing a single black strand of web silk. The cable that connected the Lorelei to the explosives began to reel out in great loops as it lofted toward the surface.

He abandoned the idea of trying to track down and destroy the explosive packages one by one; there simply wasn't enough time. Instead, he steered the Wraith back toward the Lorelei and deployed the manipulator arm. With a deft touch, he snared a loop of cable and then angled the sub around toward its source.

Even carrying the burden of heavy cable, the Wraith was still far more agile than its cumbersome mother ship. The minisub darted in close, a gnat buzzing around the legs of a tarantula.

X agilely looped his Wraith around one of the support stanchions and then repeated the maneuver again and again until all the slack was gone from the wire. Only then did he back off to survey his handiwork.

The great spider had been snared in its own web. The cable continued to deploy from the underbelly of the beast, but now it simply formed a long loop that doubled back to its source, now snagged on one of the massive outrigger legs. The remaining length of cable, still attached to the explosives, went taut a few seconds later.

Lorelei was too massive, too powerful to be held down by the weight of a few mere tons of explosives however. Her enormous propulsion thrusters hardly even strained with the effort as they heaved the amatol bricks out of their emplacements and dragged them along on the journey toward the surface.

In the dark cockpit of his Sea Wraith, X breathed a sigh of relief. Erste Welle was finished.

**In the control** room of the Lorelei, Mr. Smith eagerly watched the depth gauge as it ticked off their ascent. As the needled swept over the ten-fathom marker, he removed the safety lock from the Erste Welle trigger and let his finger rest against the large red button. The executive officer began reading aloud the intervals.

"Five fathoms…three…we're on the surface."

But for a gentle back and forth rocking, it was impossible to distinguish the difference.

Smith turned to the members of the watch with a broad smile, the earlier insubordination forgotten. "Karo As will be sorry he missed this moment."

Then he pressed the button.

**In the darkness,** the bedraggled castaways aboard the Lorelei's lifeboats did not see the great seabase rise above the surface, springing forth from the ocean's womb like an artificial island, but they certainly saw what happened next.

Deep beneath the surface there was a flash of emerald brilliance briefly illuminated the benighted Atlantic. The pulse lasted only for an instant, but the light that flashed in through the small portholes in the escape pods was bright enough for each passenger to see the faces of the others.

"That can't be good," Betty murmured.

Someone shouted: "Hang on!" and then everything went crazy.

The heavy metal walls of the lifeboat rang like a bell as the shock wave raced through the water, stunning everyone inside. The two pods tumbled end over end, driven by a wave of water that, although being nothing like the monstrosity envisioned by Nazi scientists, nevertheless crested nearly fifty feet overhead before smashing down on top of the watertight escape craft. It was, Betty would later reflect, a little like going over Niagara Falls in a metal mailbox, into which a wayward delinquent had just dropped a cherry bomb.

Pummeled mercilessly, battered, bleeding and with one or two broken bones among their number, the souls aboard the lifeboats were still grateful to be alive when the tumult finally abated. The same could not be said for those aboard the Lorelei.

As she reached for the surface, the seabase had dragged along the explosive bundles like the tentacles of a jellyfish. Because they had been rigged in a daisy chain, the bombs were all at varying depths when the simultaneous detonation occurred, and although each one created a massive outwardly expanding sphere of destructive energy, the effect was magnified along the vertical axis they shared, sending a shockwave of titanic force straight up.

The concussive force struck every soul aboard dead in an instant. No one remained to witness the Lorelei come apart at the seams. Great chunks of metal were vomited from the churning sea and shot into the air like artillery shells, but after a few seconds the sea swallowed the remains down once more.

Betty lay motionless for a long time, afraid to move lest she aggravate the multitude of injuries sustained during the chaotic upheaval, but as the ringing in her ears subsides, she heard the reassuring voices of her fellow passengers assuring one another that they were alive and—more or less—well. Then the man she knew only as Agent Greaves called out with a different report:

"I see a light! Someone's coming."

It's X, Betty thought, and roused herself to peer through one of the portholes.

They could not see the vessel that was the source of the illumination, but a pair of large searchlights swept back and forth across the dark water, finally coming to rest on the exterior of their lifeboat. Betty's heart soared as the lights grew closer, but then her joy died a little when the G-man recognized the ship. "It's the Vigilant! We're saved."

**It took more** than an hour for the Coast Guard vessel to round up the two escape pods and bring the refugees safely aboard. The ship's mess became a makeshift infirmary where the doctor went to work stitching gashes and setting broken bones, but thankfully none of the injuries proved life threatening.

Ensign Barlowe was relieved to find Hobart and Greaves nursing only minor bruises. "Well, he told me to wait for his signal, but by golly I never expected that."

"What do you mean?" inquired Greaves.

"Secret Agent X left me a message. He said he was going to rescue you all, and that I should wait for a signal. I thought he meant he'd shoot off a flare or something, but that explosion rattled our windows from miles away."

He did not elaborate on the fact that there had been an earlier explosion—smaller and much closer—to the cutter. In addition to supplying the Coast Guardsman with a prisoner—one of the invaders whom he had overpowered during the initial attack—the Agent had removed all of the timed explosive charges from the Vigilant and set them adrift in one of the ship's lifeboats, thus saving the crew from certain death and fooling the Nazis into believing the ship destroyed.

"Speaking of which," Barlowe continued, scanning the weary faces of the survivors. "Which one is he?"

"He's not here," Hobart answered gravely. "Last time we saw him, he was still aboard that undersea monstrosity."

Barlowe looked back and forth at the two men. "I'd say you fellows must have quite a story to tell."

Greaves offered a humorless smile. "Honestly, I'm not quite sure where to begin."

As they told their tale, with a lot of help from Betty Dale who had spent more than a week aboard the seabase, the cutter continued combing the water for survivors but none were found.

Secret Agent X's fate was summed up in three words: Missing, presumed dead.

## EPILOGUE: THE GREATER STORM

**The Herald did** not publish Betty's first-hand account of her experiences aboard the Lorelei. In fact, she never wrote a word of it down. To reveal the existence of the seabase and the diabolical plot to wipe out America's greatest cities would surely trigger a storm of retribution and Betty did not want to be the one responsible for sending her country into war, although there could be little doubt that such an outcome was eventual and inevitable. The Nazis had made their intentions known; they would almost certainly try again.

The newspaper did not suffer from a lack of news however. The city was still reeling from the second gangland slaughter in less than a month—this time a shootout that had claimed the lives of Luigi Petrona and several of his most trusted lieutenants, along with a number of German-American citizens whose involvement with the mob was not fully understood.

For his part, Jim Hobart returned home to his lovely wife, and for a long time thereafter, had not the slightest desire to get caught up in any adventures. There was of course plenty of catching up to do at the office, and quite a few projects on the home front, not the least of which was redecorating the nursery to a theme better more appropriate for his beautiful newborn baby daughter.

Agent Wesley Greaves returned to Washington DC, eager to submit his final report on Secret Agent X and more importantly, to commence the hunt for Nazi saboteurs that he now believed were plotting acts of terror and revolution on American soil. His first lead was waiting on his desk when he arrived; a large envelope marked with the letterhead of the Colonial Research Foundation in New York City. Inside were transcripts of coded radio transmissions between Nazi operatives and a man known only by the name die Stahlhand—the Steel Hand. The Colonial Foundation had triangulated the signals and pinpointed the source of the transmissions; die Stahlhand was none other than steel magnate and presidential advisor Henry Barton.

There was one other item in the envelope: a small card on which a brief personal message from Harvey Bates, the director of the Foundation, had been scrawled:

*A mutual friend wanted me to pass this along to you, and to offer an assurance that all our resources are now at your disposal.*

Greaves's suspicions concerning the identity of the "mutual friend" were confirmed when turned the card over and saw a single luminous letter.

**Betty Dale also** received an envelope. She found it on her dining room table one evening after returning from work only a few short days after her homecoming. The envelope and the parchment with were speckled with what looked like raindrops. With trembling fingers, she unfolded the letter.

*My dearest Betty,*

*I love you. For as long as I have known you, I have loved you, and my greatest regret is that I never told you how much I love you.*

*When I took an oath to defend my country against those who would seek to destroy her, I believed there could be no higher calling. I thought I understood the risks, thought that I was ready to die for that noble cause. I did not realize that there are greater sacrifices than that.*

*Someone once told me that it was my fate to die a lonely man. I have always believed that one day, the battle against evil would be won and I would retire to enjoy the fruits of my labors with you at my side. I realize now that such can never be the case.*

*While this war endures, there will always be danger. The risk of my own life is something I long ago came to terms with. But I have now seen how my enemies will seek to wound me by threatening your safety, and this is something I cannot allow. When I thought you were lost at sea, it nearly broke my heart. When I learned that your abduction was designed to flush me into the open, I felt like dying.*

*I wish that I could just leave all of this behind—the violence, the deception, the endless war against evil—but I cannot. That is who I am; that is the man you are in love with.*

*But I cannot… I will not put you at risk again. I love you too much to lose you. I pray that you will find happiness one day, but it will not be with me. Know always that I will never stop loving you as long as I live.*

*Goodbye, my love.*

X

It was only when her own tears began to fall on the paper, blurring the words before she had finished reading them, that Betty realized the stains on the letter were not raindrops.

**The executive secretary** to the Secretary of the Treasury was mildly surprised to see someone enter the outer lobby of her employer's private office. It was late in the day, nearly five o'clock, and it was generally considered bad manners to pay someone a visit so close to quitting time.

The handsome man in the ordinary looking gray suit did not apologize however as he strode directly to her desk. "I'm here to see the Secretary," he announced. "I don't have an appointment, but I think he'll want to hear what I've got to say. Here's my card."

# ABOUT THE AUTHOR

Sean Ellis has authored and co-authored more than 20 action-adventure novels, including the Nick Kismet adventures, the Jack Sigler/Chess Team series with Jeremy Robinson, and the Jade Ihara adventures with David Wood. He served with the Army National Guard in Afghanistan, and has a Bachelor of Science degree in Natural Resources Policy from Oregon State University. Sean is also a member of the International Thriller Writers organization. He currently resides in Arizona, where he divides his time between writing, adventure sports, and trying to figure out how to save the world.

www.ingramcontent.com/pod-product-compliance
Lightning Source LLC
Chambersburg PA
CBHW020303200626
46814CB00006BA/2055